Firefly
Island

Books by Lisa Wingate

MOSES LAKE

Larkspur Cove

Blue Moon Bay

Firefly Island

DAILY, TEXAS

Talk of the Town

Word Gets Around

Never Say Never

TENDING ROSES

Tending Roses

Good Hope Road

The Language of Sycamores

Drenched in Light

A Thousand Voices

BLUE SKY HILL

A Month of Summer

The Summer Kitchen

Beyond Summer

Dandelion Summer

Firefly Island

A Novel

LISA WINGATE

BETHANYHOUSE

a division of Baker Publishing Group
Minneapolis, Minnesota

© 2013 by Wingate Media, LLC

Published by Bethany House Publishers
11400 Hampshire Avenue South
Bloomington, Minnesota 55438
www.bethanyhouse.com

Bethany House Publishers is a division of
Baker Publishing Group, Grand Rapids, Michigan

Printed in the United States of America

Library of Congress Cataloging-in-Publication Data
Wingate, Lisa.
    Firefly island / Lisa Wingate.
        p. cm.
        Summary: "A whirlwind romance—and a leap of faith—has made Mallory Hale a mother and a rancher's wife in small-town Texas. Can she survive the wild adventure?"—Provided by publisher.
        ISBN 978-0-7642-0823-2 (pbk.)
        1. Women professional employees—Washington (D.C.)—Fiction. 2. Life change events—Fiction. 3. Ranch life—Texas—Fiction. 4. Land use—Fiction. 5. Political corruption—Fiction. I. Title.
    PS3573.I53165F57 2013
    813'.54—dc23   2012035228

Unless otherwise indicated, Scripture quotations are from the King James Version of the Bible.

Scripture quotation at the start of chapter twenty-one is from the Holy Bible, New International Version®. Copyright © 1973, 1978, 1984, 2011 by Bibilica, Inc.™ Used by permission of Zondervan. All rights reserved worldwide. www.zondervan.com.

Cover design by Andrea Gjeldum

Author is represented by Sterling Lord Literistic

13 14 15 16 17 18 19   7 6 5 4 3 2 1

For Alice Steele
and her sisters Paula and Cindy

May books and love
always bind you together

*When we no longer know which way to go,
we have begun our real journey.*

—Wendell Berry
(Written on the Wall of Wisdom,
Waterbird Bait and Grocery, Moses Lake, Texas)

Chapter 1

There are times when life is a cursor on a blank page, blinking in a rhythm a bit like an electronic heartbeat, tapping out a question in three little words.

What.

Comes.

Next?

Time and space and life wait for an answer. A blank page is an ocean of possibilities.

The producer from CNN wants to know how I ended up here. Did I realize, when I started this thing, where it would lead?

The cursor would like an answer to that question. Or maybe it is challenging me. A wink instead of a heartbeat. A wink and a little chuckle that says, *Go ahead and try*. It's like one of those bad jokes told by lonely traveling salesmen in hotel lounges: *What do a milk cow, an Irish love legend, and a political scandal have in common . . . ?*

But I couldn't make this stuff up if I tried, much less explain it. It's easier just to look out the window, scan the DC skyline that seems out of place now, and let it fool me as it whispers, *It's summertime, Mallory. It's balmy out here—can you feel it? Don't you hear the crickets chirring and the hens plucking June bugs off the porch?*

I let myself sink into the fantasy, let it wrap around me like a comfortable old shirt—the oversized sort with the neck torn out and the fabric washed so many times that the tag is bleached bare and the logo is only a smattering of color clinging to individual threads.

I imagine that I am home, not here in DC. I hear the waters of Moses Lake lapping at the shore, feel the rhythm of it beneath my feet. My eyes fall closed, and I drink in the water-scented Texas air, the oleander blooming, the sound of small bare feet tramping up the hallway, a favorite blanket dragging behind. The honey-sweet tastes of a summer morning.

I'm ready to cuddle a knobby-kneed little body in my lap, snuggle a case of bedhead under my chin, feel the soft, downy hairs tickle my neck, hear the first snuffly breaths of morning before there's any need to talk or ask questions or face the rest of the world. I'm aching for all the things I never thought I'd want, for the place that has wound its way over me like the silk of a web, soft yet strong. I am a prisoner of it, content in ways I could never have imagined. It's strange how quickly a life can become *your* life, and how hard you'll fight for it when someone tries to take it away.

CNN's Washington Bureau wants the story in my own words, so the anchor can prep for the interview. They're looking for details, the juicy sort that will pull in viewers. They wonder if I had any idea I'd end up here. They're not the first ones to ask; inquiring minds all over the world want to know.

For CNN, you'll do things you wouldn't do for anyone else. You'll attempt to flatten your life like a map, smooth your hands over it, letting nothing hide in the wrinkles. So I put my hands on the keyboard and try to go back to the beginning, to lean all the way over that accordion-folded sheet of memory and identify the start of a yearlong wild ride, at the far corner of the map.

The first time I saw Daniel Everson, I was scrambling on the floor of the Capitol building among papers and sticky notes, trying to gracefully manage a squat in an above-the-knee straight skirt and pumps that were practical enough to say, *I'm serious about my work,* yet high enough to whisper, *I am woman, hear me roar.* The suit was my favorite—the perfect thing to wear while posing for an early-morning congressional staff photo on the Capitol steps.

The papers skittering along the marble floor were in direct conflict with the upwardly mobile fashion choices. They said, *This girl's an idiot.*

"Looks like a bomb went off in here." The smooth, deep voice with just a hint of baritone was hardly welcome just then. Neither was the observation. Bomb jokes on The Hill are generally considered bad decorum, even early in the morning when the tourists haven't invaded the place in droves yet.

"I've got it," I answered in the flat, perhaps slightly hostile tone of a girl still sensitive about the idea that her father might have had something to do with her landing a new job as a legislative assistant in a senior congressman's office. I squat-stepped sideways, slid a little on the slick floor, then slapped my hand over five sheets of the massive Clean Energy Bill, now peppered with yellow flags and scribbled notes in the margin, and headed for revisions, an exhaustive proofing, and duplication. Now I'd have to collate the thing by hand before I could even work on it.

A gust of air whooshed past—the result of the nearby renovations to the Capitol building—and I heard papers tumbling into the cavernous space of the rotunda. A single cherry blossom cartwheeled past in a strange sort of slow motion. Two men in dark suits, engaged in a rapt conversation, circumvented me as if I were invisible. A sheet of paper went airborne and stuck itself to my rear end. I reached for it, playing an odd game of solo Twister, one hand holding the papers on the floor, the other reaching for the piece that was wedged against my backside. My fingers caught it just as another sheet slid past. I pinned that one beneath my remaining foot.

"Hold on a minute." The man's voice held a friendly little laugh in the undertone. I tried to place the accent. Michigan, maybe—a Yooper from the Upper Peninsula, or maybe upstate New York. Could be Canadian. His voice had a nice sound. Warm and thick, almost musical. He leaned over and grabbed the smattering of papers I'd pinned to the floor. I imagined what he was seeing—a blonde in a pencil skirt, stretched over the tile like a giant spider.

It crossed my mind that the bill was fresh from a mark-up session and definitely not for public consumption. Technically, it was my job to protect it, and when your newly retired father has spent his life in the lobbying business, you know that there are always people skulking around, hoping for leaks. "No. Really. I've got it under control," I insisted.

"I can see that." He slid the papers from beneath my foot, shuffled them into a stack, and squatted down to tap them on the floor. Handing them back, he looked at me and smiled, and just as in those classic black-and-white movies on late-night cable, the world stood still. I heard the rising crescendo of music that would accompany such a scene, heavy on the trumpets and violins.

Daniel Webster Everson—yes, that was his real name, though I didn't know it yet—had the most beautiful green eyes I had ever seen. Framed by thick, black lashes, they seemed to glow with an inner light that was almost otherworldly. His hair was wavy and dark, long enough to curve around his collar, too nontraditional for Congress. He was wearing a suit—rather well, I might add. Black with a pale blue button-down chambray shirt and a fairly sedate navy-and-gray striped tie. I wondered what his business was here. Lobbyist? Tourist who'd somehow sneaked in early? Consultant?

I wondered how in the world a person could have eyes that shade.

I wondered if he wore color-enhanced contacts.

I wondered if his father was a gypsy.

Or an actor.

He looked like a gypsy-slash-actor. The guy who would play the prince of Persia, or the pirate king, or the Jedi Knight.

I wondered if he was married.

I wondered if he wanted to *get* married. Ever. Anytime in the next decade would be fine. Really. I'd wait.

Did he live here, or was he just visiting? Did he like furry little kittens and children? Did he visit his mother on Sundays? Was the curl in the back of his hair natural? Surely it wasn't one of those horribly outdated man-perms my friend Kaylyn referred to as *merms*?

Did he like Italian food? Was he Italian?

He could be Italian. . . .

Or a baseball player. A professional baseball player. He looked athletic. Congressmen loved to invite pro athletes in for behind-the-scenes tours. . . .

I mentally cycled through all those questions in the space of an instant, before he handed me the sheets of paper, jogged into the rotunda to gather up the rest, and returned them with a smile as I was regaining my feet and trying to reel up my bottom lip. I reached for some intelligent thought, some clever comment that might indicate that this brush with

11

klutziness was just a random incident—I wasn't some ditzy office assistant, hired because of my dazzling beauty and the way I looked in a straight skirt and a good pair of Spanx.

But all I could think was, *hubba-hubba*. And all I could manage to say was, "Thanks." I felt myself blushing, which, for a thirty-four-year-old, city-wise girl who'd sworn off relationships in favor of political aspirations, was saying something. The (at that point) nameless Good Samaritan wasn't the most incredibly good-looking guy I'd ever seen, not in the fashion model sort of way, but there was just . . . something. Fireworks, I believe my great-grandmother would have called it. *Mallory*, she liked to say, pointing that knobby grandma finger at me, *a smart woman doesn't settle for a man, just to have a man. That's like buying shoes just because they're cheap. If they don't fit, what good are they?*

You wait for fireworks.

Great-grandma Louisa was from the holy city of Charleston, South Carolina, the only southerner in the family, an enigma of sorts. She believed in misty-eyed platitudes. Offered up in that long, slow Southern drawl of hers, they sounded delightful and sweet, like a taste of mayhaw jam or honey butter. She supported the idea of skyrockets and things meant to be.

I'd always thought the notion charming but sadly outdated, until the day I met Daniel Webster Everson. My heart fluttered against my ribs like a butterfly trapped in a net. I had the fleeting thought that surely he could see it. In that instant, over the jumbled carcass of the Clean Energy Bill, we seemed to be drawn together by some invisible force we both sensed but couldn't see. He felt it. I just knew he did.

And then, all of a sudden, he shattered my fantasy completely. His wristwatch—one of those geeky plastic digital kind with a million buttons and gadgets—beeped, he checked it, then smiled, wished me an upturn in my day, and hurried out of my life. Leaving me standing there, still slightly splay-footed and speechless.

I toddled off, juggling the Clean Energy Bill like an unruly baby and feeling either rejected or teased by fate, or both. On the heels of that thought, there was a still, small voice drumming out mantras from the stack of self-help books I'd read since moving to DC and shaking off the dust of my last imploded relationship. It was the longest I'd ever dated anyone, and the only reason I'd stayed two years in a career black hole at the U.S. Consulate in Milan. I'd spent the last nine months of that time trying to find a graceful way to exit without disappointing everyone's hopes—his, my family's, his family's.

When you're over thirty, single, and you date someone for more than six months, everybody decides this must be *the one*, the (somewhat delayed) start of the marriage-and-family phase of life. But some people really aren't picket-fence-and-two-point-five-kids material. I'd always known that I was better suited to a career. Political life intrigued me. I relished the power, the sense of doing something world-changing and important, the mystery of deal making behind the scenes. Like the underground rail system that connected the Capitol to the Congressional and Senate office buildings, the place was laced with hidden connections, and I delighted in figuring them out. This was the life I was meant for.

My mother hated the idea with a passion. She thought I should be looking for a suitable man, particularly at my age. In Mother's family, women *married* influence; they didn't seek it for themselves. She'd had her way with my four older sisters, but I would be the one who was different, who broke the mold, who became a deal maker myself.

Yet, as I sorted my current stack of papers and put it back

together like Humpty Dumpty, I was thinking of the guy from the rotunda. The one with the green eyes and the thick, boyish lashes.

We would make beautiful babies together. We really would.

I found myself wondering if I'd taken a wrong turn at a crossroads of fate by letting him walk away without a word. Silly, of course. He wasn't interested, or he wouldn't have left me for a beeping wristwatch.

When I dropped by my apartment to change clothes before heading to the gym that night, I called my sister Trudy—the one closest to my age, but still five years older. Trudy was teetering on the backside of thirty-nine and undergoing in vitro treatments. Today, she wasn't really interested in hearing about the guy in the rotunda. She was headed back to the doctor tomorrow to find out if the latest round had worked. Tense times.

"You could be like those people who had six all at once," I said, and Trudy groaned.

"We'd just be happy to get one, maybe two. I just want to be someone's mommy, you know?"

"Yeah, I know." I didn't, really. Maybe it was being the baby of the family, but I'd never been too confident that I'd be any good at handling the care and feeding of another person. If you failed as a mom, you'd end up on an afternoon talk show someday, defending yourself in front of millions. Trudy's life seemed pretty good to me, actually. She had a successful husband and an imports business, but none of it mattered. She wanted a baby, and the lack of one was all she could talk about.

I finally gave up on the conversation and headed off to the gym. My little cast of friends was there—rejects like me, who couldn't find anything better to do after work. We'd cleverly dubbed ourselves the *Gymies*. Most days we ended up working out and then hitting the restaurant across the street for French fried onions and Philly melts. Seems counter-productive, but when you're sampling round-robin pie and discussing career hits and misses as if you really matter to the functioning of the free world, you don't feel so much like your Love Boat is stuck in dry dock.

I ended up telling Kaylyn about the guy in the rotunda right after she confessed, somewhat sadly, that the new man she'd been eyeing at her favorite coffee shop had turned out to be a dud. Married, three kids. Gorgeous wife.

She pulled a breath when I mentioned the rotunda experience, and the guy. "Ohhh, I'll bet he's Irish," she breathed. "It's St. Patrick's Day, you know."

I paused with a bite of pie halfway to my mouth, uncertain what one thing had to do with the other. Did Irish people move about more readily on St. Patrick's Day? Take it in their minds to suddenly visit the hallowed halls of Congress? "He didn't look Irish. More . . . Italian, maybe. Or . . . gypsy. I think he was a gypsy. Or a Scottish laird."

Kaylyn rolled her eyes. "Don't be making fun of my books." Kaylyn was hopelessly hooked on romance novels. We'd known each other since prep school, and even back then, she'd had her nose in a book. She knew the names—the real-life names—of the guys dressed as cowboys, knights, and highland warriors on the covers.

"I wasn't." I shoulder-nudged her. Who was I to criticize, really? At least the guys in Kaylyn's romance novels had integrity. They fell in love and stayed that way, unlike so many of the people I worked with. Life around the movers and shakers could make you cynical after a while. "I think it's great to be a romantic."

Kaylyn nodded her approval, her pert little nose scrunching. "Mmm-hmm. Did you read *Taming the Texan* yet?"

I wasn't sure whether to confess that the books she'd loaned me were gathering dust in my apartment. Across the table, Josh, all two hundred and eighty pounds of him, was once again watching Kaylyn through lovesick eyes. Even though they shared an office at a software company, she wasn't the least bit romantically inclined toward poor Josh. He didn't look anything like her favorite cover models.

"I . . . uhhh . . . started it. There was some good . . . history," I hedged. That seemed a benign enough response.

Kaylyn was pleased. "I told you so." She lifted her straw from her cup and sipped drips from the end while Josh watched wistfully. "Wait until I give you *His Irish Bride*. It's so good. You know that if two people meet on St. Patrick's Day, they're destined, right? That's why I asked if the guy was Irish."

"So, it only works for Irish people?" I raised an eyebrow to indicate that I was in no way being sucked into any premise that came from a used paperback.

"I'm sure it works for anybody." Snorting, she flashed an eyetooth and dipped her straw back into the glass. "Except cynics. Amy Ashley does her research, by the way."

"Who's Amy Ashley?"

Kaylyn wheeled a hand as in, *Pay attention here.* "She wrote *His Irish Bride*. She's won Readers' Pick of the Year, like, five times. She does her research."

I ate a few peanuts, pretending to defer to the wisdom of Amy Ashley. "All right, all right. But the odds of my running into the rotunda guy again are a million to one. I've never seen him around before. He was probably a tourist from Hackensack. Anyway, I'm not a cynic. I'm just . . . realistic." *Is that so wrong?* "But I'm not Irish, either, so I don't suppose it matters. I think you'd have to be Irish for the St. Patrick's Day thing to work." I threw a peanut across the table. "What do you think, Josh?"

Josh helped himself to the peanut and pretended to think about it. "We could test it." Throwing his head back and his arms out, he smiled and said, "Kiss me. I'm Irish."

Kaylyn rolled her eyes and pointed the straw at me again. "All right, how about we just put our money where our mouths are. I bet—" she interlaced her hands and steepled two fingers—"a year's supply of romance novels that you see that guy again, and that he asks you out before the month is over."

"You're on, sister." Laughing, I stuck out my hand to seal the deal. I wasn't a gambling type, but it seemed like an extremely safe wager.

Across the table, Josh was shaking his head with an expression of foreboding.

He knew how many romance novels Kaylyn could read in a year.

Chapter 2

Love is a many splendored thing. There's a more classic history to that phrase, I'm sure, but I learned it from a Sinatra album—the old-fashioned vinyl kind my father played on an ugly console stereo that looked like something out of *The Jetsons.*

The night after my sixth birthday party, that song tugged me from my bed. I moved to the sliding glass doors, pulled back the curtain, and saw my father out for a late-night swim, trying to coax my mother into the pool. She was curled in a chaise lounge, wearing a long, filmy negligee. The feather-edged sleeve floated diaphanous and light on the breeze as she playfully slapped his hand away. Laughing, she let her head fall against the cushion, her gaze rising into the starry night.

She never saw him coming. Without warning, he scooped her off the chair and carried her across the patio as she protested, squealed, and told him what she'd do to him if he ruined her new loungewear. He ignored her completely and swept her straight down the steps and into the water, deep blue under the smoky patio lights. The hem of her nightgown floated to the surface, her body and his disappearing into the darkness below as he kissed her.

I'd never seen my parents behave in such a fashion, never even considered whether they kissed or hugged or got romantic like the Bradys did on afternoon cable reruns. But after watching them in the pool, I knew that love really could be the way it was in the movies. From that night on, I believed in the possibility. Even if I'd never been lucky enough to find the right guy, I clung to a yearning that made me want that kind of intensity. All of my life a still, small voice had been whispering in my ear, *If it can happen to Mom, it can happen to anyone.*

My mother was about as stiff, proper, and practical as a woman could get. If she could be swept off her feet, anybody could.

I was off my feet almost from the moment I met Daniel Webster Everson. Both in the literal sense and the figurative sense. I twisted an ankle running for a subway train the day after the spilled-bill incident, and I was wearing a walking cast later that week when I hobbled into the office of James V. Faber, honorable congressman from Arkansas. Two steps in the door, and I found myself once again face to face with the startling green eyes I remembered from the rotunda.

Congressman Faber's home district was big in poultry production and processing. Daniel was a biochemist working for the USDA, visiting The Hill at Faber's request to discuss some particulars in a pork-barrel (or in this case poultry-barrel) rider to a bill working its way through committee. I'd dropped by Faber's office to personally pick up a LOI—Letter of Intent—that would make Faber a cosponsor for my boss's Clean Energy Bill.

Suffice to say that a freakish alignment of legislation brought me together with Daniel Everson for a second time.

Or perhaps it was the Irish legend.

Choose to believe as suits you, but God does create soul mates, and Daniel Webster Everson was mine. I knew it from the first time I saw him, and by the second time, I *knew* I knew it.

I limped into his life once again carrying an armload of papers. Daniel glanced up from the leather sofa in Faber's receiving area and noticed my uneven walk and the cast, attractively embellished with Sharpie drawings by office co-workers and the Gymies.

"Looks like things haven't quite taken that upturn yet," he observed. Very astute of him. Then he laughed softly and smiled, and I forgave him for making light of my unfashionable situation.

I noticed those boyishly thick lashes again. And his smile. If I had to feed Kaylyn's romance novel habit for a year, or ten, I had to know who he was.

"It's been that kind of week," I admitted. "Month, actually."

There was a flash of something in his eyes, as quickly as a car passing at the other end of an alley, but I saw it. A look that said, *Yeah, me too. That kind of week . . . month . . . year.*

I shifted the stack of papers onto my hip and tried to look as though one arm wasn't slowly growing longer than the other. My foot was hurting. I needed to get off it. The doctor had prescribed limited walking for a couple weeks while the ankle healed. You can't limit your walking on The Hill, not and be in the know. It's a big place. My position as a legislative assistant put me about halfway up the congressional staff ladder. There were plenty of young kids hungry for advancement, and each of them had two good feet. My only advantage was charm and the fact that, even though I'd tried for anonymity, word had gotten around. People knew who my father was.

Daniel stood up like he'd been pushed out of his seat by a loose spring. He reached for the documents. "Here. You look like you could use some help with those."

The rest was history, or a whirlwind, depending on your point of view. I asked about Daniel; he asked about me. Faber's personal assistant gave us irritated looks for muddying up a congressional office with an obvious flirtation. We exchanged business cards before Daniel headed for a consultation in Faber's office. After he'd passed the snotty personal assistant, he turned around, pointed at her and made a face, then mouthed, *I'll call you*, as if we'd known each other forever.

The grouchy lady swiveled a stern look over her shoulder. Daniel made a show of turning around and heading for the congressman's door.

I giggled.

I fell in love.

My ankle didn't hurt anymore, because I wasn't standing on it. I was floating a few inches off the ground.

Within four hours, my artsy cast and I were having dinner with Daniel at a hole-in-the-wall Italian place with decor that was vintage Dollar Store. I didn't mind. The food was good, and it hadn't taken me very long to figure out that my newly discovered prince, my gypsy king, my romance novel cover guy was, unfortunately, fairly broke. He had a master's degree in biochemistry, two years of university research experience, two years of interesting stories from having traveled the world doing crop science for an underfunded non-governmental organization, and a couple years of teaching experience at a city college. His recently acquired position at the USDA was his first real eight-to-five job. He also had a healthy supply of student loans, medical bills from a car accident a few years back, and a three-and-a-half-year-old son who, that particular week, was in Ohio with grandparents.

It was a lot to take in on a first date. I had a feeling that Daniel didn't usually share so much information so quickly. I wondered how much of his life he normally offered up to women he'd just met. Then I found my brown eyes going a little green over the idea that he met other women. Ever. I felt strangely possessive.

That didn't matter, as it turned out. For the next two weeks, we were together every evening. Both of us knew we didn't want to see anyone else.

Kaylyn started hounding me to pay her romance novel bills and to admit that Amy Ashley's Irish love legend had validity. Irish magic aside, the night before Daniel's son was to come home, I was worried. Other than roughhousing with my nieces and getting them in trouble with their mothers, I had no idea what to do with children of any size, particularly not a three-and-a-half-year-old. Aside from that, I'd grown up in a family full of girls. Boys were a complete mystery.

I was trying not to classify little Nick as a stumbling block, but a sense of loss and foreboding had begun needling me, even though I didn't want it to. It wasn't mature to think of a preschooler as the competition, but I liked things the way they were. Life with Daniel was . . . perfect. *We* were perfect. Just the two of us.

I hated myself for having that thought. I really did. I knew all about Nick. He was adorable—a towheaded version of his dad. I'd looked at his pictures in Daniel's apartment. I'd laughed at many a "Nick" story over dinners and lunches with Daniel. I'd stood in the doorway of Nick's room when Daniel wasn't looking, studied Nick's toys and his little race car bed, trying to imagine him there. I'd sympathized with Daniel when he'd snuggled me under his chin and brooded because Nick had started to notice that other kids in day care got picked up by their mothers. Nick wanted *his* mother to pick him up. Nick didn't have a mother. Not that anyone could see, anyway.

"Nick's mother doesn't ever get in touch?" I asked, trying to picture her. There were no photos of her in Daniel's apartment. I suspected that was intentional. Daniel's face revealed an obvious pain whenever Nick's mom came up in conversation. "She doesn't ask to see him?"

A sigh deflated his chest beneath my cheek. "She didn't want kids. She's into her work." The bitterness in his voice worried me, if I wasn't worried enough already. I already knew that Nick's mother worked for an oil company and traveled around the world. "Nick wasn't planned," he added.

"*I* wasn't planned, either, but my mom didn't just walk out on me," I said, and then admonished myself for overstepping.

"It is what it is." Daniel's arm tightened around me in a way that made me feel good. I was reassured that I hadn't said the wrong thing. I tried again to imagine Nick's mom. I conjured an image of an executive. In my mind she was tall, svelte, with the face and body of a fashion model. Blond, probably, judging by Nick's hair. He didn't get that from his father.

"It's just harder now that he's asking, you know?" Daniel's hand slid up and down my arm, raising a pleasant tingle on my skin. I felt an expectation in that caress, in Daniel's words, in the absence of Nick's mother. There was an empty space to be filled here, for both Daniel and Nick. But I'd met Daniel only two weeks ago. How could either of us possibly know whether I was the person to fill it?

I wasn't a very likely candidate. If I met Nick now, we might only be setting him up for disappointment. On the other hand, if I didn't meet Nick, how would I continue to spend time with Daniel? With no relatives living nearby, Daniel was a full-time single dad. The last two weeks had been an anomaly.

Real life was headed this way, safely strapped in a car seat in the back of the grandparents' minivan.

"I don't usually let him . . . meet people," Daniel offered, and I felt sick. He was having second thoughts, trying to gently tell me that we needed to cool it for a while. Maybe now that Nick was coming back, Daniel was rethinking things altogether. Now that there was a child involved, perhaps Daniel was sensing the thing that men seemed to pick up on innately: I was hopelessly nondomestic. I couldn't even make macaroni and cheese, the boxed kind.

I understand. I knew that was the correct response, but I couldn't force the words out. I felt another unwanted stab of competitiveness toward little Nick. Looking across the room, I took in a picture of him dressed in a Giants jersey, a massive football helmet hiding his face in shadow, so that only a huge smile showed. I envisioned myself getting into a squat like an NFL lineman and knocking him off the playing field. I was bigger than he was. . . .

The thought was reprehensible, of course. It was only proof of what I already knew: I was the spoiled, self-centered, over-indulged, late-in-life baby of the family and would never grow up. Completely hopeless.

"So . . . then . . . what . . ." *What are you saying? What does this mean? What do you want me to say?* I reached up and rubbed my eyebrows, then pinched hard, a little pulse thrumming beneath my fingertips. The I'm-not-going-to-cry feeling stung my throat. Daniel's parents would be here tomorrow, road weary after driving from Ohio, and on their way to visit their other grandkids. Daniel and I had already established that this wasn't the best time for me to meet them. *They're a little touchy because of Nick,* he'd explained. Now Daniel was having cold feet, too.

"He's getting old enough that he notices things," Daniel remarked vaguely.

"Things?" My voice trembled a little, just getting that much out. I felt like I was groping in a dark room, waiting for Freddy Krueger to jump from the shadows and slash my heart in two. Another relationship meets its gruesome demise.

A soft little laugh-snort ruffled my hair and my thoughts. Now I was completely confused. Daniel found this funny? I was dying here. "Yeah, like the other day on the phone, he asked me why some people at Nanbee's and Grandpa's have one name, and some people have two. The second cousins, even the teenagers, who seem like grown-ups to him, are Angie, Chris, Corrie, and Zack, but the great-aunts and uncles are Aunt Tammy, Uncle Carl, and so on. The nursery ladies at their church are Miss Lori and Miss Teresa. He's all confused."

"Oh." So was I—all confused.

Daniel shifted on the sofa, forcing me to sacrifice the warm spot under his chin, so I could see him. Those eyes, those beautiful green eyes, took me in. They were so pensive, so concerned, as if an invasion of the Daddy-body-snatchers had stolen away my gypsy king.

I felt every heartbeat in my chest, felt the teary lump rising and growing more imminent by the minute. *Please don't say it. Please don't say it.*

"So, anyway, I was thinking . . ." he began.

Here it comes, here it comes. I braced myself. Or tried. For some reason, a snippet of Josh and Kaylyn's video-game programmer talk raced through my mind. *Shields, shields, raise the deflector shields . . .*

" . . . what do you think he should call you?" Daniel finished.

"I . . . huh?" My disembodied self melted back into the

carcass of the highlighted-blond, brown-eyed girl on the sofa. *Seriously?* I wanted to say. *You scared me to death for that?*

I pretended to have a tickle in my throat and something in my eye. In reality, tears of joy had begun to seep onto the bridge of my nose. "Sorry. I must have gotten a whiff of something." I fanned myself, my body hot, then cold, then hot again. My gosh. I was crazy about this man. How was that possible after only a couple weeks? "I don't know. I hadn't thought about it." *Because I know absolutely nothing about kids.* To my nieces, I was just a big kid—someone fun to play with, but completely useless at mealtime or bath time.

Daniel scratched the nape of his neck, seeming to agonize over the question. "It's just that . . . well . . . however we get him started, that's what it'll be forever. Kids are creatures of habit, you know?"

I nodded. Nope, didn't know. This whole issue had never even crossed my tiny little mind, nor could I really focus on it now. I was still stuck on one word of that sentence: *forever. Forever, forever, forever.*

"Why don't you pick?" I suggested. "I'm okay with whatever you decide."

Whoops. I instantly sensed that I'd given the wrong answer. He looked disappointed—as if I'd blown off something he considered important, indicating that I didn't understand the weight of it. "Okay, let me think a minute." I said. *Think. Think, think, think . . .*

I'm not his aunt. I'm not his mother. Well, not yet, but a girl can dream. These were changing times, but I had always been taught that children didn't call adults by their first names. My mother found the familiar way my older nieces spoke to me to be completely distasteful. Since they wouldn't use *Aunt Mallory*, she had attempted to convert them to *Tante M*, the French word for *aunt*, which, in her view, had greater hipness to it. It was a flop, unless the nieces were trying to tease me. Then, when Mother asked who'd spilled Kool-Aid on the kitchen floor and failed to wipe it up, they'd call out, *Tante M did it,* with an emphasis on the French.

It crossed my mind that whenever I did finally work up the guts to confess to my mother that I was seriously dating a divorced guy with a three-and-a-half-year-old son—at which time she would frown gravely and remind me that I was recently out of a two-year relationship—she would not be impressed if Daniel's preschool-aged child was calling me by my first name.

"How about Tante M? It's French for *aunt.* It's sort of a weird handle my mother made up. She hates it when the nieces call me by my first name."

"Tante M." Daniel licked his lips, tasting the word.

I watched his lips, felt myself swoon. Everything about him lit me up like a Christmas tree. He hadn't even tried to put the moves on me, which, considering that this was DC, was shocking. Daniel was a perfect gentleman, old-fashioned in his view of things. I found that as charming as everything else about him. I'd almost lost faith that there were guys like that around anymore, but deep inside me, there was that image of my parents romancing in the pool. I'd always known that casual relationships were no substitute for true love and lifetime commitment. Aside from that, Great-grandma Louisa had avidly assured us girls that a man does not buy the cow if he can get the milk for free. You don't forget a mental image like that one. Ever.

"But we can pick something else if you don't think that seems good." Maybe he thought the whole foreign language thing was dorky.

He shifted, bracing a hand on the sofa arm and leaning toward me. "I don't know. I'm not sure I want some other man talking to you in French." His voice was throaty and rich. "You might like him better than you like me."

"Not possible," I whispered, and he kissed me, and the storm of worry in my mind whirled off into a corner, growing smaller and smaller, until it was just a little swirl, like water spinning down the drain after a hot bath.

Not possible that I could like someone better than you. In some hidden part of my soul, I knew that *like* wasn't the word I meant. I didn't just *like* Daniel. I was in love in every way a girl could be. If two weeks was too soon to be using that word, I couldn't help it. This was it. The Amy Ashley romance novel kind of love. I wanted to be his Irish bride.

No other man I would ever meet could possibly make me feel like this, I was certain.

But as it turned out, little Nick took a pretty good stab at it the very next day. I liked him the minute we met, over a picnic of fried chicken and soggy potato wedges. I'd been burning the midnight oil at work, and the best I could do was a quick brown-bag dinner in Bartholdi Park. I was, at least, newly out of the walking cast, so the stroll over was no problem.

Nick was not only adorable, he was funny, articulate, and—perhaps because he felt the absence of a mom in his life—surprisingly attuned to women. Moments after we met, he told me he liked my hair. I'd let it dry wavy that day, and he said it was *princess hair.* I fell in love. While Nick explored the softly trickling water feature nearby, I told his father he had competition for my affections.

"Figures." Daniel let his head droop forward, his shoulders rounding in a display of surrender. "Nick always gets the girls. You should see him at day care."

"I think you're doing all right yourself." I stretched onto my tiptoes for a kiss while Nick wasn't looking. The next thing I knew, something was pushing on my knee, trying to force me away from Daniel. An instant later, I realized that it was Nick, and that we'd been caught. Guilt sledgehammered me. I'd watched the talk shows. I knew that this first meeting should have been about getting acquainted in a nonthreatening way that was easy for Nick to adjust to. Less than a half hour together, and I'd blown it already. He hated me. *Step away from my daddy,* the pressure of that little hand said. *Who do you think you are, strange-princess-hair-woman?*

Daniel and I yielded to the push in unison. There was a hand pressing on his leg, too. When we looked down, Nick was poised between us like a tiny Atlas, trying to hold two worlds apart. Daniel cleared his throat, obviously uncomfortable. He gave me a worried look. I was sorry that we hadn't waited for a less rushed time to begin introductions with Nick—maybe allowed him a few days to reacclimate to DC.

"Sorry, buddy," Daniel said, and Nick just rolled a look at him—the kind of honest scorn that comes from a little psyche not yet attuned to hiding feelings in order to make everyone feel warm and fuzzy.

We'd really screwed up.

Daniel extended a hand to take Nick's. "C'mon, bud. Let's go see the water."

I took a step back. Now would probably be a good time to exit, since this hadn't gone so well. "I should . . . ummm . . ." I thumbed over my shoulder, wincing apologetically. "Go back to . . ."

I never finished the sentence. The most amazing thing happened, and in that moment, I felt certain that angels must have been swirling overhead. They smiled down on us as Nick turned to me, his face rising into the light, his blue eyes framed with his father's thick lashes. He reached upward, fingers extended, all ten of them, as far as they would go, and in the space of a heartbeat, I understood that he wanted me to pick him up.

Daniel and I glanced at each other, and he just shrugged. "Well, I can see I'm second-rate."

I picked Nick up, swinging him onto my hip somewhat awkwardly, but he didn't seem to notice. Instead, he flashed an over-the-shoulder smirk at his dad, a pleased look with perhaps a hint of gloat in it. Daniel grinned wider and shook his head, a dark curl toying near his eyebrow. "I think someone's after my best g-i-r-l." He spelled the last word, and Nick squinted at him, trying to discern the meaning.

I felt like a queen, like a rock star, like a supermodel with adoring fans crowding in at the edges of the catwalk, fighting over me. Nick wasn't pushing me away from his dad. He was pushing his dad away from me.

Nick wrapped his little arms around my shoulders, and from that moment on, we were friends. He quickly discovered that although I didn't know how to properly cut up a hot dog into toddler bites and I could not even begin to name the characters on *Thomas the Tank Engine*, I could keep a balloon in the air for a long time without reusing any part of my body, I was pretty good with a soccer ball, and I had a poor short-term memory that made me easy to beat at the memory match card game. Time after time, it was a mystery to me which card had the purple dinosaur under it and which had the rubber ducky, and so on. Nick loved that about me. He also knew more farm animal sounds than I did, and he loved that, too. I had no idea what a goat might say, and I didn't know whether a bull would *moo* like a cow or snort like a fire-breathing dragon. Nick knew because his grandparents lived in a rural neighborhood with farms just down the road. I didn't mind losing parlor games to a kid who had yet to graduate from day care to official preschool. I was just happy that the three of us were bonding so well.

We made dinners together. We played games. We did things

on the weekends. We watched the last of the spring blossoms fall and new leaves come in. The Gymies, fearing that I'd been kidnapped by some underground government agency, began reconnoitering, sniffing out the situation, asking concerned questions.

"Don't you think things are moving a little . . . fast, though?" Kaylyn wanted to know when I called to ask Josh if I could borrow a few of his Disney DVDs for a couple days. Daniel had to go out of town to some sort of symposium about fertilizers and genetically modified super crops, and due to a snafu with the baby-sitting he'd arranged, I'd agreed to stay with Nick through the weekend.

"I mean, it sounds like you're practically moving in over there." Kaylyn's romantic notions of St. Patrick's Day magic and Irish destiny seemed to have faded away. "It's only been, like, a month, y'know."

A month? Had it really been only a month? "I'm *just* watching Nick for the weekend while Daniel's gone. I'm not *moving in*." But in the pit of my stomach there was a giddy little domestic feeling that I hadn't told anyone about. I was looking forward to spending the weekend with Nick—boiling hot dogs, working on my ability to make boxed convenience foods, watching Disney movies, and reading favorite story-books before tucking him into his little race car bed.

"What's your mom think about all this?" Kaylyn had been dragged along on enough of my mother's DC shopping visits to fully understand the undertows between Mom and me.

"I haven't . . . exactly . . . said anything to them," I admitted.

"You haven't told your parents?" Kaylyn's shock caused me to hold the cell phone away from my ear.

"I will. I will," I ground out, the pressure pinching like a hermit crab nested under the mop of hair at the back of my neck. "I'm just waiting until I go home for Easter next week.

That way, I can tell them in person—sort of ease Mom into it, so she doesn't go berserk. The whole thing about Daniel being divorced-with-kid might throw her a little. She thinks divorced guys are damaged goods. She's prehistoric that way."

"You haven't told your parents *anything*?" Kaylyn reiterated, then she covered the phone and shared the news with Josh, who was probably hard at work on the other side of their cubicle, creating fantasy characters and pixel-based swords for some new video game. "Mallory hasn't told her family anything about Mr. Wonderful or Little Mr. Wonderful."

I heard Josh's response. "Whoa. That's radical."

The conversation went on from there, Kaylyn's admonishments heaping guilt and trepidation on me until I almost gave up my quest to wrestle away some of Josh's prized Disney DVDs.

But I wanted those movies, so I persevered, and an hour later, I was picking them up on my way to grab Nick from day care. Kaylyn was concerned about my ability to handle over forty-eight hours of parental responsibility. She dredged up the issue of the little window-hanging finch feeder she'd given me for Christmas. The one that sat empty while disenfranchised birds cast wistful looks from nearby electrical lines.

"I'm not going to forget to feed the kid," I insisted as Josh caressed the stack of Disney movies, appearing to have second thoughts. "I'm *not*. Seriously, I've got it all planned out. He's just one little boy, and he's adorable, and we have a blast together. What could possibly go wrong?"

I should have known that such questions only tempt fate.

Nick picked that weekend to get the stomach flu.

I learned about thermometers and wet wipes, sensitive skin and Desitin, sponge baths, dehydration, throw up, washing sheets, washing sheets again, scrubbing stains out of carpet, and calling the emergency hotline in the middle of the night.

I also learned what fully qualified caretakers already know. The stomach flu is contagious.

By the time Daniel came home, Nick and I were a couple of washed-out rag dolls, strung across the recliner, nibbling soda crackers and blearily watching *Bambi* for the umpteenth time. Daniel went down to the Chinese restaurant on the corner and bought soup for us. When he came back, he fixed trays and then got to work cleaning up the offal of towels, clothes, DVDs, toys, and empty Pedialite bottles that had overtaken the apartment during our quest to survive. The phone rang while he was carrying an armload of stuff to Nick's toy box. He took the call in the bedroom. When he came out, he was as pale as Nick and me.

"What's wrong?" I asked. He looked like someone had died. I immediately thought of his family in Ohio. I only knew what Daniel had told me. He had a mom, dad, grandparents, and various cousins, aunts, and uncles all living within a thirty-mile radius, and a brother who lived in Boston with his wife and kids. Like my parents, Daniel's parents still owned the house he'd grown up in. I hoped the call hadn't brought bad news—a car accident or something.

"I think I just got offered a job," he said, his jaw hanging slack after the words, a hint of five o'clock shadow testifying to the fact that, in his rush to return home to Nick and me, he hadn't even shaved this morning.

"A job?" That didn't sound like bad news. Why the horrified expression?

He nodded slowly, his eyes shifting toward the bedroom doorway, as if the spirit of something large and life-altering were hovering there, and he expected it to come storming up the hallway any moment.

His next two words explained everything. "In Texas."

The course of true love never did run smooth.

—William Shakespeare, *A Midsummer Night's Dream*
(Left by Brent, who spent the night *outside* the tent)

Chapter 3

A job.

In.

Texas.

I heard it that way, as if it were several sentences rather than one. My life flashed before my eyes—two lives, actually. Two completely different possibilities. In one, I was sitting at a table with the Gymies again, a week from now or maybe a month, eating round-robin pie, engaged in yet another conversation about video game characters, Disney animation, and fascinating computer-related topics like bits, bytes, and black-hole servers. Meanwhile, Daniel and Nick were far, far away in Texas. Pretty close to the other side of the world.

In the opposing scenario, I was packing my pumps and my black suit, those knockoff designer purses I loved so much, and the rest of my worldly belongings. Outside the window, a moving man with a dolly was pushing my life up the ramp a few boxes at a time. I was headed for Texas, to some big city or other. They did have big cities in Texas—commerce, corporations, skyscraper office buildings, shopping malls . . .

I'd watched an entire season of *Dallas* reruns on DVD during a girl trip with my sisters. I could live in the world of the Ewings. Find out who shot J.R. for real.

Once again, I'd be moving far, far away from my family. . . .

My mother would have a coronary. . . .

You've only been dating the man a month. What are you thinking?

Maybe we could do the long-distance thing. I could fly down on weekends. Daniel and Nick could visit for the holidays . . .

Flying with a three-and-a-half-year-old would be a hassle . . .

Those thoughts and a dozen others raced through my mind, rapid-fire, but all I managed to say was "Oh."

"Yeah," Daniel breathed, then pressed his lips together and swallowed hard. Behind those gorgeous eyes, I could see the wheels turning, full speed like mine. I wondered where they were headed.

"Umm . . . where in Texas?" Inside me a voice was wailing, *Say something. Tell me what you're thinking.* I mentally cycled through the possibilities, calling up scattered shreds of Texology gleaned from pop culture references and office chitchat. One of the cosponsors of the Clean Energy Bill was a congressman from Texas—someplace out in the sparsely populated part, where cowboys and oil wells dotted the lone prairie.

City names swirled through my mind, potential backdrops for my potential new life. *Dallas, Houston, Austin . . . uhhhh . . . San . . . something . . . San Antonio. Abilene, like in the old song about cattle drives. Or was that in Kansas? Abilene, Kansas, or Texas?*

"Moses Lake." Daniel's answer broke through the clatter in my mind, silencing it momentarily.

Moses Lake. Never heard of that one. The word *Lake*

implied something pleasant—water, sun, surf. Texas did have coastal areas and large inland bodies of water. The Clean Energy Bill's Texas cosponsor had tucked something in there to provide financial incentives for hydroelectric power generation on Texas rivers.

Moses Lake could be good.

Keeping an open mind here.

"Where is that?" I inched into new territory, since I had no idea what Daniel was thinking and how this job offer might affect the two of us.

A baffled headshake answered my question. "I'm not exactly sure. Somewhere in the middle. There's an island involved. Firefly Island."

"But what's it near?" *Dallas, Houston, Austin, San Antonio. Give me a reference point. Someplace to anchor my fantasy future.*

Daniel shook his head again, his gaze analyzing the room, as if he were already considering the size and number of moving boxes needed. "Don't know. I didn't want to look like an idiot, asking the man a million questions. He was in a limo on his way from the airport, so he didn't tell me a lot, except that he maintains research crop plots there, as well as a state-of-the-art lab, and then he mentioned something about Firefly Island. I'm sure, being Jack West, he just assumes that people know all about him. He wants me there in a month."

Jack West . . . Why was that name familiar?

Nick tapped my hand with a cracker package, and I opened it without thinking, then handed it back to him. "There you go, peapod." Over the past couple days, I'd adopted my mother's usual endearment for anyone under the age of twenty-five, *peapod.*

"I need a map," Daniel muttered and headed for the door. "A real paper map I can look at all at once." He didn't even ask if I would stay and watch Nick. He just left. Somehow, I liked that. It implied that I belonged here.

By the time Daniel came back, he'd already looked at the map and folded it to two panels surrounding the mystery job location. Moses Lake was a tiny dot in a crease, the letters so small it practically blended into the background. Surrounding it, although not too closely, lay other little map-dot towns with names like Cleburne, Blum, Aquilla, and Walnut Springs. There was nothing of major metropolitan size nearby. Dallas, Austin, San Antonio, and even smaller cities like Waco seemed disturbingly far away, reachable only via pencil-thin strips of highway printed in an unpromising light gray.

I felt myself going queasy, my bound-for-Texas version of the future warping like an image in a funhouse mirror. Clearly, I wouldn't be following Daniel and Nick to Texas, applying for jobs nearby, setting myself up in a little apartment around the corner until such time as we'd come far enough in the relationship to merge our lives, so to speak. This place in the fold, this Moses Lake, was a life without me in it.

I could see in Daniel's eyes that he was seriously considering the trade-offs. I could hear it in his voice as he talked about the offer from Jack West, the owner of tiny, but well-funded, West Research. Daniel was more excited than I'd ever seen him. He'd heard Jack West speak at the symposium. Apparently Mr. West had heard Daniel, as well, and he was impressed. He felt that Daniel's work with genetically modified grains would fit nicely into West's master plan to develop super crops and super growth environments designed to produce food in the increasingly harsh conditions of a world plagued with erratic weather. By some standards, Daniel admitted, Jack West was a flake, or at the very least, eccentric and anti-establishment. He'd found fame in the sixties as an actor, then had a short political career before marrying into

Texas oil money. He'd inherited an unfathomable fortune when his first wife died.

While he was out looking for a map, Daniel had scoured the Internet via his phone and come up with a *New York Times* article about Jack West. As I read it, Daniel watched me, his gaze trying to bore through the side of my head and discern my thoughts. There was a sense of the room holding its breath, as if every stick of furniture and stitch of clothing, including Nick's toys, were lining up, whispering, *Toy box or moving box? Which one? Which one?*

On television, Owl was talking to Bambi and Thumper about being twitterpated, a hopeless infatuation that causes love-struck young creatures to completely lose their minds in the spring.

"I don't know . . ." I looked across the table at Daniel and thought, *Don't go. Don't do this.* I wasn't only considering myself, considering us. I was afraid for him, and for Nick. "It sounds kind of . . . crazy. I mean, you've got Nick to think about and your job and . . . well . . . health insurance and retirement . . . everything. And what about day care? Nick would have to get used to someone totally new. And then there are your parents, and your brother and his kids. They'll be so far away." I heard air slowly escaping Daniel's lips. I knew I was deflating him, but I couldn't help it. Selfish motives and genuine concern were a mishmash at this point, like multicolored blobs of Play-Doh carelessly pinched together, impossible to separate now. I didn't want Daniel and Nick to go. I couldn't bear the idea of it.

I looked at Nick, tried to imagine him growing up somewhere else. Maybe with *someone* else.

Drawbacks popped into my mind in rapid succession, and I threw them out like road spikes in Daniel's exit path. "And then there's all the everyday stuff. I mean, that town looks *tiny.* Where would you find a good preschool next year? Where would you even *live* in a town that small?"

Daniel ran a hand through his hair, drew back that little curl that hung over his forehead, making him look like Christopher Reeve in *Superman.* "That's just it, well . . . that's one thing. The place is so remote that housing comes with it. The research lab and the crop plots are actually on West's ranch, which is—I forget what he said—ten thousand acres, or something, some of it right along the lakeshore. There's housing there for the ranch hands, and one of those houses is part of the job offer. Three bedrooms, two baths." He looked at me, the expression in his eyes almost pleading with me to breathe gently on the dream, cause it to spark rather than blow out. "Nick could grow up in a house, a *real* house, instead of this dumpy little place. He could run around in the woods, build tree forts, catch frogs and lizards like my brother and I did in Ohio. It was a great way to grow up, you know? As long as we were home by dark, nobody worried about us. Mom could send us out the door in the morning, and all she'd have to tell us was to watch for snakes and be home by supper. And this place is even better than that. What kid wouldn't like to have a lake on his doorstep?"

I didn't answer immediately. I was still stuck on *frogs, lizards,* and *snakes.* I'd never lived more than a stone's throw from neighbors and a mini-mart. Even my parents' house in Maryland was sandwiched between other large houses with manicured lawns. The only lakes I'd ever spent any time on were the sort at which my father schmoozed with congressmen, senators, and their families—the kind with gorgeous resorts featuring nice, clean swimming pools and lovely cabanas. Were there beaches somewhere that weren't lined with resorts, littered with sunbathers, and dotted with colorful umbrellas? Did such places exist?

39

I felt tears pressing in, crowding my eyes and my senses. My gypsy king was gently telling me good-bye, justifying all the reasons he needed to go. I heard his voice almost in the background now, like a television droning on when you're busy with something else.

" . . . The salary isn't really any higher, but there's so much included. The house, the utilities paid, a company vehicle. It's like making twice as much as I make now. I'd be able to finally work my way out from under some bills and start putting away money for Nick's college." His eyes met mine again, and I took a small bit of encouragement from that. Maybe he really did mean to continue our relationship long-distance. I didn't see how. There wasn't a major airport in Moses Lake. "It's the difference between two completely different lives, Mallory," Daniel said.

Yes, it is, I thought, my long-distance fantasy dissolving like a mirage on a hot day. It was the difference between *us* and *you-there-and-me-here.*

"And that's not even mentioning the work." Daniel was so excited, he was talking ninety miles an hour, overloading my brain, causing it to whir. "This guy is a little . . . atypical, but he's light-years ahead of conventional science on all kinds of things, not just the super crops, but low-impact growth environments and foods that fight cancer. You wouldn't believe all the good his work could do. And he's got the funds to keep it going. Private funds. And I'll have a share in any patents we're granted. If we come up with the kind of modified seed grain I think we can, there's no telling what the bio-patents could be worth. Imagine corn that could grow in the desert, or wheat that produces under drought conditions. Imagine what that could mean."

I nodded, swallowing hard. Sue me, but at that particular moment, I didn't care about growing corn in the desert; I cared about the life I wasn't going to have. With Daniel. I'd finally found the right one, my prince had come, and some billionaire was determined to tumble my castle of cards before I could dab enough glue on it. Why couldn't Jack West buy someone else's boyfriend? Why did he have to have mine?

Because Daniel was brilliant, and he was wasting away at that USDA lab, and he was made for better things. I knew the reason. I knew I should love him enough to let him go. He wasn't happy in the job here. He was trapped in it.

His hand slid across the map, covered mine, clasped it. I felt reality staring me down like a Rottweiler, dark-eyed and malevolent.

"Come with us."

At first I wasn't sure I heard the words correctly. "Huh?"

"Come with us," he repeated, more emphatically this time, his eyes taking on a glow that pulled me in. "Come on, Mallory, think about it. We both know that we . . . us . . . the two of us and Nick . . . Something so right doesn't come along every day. I realize it's not the best timing—it's only been a month, but life isn't about waiting for perfect timing. If you're not careful, life happens while you're stuck in a holding pattern."

My heart leapt, and fell, and leapt, and fell, the rebound a little less complete each time, like the bounce of a basketball slowly losing air. "Daniel, I don't even know where I'd live in a place like that, or where I'd get a job, or . . ." *Anything.* " . . . how I'd pay my bills or . . ." Mentally, I cycled through the arguments. This was nuts. Even thinking about it was nuts.

"Live with us." His gaze tangled with mine, his free hand rising, covering my fingers so that he had me in a double grip.

"You want me to . . . move in with you guys?" It was one of the things I'd promised myself I would never do. Call me old-fashioned, and this was the twenty-first century, but I still had Grandma Louisa and her Southern wisdom about cows and milk in the back of my mind. What kind of idiot would move across the country, give up her job, her family, and everything else to move in with a guy?

An idiot hopelessly in love . . . maybe? Or maybe not. My parents had raised me not to sacrifice my principles. It was a strange dichotomy, considering what my father did for a living. Lobbyists aren't known for principles.

Daniel laughed softly, his lips forming a lopsided grin. He lifted his chin, those gorgeous eyes sparkling, mesmerizing. "I'm asking you to marry me. I've been thinking about it since I left to get the map."

I felt moisture on my hands, as if suddenly his skin had gone hot. "You decided that . . . while you were out *buying the map*?" I stammered, shocked and incredulous, though I didn't want to be. Past pain leaves behind unfortunate slug trails of cynicism. Everyone who comes into your life afterward can't help stepping in them. I'd had a man ask me to marry him on a whim once before. In the aftermath, I knew we weren't meant for each other, and maybe I wasn't meant for marriage at all.

Groaning, Daniel let his head fall forward. "Ugh . . . I'm really botching this." I felt a little tremble in his hands, but there was a resoluteness in his jaw. "I love you, Mallory Hale. I have from the first time I met you. That may sound corny. Man, I know it sounds corny. I feel like I'm channeling some sappy made-for-cable movie here, but it's the truth. I can't help it. That's all I have to offer, Mal. A sappy-sounding line, Nick and me, stomach-flu germs from the day care, and a life that looks like it might be an adventure. I don't have a lot of money or a big house, and the week I met you was probably my first and last time to rub elbows with the political power brokers. I know it's not what you planned on. I know you're used to better."

There is no one better, I thought, but instead, I said, "Well, if there's adventure and the stomach flu involved, then count me in."

Irreverent laughter spilled from his lips. "You know I'm serious here, right?"

I met his gaze, tumbled in, and saw the future. Not in the crisp clarity of photos—because I couldn't picture this over-the-rainbow life he was describing, or me in it—but in shades of color. The soft grays of mornings, the muted rose and violet of sunsets, the stark, blinding yellows and whites of middays. I saw holidays and seasons and years. Growing up, growing outward, growing old. I didn't want to live one year, one season, one day without Daniel and Nick.

"I know you're serious," I whispered. My heart traveled on the words. I felt like *His Irish Bride.* Amy Ashley was right about the St. Patrick's Day thing. She had to be. This was some kind of magic. "There *is* nobody better than you, Daniel Webster Everson. Nobody in the whole world. If you're going to Texas, then I guess I'm . . ." *Gulp.* My throat tightened. I wasn't sure I could say it. By sheer force of will, I managed to croak, "Going to Texas, too."

There. The deed was done, the promise made. A rush of emotions came at me, leaving me confused and uncertain. What did I do now? Call a moving company? Write a resignation letter for my job? Tell the Gymies good-bye, leaving Kaylyn with a blank check to buy endless romance novels? Try to sublet my apartment?

Call my mother?

Ohhh . . . my mother. I was supposed to go home to Maryland for Easter next week. I did *not* want to deliver this news in person. I didn't want to deliver this news on the phone, either. I didn't want to deliver this news. Period.

My mother would flip her lid so high, it would land

somewhere in Boston harbor. She'd have me committed. My father would hire private investigators to look into Daniel's background, or find an interventionist to deprogram me. I couldn't possibly make them understand this. *I* didn't fully understand it. I hadn't even told them about Daniel and Nick yet. And now I had to inform them that I planned to get married and move to Texas? Next month?

"You know what, forget I said anything." Daniel broke into my thoughts. I realized that Nick had come over from the television to climb into his dad's lap. The *Bambi* credits were rolling, the DVD getting ready to cycle back to the main menu. I'd watched it enough this weekend to know. "Forget I asked, okay?"

For half a second, I was relieved. I actually had the fleeting realization that, if I didn't get married and move to Texas, I wouldn't have to tell my mother. Then *Forget I asked* hit me like an unexpected right cross. He was having second thoughts? Already?

Daniel backpedaled. "I mean, don't forget I asked, but just pretend it didn't happen. When we're old and gray, and our grandkids ask how I popped the question, I don't want the story to be about a trip to the newsstand and egg drop soup with soda crackers. Let me rewind and do it right, okay? You only get to do it once."

Nick, completely confused, partially dehydrated with his eyelids drooping, burrowed under his dad's chin. My chest swelled, filling with the sight of them until I thought it might break me open. *Old and gray, grandkids, only once.* This was it. This was it, and we both knew it. I wanted to tell him that the proposal was perfect just the way he'd said it. Instead, I blinked, giving him a blank look. "What? Did you say something? So how was your trip to the conference?"

Pointing a finger at me, he winked and grinned.

The next day, at the very hour I'd first met Daniel Webster Everson, in the very same spot just off the Capitol rotunda, Daniel and Nick showed up, spit shined in their Easter suits, carrying two dozen red roses. Each gave me a ring. Daniel's came in a burgundy velvet box from a jewelry store. Nick's came in the plastic bubble from a gumball machine. Both were equally precious, but even more amazing was the fact that Daniel had secured the help of the grouchy personal assistant in Congressman Faber's office. It confirmed my suspicion that he was, indeed, Superman. My Superman.

Cheers went up in the Capitol building at an hour of the morning normally quiet. Even the Gymies were there. Kaylyn and Josh had written a special video game segment just for Daniel and me. We watched it on Daniel's computer later that evening. Daniel's little cowboy figure chased mine through a maze, and when the two finally met, he lassoed his sweetheart and said "Yee-haw!" Nick thought it was awesome. By the time he was ready for bed, we'd watched the video game over and over and over.

After Nick was down for the count, Daniel and I made plans to go home to my parents' place together for Easter, to deliver the news in person. We'd decided that, given the short time frame and all the practical details of moving across country, a quick trip to a wedding chapel made the most sense.

Everything seemed to be clicking into place . . . until the parents actually got involved. After the initial attempts to talk sense into us, the dads threw up their hands and the moms began talking on the phone daily. Daniel and I were having a real wedding, whether we had time for it or not. My mother was particularly determined that I would be married by the Presbyterian minister who had performed my sisters' ceremonies. She pulled the minister out of retirement and forced my father to throw down big bucks for last-minute tuxedos, flowers, music, wedding cake, a zillion yards of tulle, and rented candelabras at the little white church I'd attended since childhood, albeit mostly on special occasions and holidays.

Due to a surprise root canal a week before the wedding, and an inconvenient problem with the medications, I had practically nothing to do with the planning.

On an evening of gale-force May storms, with a small crowd of family looking on, I walked down the aisle in a white dress worn by my grandmother, mother, and all four of my sisters. Technically, I was homeless, and almost everything I owned was in a shipping container bound for the Texas ranch of a man of uncertain reputation.

My youngest niece panicked at the last minute and refused to walk the aisle with the basket of flower petals. Nick tugged her along and hammed it up with the ring pillow, stealing the show, but none of it mattered.

I was marrying the man I loved. I was becoming a mom. I was no longer a lone entity, but half of a whole, one third of a trio.

And all together, we were headed for Texas.

The moments of happiness we enjoy take us by surprise.
It is not that we seize them, but that they seize us.

—Ashley Montagu
(Left by Alice, Cindy, and Paula on their annual Binding Through Books
getaway. No fellas, no kids, no worries, just sisters and stories.)

Chapter 4

There's something incredibly weird about spending your wedding night in the playroom of your childhood. Your mind flashes back to games of Monopoly and Life and to teenage parties where kisses were stolen while the adults were in the kitchen refilling the punch bowl. You feel like you're doing something for which you'll be caught by your parents any moment. For some, this may lend an atmosphere of danger to the wedding night romance, but for me it was just . . . embarrassing.

It really wasn't anyone's fault that the hotel had been flooded by a sewage backup. In actuality, we were lucky. It's better to find out about the sewer problem before you check into the honeymoon suite than after. It was late by then, and my mother made the command decision to boot some of my nieces out of the place we'd always lovingly referred to as the *rumpus room*—a little guest cottage that had served as the playhouse to beat all playhouses. Mostly, I remembered it as my older sisters' teenage party spot, where I was typically not welcome after about eight in the evening.

My mother, being ever resourceful, had enlisted my older nieces to give the rumpus room an emergency face-lift while Daniel, Nick, and I spent time in the parlor with Daniel's parents. The nieces carried in leftover wedding flowers, then strung up the white twinkle lights and the yards of filmy fabric that had decorated the sanctuary during the ceremony.

The twinkle lights glittered as Daniel and I entered the rumpus room, the glow illuminating haphazard organza drapes that hid shelves of old girl toys. Diaphanous curtains hung around the lumpy sofa bed, presumably to provide us with some privacy from Nick, who was supposed to be sleeping in a hotel room with Daniel's parents, but had been clinging to his dad all night, insecure about the flood of new people. Now he was dozing and waking on Daniel's shoulder, all worn out from a day that had started with cramming our remaining belongings into a small U-Haul trailer, and had ended here in the rumpus room. We were suddenly a family of three—five if you counted Barbie and Ken, whom my nieces (the smart alecks) had dressed in wedding attire and positioned in a passionate clutch on the bed of a well-worn Barbie Dream House.

After tucking Nick into the love seat at the other end of the room, where the wall heater hummed directly above his head, so, theoretically, he wouldn't hear anything, Daniel peeked under a mound of organza in the center of the room, which was hiding an ugly pink plastic slide that had belonged to one of my nieces. Giving it a confused look, he dropped the fabric and crossed the room to me. No doubt he was wondering why the playroom was shrouded in shimmery cloth and draped with twinkle lights.

"I think Mother was trying to make our new honeymoon suite a little more appealing," I said, keeping my voice low and taking a glance at Nick. His little mouth was hanging open already. He was out. It still felt odd, having ended up here in the rumpus room together. I understood it, of course, but it wasn't much of a wedding night, especially for two people who had waited—with growing difficulty, I might add—for the wedding to actually happen. "Sorry," I whispered, snickering and dropping my face into my hand. The day had been too weird for words, right down to the point where my father tripped on the train of my gown and pirouetted into the first pew after he officially gave me to my groom.

"I think the room's pretty appealing." Daniel's voice was low and smooth, with a strong hint of *come hither*. When I glanced up, his eyes were smoldering, but he wasn't focused on me. He was checking out the Barbie Dream House. He'd noticed my nieces' work. "Wanna play with Barbie and Ken?"

I stifled a laugh with my hands, a hot flush traveling from one end of my body to the other.

"Twister?" Daniel's suggestion was throaty and playful. "Spin the Bottle?" Extricating a glass Coke bottle from the hidden toy shelves, he held it between two fingers, twisting it back and forth, one dark eyebrow fanning suggestively.

The heat on my skin intensified, boiling up from some smoldering place deep inside. "I will if you will."

"Mmm," he murmured, setting the bottle on Barbie's balcony. "I already am." Slipping off his tuxedo vest, he draped it carefully over Barbie and Ken's bedroom, admonishing, "A little privacy, please," before he crossed the last few steps between us and took me in his arms to make me his Irish bride for real.

We discovered that Barbie and Ken had nothing on us— that when you're young and in love and you're finally together, lumpy sofa beds and goofy attempts at romantic decor, U-Hauls waiting outside the door, and tenuous future plans don't matter. You're in your own world, and there's no one there but the two of you. Everything seems right, because the one thing that matters most, really is.

Sometime in the wee hours in the morning, I dreamed I was living in Barbie and Ken's dream house . . . on the African savanna, where tall amber grasses waved in an ever-present breeze.

I saw lions prowling in the distance.

Something shook the balcony, making the floor squeak and wiggle. "Donnn't," I muttered, my mouth gluey and stiff. "I'm watch-ennn . . . the l-lions."

"What?" a voice answered. A man's voice. I felt a hand on my shoulder. I tried to shake it off.

"The li-unnns," I heard myself murmur. "Biggg li-unnns."

"Mallory?" The voice was pulling me away from the savanna. I wanted it to stop bothering me. It was important that I keep a lookout for the lions. "Mal?"

More shaking. My eyes opened to blurry twinkle lights and silky white walls, billowing slightly. Where was I? "Wait . . . the li-unnn . . ." Sometime between the words *lions* and *are coming*, it became clear that the sentence made absolutely no sense.

Reality rushed over me, and I was a bride on my wedding night. In my mother's rumpus room, with a three-and-a-half-year-old silhouetted on the other side of the organza curtain, trying to find his way in. My brain leapt to full awareness, and both of us scrambled into our clothes.

"I've got him," Daniel whispered, standing up and slipping through the curtain.

Before Daniel could round him up, Nick found a gap in the draperies on my side of the bed. For a moment, he was like a little mummy, trapped between two layers of fabric, and then he emerged, sucking on his thumb knuckle, his hair tousled in little flyaway curls, his eyes droopy and huge.

"Did you get scared?" I whispered, and he nodded.

Despite all the parenting books—I had poured over a few in my crash course on step-parenthood—I did not gently-yet-firmly guide him back to his own bed. Instead, I let Nick pull the covers aside and hook a knee over the mattress.

He was halfway in by the time Daniel tracked him down. Hands braced on his sweats, Daniel heaved a sigh, looking at the two of us, Nick with his soulful eyes and me just back from Barbie and Ken's house on the African savanna. "Sorry. It's just that he's in a strange place." Daniel's disappointment was obvious as he made his way around the bed, clearly caught between the soft tug of parental devotion and the lure of further romance. A little hitchhiker in the middle of the mattress wasn't in the plan.

"Places don't get much stranger than this." I rolled over and folded an elbow under my head, gazing at Daniel in the dim light as he slipped beneath the comforter again. His arm made a bridge over Nick, linking us, and I toyed with his fingers.

"Yeah, and then there are those lions." In the glow of the lights, I saw his grin.

I quieted a laugh with the pillow. "I guess I didn't mention that I talk in my sleep." One of the many things that isn't a problem until you try to share living space. I was worried about that, deep down, though I hadn't admitted it. I'd been on my own since leaving my parents' house for college. I wasn't sure how good I would be at accommodating the needs of two other people. After finally breaking my parents' stranglehold by taking a job in Tokyo following college graduation, I'd learned to relish my independence.

Daniel closed his eyes, as if he had none of the same concerns—not a thing troubling his mind to make him lie awake. "*Now* you tell me." He smiled another sleepy smile.

I closed my eyes and willed the lions to stay away. In terms of dream analysis, Kaylyn had informed me, predators symbolized deeply held fears. The sort that make us feel like the hunted rather than the hunters. I'd been dreaming of predators for over a week. Last night it was a full-grown bear trying to get into my car and eat the Clean Energy Bill. Tonight, lions outside Barbie and Ken's house.

Even though I'd never been good about prayers—having grown up in a household that was loosely religious in the old-world sense, prayers were more of a recitation offered before special meals, at family funerals, and at church services on holidays—I offered up a silent plea.

Please help me give this everything I've got, and please let that be enough. . . .

Surely the Almighty could see the fear balled inside me, even on this most special of special days. Surely He knew that I'd looked at the large window in the bathroom of the church earlier that night and briefly contemplated how hard it might be to climb through it in a wedding gown. Panic really didn't describe that moment.

I continued my midnight prayer, offering up a laundry list of issues I thought God might want to address, or that at least probably merited notification. Sometime during the latter half, I drifted off to sleep, suddenly peaceful, the lions far away.

In the morning, I awoke to a kick in the gut. Letting out a sleepy "Ooof!" I jerked awake, the room whirling around me in a confusing swirl of sights, sounds, and thoughts.

Ouch, that hurt!

Did someone just hit me, or did I dream that?

Where am I?

What was that noise? There's someone in my bedroom! Call the police!

I jerked upright and the first thing I saw was a bare back—muscled, manly, the dim light of morning falling over the skin, making it look softer than it was. He was sitting on the edge of the bed, poised to get up. The wedding night replayed in my mind as he looked over his shoulder. "You're awake," he whispered.

"Somebody slugged me, I think." Rubbing my ribs, I pretended to be in pain, then glanced at Nick, stretched out in a star shape in the middle of the bed. Careful not to disturb him, I bunched the pillows and rested against the back of the sofa.

Daniel grinned, a smile that was half sweet, half wicked. "Want me to kiss it and make it better?"

Desire heated my cheeks, the rumpus room around me making me feel like a bad girl about to be caught in a game of Truth or Dare. "You could try. But then I have a feeling we'd have a hard time beating the rush-hour traffic." The plan was for the two of us to grab the few things we'd brought in with us and hit the road early. We had a long way to go, and since neither of us had any experience towing a trailer long distances, we suspected that our journey to Texas with what Daniel had dubbed *the gypsy wagon*, would be a slow one.

"You're so practical," he teased, and I felt an odd little pinch. Insecurity nipped, taking out a little piece of flesh, making me wonder if Daniel was worried that he might have married a killjoy—someone not very spontaneous and exciting. Someone who was too worried about beating the morning traffic to live in the moment.

A dreamer, a vagabond like Daniel, who wasn't afraid to travel the Third World with a backpack and a bicycle, would get tired of a too-practical wife, and probably sooner rather than later. He'd be sorry he married me. He would realize that all of this was a mistake.

"Whoa, what's *that* look for?" His question told me

immediately that he'd sensed sheer panic leaking into the room like radiation from a nuclear meltdown.

"Nothing." I smiled, trying to cover up, but my heart was racing, the air escaping my throat in little puffs. My lost independence wrapped around me like a giant anaconda, slowly squeezing, sensing fresh meat.

I looked at Nick, so small, so innocent, his tawny curls falling over the pillow in a sun-bleached halo. The weight of responsibility pressed hard on my stomach. *You could ruin his life. When this doesn't work out, when you can't hack it, you'll break both of their hearts. You've never been able to keep a relationship together, even under the best of circumstances.*

These are hardly the best of circumstances.

Daniel's hand found mine. He'd leaned across the bed, his arm again bridging Nick, linking the three of us. "No second thoughts?"

I forced a smile, told the first lie of my marriage. "Of course not." I tried to picture getting into Daniel's Jeep, heading for Texas with the U-Haul filled with wedding gifts, as well as Grandma Louisa's Fostoria crystal and other things we didn't want to send in the shipping container. The beating in my chest grew wilder, more erratic. The slithering coil of fear squeezed tighter.

"Guess we'd better get packin' then, Kemosabe," he said, with the gleeful abandon of a twelve-year-old kid on his way to Boy Scout camp.

"Guess we'd better," I agreed. We'd said our good-byes last night, on the theory that leaving the house before the whole crew woke up would make things easier.

Within thirty minutes, we were dressed, the suitcases were packed, and we were ready to scoop Nick out of the bed, spirit him into the Jeep, and shout, "Wagons ho!"

Unfortunately, the Great Chief had set her alarm clock for a very early hour and mustered from their beds every member of the tribe. A conglomeration of sisters, in-laws, nieces, and nephews were waiting, bleary-eyed after last night's celebration. Mom had made quiche.

She waved off Daniel's assertion that Nick wouldn't be fit company if we woke him for breakfast. "Oh, he'll be fine," she insisted, with the casual hand swipe that typically accompanied statements like, *It didn't cost that much*, or *I know you're in the middle of your work day, but guess what happened at bridge club this morning* . . .

When my mother had her mind set on something, there was no fighting it.

We roused Nick. He was cranky. Conversation around the breakfast table was drowsy and bland. My eldest sister's husband, a columnist for an Annapolis newspaper, filled me in on the sordid history of Jack West. "You know that his second wife and her ten-year-old son vanished under mysterious circumstances, right? The Mexican authorities never solved the disappearance. Two people, just gone without a trace from the family vacation home in Bocas Del Gallo. Poof." Illustrating with his hands, he leaned close, his eyes meeting mine meaningfully as my mother and sisters chatted about variations of quiche. Daniel was busy trying to placate Nick with fresh fruit in strawberry sauce.

"They didn't exonerate Jack West, either," my brother-in-law continued. "West skipped the country before charges could be pressed. No sign of the wife and the ten-year-old stepson, even after twenty years. No bodies. Didn't turn up somewhere else in the world living under assumed identities. Nothing. They just vanished off the face of the earth." He glanced surreptitiously at my eldest sister, Carol, from whom he was undoubtedly keeping this information. This wasn't the sort of bombshell Carol would handle well. "Keep your eyes peeled down there."

I blinked, swallowing a lump that had nothing to do with the horse pill prescribed by the dentist. "Geez, Corbin."

"I don't mean to kill the wedding bliss," he whispered out the side of his mouth. "I just thought you ought to know, that's all. It was a big story, back when it happened. From time to time, some news show or other picks it up again—he *is* Jack West, after all. He's a curiosity. But, hey, it's not like he's been in any *other* trouble. Well, there was that prosecution for the financial thing, but they couldn't get the charges to stick."

"Oh, that makes me feel a whole lot better. Thanks." I set down my fork, having suddenly lost my appetite. At the end of the table, Daniel caught my gaze, shrugging toward the door. Over the past weeks, he'd read every story he could find about Jack West. He undoubtedly knew about the vanished second wife and stepson. It bothered me that he hadn't told me about it.

"It's . . . interesting," Corbin whispered, scooping up a last forkful of quiche. "Let me know if you hear or see anything strange, that's all." My favorite brother-in-law was always looking for the story that would reel in a Pulitzer and a job at the *New York Times*, the holy grail of reporting, in his view. "I'm sure you don't have anything to worry about—in terms of personal safety, I mean. The man undoubtedly has plenty of people working for him on that ranch. None of *them* have disappeared, I guess."

"Oh, that's reassuring." Nothing about this move felt right. It was tying my insides in slipknots.

Corbin patted my hand. "I shouldn't have said anything. . . ." The sentence seemed to trail off unfinished, the words definitely not meaning what they said. "Forget that I brought it up. I was just . . . pawing into the story a little the other day. I didn't come up with anything."

"Are you going to keep pawing into it?"

He shrugged, falsely casual, then he cut a nervous glance toward Carol, who was giving us the fish eye. "Oh . . . I'll have an ear to the ground. Listen, don't tell Carol about any of this. She's already upset that you're moving away, and you know how your sister can be."

An uneasy prickle skimmed the back of my neck. "You'll let me know if you find out anything though, right?"

"Sure, sure," Corbin agreed, suddenly anxious to disengage.

Breakfast was soon over. When we rose from the table, one of my teenage nieces became emotional because I wouldn't be there to see her in her prom dress. My mother started crying, too. Then Carol started crying, Trudy broke down, and my two middle sisters, Merryl and Missy, joined the weep fest. Brothers-in-law scattered in all directions, anxious to exit the pool of female emotion. Daniel's parents, having been phoned by my mother, showed up for one last good-bye. Nick suddenly decided that he wanted to go home with them. Daniel's mother clutched him so tightly, I thought she might break him. Daniel's father, a big man with an even bigger heart, got watery-eyed.

Nick threw a fit when he saw the Jeep, and strapping him into his car seat was like trying to put a spider in a strait-jacket. I'd never seen that side of Nick before. I was used to handing all out-of-control kids to their mothers when things got difficult. I had no idea what to do, except stand there looking like a helpless idiot while Daniel engaged in the wrestling match and tried not to look aggravated in front of everyone.

We drove away with Nick screaming, kicking, wailing, and reaching toward the window as if he were being hauled

57

off by kidnappers. Daniel gripped the steering wheel with both hands, his muscles stiff, his jaw tense, the playful smile nowhere to be seen.

Ten minutes out my parents' door, we hit rush-hour traffic. Forty-five minutes passed as we inched our way toward the open road. By the time we made it, Nick had cried himself into oblivion. I quickly joined him in sleep, curling my body toward the window and trying to push Corbin's warnings from my mind.

To keep your marriage brimming,
With love in the loving cup,
Whenever you're wrong, admit it;
Whenever you're right, shut up.

—Ogden Nash
(Left by Herb and Charlie Hampton,
telling the young folks how it's done)

Chapter 5

On day three of the U-Haul honeymoon, we crossed Louisiana and passed into Texas. Texas was experiencing a May heat wave, and the air-conditioner on the Jeep was all but out of commission—not what you want to discover when you've been traveling through Arkansas with a carsick kid in the back. Daniel and I had our very first marital head-butting session over whether to stop at a car wash and shampoo the smell out of the backseat. Daniel didn't want to discuss anything that had to do with stopping. We were already behind schedule, and there was no way we would make it to our new home in the early afternoon, as planned.

Tucked safely in the console were Jack West's instructions as to how we were to find the place. Eerily, we hadn't heard from the man in over a week. I hadn't looked at the sheet of notebook paper where Daniel had written the directions. I was afraid to. I doubted there was anything on there like, *Turn just past the shopping mall* or *Go one block beyond Starbucks.*

Aside from that, there was the whole question of Daniel's

new boss being an accused murderer, which I hadn't even brought up, because things in the car were tense enough already.

In a map-dot town in East Texas, we stopped for gas at an old station with a rusty Gulf Oil sign swinging gently in the breeze. The station owner, Baby Ray, promised he could fix the Jeep's lackluster air-conditioning system right up. "Hoo-eee! You're gonna need it," he added. "It's hotter than who'd-a-thought-it down there already. My cousin has his headquarters over that way—leads game hunts and fishin' trips all over the state of Texas, though. Took a fella down the Trinity River last week, and the fella got a fourteen-foot alligator. Now that's some good eats, and . . ."

Baby Ray was my first refresher course in the taffy-like consistency of Southern language. It reminded me of childhood visits to Grandma Louisa's house in Charleston, where summers were sticky-hot and the livin' was slow and easy. Words rolled off Baby Ray's tongue laced with colorful metaphors like, "Don't that just put the socks on the rooster?" and "When we fried that thang up, I was full as a tick on a back porch hound, I'll tell you what . . ." As he talked, Freon continued pumping into the Jeep.

Meanwhile, I was thinking, *Somewhere around here, alligator-hunting people capture giant alligators, man-eating ones. We'll be living on the shores of Moses Lake. Surely there are no alligators in Moses Lake. Right?*

When it was time to go, Nick didn't really want to leave Baby Ray behind. Ray patted him on the head and gave him a lollypop with greasy fingerprints on the wrapper. After we got in the car, I opened it with a wet wipe and swiped off the stick.

Daniel rolled his eyes. "He's a *boy.*" As if somehow that made the consumption of toxic petroleum products okay. He smirked playfully at me and flipped on the air-conditioner as we rolled out of town, leaving Baby Ray behind.

Thirty miles down the road the Jeep's compressor froze up, promptly choking the life out of the engine. We spent the afternoon sweltering with the windows open, while searching for another mechanic who might be working on Sunday.

Daniel was mad, then irate. I'd never seen him like that— red-faced, tight-lipped, a little muscle twitching in his jawline. He looked violent and dangerous. Nowhere in my basket of preconceived marital worries had I imagined that Daniel, my Daniel, might have a side like this hidden beneath the surface. Before long, even Nick was upset. I climbed into the back- seat and helped him start a book on CD. Daniel complained about the noise. I clenched my teeth, wet-mopped my skin and Nick's with a rag, and tried to keep from throwing any more tinder on the situation.

By the time we finally found a mechanic and had the Freon level properly recalibrated, my stomach was roiling and the sun was slowly sinking on the horizon. All three of us were exhausted, smelly, and teetering near the breaking point.

"Maybe we should just grab a hotel room, have a nice dinner, and go the rest of the way tomorrow," I suggested as we drove along a narrow two-lane, snaking our way through hills thick with live oak and cedar. The idea of arriving at our future home at night scared me. If there *were* monster gators, I didn't want them sneaking up on me in the dark.

Aside from that, I didn't even have the faintest mental pic- ture of the place. Daniel had asked Jack West for information about the house, and Jack's only response had been, *It's just yer regular ranch house.*

Ever since then, I'd had an unsteady feeling about what "just your regular ranch house" might be like. On Google all I'd found was a fuzzy satellite image—massive lake, miles of undisturbed country, a tiny cluster of buildings shrouded by old-growth trees. A mystery, like everything else about Jack West and this job.

"We need to push on and get there tonight," Daniel insisted. "Besides, we shouldn't blow money on another hotel. We've already spent too much, thanks to Baby Ray." He sneered when he said it, the twitch in his jaw returning.

I sighed, admonishing myself to let it go. "Want me to drive for a while?" I was hoping Daniel would nod off, then wake up in a better mood. This don't-look-at-me-don't-talk-to-me persona was unsettling. It reminded me that, like the mail-order brides in days of old, I was married to a man I barely knew, and headed into the mysterious frontier hundreds of miles from all that was familiar.

We made a quick stop, and I took over the pilot's chair. Daniel was asleep in less than ten minutes. Nick eventually crashed, too, and I sank into the quiet of my own thoughts, strumming a tune of self-assurances to calm my ruffled spirit. I was a DC girl. If I could survive in the city, I could survive here. I wasn't some fragile little hothouse flower. I'd lived in six foreign capitols. I was . . .

Something large and shadowy bounded across the ditch and walked into the road. I jerked my attention back to the driving. A dog . . . no . . . deer. A deer. Adrenaline zinged through my body, hot like a lightning strike. I gripped the steering wheel, hit the brakes, felt the Jeep begin to slide, the trailer protesting the sudden change in momentum, skidding side to side.

Daniel bolted upright, blinking in confusion. Nick's car seat buckled forward against the seat belt, then snapped back with a pop. Daniel grabbed the dashboard. "What in the . . ."

Possible endings raced through my mind, rapid fire—

overturning and rolling into the ditch, flying end-over-end, the trailer crashing through the tailgate, hitting Nick, the Jeep flying headlong into a tree. My parents getting the news . . .

And then, just as quickly as it had sauntered into the road, the deer calmly moved to the opposite lane, leaving room for our vehicle to slide past before finally coming to a rest, the trailer cocked sideways across the center line.

We sat in momentary silence, not a vehicle or a street lamp in sight, stressed pieces of metal in the car's undercarriage letting out soft crackles and pings, as if it were catching a breath along with the rest of us.

"Is a doe-deer like at Grampy's house, Tante M!" Nick twisted to see out the side window. "And a baby one, too!" He pointed as a smaller deer scampered across the pavement to join the first one, unaware that tragedy had been only an instant away.

"Man, that was lucky." Daniel blew out a puff of tension, his hand resting on my arm, where the muscles were still trembling.

"Uh-huh." In the fringes of the headlights, I noticed a small white cross in the ditch—the kind that people plant at the site of a tragic accident. It simply read, *Blessing*, with no further explanation. Suddenly that seemed to fit the moment. Not a random stroke of good fortune, a blessing. A reminder that time was too precious to be spent fighting.

Daniel squeezed my hand and kissed me on the cheek, as if he were thinking the same thing. "I'll take over the driving, if you want. Moses Lake can't be much farther."

I didn't offer any argument. I'd seen my life flash before my eyes in the last three minutes. My fiercely independent streak was ready to curl up in a corner and lick its trembling paws. I was happy to go back to being a co-pilot.

We switched places, Daniel limping stiffly around the back

of the car and me dragging my tired body around the front, and we were off again.

"Last leg," Daniel promised as the trailer righted itself behind us. "I'm ready to get there and get out of this car." He laid his hand on the console, palm up, and I slid my fingers into his, then leaned back against the headrest.

"That sounds so good," I murmured. "When we do get there, I vote we just grab the air mattress, Nick's sleeping bag, and the sack with the pillows and blankets. Everything else can wait until morning."

Daniel nodded. "Yeah."

We drove along in silence for a few miles, until finally Daniel lifted my hand and brought it to his lips, kissing my fingers. "I love a woman who can handle a U-Haul, by the way."

My sticky, road-weary skin came alive with goose bumps, and the apprehension that had been haunting me drifted out the window. "Now you're trying to flatter me."

"Is it working?"

"Maybe." I smiled at him, filled with the returning warmth of adoration.

"My guess—in a half hour or less, we'll be pulling into our driveway," he offered.

The words *our driveway* were just settling over me, a warm and sweet-smelling bubble bath, when Daniel hit the brakes, snapping me forward against my seat belt.

"There's another one." Leaning close to the window, he peered into the night, pointing.

I turned just in time to see a deer amble into the road and stop.

"Is a doe-deer! 'Nudder one!" Nick announced gleefully.

"You've got to be kidding." I felt my mouth hanging slack. "You think it's the same deer? Maybe it's, like, messing with us."

"Can't be." Daniel shifted his hands on the steering wheel,

and we proceeded slowly forward on what would forever be known as *The Night of the Kamikazi Deer*.

Sometime later, after having passed through one small town and watched every four-legged wild animal in the county cross the road, we topped a hill and spotted what had to be Moses Lake. Around us, the moon cast a faint glow against waxy live oak leaves as we wound into the valley. Some sort of massive bird swooped across the car, then sailed over the dark expanse of water, following the moon's glistening path toward the horizon.

"Wow," I whispered, watching branches play a hide-and-seek game with stars and moon and water. Lights glittered on the lake's surface here and there, seeming to float free in the blackness—boats, I supposed. Houseboats, perhaps. I hadn't thought of the lake as being big enough that people might live on it, but Daniel had mentioned that the ranch included miles of lakeshore. I guessed it made sense that the lake would be huge.

An unexpected tingle rushed over my skin as we descended a small hill into the utter darkness, Moses Lake dipping out of sight. An aura of romance and danger simmered through me like a trail of smoke, scented with an intriguing fragrance I couldn't quite place. For the past month, Kaylyn had been sending me bits of mystery and lore pertaining to Moses Lake, and now all of it was churning in my head. I felt the history of the place slipping over me, drawing me into a mix of past and present. Comanche hunting ground, pioneer settlement, site of a secret gathering of Civil War dissenters determined to join forces with the Mexican army and cause the South to rise again. Location of a mysterious frontier settlement where all the residents had vanished one winter. To this day, no one knew what had happened to them.

Though the river had been here since time immemorial,

the lake was man-made, a product of the Corps of Engineers during the building boom of the fifties. The water's surface hid what was left of towns, farms, homes, and an old Spanish mission run by monks who came to the area with dreams of enlightenment, but eventually abandoned their vision.

"This is it. This is our road," Daniel said, turning off the highway. Gravel rumbled beneath the Jeep's tires, and when we'd bumped and bounced our way to the top of the next hill, I could no longer see lights in the distance. Except for the glow of the moon, everything around us was impossibly black, the thickly wooded hills filled with shadows that shifted as we drove. Tiny pinpoints of eyes glittered in the fringes of the headlights here and there. I didn't want to think about what those might belong to.

Were Baby Ray's giant alligators out there somewhere, just waiting for a chance to avenge the cousin who'd been hunted down and fried up into gator nuggets?

A sense of solitude cloaked the car, the weave thick and tight, shutting out sound, giving the feeling that we were stepping off the edge of the world. My lust for adventure wavered, and I found myself again wishing for a hotel room.

Daniel rested his elbow comfortably on the window frame, seeming completely at peace with the lack of civilization.

"Are you sure it's okay for us to show up so late at night like this?" I shivered as the water-scented breeze worked its way down the neck of my T-shirt.

"I gotta go tinkie!" Nick's unceremonious announcement interrupted the flow of conversation.

Daniel reached back and patted Nick on the knee. "Hang in there, buddy. It can't be far from here. Just a few minutes." He held up the paper with the directions, squinted at it in the dash light, then set it down and turned left at an intersection where one gravel road looked about as dark and unwelcoming as the other. "Here we go. Say, see ya later, stop sign."

Daniel and Nick fell into a game I'd heard them play before, talking about things as we passed, so as to make the miles speed by.

"Later, gad-or," Nick chimed in.

I wished the subject of gators hadn't come up.

"You cold?" Daniel asked, and I realized I had my arms clutched tight. All the blood had moved to the center of my body in an instinctive flight response. "Not sorry you threw in with us blokes, are you?"

"No, of course not." *Don't complain. Don't complain. Don't be a party pooper, fun killer, namby-pamby little fraidy cat.* "But what if some . . . security guard mistakes us for prowlers and shoots us or something when we get there?"

"The place is so remote, I don't think there's any need for security. That's why Jack has his research facility and crop plots there. He's pretty paranoid about people trying to spy on his work. The only houses close to ours are a little guest cottage of Jack's and an old cabin on Firefly Island. Jack has a bigger place and a ranch headquarters on another piece of land twenty miles down the county highway. His house there is massive, actually. At the symposium, he was showing pictures of the generator. Solar and wind systems power the house and barns, and he uses modified geothermal units for cooling and heating. Seriously innovative. I've never seen anything like it. He designed the whole system himself."

The two of us fell silent as an imposing white limestone entranceway came into view, dwarfing the Jeep and the U-Haul. The heavy wooden gates were closed like the barriers that protected the old Spanish missions. Daniel exited the Jeep and punched the magic numbers into a keypad inside a metal box, then slid back into his seat as the gate swung open, letting us through. We proceeded along the narrow drive toward what appeared to be a grouping of buildings ahead. Oddly, there seemed to be no lighting of any kind, other than what the moon afforded. I had the disquieting thought that maybe we really weren't expected here at all.

Corbin's story swirled through my thoughts, and I considered asking Daniel what he knew about Jack West's sordid past, but I didn't. Daniel wouldn't have brought us here if he thought we were in any danger. I had to trust in that.

"Yup, there it is." He pointed as the headlights outlined a simple, one-story Craftsman-style house with clapboard siding. The structure appeared to be of forties or fifties vintage, with a fence around it made of painted iron pipe and wire. It wasn't the sort of fence built for decoration, but more for function, to keep something in or out. *What?* I wondered. Livestock? Wild animals? The gates had been adorned with welded-on pieces of old farm machinery, as if to dress up the place a bit.

"Why aren't there any lights on?" I'd waited as long as I could to bring up the obvious.

"Not sure . . ." The hint of uncertainty in Daniel's voice was disquieting. "But that's the house—first building on the left. Jack said there are some barns and whatnot out back, and Jack's little house. I get the impression he doesn't use it anymore. The greenhouses and the lab building are a couple miles down the ranch road."

"Oh." I couldn't think of much else to say as we rolled to a stop by one of the yard gates. All three of us sat in silence, nobody willing to make the first move. The darkness was incredibly thick, the low-hanging moon hiding behind a cloud. Some sort of night-flying creature strafed the car again. It looked like a bat. The fine hairs rose on the back of my neck.

"Where is everyone?" Scanning a 180-degree circle, I could

only see one set of lights that might belong to a house—one sign of civilization far in the distance, floating beyond a swath of fathomless blackness that was either a deep canyon or part of the lake. The air smelled of water and wet limestone. "Didn't they know we were coming?" I'd expected a welcoming of some sort; Daniel's new boss or a caretaker with a key, at least. Instead, I felt like someone, or something, might be lurking out there in the darkness, waiting for us to step out of the car.

Daniel leaned over the steering wheel, squinting beyond the headlights. "I left a message on Jack's voice mail saying we'd be later than we thought, but he never answered." Squaring his shoulders, he fished a key ring and a small penlight from the console. "Guess I'll go unlock the door and see what I can do about finding some switches."

"Okay." On the one hand, I was exhausted. On the other hand, I was petrified. The two opposing forces clashed like Titans inside me. It was hard to say which one was winning. "We'll wait here." I reached for Nick, who'd managed to unbuckle his seat belts and climb onto the console to follow his dad. "Hang on, Nick. Let's just stay here and wait for your dad to figure things out." As much as it pained me to do what my mother would have done in this situation, I was happy to let Daniel venture forth while I stayed behind to protect the young. Nick squirmed into my lap, and I hugged my arms around him, resting my chin against his silky hair.

Daniel hovered half in and half out of the car, messing with the pen light, which was shuddering and blinking, threatening to fail us when we needed it most. "At this point, I'm ready to lay that air mattress down anywhere, as long as I can sleep." He swung the door shut and walked off into the night, his flashlight beam crossing the yard and bobbing up a couple steps to the house. Moments later, the glow of the penlight moved from window to window inside the house, but no lights came on.

A full fifteen minutes had ticked by before Daniel returned. He'd found plenty of switches, but none of them worked. With the penlight quickly losing steam, we had little choice but to give up on electrical power and just move in anyway. We were too exhausted to care anymore.

We unpacked the sleeping equipment by the light of a waxing moon and settled down on the floor of what appeared to be our new living room. The house smelled musty and old, until we opened the windows to let in fresh air. Outside, a blanket of stars stretched across the sky, and somewhere in the distance, I thought I heard waves gently lapping at the shore. I wondered if it was only my imagination, or if we were closer to the water than I'd thought. Did lakes have tides like an ocean—a cycle of rising and falling that followed the moon?

Nick curled up in his sleeping bag, and Daniel and I slipped beneath the quilt on our hastily inflated air mattress, the last twinkle of the pen light fading slowly into oblivion as Moses Lake rocked us to sleep with its lullaby of water and stone.

We came by night to the Fortunate Isles,
And lay like fish
Under the net of our kisses.

—Pablo Neruda
(Left by Kotoyo and Sgt. Ben [ret.], forbidden love a lifetime ago)

Chapter 6

Hawaiian mythology describes Tangaroa, the ruler of the ocean, who breathes only twice in twenty-four hours, creating the tides. I heard the legend when I was thirteen, just entering that spindly-legged and awkward stage of semi-adulthood—not a girl, not a woman, old enough to wish the beefcake Hawaiian storyteller would ditch the luau audience, mysteriously fall in love with me, and sweep me off to a life of bliss in a thatch hut somewhere. I looked into his dark eyes, saw the firelight reflected, heard the pounding of the surf. The corners of my vision narrowed, blocking out the movers and shakers for whom my father's client had planned this island meeting. I fell into the tale, felt the storyteller's love of the ocean, his understanding of it, his reverence for the vastness and the mystery of the world around us.

It wasn't in the tides that the breath of God could be found, I decided, but in the water itself, in the endless rhythm of it, ever present, ever constant, louder amidst the storms of life, softer in the peaceful times. Not a god only moving twice a day like the mythical Tangaroa, but a God moving countless times. Always. Continually. A God present in the deepest parts of our lives, sometimes crowded out by all the surface clutter as we stroll along the shore, our minds preoccupied with things that seem important. Then a wave rises higher than the rest, strokes soft and cool over sun-warmed skin, and we hear it again, the constant breath of God. We think, *How could I not have heard that all along?*

Our first morning on Moses Lake, I woke with the breath of God in my ears. It flowed softly in and out, rocking me to wakefulness in the way of a parent gently rousing a beloved child to a new day. In that misty land between sleep and reality, I wasn't certain where I was, but I thought, *This is perfect. I love it here. I want to wake up to the soft morning breeze and the scent of the water, to this peace forever.*

The air mattress shifted beneath me as I burrowed deeper into the quilt that Grandma Louisa had long ago made in anticipation of my wedding. I felt as if I were floating on the water, a ship drifting at sea. Not a thing in the world to worry about.

You're on vacation, a dream-voice whispered. *No need to get out of bed. You can lie here as long as you want.*

The smell of coffee teased my senses just as I was beginning to drift again. *Coffee. Good.* The thought registered, and a stomach rumble concurred. I rolled over, stuck my face in the pillow, fought waking and rising. As much as I'd always wished I could be a morning person, it hadn't happened yet.

The coffee wouldn't leave me alone. It wanted me . . .

A heaviness settled in, like Grandma Louisa's old Fat Cat (that really was his name, *Fat Cat*) sitting atop the quilt, weighing down the fabric.

I couldn't quite remember where I was. Memories flitted in and out like the skittish white moths that hatch in multitudes in late summer. *There was a car . . . something about the air-conditioner . . . and alligators in the road . . . no, no deer. Deer in the road . . .*

I blinked the new day slowly into focus, dapples of sunlight falling over my face. A severed head was staring back at me, its glassy black eyes gazing into the distance from beneath a massive pair of antlers. I did a clumsy upward scramble, bunching the pillow against my back. Instead of a headboard, there was a wall. I smacked my head on a windowsill.

"If that doesn't say good morning, I don't know what does." Daniel's voice and the fact that I was now a married woman took a moment to register. So far, I'd remarried Daniel in the first few moments each morning. I wondered how long it would be before I stopped being my old single self in my subconscious mind.

"Nice, huh?" he added. He was sitting on the other side of the air mattress, wearing a pair of jogging shorts and a T-shirt with the sleeves ripped off, his dark hair tousled into slightly damp curls, his long legs crossed one over the other.

He made a very appealing picture.

I blinked to gain a clearer focus, trying to concentrate on Daniel, that gorgeous hunka-hunka husband, rather than the disembodied head on the wall.

The head was powerful, though. It pulled at my gaze until I was looking sideways at it with morbid fascination. I thought of the *Bambi* movie. Bambi's father. He was on our wall, nicely highlighted by the sun filtering through a set of ancient mini-blinds that hung off kilter, a slat or two missing.

There was a *head* in our living room. A body part of a dead animal. My stomach roiled, and I wondered what was inside the head. Bones and flesh, preserved with formaldehyde or something? Was that even possible? How long could eyeballs possibly last, hanging on a wall?

Maybe it was mummified, the brains removed through the ear, like the body in an Egyptian sarcophagus. . . .

"Do you think the eyeballs are real?" I kept a sideways focus on the head as Daniel grabbed an already prepared cup of coffee and handed it to me.

He chuckled. "Of course not. They're glass. None of it's real. It's just hide stretched over a plastic form, like a . . . leather coat."

I took a sip of my coffee. *Perfect.* A random thought, an endearment of sorts, traveled through me, warm like the sip. *He already knows how I fix my coffee.* "What's it doing there? I mean, you think we're in the wrong house?" Maybe we'd misread the directions last night after all, and we were trespassing where we shouldn't be.

"What? You don't find that sort of woodsy and charming?" A hand flourish added dramatic flair. "Don't go in the bathroom, then."

"The *bathroom*?" Suddenly last night's power outage seemed like a blessing in disguise.

"And the master bedroom." He pointed toward a doorway that led to the shadowy hall where some sort of ancient velvet wallpaper was peeling off the wall. "The good news is that the place does come with electricity. I finally found the breaker this morning and turned it on." He grinned at me, and I couldn't help it, I laughed.

"Okay, but if you tell me there are stuffed dead animals in the kitchen, I'm going to be sick."

He gently shoulder bumped me, creating waves in my coffee. "Kitchen's clean. Well, not clean, exactly, but there are no dead animals. We're going to have to do some work in there. The good news is that there's a nice little café in town—The

Waterbird Bait and Grocery—and they open at five a.m. for the fishermen. The coffee's good. Nick and I brought back a breakfast burrito for you. They're good, too."

"You guys went to town without me?" I looked around the room. Some stepmother I was. Until that very moment, I hadn't thought about the fact that there was supposed to be a third person with us. A little person. "Where's Nick?" A tiny spear of panic cut through my morning fog, ramping up my heartbeat. Surely Daniel wouldn't just forget about Nick. If the lake was close enough that I could smell the water, Nick might be in danger of wandering into it.

"He's outside, with . . . someone."

"Someone?" I threw off the covers, envisioning our new boss just on the other side of the wall. I couldn't meet Jack West for the first time looking like this. I wanted to make a good impression, to help Daniel start off his new job on the right foot. "You didn't tell me there was someone here. Is the shower working?"

"Relax." Daniel snaked out a hand, palm-up, like he was going to catch the coffee cup if I dropped it. "He doesn't care, I promise. Besides, you look beautiful." His fingers caught my T-shirt, stalling me in a crouch as I set my coffee cup on the floor.

"Daniel, I'm serious. I don't want him to think you're married to some kind of . . . lazy person who sleeps all day." Based on my limited knowledge of Jack West, I was already scared to death of meeting him. I needed to be prepared.

The pull on my T-shirt increased, tipping me back onto the air mattress. I landed on Daniel's chest, and he wrapped his arms around me. "Just stay here with me a minute. We haven't had much alone time so far." A sigh softened him against the pillow. "I'm sorry, Mal. I know this hasn't been what you dreamed of for a honeymoon."

"It's been an adventure." The words were upbeat, confident, a smokescreen for what I was really feeling. The hint of brokenness in Daniel's voice rattled me to the core. I wanted to take some of the pressure off. "Listen to me." Twisting in his arms, I touched his face, turned him toward me. I saw him in minute detail, the squareness of his chin, the freshly shaven skin, the dark, arched brows, the glint of sunlight against his eyes. "I married you. You. Daniel Webster Everson. Not a road trip, or a house, or job, or a salary, or a location, or a living room wall." I waved a hand toward the severed head, hanging on ugly gold-flocked wallpaper of seventies vintage. "As long as you and I are okay, that's all I need. You and me and Nick. The three of us. You don't have to try to make things perfect for me or pretend you've got it under control all by yourself. I can handle it, okay?" *I can. I will. Somehow.* "I'm not some fragile little china doll you need to shelter and protect."

His gaze connected with mine in a way that seemed to reach into my soul. "I want you to be happy. I want to take care of you. Of us."

I felt my center turning to mush. That was the most romantic thing anyone had ever said to me. I was the heroine in a 1950's western, the scene shot with a misty lens softening all the rough edges, leaving only perfection. We kissed, and I wished we could lock the doors and spend the morning curled up together in the wedding quilt, floating on the air mattress, two lovers lost at sea.

Something crashed outside, and the serenity vanished like vapor. We jerked apart. Daniel climbed off the air mattress, and I followed.

"I've got it." He moved ahead of me into the adjoining room, which we'd come through in the dark last night. Judging by the row of old wooden windows and a painted stone footer, the long, narrow space had been an outdoor porch at one time. The kitchen doorway was off to the right, and there was an old oak desk in the left corner of the room. Apparently this area served as an office, and maybe a dining room. The floor was covered with butternut yellow carpet. It felt sticky beneath my feet, and was dotted with stains I didn't want to contemplate.

"Well . . . but who's outside?" Surely Daniel wouldn't just leave Nick out there with Mr. West. I tried to peer around Daniel's shoulder. If the new boss really was outside, I was going to bolt for the bathroom . . . if I could remember where I'd found it last night in the dark.

"Come see for yourself." Daniel opened the back door and stepped onto the wide covered porch behind the house. He held the screen until I could catch it, then disappeared around the corner as I tiptoed cautiously out.

The yard was huge by DC standards, an acre or two at least, enclosed by the iron pipe fence with rusty mesh wire over it. Ancient-looking stone footpaths fanned out from the porch, one leading to the driveway gate, another leading to an old garage building on the left side of the house, and a third heading directly across the backyard to what appeared to be another house, smaller than our own, with a low-roofed front porch that somehow looked empty and barren. From the overgrown flowerbed in front, a cement angel watched me. Sunlight glittered against the water in the birdbath at her feet, casting shifting ribbons of light over her skirt. A yellow butterfly sat on the basin rim, fanning its wings.

I thought of the woman and the little boy who'd disappeared. Jack's wife and stepson. Was the birdbath hers? Had the little boy chased butterflies in that very garden? Had she planted the irises that now bloomed thick along the foundation? Even with the gardens gone to seed and most of the paint faded off the porch furniture, that place had the look of a woman's touch. There were lace curtains in the windows. Had she sewn them herself?

Shaking off the questions, I surveyed the roofs of barns and outbuildings beyond the little house. A grassy hillside dotted with pecan trees lay beyond. In the distance, the azure waters of Moses Lake peeked through. From the looks of things, it was close enough to walk to, but even though the view was beautiful, it was eerily empty. As far as I looked in any direction, there wasn't a single sign of another human. The ranch was like a tiny island in a vast wilderness.

I stood there feeling out of body, lost, vulnerable. Was this what it would be like here all the time—just Daniel and me, living in this house with no one else around? Even straining my ears into the distance, all I could hear were the sounds of crickets chirring, the rustle of the breeze in branches, the ragged caw of a bird.

"Daniel?" I called, stepping off the porch and onto the stone path. "Nick?"

Something black, white, brown, hairy, and rather large rocketed from the corner of the house and flashed by in a blur. Nick was chasing it with his arms outstretched, laughing and squealing, calling, "He gots it! He gots it! C'mere, doggie!"

Doggie? I watched as what looked like at least a hundred pounds of dog circled the yard. Hair, slobber, and clods of grass flew as it rounded a bush near the stone footpath, then doubled back, racing past Nick before making another hairpin turn. The two played a wild game of keep-away, the dog cavorting back and forth in front of Nick, and Nick jumping and diving, trying to grab something from the dog's mouth.

Whose dog? There hadn't been a dog around last night. When we'd pulled in, the place was as quiet as—I hated to even think it in view of Corbin's wedding-breakfast revelations—a graveyard.

Daniel's arm slipped around me, and I jumped. I hadn't even realized he'd come back up the path.

"What's that?" I motioned to Nick's playmate.

"A dog."

"But where did it come from? It looks like a . . . hairy Rottweiler or something. Should Nick be playing with it?" Growing up, I'd had a friend whose father kept a Doberman in the backyard. My mother wouldn't allow me over to that house to play. She was afraid I would be mauled.

"Stock dog. Australian shepherd. His name's Pecos."

Pecos . . . So, someone *had* been here this morning while I was sleeping, and left behind . . . a dog?

"Well, who does Pecos belong to?"

"I don't know." Daniel's fingers smoothed over my skin as Nick caught the dog, wrestled a tennis ball from his massive jowls, and then tossed the ball across the grass, sprays of slobber flicking off in all directions, catching the sunlight.

I had the urge to grab Nick and wash his hands. I could hear my mother saying, *Good heavens, the germs!* "You didn't ask?" Was it a good idea to let a small child play with a strange dog? As much as I was aware of my newcomer status in this threesome, sometimes I wondered if Daniel was too casual about things.

"He doesn't talk much."

"Who?"

"The dog."

A little chuckle attempted to chase my worries. "No, I mean whomever the dog was *with*. You didn't ask who he belongs to and whether he's safe for children? I mean, dogs can maul little . . ." I bit my tongue just as Daniel's arm stiffened. This whole stepparent thing was complicated.

"His name's on his collar." The answer was flat, a little clipped. The meaty, manly hand stopped caressing and instead settled on my elbow. I felt slightly off-balance. There were so many new things to figure out at once. Where did my parental responsibilities for Nick begin and end? At what point was I supposed to start acting like his mother, instead of a casual family friend? Would that process occur naturally, or should we plan it? Everything had happened so fast that Nick was still calling me *Tante M.* We hadn't even talked about whether to change that, and how.

Had Daniel thought of any of those things?

He seemed to have none of my worries. "They're fine. We had a couple dogs like that when we were kids. They're good dogs. I did a genetics thing on the breed in grad school. That one's a tri-color pattern, but if you take two with the blue merle color pattern and breed them, there's a sixty-seven-percent chance . . ." He went on with facts and figures having to do with canine genetics and white puppies born with inherited recessive something-or-other, causing blindness, deafness, or stillbirth.

The science talk dissolved into a background hum as I watched Nick and the dog. Finally, Daniel squeezed me and said, "I'm boring you, aren't I?"

"No, not at all."

"Why don't you go on in and get your shower? Mr. West— or somebody—will probably show up here pretty soon. The manager and the ranch hands do most of their work over on the main ranch, but they come by here daily to feed and check on the animals. Someone was by this morning while Nick and I were gone. That's probably how the dog got here."

"Okay." I wished I hadn't missed the trip into Moses Lake. I wanted to know what it was like. "How was the town, by the way—other than the bait shop café—what did you call it? The Waterbird?"

"It's . . . small."

I decided not to ask for details. Sometimes it's better to take things in little bites. I chose not to explore the house, either, but went straight back the way I'd come. I stopped in the living room long enough to get clothing from my suitcase and nibble the breakfast burrito Daniel had left for me in a paper sack, then proceeded to locate the bathroom.

I discovered a few things I hadn't seen last night in the dark. When I came out, Daniel was sitting on the back porch. He greeted me with a Cheshire-cat grin as the screen door smacked shut.

"Well, how'd it go?" His lips twitched at the corners, anticipating my reaction to the bathroom.

"There's a *stuffed* mountain lion—with a bird in its mouth—hanging over the shower stall." Tucking my hands between my legs, I took a seat on one of the old metal office chairs that served as porch furniture.

Daniel choked on a withheld snicker. "Technically, it's a bobcat."

"It *watched* me take a shower," I added, and he laughed out loud.

"It's not funny," but I could feel my cheeks tugging. What else could you do with a stuffed bird-eating bobcat in the bathroom, but laugh at it? "You realize we can't, in any way, tell my mother about this. She'll send in a SWAT team."

"Yeah, you're gonna have some issues with the kitchen, too. It's kind of . . . bare bones." Daniel shook his head, but he was grinning. "I think Jack said something about this place having been a hunting lodge over the years."

I groaned. My curiosity about the kitchen floated on a wave of dread. Maybe I wouldn't even go look. Maybe I'd just stay here on the porch all day and watch the trees sway overhead and the water twinkle in the distance as Nick played in the sand while a stranger's dog stood guard over him, all signs of human activity remaining strangely absent.

Maybe I would just close my eyes, listen to the breath of God, and let it rock me along until finally I woke in the real world and discovered that all this was just one of those silly dreams, like the lions outside Barbie's Dream House, or the bear trying to make off with the Clean Energy Bill.

I was probably talking in my sleep, and Daniel was probably laughing, especially at the part about the bobcat over the shower stall. . . .

All things which make noise on the side of the path,
Do not come down the path.

—African proverb
(Left by Aaron Anderson, who just found out the cancer's gone)

Chapter 7

I had an unfavorable opinion of Jack West before I ever set eyes on him. Aside from the unsolved murder issue, my first reconnaissance mission inside the house ignited an inner simmering that had nothing to do with the spicy breakfast burrito. My dislike for the man grew each time I opened a cabinet door, peered into a dark corner, or looked inside one of the tiny, dark, musty-smelling closets.

The size of the closets wasn't the problem. The real problem was that they were already occupied. When I opened doors and turned on lights, the current residents scampered in all directions, fanning away from the light like drops of rain on the windshield of a car going seventy miles per hour. They disappeared beneath the layers of old wallpaper and cheesecloth that hung over dirty, loosely pieced slats of wood.

In dark corners dust motes gathered, filled with Brillo-like wads of human hair, animal fur of some kind, bits of rodent-eaten cardboard, the droppings that mice leave behind, assorted body parts from crickets and spiders, and the kind of giant roaches that slide quickly between wallboards. The kitchen cabinets were similarly objectionable, although some-one had lined the edges of each shelf with baby-blue powder that I had a bad feeling was intended to kill the roaches.

As disturbing as I found the mess in the cabinets, the mice didn't seem to be bothered by it in the slightest. I saw two of them, and evidence of more. My mother had often preached about the disease-carrying potential of rodents and insects, and as much as I was determined not to become my mother, I'd never in my life been in a place this repulsively filthy or filled with vermin.

There was no way we were unpacking the U-Haul here, much less the shipping crate when it arrived in a day or two. I wanted to grab my suitcase and purse, run out the door, and never come back.

I wanted my mommy. But if my mother saw this place, she'd have me hospitalized and checked for communicable diseases. I couldn't believe I'd slept here last night. On an air mattress. On the floor. No telling what might have been crawling underneath, over the top, under the covers, back and forth over my skin . . .

The sound of a vehicle rattling up the driveway interrupted the horror-movie scene in my mind as a shudder descended down my body.

I seized the only ray of hope I could come up with: Perhaps the person in the white truck was a ranch worker. Perhaps Jack West was out of town—Daniel had said his oil-company offices were in Houston—and he had no idea what shape the house was in. Perhaps whoever was supposed to prepare the house for move-in had failed to do it. Clearly this place had been sitting empty for a while, given over to the closet critters and the stuffed heads on the walls.

Taking a deep breath, I unclenched my hands and shook out the tension. Maybe communications had somehow broken down, and Mr. West didn't realize we were arriving so soon. No man in his right mind would lure a research scientist with a master's degree and his family halfway across the country to live in a place like this.

No man in his right mind . . .

Outside the window, Daniel stepped away from the U-Haul, and Nick trotted curiously to the gate, trailed by Pecos the dog. I squinted through the dirt-encrusted glass as the truck rolled to a stop and a man stepped out, the patchy shade of a magnolia tree slipping over his cowboy hat and faded pearl-snapped western shirt. He was tall, a head taller than Daniel even, and broad-shouldered with a thick build. His knees bowed outward slightly, his jeans tucked into boots that accentuated the arc.

Grabbing a napkin from breakfast and wiping greasy dirt off the inside of the window, I tried to get a better view of my first honest-to-goodness cowboy. He very much looked the part. He even had a bright red bandana tied around his neck, just like in the movies. I was suddenly enamored. I'd never met a real live cowboy. I'd rubbed elbows with a few congressmen and senators who claimed to be, but this man was authentic. Most certainly, this was not Jack West. Even from here, I could see that his shirt was threadbare, a piece torn away near the elbow. His jeans had holes on both front legs where car keys or loose change had worn through the fabric. This was no millionaire, but a workingman. Perhaps he was the ranch foreman Mr. West had mentioned in his communications with Daniel.

The cowboy and Daniel greeted each other with a handshake, and something about it stopped me just as I was about to move toward the door. My heart did a quick flip-flop in my chest. The burn started in my stomach again. A fluttery, panicked feeling beat its wings with the desperation of a sparrow trapped in the rafters of a shopping mall. Sometimes you can tell exactly what's being said, just by watching a conversation. I knew even before the stranger turned to follow Daniel to the house—this was the man himself, ragged cowboy clothes or not. This was the infamous Jack West. And it was clear from the body language that he wasn't one bit surprised we were here. It was also clear that no apologies were being offered, which meant that he didn't see any problem with moving a family into a filthy, smelly, vermin-infested house.

I felt our lives sliding off a cliff. If there was one thing my father, who was a fantastic judge of people, had taught me, it was that present behavior predicts future behavior. *Most people will tell you who they are within the first five minutes, Mal,* he'd advised me when I left for my post-college embassy job in Tokyo. *You show me someone who doesn't care what kind of first impression he makes, I'll show you someone who's the center of his own universe. Look out.*

I felt sick. No one who intended to treat an employee decently would begin a relationship this way. Daniel and I had just made the biggest mistake of our lives. We'd quit our jobs, we had almost no savings to fall back on, and nearly everything we owned was in a shipping container headed to Texas. We were trapped, hopelessly entangled, like the rat pills and the cricket legs in the dust motes.

Tears pressed, and my last romantic thoughts of this move to Texas as one big adventure faded like a mirage on a hot day. I wavered between running for the bathroom or choking down the emotion and greeting Jack West properly. Years of being dragged along to boring lobby-sponsored family events had taught me the art of the pasted-on smile. I knew how to pretend to be happy when I wasn't, but some situations are beyond even the pasty smile. Our future was involved here. Our family.

They were headed this way now, Jack striding up the foot-path with Daniel. Nick followed along, Pecos at his heels, both of them darting surreptitious looks at Mr. West's hulking frame, as if they couldn't decide what to make of him. He gave no regard to either of them. Apparently he wasn't interested in friendly dogs or adorable children. Another one of my father's bits of advice: *You can assess a man by how he reacts to those most vulnerable.*

My head swirled, and I turned to make a dash for the bathroom, but something strange happened. I can only describe it as the essence of the Ellery women inhabiting my body. I could hear my mother and Grandma Louisa Ellery whispering in my ear. Invisible hands pulled me upward like a puppet on strings. *Stand up straight,* Grandma Louisa commanded. *An Ellery woman does not bow to anyone.* My mother added, *Make a good impression. A wife can be her husband's best asset, if she knows how to present herself. . . .*

I greeted Daniel and Jack West as they stepped into the sunny porch-like room with the old oak desk and the icky yellow carpet. Jack West was even larger and more intimidating in a confined space. He was six foot five at least, with ruddy skin, black eyebrows, and a thick head of gray hair that tumbled from his straw cowboy hat when he took it off to mop his forehead. His piercing blue eyes were cool and aloof in a way that brought Corbin's rumors to mind again. Daniel's new boss had the countenance of someone who could murder two people, hide the bodies, and not be haunted by his own conscience.

He had the hands for it, too. His broad, long-fingered grip compacted the bones in my knuckles when he greeted me. He didn't smile along with the crushing grip, but merely met my gaze, as if the display of strength were more of a test than anything. I squeezed back. The Gymies would have been proud. All those pre-wedding workouts were good for something.

"Y'all are settled." Jack West's words were more of a statement than a question, requiring no answer. His slow drawl, more Southern than western, echoed through the room in a baritone perfect for voice-overs. He seemed oblivious to the echo and the lack of furniture or boxes in the house. If he wondered why we hadn't moved anything in, he didn't ask. His gaze swept the chalky, slightly crazed paint job on the walls and then skimmed the stained yellow carpet without interest.

"Uhhh, no, not . . . exactly . . ." I stammered. *This house is a wreck, have you noticed?*

Beyond Jack's broad shoulder, Daniel took a step to one side and widened his eyes with an almost imperceptible headshake. He'd been watching me go into panic mode about the house all morning. He'd even joined me in panic mode several times. He'd agreed that surely there was some mistake, and Jack West was not aware of the condition of the house. Now Daniel seemed to be taking it all back. He was giving me the don't-rock-the-boat look.

I sent an eye-flash back at him when Jack's attention darted to the dog barking outside. On the back porch, Nick had found the tennis ball, and he and Pecos were playing keep-away again.

In the few seconds while Jack's attention was elsewhere, unspoken dialogue pinged back and forth between Daniel and me with amazing clarity, considering that we were new at this marriage thing. All of a sudden, we could read each other's minds. I understood quickly and clearly that Daniel had just found out Jack West thought the house was shipshape as is, or at least that it was good enough for us. The very idea I'd been trying to backhand away was now landing smack-dab in the middle of our reality.

"Swimmin' hole down at the creek," Jack said flatly, seeming to be talking about Nick, though it was hard to tell. Jack was one of the strangest people I had ever met, and considering that I'd grown up in and around DC, that was saying something. "Rest of the hired hands' kids like it. Or the lake. Save on bathwater."

While the bathwater comment was weird, I took heart in the fact that he seemed to be suggesting something fun for Nick to do. Maybe he did have some sentiment toward children, after all. Someone who cared about kids couldn't be all bad. The term *rest of the hired hands* bothered me, though. Daniel wasn't a hired hand; he was a scientist, a business partner, a part owner in any future bio-agricultural patents developed here.

"We haven't really looked around at all." Daniel's answer had an uncertain, almost apologetic quality.

I felt the need to be honest. No sense starting out a business relationship without the terms negotiated. "We've been looking at the issues with the house . . . cleaning . . . and some repairs . . ." My mother would *not* have been pleased with me for piping up rather than waiting for my husband to do it, but there was a great big elephant in the room, and it was standing on my toes.

Daniel lost his balance and took a quick step backward, his mouth dropping open. He sent a warning grimace my way.

Jack gave the house a cursory glance that changed from slightly surprised to patently disinterested in the space of a second or two. His tree trunk arms rested above the thickened midsection of a sixty-something man who obviously worked to keep in shape. "Ranch account at the hardware store in Moses Lake. Need anything—paint, lumber, carpet cleaner—get it there. Put it on my charge."

How about a flame thrower? I entertained a mental image of blasting the interior of the house, just nuking everything.

"What about an exterminator?" I asked, and Daniel coughed softly, mortified.

Jack started for the door, dismissing the issue offhandedly. "Ask at the hardware store. They'll tell you what to use. Sprayers are in the equipment shed behind my little house out back. The shed's unlocked, the little house is locked. No one's welcome in there—or out on Firefly Island." He turned a hard look my way, as if making certain I understood.

Time seemed to hitch for a moment. The look in his eye sent a sharp, icy sliver straight to my stomach.

"Pack a little steel wool or caulk wherever the mice come in, if you're bothered by it." He reached for the screen door, and Nick moved out of the way on the other side. "Get some new screen for this thing, too. Lake breeds mosquitos. They'll suck you dry while you sleep." Pulling the door open, he stepped through, then walked toward his truck with long strides.

All I could do was watch him go and stare at the screen with my mouth frozen in a weird sneer. "What was that . . . ? Is he serious?"

Daniel hovered, seeming shell-shocked, then he rubbed his forehead roughly and started after his new boss. "Now wasn't the time to bring up the house."

The words went in like an arrow, and I instantly felt betrayed. "I thought *you* would bring it up, and . . ." I bit down on the sentence, severing it before it could become a return volley. It wouldn't help for Daniel and me to fight. "It's ridiculous that anyone would expect people to live this way, Daniel. The house should be fit for habitation, at least. A bottle of bug spray and a jug of paint from the hardware store aren't going to fix what's wrong here. I don't know how to paint a

house or . . . exterminate bugs . . . ." A shudder of revulsion
went through me.

In the yard, Jack West had stopped to investigate the ripening fruit on a small tree. They looked like plums, although
I'd never seen a plum in the wild before.

Nick progressed slowly in Mr. West's direction, one step at
a time, curious about the tree, or the man, or both. I wanted
to run outside and snatch Nick away, like a mother protecting
a child from getting too close to a snarling lion. "And steel
wool? We're supposed to crawl around God-knows-where
and figure out how the mice are getting in? If the mice have
been there, I don't *want* to go there. We can't stay in this
place, Daniel."

Jack picked a plum off the tree and took a bite. Beside
him, Nick imitated, though they weren't talking. The dog, I
noticed, kept himself on the other side of Nick, away from
the hulking man in the cowboy hat. Jack pointed a finger at
Pecos, commanding him to proceed to the pickup, but the dog
refused, instead moving closer to Nick's legs. Jack responded
with an unhappy scowl. Apparently, on top of everything
else, we'd stolen the boss's dog.

A giant, chicken-sized bird of some sort landed on the
fence. Jack threw a half-eaten plum either to it or at it; I
couldn't tell. The bird flapped down from the fence and chased
the plum as it rolled to a stop. Nick laughed and threw his
plum, too.

Daniel reached for the door, the motion quick, his gaze
distracted. In the yard, his boss was clearly waiting for him.
"Be realistic, Mallory," he snapped, suddenly morphing into
the stiff, impatient Daniel I'd met only yesterday during the
broken air-conditioner incident. "We can't change our life
plan because the closets are dirty."

The torn screen flapped as he opened it and walked out.

A moment later, he and Jack rumbled off in the white truck, while Nick stood at the fence near the U-Haul, where boxes of Grandma Louisa's Fostoria waited, still lovingly contained in cardboard and paper.

I briefly considered becoming a runaway bride.

If it hadn't been for poor little Nick and the fact that I couldn't figure out how to carry my grandmother's Fostoria on a bus, I might have done it. I'd never seen this side of Daniel before the wedding. I didn't like it. I didn't like being spoken to as if I were a minion, as if my thoughts didn't count for anything.

I went inside and paced the kitchen, feeling desperate. Finally, I did exactly what all the bridal advice columns tell you not to do after your first big fight: I called my mother.

She didn't want to talk to me. She'd read the advice columns, too. Aside from that, she'd married off four daughters already. She said that she'd always made it a policy not to meddle in her children's marital affairs. Which was so much hooey. She meddled all the time.

She gave only one piece of advice before she told me that she was hanging up because I should not be calling my mother just days after the wedding: "Say you're sorry, Mallory, even if you're not feeling that way. Marriage is about sacrifice. A wife must, at all times, realize that a man's ego is fragile. He needs to feel that you trust him to be the head of the household. Take the blame for starting the fight. It won't hurt you. Women lose their wits over a mouse in the house all the time. No one expects us to know better."

My indignation fumed in a dozen different directions, sending off molten spears like a sparkler . . . no, a sunspot. More like a sunspot. The kind that burns at a bazillion degrees and alters tides thousands of miles away. "The fight *wasn't* my fault." Suddenly I was supposed to relegate myself to the role of quiet cleaner-upper and soft-spoken apologizer? My life was supposed to be all about keeping the peace, no matter how I felt on the inside? I was supposed to become *my mother*?

This was not at all what I'd bargained for. This was not me.

A sickening premonition materialized, a dark vision. I imagined the girl who had confidently walked the halls of Congress in her favorite designer suit, but in the vision, she was disappearing day by day, until she vanished completely. A victim of death by acquiescence.

"I'd better go," I muttered.

"Say you're sorry," insisted my mother, whose policy was not to interfere.

"I love you, Mom." The end of the sentence choked in my throat. I wanted my mommy, but I wanted her to be on my side.

"All married couples have fights."

"Bye, Mom."

"Don't sulk. That's a bad habit of yours."

Who *was* this woman talking to? Me? Sulk? I never sulked. Sulking was for wimps.

"And never go to bed angry."

"*Bye, Mom.*" *I love you, but you are not telling me what I want to hear.*

"You're always welcome back at home." There was a catch in Mom's voice now, and I felt myself crumbling as she quickly tried to mollify the interference implied in that comment. "If Texas doesn't work out . . . for the two of you, I mean. You three can turn around and come right back. This house is too big for just Dad and me. . . ."

My low point sank lower, a raft with air hissing from it. Mother had managed to come up with an alternative worse than living in Texas on the property of a possibly homicidal maniac—moving my new family in with my parents.

I, quite wisely, ended the phone conversation there and called my sister Trudy, instead. She was upset with her husband, because he wanted to give up on the in vitro procedures if this next one didn't work. He was in favor of surrogacy or adoption.

I commiserated with her, and when she finally got around to asking why I'd called, I couldn't bring up the house-mouse fight or the stuffed-bobcat thing. Both seemed shallow, compared to Trudy's pain.

The hormone shots had given my sister mind-reading abilities, though. "Did you two get in a fight?" Her voice had a knowing undertone.

"Huh?"

"Did you call Mom?" The way she said it, as if it were a foregone conclusion, pushed blood into my cheeks. *Dork of the world. Right here. Big red arrow, pointing to Moses Lake, Texas.*

"Yes." There's no point lying to your sister. Sisters know.

"Did she tell you to get over yourself?" Trudy was holding back a laugh.

"Yes. You don't have to sound so happy about it, though." That long-way-from-home feeling grew potent and heavy. "She said that right before she told me that Daniel, Nick, and I could come back and live with her and Dad if we needed to."

"Ouch," Trudy chuckle-groaned. "Which option sounds best?"

"Getting over myself." I glanced at the clock on the scary gas stove that looked like it had been there since 1940. I was hungry, and there was no food in the house. Any time now, Nick would want something, too.

"Guess you have your answer, then." Leave it to Trudy to drive the point home.

My cell phone beeped a low-battery signal. "Hey, Trude, my cell is going dead. If this thing cuts off, I love you, 'kay?"

"Man, you *are* homesick." She didn't return my sappy endearment. Trudy was anything but sappy.

"I'll be all right." *I hope. I will, right?* "It's just been a long day, already."

"Hang in there, Wheezy." Her use of the nickname, which I had been saddled with ever since having a little nasal problem as a baby, was her idea of getting warm and fuzzy.

"I am. It was a dumb argument. I admit it."

"Most of them are. Actually, I should go apologize to Andy. These hormones have turned me into a part-time barracuda."

"Part time?"

Trudy snorted. "Very funny. Kiss and make up, first chance you get. That's the good thing about fighting. When it's over, you have a new appreciation. Just remember, if you're going to argue, argue against the point and not the person. You can change your position on a point, but once you step over that line and criticize who he is, you can't go back. There's no sense bothering, anyway. People really don't change. They are who they are."

"I'd better go before the phone cuts off."

"You know how I knew that you'd called Mom, right?"

"Huh? Well, no. How did you know?"

She laughed, a soft, tender sound that felt like her wrapping her arms around me from hundreds of miles away. "All of us did it. Before the cell service went to free long distance, Mom used to include prepaid calling cards in the wedding gifts. She started that after Caroline and Merryl called collect, and the bill was horrendous. You're the first one not to make it a week past the wedding, though. Andy and I had been in Hawaii for seven days before I called Mom."

"Well, at least I get to be first at something." There was

comfort in knowing that my settled, sane, still-happily-married sisters had gone through this sort of thing, too. Maybe Daniel and I weren't such a mess after all.

"Take my advice. Kiss and make . . ." Trudy was gone. Time expired. Battery dead.

Despite the fact that Daniel had left the Jeep hooked to the U-Haul after he'd backed the trailer near the yard gate, I grabbed my purse and made up my mind to drive into Moses Lake and seek out the café and the hardware store. The Gypsy Wagon would just have to ride along, since I had no idea how to unhook it. Nuclear bug bombs and acres of steel wool were in our future.

From the kitchen counter, a brown mouse sat up on its delicate little hind feet and waved good-bye, having no idea what was headed its way.

Chapter 8

Welcome to Moses Lake! If you're lucky enough to be at the lake, you're lucky enough, the sign at the edge of town read. Ancient-looking rock pillars supported the weathered wooden timbers, casting a shadow over the words and sheltering a spray of purple wildflowers. Considering that it had been a fairly mild night, it was hot today. Downhill from the sign, the waters of Moses Lake glittered in cheery patches between the trees. Boats crisscrossed the twinkling surface, leaving foamy white trails. Near the shore, docks of various vintages floated with brightly colored canoes, faded paddleboats, and pontoon craft tugging at their leashes, eager to be released to the water.

I had the strangest urge to pull over and abandon the Jeep and the trailer, which was catching wind today and weaving like crazy. I pictured myself running down the hill, hopping into a speedboat, and taking off across the water to the hills on the opposite side. They seemed wild and unspoiled, no docks, houses, or boat sheds marring the rocky shore. I could build a thatch hut there, hide away from everything. . . .

"I wanna go swimmin'!" Nick piped up, poking his finger against the window glass, leaving behind smudgy dabs of enthusiasm. If Nick felt at all out of place in this new life, it didn't show. He seemed as comfortable with the house and yard, with the town of Moses Lake, as if he'd always been here.

"It looks like fun, doesn't it?" I agreed. "Maybe we can do that later, but right now we have to find the hardware store and a place to get some lunch and some groceries. Doesn't that sound like fun, too?" The question sing-songed upward in an attempt to win Nick's cooperation. Truth be told, I didn't have much experience being alone with Nick, other than the weekend of the stomach flu when he was too sick to argue about anything. Beginning with our departure from my parents' house, I had seen Nick throw some fits my sisters would have classified as *snotty humzingers*, a description that had been in our family, not coincidentally, since I was little.

I'd been in public with my sisters a few times when one or more of the nieces opted to go the route of the snotty humzinger. The great thing about being only an aunt was that I could step away and pretend I didn't know those people. With Nick, I was responsible. I had no idea how to singlehandedly quash a zinger. So far, I'd been able to pretty much leave the discipline to Daniel.

The weight of parenthood fell heavily on my shoulders as we drifted past the Moses Lake sign. What qualifications did I have for guiding and shaping a small, fragile, developing human being? What if I screwed him up totally?

I glanced in the rearview mirror, and Nick was gazing toward the water with his brows slightly lowered. He craned to see the lake as we passed a small Corps of Engineers building and then a little rock church with a park along the lakeshore in back. In the picnic area, kids from a day care or a school were playing in the shade of sprawling pecan trees near the water's edge.

"Ohhhhh . . ." Nick breathed, straining toward the window. "Look, there some kids-es!" His hand pressed flat against the glass, as if he were trying to reach out and touch the excitement.

"They're having a picnic." *Please, no zingers. Please, no zingers . . . We can't stop and play with the kids. We have steel wool and bug bombs to buy.* "Maybe we can get your dad to go on a picnic with us after we get home."

"I wanna go wit' the kids-es." A lonely little whine frayed the last word.

"I bet the hardware store has candy." *Redirect, redirect.* Where was that hardware store? "Tell you what, though, let's go find the café first. I'm hungry. Are you hungry, Nick? Remember the place you went with Daddy this morning? Can you help me find the way there?"

Nick didn't answer. He was too busy watching the kids as we passed by. I couldn't blame him for wanting to hang out with them. He was used to being surrounded by children every day. Daniel and I weren't much of a substitute for playmates his own age, and even Pecos the dog couldn't really make up for all the friends Nick had left behind in day care. Once we were settled here and had our finances back in order, maybe we could find some kind of preschool for Nick. I could use the time to look for a job, but for now getting the house in order had to come first.

Taking in the town of Moses Lake, I felt my hopes for future job possibilities shrinking. The place was tiny, just a few things on the edge of town: a convenience store that served Chinese food, a bank, the Harmony House Bed and Breakfast, and the church. Beyond that lay a little strip of old stone buildings with high false fronts—dollar store, hardware store, a few antique shops, and a smattering of other things. No office buildings, no government facilities, no global corporations.

What could I possibly do with a degree in political science and foreign language in a place like this? The nearest town was Gnadenfeld, which we had passed through on our way in last night. It was larger, with a Walmart, various restaurants, new housing developments, and a fairly impressive-looking school building, but there was no business and industry section there, either, other than some sort of massive food processing facility.

I'd never find anything in my field around here, and if I didn't work, what would I do with myself? Who would I be?

Stop. One thing at a time. The words came from outside my head as much as within it—as if someone were trying to deliver a cosmic chill pill, telling me to lay off the expectations. Just let things happen.

I tried to allow the placid rhythms of Moses Lake to wash over me as Nick and I proceeded through town, following signs to the Waterbird Bait and Grocery. When we rounded the corner and the place came into view, I had an uneasy feeling about eating there. With a rusted tin roof and an odd configuration of rooms and additions, the building looked like it had metamorphosized over time, growing out of the lakeside hills with no particular plan in mind. This was the spot Daniel had mentioned—the origin of this morning's delicious breakfast burrito? It looked more like one of the fish markets in Mexico.

In the backseat, Nick was already working his shoulders out of his safety harness as we turned into the gravel parking lot and the vehicle slowly drifted to a stop. "Can we get some fishies? And some wo-r-r-rms." Stretching the last word, he lifted his little fingers and wiggled them in a crawly fashion.

I could only guess he'd gotten that from his dad. Nick and Daniel were similar in so many ways that it was hard to imagine, other than the blond hair, where Nick's mother was in the picture. Nick seemed to be a one hundred percent copy of his father, or maybe I just wanted to feel that way. It bothered me when I really thought about the fact that Nick had a mother out there. I wondered if, on some random day, she would awaken to what she was missing and come back to stake her claim. On Nick. On Daniel.

I worried that I would never really be Nick's mom, but I hadn't admitted that to anyone. I'd even denied it to my sisters when the subject came up. *Nick's biological mother doesn't have any interest,* I'd said, but every time I looked at Nick, I couldn't imagine how that could be true. How could anyone not want him?

"I think we'll just get something to eat today," I said and came around to finish springing Nick from his car seat. He smiled as I did, and stretched his arms toward me as if it were completely natural.

"I wanna eat fishies and worms!" He gave an evil giggle and made crawly-hands against my shoulders. I got it that he was trying to do a gross-out on me.

"Fishies and worms?" I asked, hip-butting the door and tipping him forward at the same time, so that I was leaning over that adorable, mischievous smile. How in the world could I have been worried about that face pitching a snotty humzinger? He had to be the cutest kid who'd ever lived.

"Oh, you are so funny." I tickled under his arms with my thumbs as his legs wrapped around me monkey-style. "What color fishies and worms?"

"Red fishies and gween wor-r-rmies!" Nick squealed and did the crawly hands again, giggling. "Big, squi-sy gween wor-r-rmies! The wittle cweam fill kind." He quoted a line from *The Lion King*, where Pumba bites into a particularly delicious bug.

"Eeewww!" I shook him upside down. "Did your dad feed you worms this morning?"

"Ye-h-h-h-es!" Nick laughed, letting his hands fly free.

"We'd better shake those worms back out, then. Boys aren't supposed to eat worms." I bounced him a few more times, until his face turned good and red, and he was laughing breathlessly. Roughhousing with kids, I could do. I could stir them up until they were so hyper they wouldn't sit still for a week. It was one of my best Tante M skills.

It didn't occur to me until I'd turned Nick upright and set him on his feet, that maybe getting him all stirred up before lunch wasn't the best idea. He jittered and tugged on my hand as we walked toward the door, and the moment I let go of him at the deli counter so I could look at the menu, he was gone. Like a Ping-Pong ball with a good spin on it, he bounced around the store, leaving fingerprints all over the fish tanks in the bait section along the side wall, sticking his hands in the worm dirt, bothering three ladies at a corner table, then snagging a pack of gum from the candy aisle as I was ordering lunch and waiting for our food. I rounded him up just as he was about to stick his dirty little fingers into a warmer full of sausage biscuits. At that point, he wasn't happy to be corralled.

The elderly man behind the counter, who was working from a wheelchair, smiled tolerantly as I swung Nick onto my hip. "You hungry, little fella?" He smiled at us over tissue-lined chicken finger baskets.

Nick answered by burrowing his face into my shoulder, refusing to speak.

The old man chuckled, then tried again. "Looks like since breakfast this morning, you done developed a case of acute

Need-a-Nugget. You bring your mom back here for some lunch?"

Nick stopped burrowing in. Leaning back against the circle of my arms, he squinted at me, as if he were looking for the answer to that question, wondering if I knew the answer. *Did you bring your mom back . . . your mom . . .*

Blood prickled into my cheeks, and I found myself caught in a moment for which there was no blueprint in my life. This was the first time the question had come up. At what point did I tell people that I was Nick's stepmother? I wimped out on it completely and grabbed a French fry from the chicken nuggets basket, handing it to Nick. "I think we've got a case of Need-a-Nugget, all right."

I pretended to be busy digging a wet wipe from my purse, opening the packet, and swiping the worm dirt off Nick's hands as the man behind the counter fixed our drinks. Nick wiggled down so he could snatch another fry. The old man grinned at him over the sodas and tapped Nick's hand with a craggy finger. "You remember my name, young fella?"

Nick backed away a step and shook his head.

"Pop, like lollypop. Pop Dorsey. You remember that now?" The old man's hands disappeared below the counter momentarily, and Nick watched with expectation, clearly having been through this drill before. A green lollypop was soon on its way to Nick's chicken basket.

Nick nodded, licking his lips.

"He can have a lollypop, can't he?" Pop Dorsey turned to me after the fact.

"Sure. Thanks, that's very sweet. What do you tell Mr. Dorsey, Nick?"

"No *mister*, just *Pop*," the old man corrected. "I'm Pop to kids of all sizes and stripes. Been running this place too long to be anything else." He stuck out a hand to shake mine.

"Yer husband said he moved here for his job, but he didn't say whereabouts."

"At the West Ranch," I answered. Pop Dorsey lifted an eyebrow, and I felt compelled to explain further. "My husband will be working in the laboratory out there."

It still felt strange to say those words, *My husband*. It was hard to believe that a little over two months ago, marriage wasn't even on my radar. I still felt as if the man behind the counter should roll his eyes and say, *Yeah right, like I believe that*.

But instead, some private thought swirled behind Pop Dorsey's cloudy gray eyes, and a wrinkle sketched lines of concern on his forehead. Nick paused, his hands motionless on the edge of the counter, as if even he felt the undercurrent. A cold sensation crawled up my back, making the skin tight and itchy.

"You livin' out there on the ranch?" Pop Dorsey asked with more than ordinary curiosity.

"Yes. At the old headquarters, I think it's called. The house came with the job. We'd be foolish not to take advantage of the offer." The explanation was meant to convey that we weren't homeless or destitute, but what I got back was the sense that Pop Dorsey thought we'd be better off living somewhere else.

"Kind of out there by yourselves at the old headquarters." He slid my drink closer to me, and his fingers brushed mine, pulling my gaze to his in a way that held both of us in a bond of things unsaid. "I know that house. Used to look after cows on the ranch, years back. That was back when Jack West's second wife was there. Before she was . . . well, anyway, that was a long time ago."

An empty, hungry, unsteady discomfort swirled inside me. I felt a little sick. What did Pop, who gave suckers to kids and welcomed newcomers to Moses Lake, know about our new boss that I didn't know?

"The house needs some work, to tell you the truth." I felt myself teetering on the ragged edge of starting a rant, but wisely chose to keep it to myself. "We'll get it done, I'm sure." Of all the strange things, tears pricked my eyes. I felt . . . completely disoriented.

Pop Dorsey seemed to sense it. "Well, you need any help—need to know the number for a good carpenter, anything like that—you come talk to Pop, y'hear?" He looked up as the cowbell on the door clattered, announcing another customer.

I bit down on my emotions, swallowed hard. "Thanks. I will." Things could be worse. At least Moses Lake was turning out to be friendly, even if the town was small.

"Len, over there, has been doin' some light carpentry work recently," Pop offered, tilting his head toward the customer coming in the door. The man was thin and stooped, his ragged shirt and dirt-encrusted jeans drooping over his body like the cleaning rags my grandmother's maid tossed over the piazza railing. His hair hung in gray strings beneath a faded ball cap, and several teeth were missing when he smiled. He reminded me of the homeless people who inhabited sheltered spaces in DC.

He didn't look like anyone I would want in my house, or around Nick. It wasn't the most charitable reaction, but I couldn't help it. My mother had always been particular about the people we associated with, even those she hired for housework and gardening. They came from a professionally managed service where background checks were performed. They arrived in clean uniforms and were dignified and well-spoken.

Some attitudes rub off, whether you want them to or not. "Oh . . . well, I'll have to see how things go. But thanks."

Nick turned and waved at the man by the door, his little

face lighting up, his head craning side to side, as if he were watching for something more. "Where *her* go?"

I blinked, looking at Nick. *Her? Her, who?*

"Ubbb-Birdie's at the p-p-picnic," the man stammered, his speech slow and slurred. "Www-with the uhh-kids. I ugg-gotta get some . . . s-s-some more udd-drinks."

Pop Dorsey waved a finger toward a stack of Gatorade cases by the door. "Got it right there for ya, Len. Just tell Miz Zimmer I'll put it on her summer school bill, and someone from the district can come by and pay it whenever."

I gathered Nick and our food, and moved away from the counter, anxious to exit the conversation.

"Don't forget to sign the Wall of Wisdom while yer here," Pop Dorsey called after us as we slid into a table with a chipped Formica top and torn red vinyl seats. "And you three sisters, too!" He addressed the women at the corner booth, who'd just finished sharing a slice of pie.

"Oh, we will. We already grabbed a Sharpie," one of the women answered, then held up a pen and pointed to the back wall, where the windows overlooking the lake were surrounded by Sharpie-pen notations of all sorts. Amid the graffiti hung handmade wooden plaques with quotes like *Good things come to those who bait* and *Early to bed, Early to rise, Fish all day, Tell big lies.*

One of the women in the corner booth leaned toward me, her expression warm beneath a shock of short reddish-blond hair. "It's good luck," she offered. "The legend goes that if you sign the Wall of Wisdom with someone, you'll always return to Moses Lake together. Cindy and I just started remodeling a little lake house here, so we're hoping it works. Paula lives all the way in Florida—" she patted the hand of the brown-haired sister— "When we all get together, it's a big deal. It's terrible having your sister move halfway across the country."

"Yes, it is." All of a sudden, I missed my sisters. I wished they were here, where we could snuggle into the corner table together and talk about what to write on the Wall of Wisdom. "I have four of them—sisters, I mean. I just moved to Texas, and they're all in the DC area." My voice trembled on the last words, which was so unlike me. I'd lived all over the world, by choice, in fact, but now a wave of homesickness was so thick in my throat that I felt like I might suffocate. My sisters were hundreds of miles away. They wouldn't be coming here anytime soon. Visiting would be a major undertaking of clearing schedules and arranging flights.

"Oh, you poor thing," Paula offered. "I know what it's like to be the one living away. You should do what Alice and I do. We call it our Binding Through Books club. We read books together, then every three chapters, we have a little meeting about it over the phone. It's a lot of fun."

Alice, the red-haired sister, nodded and smiled, the Wall of Wisdom quotes reflecting off her glasses. "You could start a Binding Through Books club with your sisters. All five of you. When you're on the phone talking about a story, it's just like you're right there together."

"Thanks." I forced a weak smile and pretended to be busy getting Nick and the food settled. I could just imagine what my sisters, with their ridiculously busy lives, would say if I suggested we read together and have regular phone-in book club meetings. They'd probably remind me that, for years, I'd been notorious about taking weeks to even answer personal emails.

Alice shoulder-bumped the third sister, who was giving me a sympathetic smile. "Cindy, write down some ideas for her." She sent a wink my way. "Cindy works in a bookstore in Dallas. She knows all the latest. She's our source."

"Sure, no problem." Tucking her blond hair behind her

ear, Cindy took the Sharpie, turned a paper placemat over, and tapped the tip of the pen to her lips. "Okay, let me think. What kinds of things do your sisters read?"

In truth, I had no idea, so I described my sisters' personalities instead, and Cindy went to work on a suggested literature list that would help me remain connected with my family across the miles. She handed it to me as the Binding Through Books girls cleaned their table and moved to the Wall of Wisdom to leave their favorite quotes behind.

Nick paid little attention. He was busy keeping an eye on the door as Len came and went, carrying out boxes of Gatorade and bags of ice.

"Did you meet that man this morning when you were here?" I asked, knowing that he must have.

"It's Birdie's gam-pa," Nick offered, smiling up at me, a fry dangling between his teeth. He munched it into his lips without touching it, then waited to see if I'd noticed.

"That's a good trick. Watch this." I threw a partial fry in the air and caught it in my mouth—hours and hours of being a bored, lonely youngest child does have its benefits. You have plenty of time to perfect skills, like catching food as it flies through the air.

"Woooooo!" Nick breathed, and we were sympatico again. I loved these moments, when we were just enjoying each other. Something about having Nick's adoration soothed the pain of missing my sisters. He made me believe I really could be someone's mother.

A happy camaraderie settled over us as we started in on our chicken nuggets. Nick chattered on about his visit to the Waterbird that morning, when he'd sat at the table with his dad and met several "fishing men," as well as a little girl who was apparently Len's granddaughter. Birdie had shown him a smiley face and a place on the Wall of Wisdom where she'd signed her name. Nick trotted over and pointed it out to me, and I saw her writing there, B-i-R-D-i-E in uneven red print.

Looking at the wall, I tried to imagine where the girl might live, what her life might be like. I watched Nick skipping back to our table, completely unaware of the whirl of thoughts in my head.

This place, Moses Lake, was so foreign, so different from anything I'd ever known. How would I ever fit in here? How would I ever make the ranch or this little town my home?

The questions taunted me as Nick and I watched the activity on the lake below and finished our meals.

After we cleaned up our table, I walked to the back wall and stood a minute, studying it. The Wall of Wisdom was exactly what the name implied—a place where locals and passersby had left little bits of themselves, quotes, words of advice, wisdom ranging from *Never test the depths of the water with both feet* to a quote from Anne Frank: *How wonderful it is that nobody need wait a single moment before starting to improve the world.*

Moses Lake was like that wall, I realized. The mixture of people who lived here, who visited here, who spent time in proximity and were not carefully homogenized like the people I'd grown up with and lived among until now. This was not a place where you could select the right neighborhood, the right schools, the right stores, the right job, meet all your needs among your own kind. In this tiny town, the people were too few to be divided. They had no choice but to live all together in the pockets of civilization tucked among the rocks and hills.

I wasn't sure how I felt about that, but the clearest emotion I could identify was discomfort . . . or fear. Maybe fear was a better word for it. Was I ready for a life like this? Did I really want it?

Was I more like my mother than I cared to admit—afraid that if I brushed elbows with the masses, something might rub off?

Was I a *snob*?

"Y'all need a Sharpie?" Pop Dorsey called. A forty-something woman had entered from a door behind the counter. Judging by the body language, I guessed that she was family. Pop's daughter, perhaps. They had the same eyes.

"It's good luck to sign the wall," Pop reminded.

"I'll have to think about it a few days," I said, trying to sound cheerful and light, not as if I were engaged in a moment of deep spiritual questioning. Part of me was afraid of what that wall represented, of who it represented. "I want to make sure I come up with something good." Suddenly in a hurry to be out of there, I grabbed my purse from the seat, bought a few groceries, and then Nick and I headed for the door.

"Welcome to Moses Lake. Be careful out there, 'kay?" Pop called after us, and when I turned around, I noticed that he and his daughter had their heads together, but their worried looks were directed my way. I had a feeling they were talking about Nick and me . . . and the West Ranch.

The chill came rushing back, raising a flush of goose bumps as we exited the Waterbird and climbed into the Jeep. I wanted to forgo the hardware store and hurry home, but home wasn't a safe refuge either. In not so many hours, darkness would settle over the hills again, seep into the valleys, and color them a fathomless black. The current residents of the house would slip from their shadowy hiding places and canvas the walls and floors.

A stop for extermination equipment was a must.

The trailer made a squealing, grinding sound as I drove through town and pulled into the hardware store parking lot. I didn't look back to see where the noise was coming from but just unloaded Nick and started toward the door. Whatever was going on with the trailer would have to wait until we got home.

The hardware store was quaint and old-fashioned, with a high ceiling downstairs, an ancient Otis freight elevator in the back, and an open area in the center. Stairs led to a second story wraparound balcony containing an assortment of clothes, shoes, hatboxes, and store displays that looked like they hailed back to the fifties. When my mother finally did come to visit, I'd have to bring her here. She would love the nostalgia of the place—the feeling of stepping back in time to an era when store walls were lined with richly polished wooden shelves offering everything from penny candy to nuts and bolts in multi-drawered cabinets that would be worth a fortune in an antique mall.

A friendly, dark-haired teenage boy was working behind the counter. *Dustin Henderson*, his name tag read. He was well-spoken and seemed sympathetic to my vermin problem. He said I sounded like his mother. She couldn't abide crawly things in her house, either. Fortunately, Dustin knew quite a bit about how to get rid of them. By the time he rang up my mountain of bug bombs, steel wool, caulking, and a new catch-and-release form of mousetrap, I was feeling a little better about things. He made it sound like a simple enough proposition—plug the holes around plumbing and so forth with steel wool or caulking, open all the closets and cabinets, cover the countertops, and nuke the place with bug bombs. This procedure had worked in the house Dustin had moved into with his mother and new stepdad, who also happened to be the county game warden. Their new house had been sitting empty awhile before they acquired it, too.

At the front counter, I added some elbow-length plastic gloves and a facemask. Glancing at the promotional photo of a woman wearing the bubble-like mask over her mouth and nose, I imagined myself geared up and ready for battle. A laugh teased my throat. I'd have to text a picture to Kaylyn and Josh. This was so far from *His Irish Bride*. Really.

Actually, the Gymies would probably get a kick out of seeing the hardware store, too. They wouldn't believe this place. With its collection of old cabinets, assorted merchandise hanging on cardboard display cards, and the freight elevator where Nick was now pretending to be Buzz Lightyear, it really was something to see. The only things missing were old men playing checkers and lovers sipping sarsaparillas while strolling along the sidewalk, parasols and brightly wrapped packages in hand.

I grabbed my phone and snapped a few pictures, then emailed them to Kaylyn with a quick text. *In the hardware store buying nuclear bomb for house mice and bugs. Look at this place!*

Dustin waited patiently until I was done. "That oughta take care of it." He slid my sack across the counter. "It flushed out everything at our place but the scorpions. My stepdad had the feedstore order some stuff for that, but I can't remember what it's called."

I didn't answer at first. I'd allowed myself to be momentarily lulled by the ambiance of the hardware store. The soft light from the second-story windows made the place seem quiet and contemplative. I was thinking that hopefully by the time I got back to the house, Daniel would be there, and he could do the steel wool stuffing and bug bomb detonation. This was a job for a real man, and now was as good a time as any to get over the tiff we'd had. Daniel and I fighting wouldn't help anything. . . .

That one word yanked me back like a bungee jumper.

Scorpions . . . Did he say *scorpions*?

"What?" Scorpions lived . . . well, somewhere on the Discovery Channel, didn't they?

"They're not, like, the deadly kind or anything. They just sting really bad." Perhaps Dustin could see the blood draining from my face, or perhaps my eyes bugging out tipped him off to the fact that he was face-to-face with a woman on the edge of hysteria. Suddenly he was in a big hurry to help the guy shopping for plumbing supplies in the back of the store. "The scorpions are more over on our side of the lake, I think. Anyway, have a great day."

He was gone before I could gather Nick and my sack of ammo. I walked out the door, watching the ground and thinking of old western movies filled with wicked-looking creatures with lightning-fast curly tails.

Before pulling out of the hardware store, I texted Kaylyn. *Hardware store guy just told me the scorpions are mostly on the other side of the lake. Wondering if this qualifies as good news . . .*

Looking down the main street of Moses Lake, I considered finding the feedstore and asking for more particulars, but on the theory that focusing on a problem can create it where it doesn't exist, I decided to head for home before I learned anything more about what might be hiding in the shadows there when I arrived.

The everyday kindness of the back roads more than makes up
for the acts of greed in the headlines.

—Charles Kuralt
(Left by Dan and Theresa Lohman,
touring Texas in their vintage motor home)

Chapter 9

Standing there looking at the tire, I had a terrible, horrible sinking feeling. This was bad. Very, very bad. The U-Haul was tipped askew, the rubber part of the tire hanging in shreds on the metal inner portion. Even I, who knew not beans about cars and trailers, knew that flat tires didn't end up in this condition unless you'd been driving on the flat for a while.

I recalled my father berating my mother for something similar years ago, telling her she should have stopped and called for roadside assistance instead of remaining on the highway, obliterating the tire, and ending up marooned in the center median on the way home from one of my sister's cello lessons. "Well, how was I supposed to know?" she'd insisted, her eyes big and tear-filled. "I thought if it really needed to be changed, a buzzer would go off or a light, at least. The car should—" sniff, sniff, a delicate dabbing around the eyes, an attempt to salvage mascara, and then—"say something."

My father, saint that he was, lost his angry look and laughed instead. "Mar . . . ger . . . ie," he coughed out between puffs. "Sweet . . . heart." And just like that, he was taking her in his arms and soothing away the trauma of the tire incident.

"I swear, she gets away with everything," Trudy, thirteen-going-on-thirty then, muttered in my ear. She was mortified that her friends might have seen us being delivered home in a tow truck with Mother's car dragging along behind, little tufts of grass hanging from the axle. "If *I* did that, I'd be grounded for, like, the rest of the year."

I didn't really understand Trudy's complaining at the time. I couldn't relate to my sisters' tendencies to be strangely jealous of how much my father loved my mother. I never coveted my mother's role or admired it. My father's role looked better. He was the one in charge. The decision-maker. The one whisking off to exotic locations in private jets and limousines.

But now here I was in an empty parking lot, having clearly pulled *a Mom*, as Trudy had liked to refer to incidents like this.

I looked around as Nick tapped his window from inside and enthusiastically inquired, "We gotta fat tire?"

Then I felt like a total ignoramus. Even a not-quite-four-year-old could diagnose the problem. I'd heard the scraping sound back there, felt the U-Haul weaving around since Nick and I had left the house to drive to Moses Lake. I'd assumed it was the wind, or that the trailer was wobbling because the road was bumpy. Stupid. Really stupid.

"Uh-huh," I answered. "Do you know how to fix one?"

"Okay." Nick began wiggling out of his seat belt, happy to give it a try. His Hot Wheels cars had flats all the time. How much different could this be?

"I think we'd better call your dad." I leaned into the car to grab my phone, popping it off the car charger.

Nick, halfway out of his safety harness, rolled his head back and yawned, studying the ceiling as I stood in the driver's side door and tried repeatedly to get Daniel on his cell. No answer. I left messages, texted, waited, muttered, complained, then finally gave up. What were the odds of finding a wrecker in this town? Could wreckers even tow a broken trailer?

I tried staring at the mangled tire some more, hoping to shame it into repairing itself. Unfortunately, I'd killed it beyond dead. And I was no U-Haul expert, but I did know that there was no spare tire for the trailer. Daniel had grumbled about this fact when we were at the rental place back home. The attendant claimed that was because spare tires tended to mysteriously vanish before trailers were returned. If we had a breakdown, we were to call the U-Haul hotline number for help. I wondered how far, exactly, the nearest U-Haul roadside assistance mechanic might have to travel to reach me in a church parking lot in Moses Lake. I had a bad feeling this was not going to be a quick process, and right now the folder with the U-Haul numbers in it was sitting on the counter in the ranch house.

"Where all them kids go?" Nick asked, when he saw me looking at the building. The place was quiet and empty now, the park along the lakeshore deserted. We could walk back to the hardware store, hang out until Daniel finally noticed that we'd been trying to get in touch with him. My new friend Dustin would probably help us out. . . .

I shared the plan with Nick, and he frowned, giving me a tired look. The red rims around his eyes testified to the fact that it was well past his usual nap time.

"All right, here we go." Before striking out, I attempted one last, desperate call to Daniel. He didn't answer, and in some inexplicable way, I felt my irritation transferring to him. He could have unhooked the U-Haul before he left with Jack West, at least. Hadn't it even occurred to him that Nick and I would need to go to town for lunch and some groceries? He'd clearly been away from the house for hours, and he hadn't even called to check on us?

My mother's advice flew away like a sparrow with an alley cat on its tail, and I stood there stewing, resentful and abandoned. *He couldn't explain to his boss that he needs to go home? That he has a family to take care of? That we have to get the house into some kind of shape for us to sleep in it, and . . .*

A rusty red four-door pickup with some sort of a cage on the back rolled into the parking lot, derailing my personal tirade. Holding Nick's hand, I turned and watched the vehicle veer in our direction. When the angle of the sun changed, I caught a glimpse of the driver. Cowboy hat, tall, thin. A child was sitting next to the driver . . . a little girl with ponytails . . . no, not a girl. A dog. In the back of the truck, a larger animal of some sort was circling in the cage. Shading my eyes, I tried to see what it was.

"Wook!" Nick pointed enthusiastically. "It's a g-raffe!"

"That's a . . . llama, I think. . . ." Although I was just guessing, too. The black-and-white polka-dotted creature was like nothing I'd ever seen. I didn't know llamas came in two-tone.

"Ohhhh," Nick breathed. "Woooo."

The llama stuck its nose through the railings as the vehicle stopped, and the cowboy got out, followed by the dog. "Flat tire?" The voice was barely audible over the rumble of the truck's idling engine; however, I quickly realized that the driver was not a cowboy, but a cowgirl—a tall raw-boned woman wearing a loose-fitting T-shirt and jeans that looked like they might have come from the men's department. Her cowboy boots were covered with dust and dried mud, and a ring of dirt around her straw hat testified to the fact that it had been sweated in a time or two. Her long, gray-tinseled brown hair was braided behind her back, and the tail hung over her shoulder, the end bound with a green rubber band that appeared to have been salvaged off a newspaper somewhere.

With a strange fascination, I watched her approach, the dog trailing behind her, heeling perfectly, though there was no leash. I'd never seen anyone quite like this ruddy cowgirl woman before. She moved across the parking lot, loose limbed and relaxed, but all business, in a country sort of way. "Got a flat tire?" she asked again. She tipped her head to one side slightly, and so did the dog, as if both thought I might be a little daft.

I realized I'd been so busy looking at her that I hadn't answered. "Yes, yes, I do have a flat tire. Mangled, actually."

Nodding, she gave me little more than a cursory glance before proceeding past me to get a better look at the leaning rental trailer. Nick and I followed in her wake like tourists having spotted a movie star in some Hollywood restaurant. "Yeah, they don't put spares in these rentals, either," she observed with an obvious note of disgust, then leaned over to take a look at the tailgate of the Jeep, where the vehicle's spare was hanging. "Well, that thing won't fit it."

"No, I didn't think it would." As if it had even occurred to me that the Jeep had a spare tire of its own. I wouldn't have known what to do with it, anyway.

Glancing up and down the street, the cowgirl woman sucked air through her teeth, a critical sound, I thought, and I wondered if it was aimed at me. Strangely enough, the animal in the back of the truck made the same noise, showing teeth that looked startlingly human. Nick slipped from my hand to move a few steps closer. "I wanna see," he whispered.

"Don't go too close." I watched him from the corner of my eye as he moved toward the pickup one tentative step at a time.

"Trixie won't hurt 'im," the cowgirl said, shooing Nick

onward. "She likes kids. She's my pettin' llama for school visits, that kinda thing."

"Oh." So it *was* a llama, and llamas did come with polka dots. I'd learned something today as a result of the flat tire fiasco. My father had always said that an experience you learn from is never a complete waste.

Nick moved closer to the pickup truck and stood with his hands on his hips, looking up at the llama. The llama looked down at Nick, pressing its nose to the bars as Nick squinted to get a better look at the animal's teeth.

"It's okay, you can pet her," the cowgirl told him. "Al Beckenbauer."

I realized she was introducing herself to me.

"Mallory Everson." I reached out to shake her hand, and she crushed me in a big, bony grip that reminded me of Jack West's. Beneath her leathery skin, lean forearm muscles bulged. I tried to gauge how old she was, but it was impossible to tell. Somewhere between forty and sixty, but she probably looked older than she was. Her skin was sun-freckled and latticed with tiny dry-weather cracks. Her face was free of makeup, other than maybe a little ChapStick. She had an air of confidence and self-sufficiency that, quite honestly, made me feel sort of froufrou and incompetent. Wimpy, really. I'd never thought of myself that way before, but Al Beckenbauer was intimidating. I had a feeling she changed her own flat tires. Probably barehanded, without a jack, and she undid the bolts with her teeth.

When I pulled my fingers away, I fought the urge to shake the circulation back into them. Sweat dripped down my back, and I wondered at the quickest remedy for my current predicament. If it didn't cost too much, maybe I'd just pay to have the thing fixed and not say a word to Daniel about it. I was an idiot for having done such a number on the tire. "Any chance there's someplace here in town that could put a new rubber part on the . . ." My grasp of the proper terminology lacking, I settled for, " . . . thing?" What was the metal part inside the shredded rubber called, anyway?

Al shook her head, her salt-and-pepper braid slipping off her shoulder and tumbling down her back in a heavy coil. "Not here in Moses Lake. Ranchhouse Tire probably has replacements this size, but that's over in Gnadenfeld."

We went on to discuss options—call U-Haul for a repair, unhook the trailer and leave it here, or leave both the Jeep and trailer behind . . .

A school bus rumbled into the parking lot and drifted to a stop near the edge where a thick patch of forest cast heavy shade. As Al and I watched, a line of children appeared like wood sprites from among the trees. At the head of the group, a young woman in a long denim skirt walked backward, a hiking stick waving in her hand as if she were directing an orchestra. The kids watched her with rapt attention. "Five plus two!" she called out, and the kids returned, "Seven!"

"Three plus three!" she called, and the crowd answered, "Trixie!" Though not in unison. The math lesson was down the tubes the minute the kids spotted the llama. Anarchy broke out with a chorus of excited squeals, cheers, and pleas of "It's Trixie! Can we go see Trixie? Hi, Trixie! Trixie, I love you! Trixie! Trix-eee!" Even the teenage helpers at the back of the line seemed excited to see Al's llama.

Trixie and the truck were soon surrounded by fans, and Nick disappeared in a squirming mass of little bodies. I was struck by the fact that he was right at home almost instantly, laughing with the other kids and pointing as Trixie pressed her nose through the bars and offered a llama smile.

The teacher crossed the parking lot, greeted Al, and introduced herself to me—Keren Zimmer. Keren was a beautiful girl, with soft features and wide, kind brown eyes. Her thick blond hair was coiled in a bun on the back of her head. Like Al, she wasn't wearing any makeup, but she didn't need any, either.

"Keren's your other side-pasture neighbor," Al offered brusquely. "You've got Keren's family on your west fence line, and my ranch on your east fence. 'Course, with all the land around that place you're on, it's quite a ways to the fences." The last statement had a hard edge that reminded me of my chat with Pop Dorsey in the Waterbird store. Whenever the West Ranch came up in conversation, there was an undertone of taboo.

I registered the fact that I hadn't told Al where we lived. How did she know? Was word around town already? Were there so few newcomers here that our arrival was news, or did it have something to do with the fact that we were associated with Jack West?

"You're next door to the West Ranch?" I asked.

Al nodded. "Saw your U-Haul at the gate earlier."

I tried to hide the note of suspicion jingling in my brain. When I'd pulled out the gate a couple hours ago, there wasn't a vehicle in sight.

"Oh, *you're* the ones moving in at the old West Ranch." Keren seemed unaware of the undertow in our conversation. "We *are* neighbors, then. If you ever need any help, directions to someplace or anything like that, just call me. We're in the book. I'm usually home after two thirty in the summer. In the mornings I have summer enrichment with this crazy bunch." She nodded toward the llama admirers.

"Great to meet you." I watched Keren's students jostling for position. Nick was laughing and shoulder-butting with a little dark-haired girl maybe a year or two older than he was. "I didn't see any houses when I looked around this morning. I didn't know there was anyone nearby."

"Our place is down in a draw." Keren paused to tell two boys not to climb on each other, then turned back to me. "You wouldn't see it, but if you go on up the road to the west, you'll pass by our gateway. It says *Zimmer Dairy* on it. Stop over and visit anytime." She eagle-eyed the kids again, then smiled. "Your little boy's having fun over there. You know, it's too late to officially sign up for summer enrichment class through the school, but if you want him to get to know some kids, you're welcome to bring him to the class anytime. He wouldn't be able to ride the bus from campus because of insurance, but you could just meet us wherever we go that day. We can always use parent volunteers. A lot of these kids come from home situations where they just don't get much adult time—not the kind they need, anyway. We'd love to have you and ummm . . ." She motioned to Nick.

"Nick," I offered.

"And Nick. We do everything from gardening to nature study. It's all free. Quite a number of our kids are low-income, so it funds the program, and . . ." She paused to take stock of the group, which was starting to look like a bunch of teenagers at a Justin Bieber concert. "I'd better go get them on the bus. If we don't head out, I'll have parents all over the school parking lot, looking for their kids. Sorry I can't be more help with the tire."

"We'll get it taken care of," Al replied. As Keren herded her kids to the bus, Al again listed my tire-crisis options.

"I think, if you'll just give us a ride back home, I'll call the U-Haul roadside assistance number and have them come and take care of it. Surely someone from the ranch can bring us back here to get the Jeep later." I'd finally arrived at the point where abandoning Grandma Louisa's Fostoria and riding home with a llama hardly even seemed like a wrinkle in the day.

On the way back to the ranch, Nick dozed in the backseat of Al's truck, and the llama pressed its nose against the rear window, seeming interested in the conversation as I learned more about Al Beckenbauer. She lived alone on four hundred acres she had inherited from grandparents she saw only occasionally as a child. She raised goats for milk, as well as mohair goats that were sheared periodically for their hair, like sheep. I'd never known where the mohair in sweaters came from, but now I did.

As we turned into the driveway at the West Ranch, Al fished a photo from the clutter on the dashboard and showed me what an award-winning mohair production animal actually looked like—sort of similar to a sheepdog, but with horns and dainty little feet. I wished Nick were awake to look at the photo, but he was out cold when we rolled to a stop at the house. Rather than parking beside the gate as we usually did, Al stopped the truck parallel to the fence, with my door facing it, the motion seeming to indicate that I should make a quick exit. She leaned over the steering wheel, checking the barnyard and seeming antsy as I opened my door and reached into the back to get Nick out. He lay limp on my arm, and I stood there trying to figure out how to take the car seat and my grocery sacks from the vehicle with Nick hanging over my shoulder.

"I'll get it. I'll just pile it by the fence there for you." Al checked the barnyard again, her gaze shifting back and forth acutely. Sliding from her seat, she muttered something, but I only caught the last words. " . . . before that old coot takes another potshot at me."

I turned in the gateway. "What?"

"Nothin', never mind." She waved me off, hurrying to unload my things and stack them by the fence. "I'm outta here."

"Okay . . . well . . . thanks." I shifted Nick on my shoulder as she returned to her truck. With a spit of gravel and a puff of diesel smoke, Al was gone, the llama watching through the bars, looking as confused as I was.

I had the sinking feeling the old coot she was talking about was Jack West. He *shot* at the neighbors? Surely not.

That had to be just figurative language, I told myself as I took Nick to the porch and laid him on the wide wooden swing. Then I went inside and dragged the air mattress to the porch and settled him there. While bug bombs were not my forte, Dustin had given me a few tips—clear the house, close all windows, open all closets and cabinets, stuff everything you can in the refrigerator so you won't have to wash it later, and so forth. After completing all preparations, set off the bomb farthest from the door and work your way out as quickly as possible.

I moved through the steps one-by-one, just as Dustin had described. There was a sense of satisfaction in it, as if I were singlehandedly conquering the wild, so to speak. I took a photo of myself wearing the rubber gloves and the mask, getting ready to set off a spray bomb. *Only one day in Texas, and I'm a regular frontier woman. LOL!* I added, and sent the photo off to the Gymies.

By the time I'd finished setting off the bombs, then called for U-Haul repairs, all I wanted to do was crash on the air mattress beside Nick. I didn't care that some sort of menacing-looking yard fowl were pecking around in the grass not far away, or that the angel fountain by the little house made me think of Jack West's dead wife, or that scorpions had been mentioned in the hardware store. *They're mostly on the other side of the lake,* I assured myself as I let my eyes fall closed. Considering that it was only midafternoon, it had been a very, very long day.

A dream slid over me as I fell asleep, the image so clear

and potent that it seemed real, rather than a conjuring of my subconscious mind. In the flower garden of the little house, the angel statue grew in size, the wings fading, the skin losing the cold pallor of stone and taking on life, until a woman, not a statue, stood among the irises. The breeze lifted her blond hair as she walked slowly up the stone steps to the house, a white sundress swirling around her legs.

I watched her cross the porch, her body disappearing into the shadows. Before opening the door, she turned and looked at me, but I couldn't see her face.

She was trying to tell me something, but I couldn't hear her.

She opened the door to the little house, and a child's laughter spilled out, and then she was gone.

A quiet sleep slipped over me.

When I awoke, long rays of evening sun were slanting across the porch, and a chicken was watching me from less than forty-eight inches away, its head notching back and forth curiously. Nick was gone. I jerked upright, panicking before I noticed a note lying atop the air mattress.

Opened the windows to air out. U-Haul called. Trailer fixed. Sorry I missed all that. Can drive you back to town later.

Walked down to the lakeshore with Nick.

Past the barn.

Through the back gate, down the path.

Come find us.

Beneath that, Daniel had signed his name, and Nick had drawn a lopsided smiley face. Apparently Daniel wasn't in any rush to rescue the Jeep and the trailer. Surely, we should go pick it up. Evening was setting in, and Grandma Louisa's Fostoria was at risk.

On the other hand, I was sweaty and sticky, I'd been admiring the lake since our arrival, and wading in cool water sounded like heaven. Maybe the U-Haul situation could wait. There was a pickup truck parked by the yard gate now, and I assumed Daniel had the keys to it. The Jeep and the U-Haul were probably safe enough where they were. It was a church parking lot, after all.

I followed Daniel's directions, walking past the little house, where I purposely did not look in the direction of the angel-woman statue, and then past a weathered red barn where horses watched me from dusty stalls. Beyond the barn, what looked like a wagon trail led across a field of pink wildflowers blooming in tiny bouquets beneath the dappled shade of ancient live oaks. My feet crunched on the rocky, milk-colored limestone soil as I walked, and bluebirds skipped along the path, the sun catching their feathers in impossible bursts of color before they flitted away. The air was fresh and water-scented, with not a hint of exhaust fumes or concrete—just the elemental scents of water, earth, and sky.

When the lakeshore came into view beyond the trees, I spotted Daniel and Nick in a little cove where the cedars opened along the rocky shore. The two of them were beautiful there together, Daniel immersed chest-high with Nick clinging to his neck. I stood for the longest time and just watched them, took in all the separate pieces of the picture they created together, studied them the way you'd study the brushstrokes of a master artist. The clear water sliding over skin, Daniel's tanned and ruddy, Nick's fair and fine in texture. The droplets flicking off the dark curls of Daniel's hair as he stood and shook his head, the shimmering spray making Nick laugh. Daniel's smile, Nick's smile, the ways their mouths were different and yet the same. The way their eyes met. The love between them. The evening light touching the water. Little feet kicking rapidly, big feet swishing smoothly, parting the water without a sound.

I wanted to freeze the moment, every tiny and perfect bit of it.

These are my guys, I thought. *My husband. My son.*

They swam to the shore when they saw me, and both of them tried to tempt me into the water.

"How about I just watch? I didn't bring a towel or a suit." I fully intended to wade in the shallows, though I didn't plan to get my clothes wet.

"Awwww," Nick complained, then ran into the water and did a belly flop with his arms spread out.

Daniel braced his hands on his hips, his arms stiff, the muscles tight. "How about you come over here." His eyes had that smoky look.

I thought of my father dragging my mother into the pool in her fancy loungewear. Now I wondered if there had been a fight involved that evening. Were they kissing and making up?

"Promise you're not going to drag me in." I took a step closer.

"You'd like it." He smiled a cute, crooked, slightly roguish smile.

"I'm not kidding." The practical side of me was already thinking about how much trouble it would be to deal with sopping wet shorts, and the fact that I was wearing the only bra that wasn't packed in a box somewhere.

Daniel's lashes lowered to half-mast. He ran his tongue along his bottom lip, as if he were considering coming after me—or at least he wanted me to think he was. We stood at a stalemate for an instant. Then he broke it with a wink. "All right. I don't want you mad at me anymore."

Somehow, in the weird way that you know things when you have a connection with someone, I knew the fight was over. Despite the advice of talk show hosts and relationship books that say issues should be talked out, I just wanted the big, ugly cloud between us to be gone. I crossed the empty space, kissed him, felt water dampening my clothes.

"Although you're cute when you're mad," he murmured against my lips.

"Don't *even* . . ." I considered giving him a shove and sending him stumbling back into the lake. He would come after me for sure if I did, though.

His eyes caught the light. "You are, you know."

"C'mon swimmin' wit' me, Tante M!" Nick called, oblivious to the ongoing dance of reconciliation. He repeated his invitation a second time, but Tante M was busy at the moment. She was learning, right there on the side of the lake, all about kiss and make up. A drop of water slid over her chin, then raced down her neck and under her shirt, tracing a line down her ribs.

It didn't feel one bit cold. In fact, it sizzled all the way.

Maybe, she decided, a dip in the lake didn't sound so bad after all.

No man is an island, entire of itself;
every man is a piece of the continent, a part of the main.

—John Donne
(Left by Clay Hampton, in town for an overdue family reunion.)

Chapter 10

In my first month on the ranch, I developed an addiction to email, texting, and long-distance phone calls—three things I'd considered largely time wasters in the past, outside of doing office business. For years, I'd admonished my nieces not to clog my inbox with email jokes and cute photos of puppies wearing Halloween costumes. Who had time for such things? Why would you want to make time?

Now I knew the answer: Because you felt like if you didn't talk to someone, the men in white coats would soon find you babbling unintelligibly, bubbling out mad laughter and gut-twisting sobs, all while finger painting your name on white walls with white caulking and tossing bits of steel wool in the air, just to watch them drift slowly downward in the window light.

I was, quite literally, losing my ever-lovin' mind, and the mice knew it. They, and the roaches, and spiders the size of my fist, and finally the scorpion that was staring at me from the opposite pillow one morning—they sensed that they were close to winning the war. I was on the verge of cracking and abandoning the house, married life, Texas, and the whole frontier adventure thing, in general.

My sisters had almost laughed me off the planet when I'd mentioned the long-distance Binding Through Books idea. They were too busy for something like that.

Little by little, even Trudy, my favorite sister of all, was trying to gently abandon me. "I love you, but you're filling up my email inbox, and I can't be checking my phone and clearing out texts all day long, Mal. Come on, a few months ago you would have told me the same thing."

"No, I wouldn't have," I whined, sitting at the dining room table with my feet curled into the chair after my scorpion wake-up call. The worst thing was that in my panic to get out of the bed, I'd flipped the invader off the sheets, and I had no idea where it was now. "*I* wouldn't do that to *you*, Trudy."

"Oh, *puh-lease*." Trudy was in a mood today. Hormones again. "How many times in the past couple years did I call you about doctor's appointments, and you were like, 'Hey, Trude, I'm in the middle of something, can I call you back?' And then you'd never call back?"

"Yes, I did. I called back." But Trudy was right. I'd been a lousy comforter and counselor when people needed me. I was used to being the focus of family attention, the baby girl who could do no wrong. I'd never had to focus my attention on other people.

"You know what you need?" Trudy asked, and I sensed another lame brush-off coming. "You need a journal. You should write all this stuff in a journal. Maybe you'll turn it into a book someday—like Swiss Family Robinson, only you're marooned on a lakeshore in Texas. Just think how funny that scene of you putting on the rubber gloves and the medical mask or dragging the stuffed deer head and the bob- cat to the garage would be. Or that business about thinking you had ghosts and finding out it was squirrels in the attic. Now, that was a riot. If you wrote it down, you could keep it all in one place."

"I don't *want* to write a book." A prickly lump, much like the ones that had stuck to our socks when Nick and I walked to the creek the day before, rose in my throat. A cocklebur of emotion. My moods were all over the place. I barely recognized myself anymore. "I just want to *talk* to somebody. It's so . . . *lonely* out here. Daniel works all the time. Jack treats him like he's some sort of personal assistant—or slave. Slave is more like it. Like Daniel is his minion, 24/7. Jack goes off on these bizarre tangents about weird new inventions, but he doesn't ever *show* Daniel anything. It's like he's paranoid that Daniel will steal his technology. The longer we're here, the more I'm sure the man is nuts, and not in a good way. Honestly, it scares me. On top of that, there's the birdbath statue out back. I'm telling you, Trudy. It's like it's watching me when I go out there. And there are yellow butterflies sitting on it every time I look, and then I've had, like, five dreams about the blond lady."

I paused to take a sip of my coffee, trying to clear my head. Trudy didn't interject. She was only halfway listening, but she hadn't hung up on me yet, so I went on. "The only good news is that Jack left town this morning, for his offices in Houston. It sounds like he'll be gone for a while. Maybe we'll finally have some time to try to figure things out. It's like there's not really any job here for Daniel. Even the ranch hands avoid us. There's this weird sense that everyone is . . . waiting for something to happen—the ranch hands, the people in town. Everyone. Daniel's starting to worry that these bio-crop patents Jack hired him to work on are just a fantasy. I mean, when they're together Jack blathers on about powering cities with giant replicas of this tide wheel thing he built on the lakeshore. And then there are his theories on cattle genetics, and the whole Firefly Island thing. Did I tell you about Firefly Island? The other night when Nick and I drove out to the pasture to look at the moon, I swear I saw lights moving around down there on Firefly Island. And then when I went to bed, I dreamed that the blond lady was out there. She was trying to get me to swim across to the shore, but my legs were like lead. Daniel woke me up, just as I was sinking underwater. He said I was talking in my sleep, saying all kinds of strange things. He said I didn't even *sound* like myself."

" . . . or a blog," Trudy answered, as if she hadn't heard a word I'd said. She was working as we were talking, her fingernails clicking on the keyboard. "You should write all of this in a blog—well, not the personal stuff about Daniel's boss, maybe, but the stuff about the mouse wars and your walks with Nick. Then we could all read it and send you comments and stuff. And then Mom would stop calling me, asking what I've heard from you. She's trying to go by her Non-interference Newlywed Rule, but that just means she calls me constantly for information. I don't have time to do the binding book . . . book binding—whatever that's called— sisters book club thing, but I'd read a blog. You could get information to all of us at once."

"I don't want a *blog*. . . ." I spit out the last word. Blogs were for people who liked to write. That wasn't me. "Now you sound like Kaylyn. She and Josh made me this goofy- looking cyber-page with some of the pictures I sent them. They put my head on this cartoon body that looks like Annie Oakley and called me The Frontier Woman. It's funny, but . . . ummm . . . no way."

"At this point, I think it's either a blog or professional therapy, and where are you going to find a shrink in Moses Lake?" Trudy's store phone rang in the background.

"I don't want a shrink. And I don't even do Facebook, for heaven's sake. I'm not a techno nerd." Even Trudy, my favorite sister, didn't love me anymore. The world really was coming to an end.

"But you just said your friends will help you. Your little Gymies. They would rather read your frontier stories all in one place instead of getting nine million texts and emails all day long. It'll be like Green Acres meets Wild Kingdom."

"It's just not *me*," I muttered, uncoiling my legs. Sooner or later I'd have to go tear the bedroom apart, find that creature that was loose in there, and dispatch it. Fortunately, Nick was outside, as usual, happily playing in the dirt underneath a tree with Pecos the dog. "I *hate* it here." The words gurgled out in a partial sob. I was having that urge again, hearing the voice that said, *Just get in the car and go. Just leave before you're in any deeper.*

Outside the window, the sunlight stroked Nick's hair, painting it a soft spun gold. How long would it take for him to forget me, for even the memory of me, of us, to no longer exist?

"Hang in there." Trudy's voice was warmer, the words not just an effort to put me off. "Everyone goes through adjustment problems in the first months of marriage. And you've got more than the normal stuff to handle, and you've had a whole life of your own before now. Plus you're dealing with parenthood, a move, and job problems. It's normal to feel a little lost."

It's not normal, I thought. *It's not. I've lost me. I'm losing my mind.*

But I didn't say it. I couldn't confess, even to Trudy, that I'd had the urge to run away. I couldn't confess that to anyone. I was ashamed of it.

This marriage thing, this forming of a new life, was so much harder than I'd ever thought it would be. It was like walking into the lake in my dream. The water was filled with bands of hot and cold current, the bottom under my feet invisible, littered with obstacles, hiding crevices I couldn't see until I got there. Love skimmed over the surface like a sailboat, grabbing me up and carrying me along one minute, the speed dizzying, the view passing by so quickly I couldn't take it in. The next minute, my little love boat was swamped in a storm, overturned, the sail pointing toward the murky depths, everything upside down. I was trying to swim with legs of lead. I'd never thought of love this way—as something that moved with the ebb and flow of currents. Push and pull. Joy and pain. Fear and trust. Falling, and trying to balance, and falling again.

Conflicts crowded my mind as I said good-bye to Trudy, then ransacked the bedroom, searching for the terrifying, whip-tailed invader now lurking somewhere in our house. I couldn't find it, of course. I imagined it hiding in my shoes, Nick's pajamas, my clothing—which was still hanging in wardrobe boxes because I refused to put anything in the closets until I'd solved the mouse and bug problems. As far as I could tell, I'd made only a small dent in it with all my steel wool stuffing, caulking of cracks, and the little box-like mousetraps Dustin had sold me at the hardware store. I used them to capture the mice and then take the tiny doe-eyed creatures far from the house, where they could be released into the wild. The place where mice were supposed to live.

Each time I went through the process, standing in one of the pastures where the tumbledown remnants of an old home-stead dotted the top of a barren hill, I gazed at the view in all directions—the lake glittering below, its watersheds and inlets hidden in thick folds of green, the mountains of Chinquapin Peaks melting skyward in the distance. Around me, spiny prairie grass waved softly, dotted with wildflowers, prickly pear cactus, and sword-like yuccas with tall stalks rising from the centers, last spring's flowers now only dried bell-shaped remnants. I took it all in, all this strangeness, all this foreign-ness, while Nick investigated blue-tailed lizards, lines of red ants walking along the ground, or wild turkeys foraging in the ravines. And I thought, *Is this me? Could this ever be me?*

I felt like I was watching a movie sometimes, superimposing my face onto a character's body. Occasionally, I wondered about the people who had come here first, who'd built the tiny, square house, the outhouse in back, the barn that now leaned against a mesquite tree, the old windmill and the stone tanks that held the water it pumped. What were they thinking when they arrived? Why did they come? Who was the woman, the sturdy pioneer wife who kept this house, who probably raised an entire family in such a small space? Was she ever lonely? Did she spend long days with only the mice and the scorpions for company? Did she struggle with it?

Did she ever think of leaving? Did it ever cross her mind to break the ties, to run away?

A mouse dashed across the bedroom, and I hardly even noticed. I imagined it and the scorpion having a facedown like gunfighters in a miniature OK Corral. I took note of the spot beneath the ancient closet wallpaper where the mouse had disappeared. I went after the steel wool. I stuffed and packed. Fifty years of dust and mildew puffed out in little clouds each time I disturbed the old cheesecloth backing.

I thought about my apartment in DC. That clean, orderly, and cheesecloth-free apartment. No stowaways. No men and boys dropping trails of shoes and laundry as they passed through the house . . . laundry that would have to be picked up with two fingers, carried to the bathroom, and shaken vigorously over the bathtub, because who knew what might take up residence in a shirt left lying on the floor?

I hadn't put on a pair of shoes without first checking inside them for a month.

I looked across the room at the wardrobe box with my suits and pumps still nicely packed inside, and the next thing I knew, I was sitting on the edge of the bed, gasping out great, wrenching sobs. The emotion, the despair welled up and was overwhelming, a tsunami of grief that was frightening in both its intensity and its very existence. Just last night, I'd decided I was over all this. Daniel and I had sat on the back porch, listened to coyotes singing a chorus in the distance, and watched as a massive full moon outlined thready clouds in glistening silver. Inside the house, I'd heard Nick talking to his toys in his little race car bed as he drifted off to sleep. It was the most perfect of perfect nights, the heavens a blanket of stars, the waters of the lake casting off a cool, moist breeze.

Daniel had tucked me under his arm on the porch swing, his body warm against mine, his breath stirring my hair. I felt loved. I felt completed in a way I never had before.

It was a moment of glory, of earthly perfection like none I'd ever experienced. A shadow of what heaven must be like, when all the cares fall away and love is perfect.

Daniel and I had finally slipped off to bed together as a breeze kicked up, the clouds thickened, and a soft rain began to fall. We'd made love, fallen asleep curled in each other's arms, floated on our own little mountaintop, no one else in the whole wide world.

Now, here I was, tumbling off that mountain in the hardest way. Over the sight of a scorpion and a mouse. Worst of all, I felt such anger, such resentment, such a sense of loss. I was angry with Daniel for bringing us here, for being so devoted to this job, for *having* a job, always being gone when something went wrong in the house, for using me as a built-in baby-sitter for his son . . .

The last thought shocked, stabbed, wounded. *Our son.* Nick was *our* son. I loved him already. I wanted to be his mother. I treasured the simple, gentle moments when the two of us were together—chatting as he played in a bubble bath, or when we walked to the creek to watch the minnows, or strolled along the lakeshore hunting for arrowheads or the fossilized shells of ancient sea creatures. I loved those moments. I loved Nick's smile, his laugh, the way he adored me. I loved him.

What was *wrong* with me that I could be sitting here resenting him?

This place was making me come completely unhinged. Somehow, I had to get control—control of the house, control of my thoughts and my emotions. This had to stop.

The back door opened, and I heard Nick racing through the kitchen, leaving the door flapping behind.

More flies. He's letting in more flies. The thought was quick and sharp. With horses and cattle living nearby, there was no end to the fly problem, either. They clung to porch roofs in the evenings in a giant black mass, hung on the door facings, slipped inside in droves each time Nick came and went. The flies crawled on the kitchen counters, on any food left out. On my face as I was waking in the mornings. Everywhere. The flies were everywhere.

"Nicholas!" My voice sliced through the house, and I was up from the bed, stalking toward the kitchen before I had time to think. "Close that door! How many times have I told you not to—"

I rounded the corner into the dining room, and there was Nick, at the other end of the ugly yellow carpet, frozen in place with a bouquet of tiny white wildflowers in his hand. He'd stopped two steps onto the rug, left behind a pair of wet, muddy little tracks, and a trail through the kitchen. His eyes were huge, his mouth dropping open, uncertain.

Everything in me melted. My tears welled again, but they were a different sort of tears. "Hey," I breathed, crossing the room. "Hey, what've you got there?"

His eyes rounded upward, sparkled with life again. "It's all in da yard!" he cheered. "Flowers! Be-yoo-de-ful flowers! I gotted you a pres-it!"

"You did?" I whispered, scooping up Nick and the flowers all in one. He held them to my face, and I smelled the overwhelming sweetness, the intoxicating combination of nectar and sweaty boy child. Outside the window, the yard was filled with tiny white flowers on single stalks. They'd appeared overnight. A miracle. A thousand tiny miracles. Flowers where there had been no flowers. "They're beautiful. They're amazing. Oh, baby, how did you know I needed someone to bring me flowers this morning?" I hugged him close, rocking him back and forth as his sandy feet swung against my thighs.

His arms stretched around me, the fistful of flowers pressing against my shoulder, their sweetness encircling my senses. "I jus' knowed," he whispered. "Somebody told my mind."

Closing my eyes, I reveled in the moment, felt the holiness of it. *Let me remember this. Let me remember this the next time I'm angry.*

I didn't care if a hundred flies came into the house through that open door. I didn't.

Nick and I went outside and enjoyed the flowers. We picked tiny bouquets and put them in glasses all over the house, filling the rooms with fragrance. By the time we finally left for town to visit the feedstore and inquire about the magic scorpion eradication powder Dustin had mentioned last month, I had recaptured my sense of Zen. I'd spent some time with the caulking gun, sealing up cracks around the bedroom window sashes and baseboards, convincing myself that the scorpion must have used one of those entry points, and that by now it was back outside. With the cracks sealed, it would not be able to get back in, surely.

When the man in the feedstore, which was in an old tin building that had the quaint look of a little country trading post, told me that scorpions hide in cool, dark places during the day, and come out at night, I did my very best to ignore him. I imagined the scorpion permanently entombed in a layer of rapidly drying caulk. I also did my best to disregard the feedstore man's warning that scorpions traveled in pairs.

"Best thing's to get you a black light and hammer," he advised. "Put you on some good shoes, grab the hammer, and just carry that black light around your house when it's good'n dark. Scorps glow in the dark. You see 'em, you smash 'em good and dead. Don't try to drown 'em down the sink. They just come back up your drains. Flush 'em live, and they can come back up the commode, and you don't want that."

The feedstore man and I locked eyes and shook our heads in unison. I imagined scorpions hiding underneath the toilet seats, lying in wait. Dark places. They liked dark places, like the undersides of toilet seats . . .

I glanced over my shoulder at Nick, who was having fun with a bucket of multicolored plastic worms nearby.

"Careful how you pick 'em up, even after you use the hammer," the man added. "That tail can still sting after you smash the guts out." He curled his finger into an arc and made a quick striking motion. "Like rattlesnakes, y'know? You don't go picking 'em up by hand, even once you think you got 'em dead. That rattlesnake head'll still get ya. But with scorps, it's the tail." He slapped a hand on the counter, and I jumped a foot in the air. "I'll have them insect granules in for ya, day after tomorrow. Just sprinkle it 'round your house and near your doors, then water it in good with the hose and keep the little guy off of it until it's dry. Oh, and indoors, don't let the beds touch the wall or the blankets touch the floor, and wrap all your bed legs with duct tape, sticky side out. That'll keep them scorps off at night."

"Ohhh . . . kay. Thanks," I murmured, vaguely conscious of several men walking in from a warehouse where large stacks of Purina livestock chow were stored. "On second thought, give me two bags of the scorpion-killer. I may just dig a moat around the house and fill it with the stuff . . . after I surround all the beds with duct tape."

The man behind the counter laughed, then wagged a finger at me. "That's funny. I like a woman who's got a sense of humor about her varmint huntin'."

"Listen, I'm a varmint-killing machine," I joked, feeling as if I were hanging out in the halls of Congress, bantering with other staff members about legislators and stacks of paperwork. Lately, it seemed like I had at least three different personalities, and any one could come out at any given time. I liked this particular one. She could handle things. Occasionally, I wondered if Daniel was avoiding coming home not because he was busy with Jack, but because he had no idea which *me* would be waiting there.

"Got problems in the ranch house?" I turned to find Al Beckenbauer approaching the counter, her lanky, confident stride making me feel a little less like Xena the Warrior Queen of Varmint Hunting. Today Al was wearing jeans and a tank top with an old denim shirt loose over it, the sleeves torn out, her arms bare and brown.

She probably kills scorpions with her bare hands, I thought, and then the idea seemed inexplicably hilarious.

"There was a scorpion in bed with me this morning," I told her.

"Been there." She offered a one-sided grin, her wind-chapped lips curling into dimples at the corners, revealing straight white teeth that seemed out of place against the ruddy backdrop. "Hate it when that happens."

Al Beckenbauer shuddered. Actually shuddered.

I marveled at the thought and I decided I really liked her. We had something in common. We both hated scorpions in the bed. Just two rancher chicks, trying to survive in the wild country.

Al tapped the pad where the feedstore man was writing up my ticket. "Scratch that and order her some diatomaceous earth. Fifty-pound sack. And an applicator. Put it on that worthless old so-and-so's bill." Hooking an elbow on the countertop, she angled her head and squinted at me. "Spread it around your yard, especially by the house, and in the attic, and in the cabinets under your sinks, too. It'll work, and you don't have to worry about it with your pets or the boy. Wear a mask when you put it out. Don't breathe the dust, but after it settles overnight, it's fine. It's organic. Good for the dog, if you have one. It'll take care of fleas in your yard, too. If the old so-and-so who owns that place gives you any trouble, you tell him Al Beckenbauer said to leave it in the yard a few weeks and see if you can find a flea out there. He'll like that." Her lips pursed, and she glanced sideways at the feedstore man, who sucked in a breath and shook his head.

"You're gonna get this poor girl in trouble, Al." Clucking apologetically, he focused on me. "Those two aren't good neighbors, in case you hadn't noticed yet."

"I've hardly been out of the house," I admitted, because that was the most benign thing I could come up with. It was clear enough that everyone gave Jack West a wide berth. With the exception of Keren Zimmer timidly stopping over with cookies the day after I flattened the U-Haul tire, no one had come by, and no one in town seemed willing to explain the hands-off reception we'd been getting. West Ranch did a lot of business in the area, and I had a feeling that people didn't want to alienate Jack's significant cash reserves by revealing the skeletons in his closet.

"Pfff!" Al blew a tight puff of air. "Anything organic, that man won't use it. Just spray poison all over everything. Dump a little more pesticide in the water supply. It's his world. We're all just livin' in it."

I snapped my lips shut on an answer. I so wanted to spill the whole story of our month-long odyssey at West Ranch and ask the obvious question: Is Jack West as crazy as he seems? Did he really kill his wife and stepson? And what's with this Firefly Island business? Why all the secrecy there? Has anyone else seen lights moving around out there at night? Why is the causeway that goes to the island protected by a locked gate? Why has he pointed out repeatedly that Firefly is off-limits to everyone? Does anybody know?

Instead, I said, "I'd much rather go with the organic stuff. I mean, there's Nick to think about, for one thing. He plays in the yard all the time. I don't want to use anything that's not good for him. Mr. West is out of town for a while, so he won't know what I put out. Honestly, if I see one more mouse, bug, or creature with an exoskeleton running across my floor, I'm going to commit hari-kari. At some point, I really want to be able to put my clothes in a closet without having something nest in them."

Both Al and the feedstore man chuckled, but Al seemed to understand. She took a pencil from behind her ear, signed a ticket for the clerk, and then pointed the pencil at me. "I like you. I'm headed to New Mexico for a week or so to see a man about a sheepdog, but you give me a call after I get back. I'm in the book. A. C. Beckenbauer."

"Oh . . . okay." I had the sense that I'd made my first friend in Moses Lake.

Nick came over and stretched upward to set a handful of squirmy rubber worms on the counter.

"Oh no, honey, we don't need those," I told him gently. "We have enough of the real kind at our house."

Al turned away from the counter and headed for the door. "Sack up those fishin' worms for the boy, Stan. Put it on my account. If he's gonna live in Moses Lake, he's gonna need to be a fisherman."

*The journey between what you once were
and who you are now becoming
is where the dance of life really takes place.*

—Barbara DeAngelis
(Left by Grandma Bette,
changing lives through Scouting for forty-three years)

Chapter 11

With Jack still gone to his offices in Houston, life took on a more relaxed pace. Daniel drove Nick and me around the ranch in the old pickup truck that was for his work use. The sheer size of the place awed me. We could literally travel for miles, bumping along rutted truck trails, white dust billowing behind us, rising and falling and always landing on property that belonged to Jack West. All part of his strange empire. All under his control.

I'd seen wealth and excess in DC, but never anything like this. It was still hard to comprehend. Everything his, as far as the eye could see—pastures filled with horses and cattle, plots of wheat growing in thick, silty black soil left behind by floods along the river before the lake was built, test fields of corn and various grain crops planted in all sorts of locations, from rocky hillsides to marshy valleys.

I marveled at starts of corn seeming to take hold on a hillside that looked like a gravel parking lot. "It's not perfect yet," Daniel remarked. "According to Jack it'll grow, but it won't yield. He's hoping I can solve the problem, and then we'll apply for the patents. Of course, that would require him to actually let me into the lab rooms, show me the data files, and leave me alone there long enough to work."

"He still hasn't even *shown* you the research?" Unease inch-wormed over me. I rubbed goose bumps away, felt a string of caulking on my skin, and began scratching it off. When Daniel had stopped by the house to pick us up, I was crouched in a closet, up to my elbows in home improvement goop. I'd felt someone touch me on the shoulder, and I'd screamed like a banshee, shooting out caulking like silly string.

Daniel shrugged. "A little. Sort of. He left me with a key to the lab, so that's progress at least, but there are several doors that the key doesn't open. I can't really do anything except water the control group samples in the contained environ-ments and dust the furniture."

I scratched off caulking, watched Nick play in the dirt nearby, and tried to decide what to say. We were having such a nice afternoon, I didn't want to spoil it. I wanted to pre-tend that Jack didn't exist, that Daniel and I were on a vaca-tion getaway. Just a young family, happily passing time in a beautiful place where ancient trees shaded pastures and little bouquets of Mountain Pinks grew on hillsides near cedar-shaded shores and high limestone bluffs. The water was rife with boats today—skiers and fishermen, families enjoying pedal boats, kayakers spending a beautiful summer afternoon under a wide cloudless sky.

Playing beneath a tree not far away, Nick pointed at a skier who caught an edge and tumbled end over end before slapping the water in a belly flop. "Whoa! Woo-eee!" he cheered. Dan-iel had promised Nick that they would take the new fishing worms down to the lake and do some fishing this evening. We'd tucked swimsuits, towels, and newly purchased fishing poles into the back of Daniel's ranch vehicle. We both knew that he'd better make good on the fishing promise before Jack showed up and turned our lives upside-down again.

On the way back to the house, we crossed through a three-hundred acre high-fenced area where Jack kept exotic animals of all sorts—everything from Thomson's gazelles to antelope, beautiful fallow deer with massive antlers to mountain sheep with giant, curled horns. All just waiting for Jack West to find himself in the mood to shoot something. The containment area was an exotic animal business on paper, but according to what little Daniel had learned, few animals raised here were ever sold.

Nick pointed at the animals and called out, "Wook at dat one! Wook at dat one! He's a big one!" as we drove along through Jack's private safari. At the far end of the containment area, Daniel stopped to make sure the laboratory complex was locked up for the day. Comprised of several long, low stone buildings that had been poultry barns decades before, the complex looked innocuous from a distance, but up close, I could hear the hum of equipment. Our reflections shimmered in a massive metallic sign that hung on the front of one of the buildings. *West Research* it proclaimed, the chrome letters looking like they belonged on a steel-and-glass office building somewhere. *Don't let it fool you,* Daniel had said the first time he'd driven me by the lab buildings. *This place is state of the art.* He'd gone on to tell me about the greenhouse-style growth environments, where temperature, moisture, hours of sunlight, and soil conditions were controlled to perfectly duplicate various climates. A wind and solar power generation system provided electricity, and water was supplied partially by windmills and partially by a device Jack was developing to collect moisture from vapor in the air.

Jack West was as brilliant as he was strange, and as mysterious as ever.

Nick, Pecos, and I waited outside with the vehicle while Daniel checked everything. Daniel had taken us into the lab the day after Jack left town, but the surveillance cameras inside gave me an uneasy feeling. I felt like we were being watched, and if we were, I didn't want Jack West thinking that Nick and I had been snooping around. The man still gave me the willies.

I tried to put Jack out of my mind as Nick and Pecos wandered off to some nearby equipment to play. Pecos stood by faithfully while Nick crawled onto a green tractor and pretended to drive, as he'd seen the ranch hands do. When the men passed by our house occasionally, Nick always stopped what he was doing and waved wildly at them, hoping they would pause to let him ogle whatever machinery they were using, but so far, the ranch hands had continued to steer clear of us. I felt like a pariah most of the time.

"Looks like Nick found a redneck jungle gym there," Daniel observed as he came out of the lab building. He paused to punch in the security code before crossing the distance between us. His hand slid warm and solid through the curtain of my hair and rested on my shoulder, his fingers rubbing softly there.

I leaned into him, enjoying the moment. Around us, the golden light of afternoon faded into softer hues, the hills casting veils of shadow and sun. Nick was talking up a storm, giving instructions to Pecos, pretending to be doing some very important job with the tractor, but I couldn't quite hear the words. "Thank goodness for that dog." In our weeks at the ranch, Pecos and Nick had become inseparable, and if anyone remembered that the dog was actually Jack's, no one said so.

"As soon as we get a little time to breathe, we need to

do something about that." Daniel pointed at Nick, and his fingers paused against my skin.

I sighed, reluctant to discuss future plans, or what we should do once we had a little breathing room. I was breathing right now, and it seemed like enough for the moment. The longer we stayed at West Ranch, the more I was sure we needed to leave. That wasn't what Daniel wanted to hear. But there was something just not right about this whole situation. It was becoming more and more clear that Jack West didn't care what happened to our family, as long as he got whatever it was that he wanted from Daniel.

I couldn't help wondering: What would happen the minute he didn't?

"Okay . . . do something about what?" I asked hesitantly. Nick and Pecos had moved to the next piece of equipment, an odd-looking apparatus sitting in the weeds, gathering rust. It looked like a narrow gangway that might be used on a ship, but with a single set of wheels in the middle, so that it could be moved around like a trailer. Alone, Nick could walk along it without tipping it end to end, but he had just discovered that the presence of Pecos added enough weight to cause the entire structure to tilt back and forth, bouncing lightly on the ground when it hit. With their combined mass, Nick and Pecos had created a giant teeter-totter and they were enjoying it, the dog wagging his stubby tail and Nick laughing and talking.

"He's over there *talking* to a *dog*," Daniel observed. "He needs some real friends. Other kids."

"He and Pecos have some good conversations." I'd never had a dog, but Pecos was growing on me. Most of the time, he kept the wandering peafowl, chickens, and guinea hens out of the yard, and he was extremely protective of Nick. I felt certain that, were anything dangerous to sneak in, like the rattlesnakes I'd been warned about but had not seen *so far*, Pecos would chase them away. He didn't allow anything near Nick, including Jack West. You had to wonder what kind of a man is considered a threat by his own dog.

"I'm serious." Daniel stretched his neck side to side, the bones crackling. The tension in him was palpable, flowing into me even as I tried to resist it. I didn't turn to look at him. I knew what I would see. Exhaustion, a new network of furrows and worry lines around his eyes. This job, and all the ways it wasn't working out, nipped at him constantly, even with the boss far away. Jack West's eventual return was the King Kong–sized monkey on our backs, even during quiet moments like this.

A question hovered unspoken. It teased the surface more and more now, when Daniel and I were alone. He wondered if I blamed him for this. If I was disappointed. If I was sorry I'd said yes the night he looked across the map and proposed. If I regretted this marriage. He hadn't asked outright, and I didn't want him to, for fear that no matter what I said, he would see how completely out of place and unhappy I was here. He would know that at least a half-dozen times a day I held my head in my hands and thought, *I can't do this. I can't.*

I wanted to be strong, and bold, and fearless. But instead, I was afraid and tired and lonely and worried.

Daniel's observation about Nick brought up another issue that had been niggling me. I'd watched Nick's eyes light up whenever we happened to see the summer enrichment kids in Moses Lake enjoying a picnic in the park behind the church, or sitting outside the convenience store eating ice cream, or helping to plant gardens in a courtyard between an antique mall and a little Books and Java store.

I knew Nick was lonely, that he was left to his own devices, forced to make a playmate out of a dog for hours on end while I worked on the house. I wondered what my mother would say about Nick and Pecos walking back and forth on the makeshift carnival ride, Nick chattering up a storm. Was it healthy for a kid to spend so much time talking to a dog?

Keren Zimmer had invited Nick and me to the summer program twice now, but I hadn't taken him. The truth, if I let myself give it a voice, was that I *needed* Nick. I dreaded the idea of him moving onward into friendships, activities, playdates, and preschool. I was scared to death of being left all alone here.

"One thing at a time, okay?" I rubbed Daniel's arm, intertwined my fingers with his where they curved gently around my rib cage, cupping the two of us together. "I just . . . feel like we're so . . . unsettled right now."

"Okay." Daniel's chin scratched against my hair. "Thanks for looking after Nick. I know I haven't been much help."

My emotions did a strange loop-de-loop, and words came before I even knew what was happening. "Of course I'm looking after him. What else would I be doing?" There was a sharp edge, a tinge of resentment I didn't want to feel. Daniel had a new job, odd though it was. Research lay in his future, hopefully. Discoveries. Achievements. Meanwhile, I was stuffing steel wool in gaps and talking about *Veggie Tales* and *Thomas the Tank Engine*. I was looking around town and realizing that my career in politics was done.

Daniel angled away, dark brows painting concern over brooding eyes. "I didn't mean anything by that. Just that I feel like I've been AWOL a lot, that's all."

"Sorry." To my horror, tears crowded my vision. Looking down at my hands, I pretended to be busy picking off little flecks of caulking. "I know what you meant. I'm all over the place lately. I don't know what's the matter with me. It'll get better." Would it? What if it didn't?

Daniel took one of my hands and brought it to his lips, caulking and all. His kiss touched just beside the modest diamond ring that symbolized the commitment made on a rainy evening in a little white church. "You're amazing, Mallory. I get wrapped up in everything, and I don't say it enough." He inspected my white-speckled fingers, kissed them again. "Who knew you had all these hidden talents?"

"Pppfff!" He was buttering me up now. And it was working, of course. I was putty in his hands when he looked at me like that. After weeks of filling cracks in closets, I knew all about putty. I was on intimate terms with it.

"All that steel wool packing and closet fixing . . . the way you stuck that wallpaper back in place, the catch-and-release mouse program . . ." Daniel trailed off as if to indicate that the list could go on and on.

"Don't stop." I tipped my chin up and fluffed my hair with exaggerated grandiosity, imagining myself posing like Angelina Jolie, only shorter and blonder and more . . . clueless. The urge for tears vanished as quickly as it had come. When Daniel and I were close like this, everything vanished. Wasn't that the definition of love—a devotion that could eclipse everything? "I want it all."

"And then there's the caulking . . . the way you lay it on there so smooth and even. I love a woman who can handle a gun."

I felt a blush travel through my entire body, just the way it had the day Daniel and I met. The rush was as heady and as fresh as ever. Just as thrilling. If there hadn't been a three-year-old and a dog nearby . . . "Excuse me? How much time have you spent with gun-toting women, Daniel Webster Everson? And with *whom*, exactly, might I ask?"

"None . . . until this woman," he answered smoothly. "But I like it."

Skyrockets and butterflies. I was melting. Just melting. I wanted to call Jack West and say, *Listen, you can have him from eight to five, but at five-o-one, he's M-I-N-E, mine.*

The noise of a truck rattling up the cow path disturbed the normal hum of boats in the distance, birds chirping, and trees swaying overhead. As always, the approach pulled the strings of tension tight, playing an unpleasant tune. *Please don't let it be Jack West. Please don't let it be Jack West.*

Once Jack returned, these long evenings together would be gone. Daniel was never willing to point out to Jack that we needed family time. He was afraid to. He'd already observed that the slightest thing—a gate chained too loosely by one of the ranch hands, a windmill that hadn't been properly greased, ranch equipment poorly parked or left in less than optimal working condition—could set Jack off on a red-faced tirade of phone calls and threats.

Daniel stiffened and took a few steps away to get a better view of the vehicle approaching. "Oh, that's just one of the ranch hands." The tension in his shoulders eased. "Tag, I think. Jack's horse trainer. I gathered that while watching Jack ream him out one day, not because anyone officially introduced us. I don't think he has a clue what I'm here for. None of them do. When we run across one of the guys, they still look at me like I just landed from another planet."

Peeking around the corner, I observed the tan ranch truck, its paint job pitted and marred by dents, dings, and rows of short scratches along the hood. "You'd think Jack would explain it to them." I couldn't keep the irritation from my voice. Daniel deserved so much better.

The driver rolled down his window, and I could see that there was a teenager and a little girl in the truck with him. After the introductions, I realized that the teenager, Chrissy, was actually the little girl's mother, and probably a little older than I'd guessed. Maybe twenty-one or twenty-two. Tag couldn't have been past his early twenties, himself. I tried to imagine being their age, working here, raising a child.

Tossing a mop of curly red hair over her shoulder, Chrissy stretched across her daughter, McKenna, who was belted in a booster seat between them. "Hey, I'm sorry we haven't been by to meet y'all." She gave her husband a sideways smirk. "Dingbat here told me y'all were Mr. West's relatives."

Tag jerked a hand in the air, then let it fall to the steering wheel. "That's what Floyd said he thought, and he's the ranch manager. How am I supposed to know if Floyd don't know?"

Chrissy responded with a petulant eye roll, then pointed at Daniel but directed her comment to me. "Anyhow, your husband does look a lot like Mr. West's son, so it's not hard to figure how Floyd made that mistake, considerin' that your husband and Jack West are cooped up together all the time. I've never actually met Mason West, and far as I've ever heard, Mr. West and his son do *not* talk, period. But there's plenty of pictures in Mr. West's house up at the big ranch headquarters. Tag and me take care of the place anytime Mr. West's out of town. But anyway, just so you know, Tag and me and McKenna aren't normally this snotty. We just figured anybody who could stand to spend that much time near Jack West *had* to be related to him. We thought maybe him and his son were getting back together. Everyone's been all stirred up about what that might mean, by the way."

Tag gave her a warning glance and tried to hide it by tugging on his hat brim. There was a whole paragraph in that look, and I didn't like what it said.

Chrissy would not be shushed, though. "Pfff! Don't try to hush me up, Tag Reese. I'll say what I want to about that man. He isn't here to hear it. Thank-the-Lord-and-phone-the-saints for that."

Daniel and I traded sideways glances the way customers might when the first person in line is harassing the checker at Walmart.

Chrissy turned back with a quick flash of eyelashes, like we were talking girl-to-girl now. "So, anyway, is he drivin' you crazy yet? Mr. West, I mean? It's hard when you're new around here. Tag and I've been here nearly a year, but the first six months was about as nice as havin' a picnic in a cow pie." She paused for a breath, her gaze shifting between Daniel and me expectantly, like she was ready to get down to some good gossip.

"We're still learning our way around," Daniel's reply was cautious. He squeezed my hand in a way that said, *Does this girl seem crazy to you?*

"I've been busy with the house, mostly," I hedged.

Red curls bounced pertly over Chrissy's cheek. "Whoa, you from New York or someplace?"

"DC."

"It *sounds* like it." Tucking the loose hair behind her ear, she leaned closer to the window. Compacted in the booster seat, her daughter squirmed and whined, "Mama!" She was a miniature of her mother—creamy skin that was a patchwork of freckles, big brown eyes, wisps of curly red hair, a pert little nose, and cupid's bow lips. Right now they were turned downward into a frown.

Chrissy responded with a quick, "Hush up!" Then she turned back to us. "So, we're headin' down to mess around at the beach across from Firefly Island for a while, since Jack's not here to have a hissy about it. Y'all wanna come? McKenna would love to play with your little boy. She's got kids at the day care during the day—I work in Gnadenfeld at the City Drug. If you ever have a prescription, just call me and I can bring it by for you on my way home—but McKenna doesn't have anybody on the ranch to play with. One of the other guys is single. Floyd, the manager, has kids that're grown and off on their own, and the other three have kids that're in high school. We'd love to have your little boy over sometime."

"Oh, well, I . . ." The flood of information clogged the synapses in my brain, waiting for processing. Chrissy's train of thought seemed to jump back and forth across several tracks.

"Sure, that sounds like fun." Daniel gave me a pleased look, as if to say, *Hey, we wanted a friend for Nick, and here one is.* "Nick would like that. And I've been wondering how to get down to that beach across from the island, too. So far, I've only seen it from a distance."

Chrissy pursed her lips in an expression that made her look more like Congressman Faber's persnickety old secretary than a girl just a few years out of high school. "Tag won't take me down there unless Jack West's out of town. He's afraid I'll swim over to Firefly Island and get us fired. I guess y'all probably already heard that *nobody's* allowed on Firefly Island. I figure that's where the b-o-d-i-e-s are buried." She glanced at McKenna when she spelled out the word.

Tag sighed and rolled a look our way, as if to say, *Now you see what I deal with every day of my life.*

In the center seat, McKenna pushed her mother out of the way and peered over the dashboard as Nick and Pecos started toward us. From the bed of the truck, a short-haired gray dog barked, wagging its stubby tail.

Tag wheeled a hand, an amiable grin forming beneath the blond mop of an old-fashioned handlebar moustache that was pretty respectable for someone so young. "Why don't y'all just hop in back? Your truck's not four-wheel drive. Prob'ly won't make it where we're goin'."

I glanced at Tag's vehicle, wondering what he meant by *in the back*. While some of the ranch trucks were of the four-door variety, this one was not. Surely, he didn't mean for us to ride in the open bed, with the dog . . .

But he did, of course, and I was quickly introduced to the concept of the cowboy convertible. After grabbing the swim stuff from our vehicle and doing a quick change behind the lab building, we rattled off, Nick up front because McKenna insisted on it, Daniel and me in the bed, balanced on the spare tire, and the dogs leaning against the tailgate, tails wagging with enthusiasm.

As we jounced across the hills, rolling over rocks, chuck-holes, and small trees, the dogs nipped the air joyously, Nick giggled in the front seat with his new friend, and Daniel and I clung to a tire in the bed, laughing at the dogs. Suddenly I realized that in this lonely, desperate first month here, I'd been so focused on the life I'd left behind that for the most part, I'd been missing the fun of where I was.

No more, I promised myself. From here on out, I was going to stay focused on the here and now. The present. The gift of limestone hills, live oak trees, and rides in a cowboy convertible with the lake breezes ruffling my hair. If I couldn't control the circumstances, at least I could control my attitude toward them.

After a white-knuckle ride across the pasture on what looked more like a mountain goat trail than a road, I finally saw the lake below. It appeared and disappeared as we bobbed over several small hills. The breeze was cool and sweet, the scent implying open water and endless sky. The tires churned madly on the way up the final boulder-strewn slope. Grabbing the side rail, I stared straight down into a canyon and briefly reevaluated the wisdom of riding in the back of the truck. And then all of a sudden the vehicle lurched over the hill, the kids squealed, and Chrissy tapped the back window, pointing toward the view splashed before us like an artist's rendering.

My heart quickened with a primal sense of discovery, of having found something I wouldn't have believed could really exist. I'd never seen a place like this—the meeting of water, land, and sky intertwined in such an untouched and perfect way. I breathed it in as we rolled down the incline and drifted to a stop on a rocky slope by the lakeshore.

Daniel hopped out of the truck and made an agile landing on the gravel, then stopped and reached for me. "Here," he said, smiling. "Careful." He held my hand as I exited less than gracefully. Tag and McKenna opened the tailgate of the truck, and the dogs jumped out, then cavorted around the vehicle, sniffing patches of milkweed and rooting in nests of last year's leaves.

"Come on, Mallory," Chrissy beckoned, turning and walking backward. "You can get a good look at Firefly Island from downshore by the causeway."

I hesitated, feeling a little guilty. Daniel, Nick, and I had so little time together as it was. I wanted to watch as Nick explored the new stretch of territory and tried out the fishing worms he'd been keeping in his pocket.

"Go ahead," Daniel urged. "We'll be here."

Chrissy gave Tag a petulant look. "See how *nice* he is?"

Tag scowled, and I tried to politely pretend I didn't notice.

"He's such a poo," Chrissy complained as we walked toward the island, where a man-made causeway and a private road connected Firefly to the rest of the world. Up close, the earthen-and-stone causeway was impressive.

"Wow, that thing is massive," I commented. At some time in the past, a great deal of effort had gone into making sure the island was accessible. Now an iron fence, a locked gate, and a plethora of No Trespassing signs prevented any public entry.

"Yeah, no kidding." Chrissy agreed. "I'd so love to see what he's hiding out there. Floyd's been working on the ranch forever, and he says that Jack's second wife, the one who *disappeared*"—she punctuated the word with finger quotes— "along with Jack's little stepson used to spend a lot of time on Firefly. It was, like, her favorite place on the ranch. There's a cabin on the island, and she'd go there a few days at a time. Probably whenever she wanted to get away from Jack West, I bet. Anyhow, after she and her son *vanished*"—finger quotes again—"off the face of the earth, Jack put up the gate across the causeway and all the No Trespassing signs. Tag doesn't like me to say it, but I think he hid somethin' there—somethin' really bad."

A chill danced over me as we stopped walking and stood looking across a short expanse of water at the shores of Firefly Island.

Chrissy pointed. "You can see the roof of the cabin through the trees a little bit, if you look . . . right there, see?" She glanced over her shoulder toward the men, as if to make sure they were still nearby. "Lights move around on the island at night, too. Tag says I'm making it up, but I'm not. One night, Tag and me were out lookin' for a lost colt in that pasture just across from your house. I was right there on the hill where the old homestead is, and I looked across toward the lake, and I saw a light moving around on the island. I don't believe in ghosts, strictly speakin'. My mama raised me in church, but it made the hair on the back of my neck stand up like hen scruff, I'll tell you."

The hair on the back of my neck stood up, too. I stared into the tree shadows of Firefly Island and wondered what might be concealed in the thick growth of elms and pin oaks.

I wasn't sure I wanted to know. It was surreal, being here looking at that place I'd had so many strange dreams about. In the dreams, I was standing right where I was now—on the shore near the causeway.

A shiver went through me, and I almost felt as if I could see the blond woman from my dream, watching me. "We should probably go back," I suggested, and Chrissy was already turning around, as if this place made her uncomfortable, too.

On the return trip down the shore, she filled me in on ranch history and invited us to Sunday services at the little church in Moses Lake. I'd been thinking about issues like church. One thing this upside-down life in Moses Lake had done was begin to cure me of the notion that I could get by on my own, that I didn't need anyone's help. I'd sent up more prayers in the last month than in the past five years combined. Even that seemed wrong—the hallmark of an overbooked, self-centered life. There had been people around me who'd needed prayer over the years. I just hadn't thought to give them any.

Now I didn't have much choice, other than to pray. I had control of almost nothing in my life. Prayer seemed the only option left.

Nick and McKenna were playing in the shallows with a minnow net and a bucket when we reached them. Nick's face lit up as we came closer. "Wook!" he breathed in sheer amazement, then headed toward me. He was carrying a green bucket in a bow-legged run, the water inside rocking and sloshing.

"What've you got?" My heart filled with Nick's smile, with the look of sheer adoration he gave me as he lugged the bucket. In the space of an instant, I felt it again—the crumbling of an old part of me, the growth of something new. The changing of my heart into a mother's heart. It happened at the strangest times, in the most unexpected ways. Nick looked at me, and the love I felt for him was almost painful in its intensity. I'd never known I had it in me, the capacity to love this way. I adored my nieces, of course. I always had. But when Nick looked at me, my mind tumbled through nights and mornings, seasons and years in the future. I saw birthday parties and first days of school and first girlfriends, Christmas mornings filled with surprises, Easter egg hunts, bedtime stories to read, bad dreams to kiss away, goals to nurture, hurts to soothe, joys to cheer, and nights side-by-side trying to figure out algebra homework . . .

I saw a future like none I'd ever imagined. I wanted it, every minute of it. Even whatever time we would spend here in Moses Lake.

Leaning over as Nick drew close with the bucket, I felt the soft, golden glow of the moment. I made a promise to myself and God. *I won't wish away another minute. Not a single one. I will build a life here, in this . . .*

Nick stumbled over a rock, the bucket sloshed sideways, and a wave of water headed my way. The moment drifted by in slow motion—the water catching the sunlight, tiny, silver fish glittering as they sailed through the air, the bucket tumbling end over end, Nick's hands splaying out, and then . . .

The wave hit. I tasted dirt and algae. Something wet, scaly, and squiggly slid down my shirt. I stumbled backward, sputtering, spitting, and squealing.

Nick screamed, "Don't squish the fishie, Tante M!"

Chrissy grabbed the front of my shirt and tried to shake the fish loose. McKenna scrambled to shore and started rescuing the stranded captives, and near the pickup, Tag slapped his leg and laughed. My husband, my soul mate, the gypsy-king love of my life who had, just over a month ago, sworn to honor, cherish, and protect me . . . the man I'd just promised God I would appreciate every moment of my life from here on out . . . doubled over and laughed right along with him.

Some prayers are tested before you even get them out of your fishy-tasting mouth. Either that, or God was telling me to lighten up on the philosophical rhetoric and just enjoy this singular, unexpected instant in my perfectly imperfect life.

The tiny fish fell into my hand, and I tossed him into the bucket, then Nick and I dashed to the shore to add water, laughing as we ran.

There is no greater agony than bearing
an untold story inside you.

—Maya Angelou
(Left by Sierra McVeigh, who'll be a famous writer one day)

Chapter 12

The morning after our swim near Firefly Island, I woke with the dreadful realization of what I'd done.

I, Mallory Hale Everson, had broken my own sacred oath.

I had joined the social media revolution.

In my rush of ridiculous Zen and overwhelming personal epiphany after the evening by the lakeshore, I had come home and looked up the password for the blog Kaylyn and Josh had created for me. When I opened it, there were the photos of the ranch around the edges, and up top, the picture of me with my cartoon Annie Oakley cowgirl body had been replaced with a photo of me standing near the old homestead where I centered my mouse-release program. The image was lop-sided and snapped from a funky angle, so that I looked like the Jolly Green Giant of mouse control. Nick had taken it.

In the quiet of midnight, with Daniel and Nick sound asleep, I'd started writing about the cataclysmic shift of the soul I had experienced along the shores of Moses Lake. I wrote about the sound of water stroking earth, the rustle of evening breeze, the slow darkening of the day, the kids

laughing, the unexpected splash from the bucket, the scramble to rescue dispossessed fish, including the one in my shirt. I wrote about the first stars twinkling to life above Chinquapin peaks, a fingernail moon rising, a gentle breeze breathing perfection into the air, the sky, and the night.

In those moments, I'd known that something new was being formed in me, too, created so gently that I hadn't even realized it until that evening by the shore. I was becoming Nick's mom in every possible way.

I wrote about the rush of love, the changing of a woman into a mother—a process that happened without conscious thought, as if the heart knew what the mind and body took time to learn. Love is the one thing that matters. That makes everything else matter. That makes everything worthwhile.

When I closed the laptop and trundled off to bed at two in the morning, I was filled with catharsis, heady with it, even. I felt as if I had created something beautiful, experienced a breakthrough, shared myself in a completely new way.

In the cold light of morning, I wanted to shoot myself in the head. I had become one of *those* people—the sort who poured their lives onto an electronic page for the entire world to see.

I hurried to the computer to erase the whole thing, but in my state of euphoria the night before, I'd sent out email invitations to my sisters, who were on the east coast and by this time already active on their computers. Kaylyn and Josh had been automatically notified of the activity on the blog site, and last night via iPhone, they'd shared the news with the Gymies, one of whom had worked on The Hill with me. She'd shared the link around various Congressional offices. Word was spreading like wildfire.

A strange thing happened over the next few days as I contemplated tossing myself off the cliffs and into the lake. People actually liked what I wrote. They sent notes and left comments on the blog, and when they did, the feeling of connection was heady and satisfying. Like an addict looking for a fix, I found myself checking the page several times a day. In the comments, I learned things I'd never known about old friends and former coworkers. Many had experienced similar life epiphanies in situations alike and different from my own.

I was not alone in the human condition.

And then, on the third day in the dark of midnight, I did it again.

I blogged about taking Nick to help little McKenna and her dad bottle-feed an orphaned foal they were keeping in their backyard. I wrote about the interdependence we all share, how none of us are meant to go along the path alone. I wrote about the vulnerability of the little spindle-legged colt, about how he'd been found standing in a ranch pasture alongside his dead mother. A middle-aged couple from Dallas, city folk on their way to a bed-and-breakfast down in the Hill Country, had seen him. They'd taken the time to turn around and make sure everything was all right. They'd saved his life with a short detour and less than an hour of their time. *How often,* I wondered at the end of the story, *do we pass by a need, a life that could be changed with the smallest bit of effort? And it's not that we don't care but that we're driving so fast, all we see are the fence posts flashing by on the side of the highway?*

Maybe the first step in changing the world is in slowing down and looking through the fences.

People liked the story of the orphaned foal. I'd added photos, and people loved those. Nick, McKenna, and Mugsy the foal were cute together, the giant milk bottle extended between them. Oddly enough, I had some talent for photography. I loved working with the lighting and the angles. I had started carrying the camera everywhere I went, looking for shots.

Later that week, when Jack West reappeared at the ranch and life turned upside-down again, photography and the blog became my lifeline. Kaylyn and Josh added new photos to the background and beefed up *The Frontier Woman* headline with fancy scrolling that looked like something from the Old West. More followers signed on. Former coworkers who were still slogging away in dank, cave-like basement offices enjoyed reading about the wild life. Suddenly the world that had been small and isolated was large again, filled with people who wondered about what might happen when a former apartment-dwelling city girl was dropped in the middle of ten thousand acres without a superhighway or a Starbucks in sight.

Even the Binding Through Books ladies found me, while thumbing through Moses Lake Google searches. Cindy, Paula, and Alice were back in Moses Lake for their annual sisters' vacation. They were scheduled for a photo shoot with a photographer from *Woman's Day* magazine, doing a story about their Binding Through Books club. Since I hadn't been able to persuade my own sisters to do a long-distance book club with me, they offered to let me come watch the photo shoot. I took them up on it, because I thought it would be a great story. It wasn't every day a major magazine sent someone to Moses Lake.

I stayed up all night reading the Binding Through Books sisters' latest book selection, then I went to Alice's well-weathered cottage on the other side of the lake. Somehow, I ended up making it into a few of the photographer's shots, and two days later, I was on the magazine's Web site, along with a little blurb about my blog and how I'd come to be The Frontier Woman.

The blog had several hundred new followers almost instantly. Josh and Kaylyn were amazed.

"*The Frontier Woman*'s got a ton of hits for a site that's only been active a few weeks. I'm not surprised, though. It's like you're writing about a whole different world," Kaylyn told me on the phone as she and Josh lingered over lunch in their office, reading about my photo shoot with the Binding Through Books sisters and yesterday's cattle roundup at the main ranch headquarters.

An amazing thing had happened to me in my first weeks of blogging. Because I was writing about adventures, I started not only to seek them out, but to see them all around me. In seeing the adventure of this place, I'd begun to truly live my life, rather than hiding from it and complaining about it. "The cattle roundup was really western, like *in-the-movies* western," I told Kaylyn. "And, hey, did you see the pictures of the wild turkey nest outside the back gate? Nick and I found it on our walk down to the creek a couple days ago. She has *eggs* now. I asked our neighbor, Al Beckenbauer, and she said gestation on a wild turkey egg is about a month. Nick and I started a calendar, so we could mark off the days." Among other things, I'd finally made that call to Cowgirl Al and admitted that my mouse and vermin eradication program was not working. I needed help. We'd purchased supplies at the hardware store and started working on the closets.

"I saw the picture of the nest," Kaylyn answered. "That's so awesome. Josh says to tell you he ordered a turkey sandwich in your honor today."

I heard Josh in the background adding, "Subway Fresh Fit, baby. Tell her I'm eating healthy so I can get on a horse and round up some doggies whenever I get a chance to come down there."

"I heard him," I told Kaylyn. "Tell him he's welcome anytime. Now that Al's helping me fix the closets, house-guests might not wake up to the Wild Kingdom. Al says the only thing to do is line the closets with paneling, then caulk everything and paint it all to seal out the smell. And seal around the doors, windows, and plumbing really well. We redid Nick's closet and the hall closet last week. This week, the master. I passed the information on to Alice, for her lake house, and now I'm the book sisters' hero. They found a scorpion in the bathtub right before the photographer came."

"I sense another how-to story coming on," Kaylyn laughed. "You're, like, the home handywoman anymore. Nice job on the tile around the bathroom sink, by the way."

"Can you come do my bathroom?" Josh chimed in, and all of a sudden he was louder. Kaylyn had put me on speaker. "Hey, look, the cattle roundup has sixty-nine comments already. The turkey might lose the top spot. And there's nineteen new followers. Who are these people?"

I'd wondered that, too. Who were all these people, and why were they so interested in life here? "Al showed me how to do the tile. She says as long as I don't—and I quote—'Point that dadgum camera at her and try to put her on the blog,' she'll help me. I'm telling you, that woman knows how to do everything." I'd become enamored with Al Beckenbauer, in a strange sort of way. She was amazingly competent, and for whatever reason, she'd decided to take me under her wing. It was hard to say why, because we were as different as night and day. I like to talk; Al preferred to work in silence. My refrigerator was filled with prepackaged convenience foods; Al churned her own butter and grew her own pesticide-free vegetables. I knew nothing about animals; Al surrounded herself with them. In addition to a half-dozen mismatched dogs and countless cats, she had a pet pig and miniature horse that, as far as I could gather, wandered in and out of her house, pretty much at will.

"So, did I tell you we're making goat's milk soap in the next few days?" I asked. "I might even learn to milk a goat."

"Uh-oh," Kaylyn quipped. "I feel a future YouTube sensation coming on."

"Jerry Springer moment. Goats unplugged," Josh added.

The three of us laughed together, and I felt strangely euphoric, my emotions taking an upsweep, like a roller-coaster car whipping over a hill and around a curve. I couldn't stop laughing.

"It wasn't *that* funny," Josh observed.

"I n-n-n-know," I giggled out. "Stuff just—" giggle-giggle-snort "—hits me . . . some . . . some . . . sometimes . . . lately. I'm s-s-s-sorry."

I was still trying to catch my breath as we signed off. Even with my newfound interest in being The Frontier Woman, I wondered if I really was a basket case. Maybe I was becoming like one of those miners who'd stayed too long in a shack in the gold fields, all alone. For the most part, now that Jack had returned and once again clamped his iron fist over the ranch, my days were just Nick and me. Daniel was tied up with Jack and still trying to establish what his job was here. So far, they'd spent time doing everything from driving to San Antonio to look at farm equipment, to picking peaches from a ragged tree near a tumbledown homestead. Jack wanted the peaches to become peach pie. Right now a whole bucketful of them was slowly going bad in my refrigerator.

The thought of the peaches dulled my euphoria as I set the cordless phone in its cradle. Daniel and I had tumbled into a fight over the bucket of fruit. He'd come home in a foul mood the night he brought it in. I'd wanted to tell him about the blog, and all Daniel wanted to talk about was me whipping up peach pies to mollify Jack.

The War of the Peaches had been ongoing for three days, but I was in too good a mood for it right now. I had it in mind to end the fight by actually attempting a peach pie, even though I didn't know pie crust from Pop-Tarts. I'd talked myself into it by deciding that I would photograph the entire process and use it as a blog. I was going to call it *Pie-Making for Dummies*. Somehow, the idea of domesticity seemed less old-fashioned when you were sharing your efforts in cyberspace.

I knew I needed help, though, and the plethora of fancy pie recipes on the Internet were too hard to sort out. The month before, while Daniel and I were moving the stuffed dead animals to the garage building for storage, I'd noticed a dusty red-and-white-checked Betty Crocker cookbook, exactly like the one my mother had. It was just sitting on top of a box of rusty pans in the corner. The sight of it had filled me with nostalgia. Clearly, whoever had left it there wasn't coming back for it, but I couldn't imagine what use I would have for a cookbook, so I'd left it where it was. Now it seemed like the perfect answer to the peach pie problem. My mother swore by the recipes in Betty Crocker.

I put on gloves and Daniel's rubber boots before heading out to the garage. The long, narrow building was a scary place, littered with cast-off belongings from former ranch residents, as well as bits of rope and chain, ancient garden tools, and broken yard-mowing equipment from days gone by. Huge iron meat hooks hung from the rafters overhead, along with a single light bulb, which didn't provide much illumination. It looked like a place where snakes, bats, and . . . who knew what else might hide.

When I stepped inside, something was scratching and

gnawing in the far corner of the room. I didn't investigate, but crept across the uneven concrete (as much as it's possible to creep in oversized rubber boots) and snatched the cookbook off the stack of pans. A cross-stitched apron was lying underneath. I held it up with morbid fascination, letting the dingy window light shine through the moth-eaten fabric. Had it belonged to Jack's wife? Had the woman who'd disappeared worn this very apron?

Dropping it, I rushed across the room, stepped into the yard, and slammed the door. In the overgrown gardens of the little house, the concrete angel watched me from a patch of sunlight. A yellow swallowtail butterfly sat on her outstretched hand, slowly fanning its wings. Shuddering, I turned away and hurried back to the house, then dusted off the cookbook before taking it inside.

The peach pie recipe was easy to find. The page was turned down, and there was a note in the margin. *For Cynthia's wedding.*

Cynthia. Was that the name of Jack's second wife? Or had she written those words herself? Could this cookbook have been hers?

A chill slid over me, tickling like the stroke of a feather.

"Okay. All right. Stop it already." A shudder rattled my shoulders, and I grabbed my phone from my purse, then quickly made a list of the ingredients required for peach pie. A trip to the Walmart in Gnadenfeld would give me time to gain some perspective, I reasoned.

The cookbook probably wasn't even hers, anyway. I was letting my imagination run completely amuck.

But even as the reassurances cycled in my head, I made it a point not to look toward the little house as I gathered Nick and proceeded toward the car.

The drive along the rural highway was peaceful, as

always—a chance to compose my thoughts and enjoy peek-a-boo views of the river. Near town, the roadsides were graced with stately old farms surrounded by picture-perfect green fields, tall hip-roofed barns, and large stone houses. The town itself was a study in contrasts. I'd read a newspaper article about how various Mennonite families had formed the community in the fifties when they were forced out of their valley by the Corps of Engineers' plan to dam up the river and build Moses Lake. Now Gnadenfeld was home to many thriving Mennonite-owned dairies, as well as other businesses catering to tourists in search of a day trip into a simpler time.

Despite its humble roots and charming Mennonite bakeries, Gnadenfeld was also the home of a large Proxica Foods production facility that was squarely on Al's environmental enemies list, right beside Jack West. Last winter a huge scandal about Proxica's chemical contamination had broken wide open, and the cleanup was still ongoing. According to Al, even though Proxica had been forced to pay massive damages, nothing could eclipse what they'd done. Al had been active in helping Gnadenfeld recover from the impact of the bad publicity, so that the tourists would return. The town was one of Al's pet projects.

My interest in Gnadenfeld was much less noble than Al's. The town had a Walmart, and when you're living so far from everything that is familiar, stepping into a Walmart feels pretty much like heaven. Unlike my day-to-day shopping in Moses Lake, where baitfish, live worms, milk, and soda pop were stored in disturbingly close proximity, in Walmart, the live fish were all the way on the opposite end of the store from the groceries. Call me fussy, but it seemed like it should be that way.

For his part, Nick was a good shopper. We talked about

the colors of T-shirts, the pictures on CD covers, the letters on product labels.

Nick watched commercials and liked to repeat them. "There a Pine-Sol!" he said and pointed to the shelf, then raised a brow and added disdainfully, "Oh, and they got that bawgin bwand pine cleaner. It leaves diwt behind." I was fairly certain Nick was the smartest kid on the face of the earth.

In the baking section, we ran into a familiar face. Nick remembered Keren Zimmer immediately and asked her where all the summer enrichment kids were. "They've gone home for the day." Keren smiled and tousled Nick's hair. "I came over here to get some fertilizer for our garden that we all planted together. Did you know we had a garden? It's right there in town, in the little courtyard beside Books and Java. All the kids worked on it together, and tomorrow we're going to pick green beans, cook them at the church, and see how good they are to eat."

"Awesome!" Nick cheered. "I wike beans!"

I laughed and patted Nick on the back. What a great kid. I was fairly certain he hadn't seen a real live green bean. Not on my watch. Getting away from the prepackaged convenience foods and learning to make something real was on my to-do list. Al had been after me about it. Anything that came in a box, bag, or Styrofoam container, she was strictly against, especially for developing humans, like Nick.

"You all can come and help us with the garden, whenever you have the time," Keren reiterated her invitation from weeks ago, turning to me with a smile that was welcoming and a little timid, as if she felt more comfortable relating to children than adults. "We water the garden every day, but on Tuesdays and Fridays we do our science lesson there. We pull weeds, add compost from our compost bin, and pick the vegetables if they're ready. The garden is a new thing I'm trying to get started. I'm hoping I can carry it into the school year. The kids up in Chinquapin Peaks live with such rampant food insecurity. Many of the homes don't have enough groceries in them, especially at certain times of the month, and what they do have is usually high fat and low nutrition. The kids don't know how to eat vegetables or how to cook them, and a lot of times, neither do their parents. But here's what I'm finding with the garden—it's different when kids grow it themselves. They want to eat it because they had a hand in making it. It's like feed a man a fish or teach a man to fish. If we can get these families started growing food and show them how to preserve it, they'll have healthy food and they'll feel good about where it came from."

"That sounds fantastic." I was vaguely aware that I'd completely misjudged Keren—stereotyped her, really. The conservative clothes, the long hair bound into a bun. I'd imagined her to be unbelievably sweet, unrealistically naïve about the world, bland, and not someone I'd really want to cultivate a friendship with. Not hip enough. Not interested in anything I was interested in. In reality, she was a force to be reckoned with, a young woman determined to make a difference.

Her enthusiasm radiated like light from a supernova. "I think it will be, if I can just get the money we need and the cooperation of the parents. I'd love for every family in the school to have a supper garden. Growing up, all I ever saw were Mennonite homes. Everyone we knew grew vegetables in the summer, then put them up for the winter. We all had tomatoes ripening in our cellars until after Christmas. We hardly ever had to buy vegetables."

"That's amazing." Keren made me want to run right out and plant a garden. I thought about my upcoming peach pie adventure. There was something earthy and primal about rendering sustenance from the most basic of components.

A strand of blond hair teased her cheek, and she pushed it away purposefully. She seemed to want something from me, but I couldn't imagine what it might be. "I never knew there were places like Chinquapin Peaks. I really didn't. Not until I started teaching last year."

"That must be really hard to deal with sometimes." I thought of the story of the foal, of what I'd written at the end of it. Sometimes, changing a life wasn't as easy as taking an hour out of your trip to a bed and breakfast. Sometimes, it required much more work than that.

"Several of my kids come to school so hungry on Mondays. I have to feed them before I can teach them." She looked at Nick, probably thinking what I was thinking—that Nick would never know what it felt like to show up for school with an empty stomach. "Anyway, I'm boring you. I'm sorry."

"No . . . no, it's interesting." Right now, I wanted to go over to the gardening department, whip out the credit card, and buy Keren whatever she needed. Then I realized that when Nick started school—next year for preschool or the following year for kindergarten—he would be walking through the doors with the kids who came from those houses Keren was describing. I didn't want him to learn about that reality.

Having been given an upper-crust education all my life, I'd never had to contend with such things. I couldn't imagine placing Nick, with his sweet nature and open, innocent personality, in such a situation. He would be exposed to bad language, bad behavior, a myriad of grown-up information shared by kids who'd already seen too much of life.

I wondered if there was a private school anywhere within commuting distance, where we could enroll Nick. Where he would be protected.

I blushed, imagining that Keren could see the questions scrolling through my brain.

Almost without thinking about it, I found myself leading the conversation to more comfortable things—away from hungry kids and supper gardens, to peach pie. Keren, having no idea of the war of conscience inside me, happily shared tips on how to easily peel peaches by dipping them in boiling water, then in ice water. She showed me where to buy refrigerated piecrust—much easier than making your own and almost as good, she assured me. By the time we parted ways, I felt competent to bake a peach pie, if not to save the world. I'd almost managed to scoot supper gardens and hungry kids completely out of my mind.

On the way back home, Nick was so preoccupied with a new Pez dispenser that he'd already forgotten about Keren's invitation to help with the summer enrichment garden. We'd bought some green beans in the produce department, though I wasn't sure what I'd do with them. Eventually Nick fell asleep clutching them in his car seat, along with the Pez dispenser.

When we pulled into the ranch, he was wide-awake and ready to play. While he and Pecos went to work digging in the sand pile, Betty Crocker and I got busy in the kitchen. I discovered two things: Number one, Betty has a talent for making things look easier than they are. Number two, I would probably never make a living baking pies. Eons had passed by the time I'd skinned the peaches and soaked the tags off the blue glass pie pans I'd received as a wedding gift. After that, I pitted, sliced, sugared, and struggled through sealing the crust, all the while taking pictures and thinking of what I would say about a non-pie-baking girl's afternoon with Pillsbury and Betty Crocker. The story was starting to hum in my head, making me laugh, despite the fact that my lopsided pies weren't likely to grace the cover of *Woman's Day* anytime soon.

"Thank you, Betty," I said and picked up the cookbook before preparing to commit my creations to the oven. Something white and rectangular slid from the pages and fluttered to the floor. An envelope. I stood looking at it before picking it up and turning it over. The flap was open, a letter on faded yellow paper inside.

Something tightened the muscles in my neck as I read the three lines of text, hastily scrawled on the paper, the writing seeming rushed and uneven.

Will meet you on the old dock at eleven tomorrow night. Please, please don't say anything to anyone. Still so unsure, and must think of the children. So very afraid now . . .

My stomach clenched, and a sick feeling gurgled up my throat. Who had written that note? When? Was it *her*? Had she written it? Was she running away from Jack West? Was she afraid of him? Had she sensed that something terrible was coming?

But she mentioned *children*. Jack's second wife only had one son. Could she have been expecting another? Was she pregnant when she died?

Or was this letter completely unrelated to Jack? Could it have been written by someone else who lived on the ranch . . . perhaps a woman meeting a lover on the lakeshore?

There was no way to know.

Outside, a peacock called, and I suddenly realized that I hadn't heard a peep out of Nick in forever. How long, exactly? I wasn't even sure. I'd left him in the yard with Pecos when I'd started the pies. . . .

But that was . . . I glanced at the clock. Over two hours had passed.

I had the moment of panic that comes from realizing you've zoned out in a potentially dangerous way. Normally I kept track of Nick's whereabouts by listening for the sound of his chats with Pecos, the high whine of tricycle wheels on the back porch, or the rattle and crash of Lego avalanches in the bedroom. Even with my limited parenting experience, I'd learned that boys are easy to track via sound. Daniel and I had made sure to put things like cleaners and paint thinners on a high shelf, so that Nick could have the run of the place.

But I'd been so preoccupied with the idea of baking the perfect pie and sharing my adventure with the world that I hadn't been listening. I hadn't even looked out the window.

"Nick?" I called, thinking maybe he was in his room, reading or coloring. "Ni-i-ick?"

No answer. No sound.

"Nick?" I held my breath, strained into the silence. Nothing. I had the eerie feeling of being utterly alone in the house, a terrible sixth sense I didn't want.

My mind rushed ahead, the pie story giving way to horrific scenarios. What if he'd discovered some dangerous chemical tucked in the back of a closet that I'd failed to check? What if he'd gotten into something? What if he'd put a Lego or another small toy in his mouth and silently choked on it? Or somehow gotten the mini-blind cords loose and accidentally tangled one around his neck, or . . .

What if he'd figured out how to open the gates, then left the safety of the yard? There were all sorts of potential dangers out there. Horses in the barn, cattle in the pasture, wild animals hiding in the woods, coyotes that howled at night, rattlesnakes curled up in the shade beneath prickly pear cacti . . .

"Nick?" My voice cracked the silence, high, sharp, demanding. "Nick, if you can hear me, answer right now! Where are you?" Wiping flour on my shorts, I ran to the back door, pushed open the screen, yelled into the yard, listened, threatened, and listened again. Nick had never hidden from me before—not unless we were playing our little games of hide-and-seek. Surely he could tell from my voice that I wasn't playing now.

Panic swelled as the echo of my voice died. The yard was sun-filled, incredibly still. Nick's little collection of toys sat basking in the golden light, a tiny yellow bulldozer with a mound of sand piled in front of it, poised for action, a miniature stack of tree bark ready to be used in the building of a fence or a house. Nick seemed to have abandoned his game in midstream.

Letting the door fall closed, I hurried through the house, checking every place I could think of, yelling Nick's name. Tears blurred my eyes and my heart hammered, the sound beating faster, faster, faster. When I'd gone through the house again, I checked the yard inch by inch, every bush, flower bed, and hidden space. There was no sign of Nick anywhere.

Fear like I had never experienced seized me as I raced back to the house, stumbled through the door, and grabbed the phone. I tried Daniel's cell. No answer. My hands trembled as I searched for the West Research lab number in the yellowed Rolodex Jack had given us.

"Please, please, please . . ." Moments seemed to stretch painfully as I waited for Daniel to pick up. He'd told me he would be in the lab all day, since Jack was gone to some sort of business meetings in Dallas.

One ring, another, another. What was I going to say? *I've lost Nick? I don't know where he is? I forgot about him while I was trying to bake those stupid peach pies to keep Jack West happy?*

"No, *no* . . ." The click of the answering machine left me desperately alone. "Please, God. Please let him be all right . . ." There was water all around us—the shallow creek behind the barn and the lakeshore across the pasture. Could Nick walk that far? Would he? Could he have set out for the lake on his own? He didn't even know how to swim without his floaties. . . .

I imagined Nick slowly walking into the water, the waves sweeping over him. No. No, he couldn't be by the water. The yard gates were all closed. The latches were too heavy for Nick. Where could he have gone?

Was it possible that someone had taken him from the yard? Who? No one ever came here but the UPS man and the ranch hands. None of them would have let Nick out of the yard without telling me. The dog was gone, too. Pecos never left Nick's side. During our weeks at the ranch, they'd become so tightly bonded that Pecos slept on the ground outside Nick's window at night.

I called the lab again, got the answering machine. "Daniel, I need you. I can't find Nick!" I slammed the phone into the cradle, paced the kitchen, trying to think. Should I get in the car and drive down to the lake, look for Nick there? What if he was still somewhere around the house? What if he came back, and I was gone? I needed help. I needed somebody. Who could I call? Al didn't carry a cell phone, and she wouldn't be in the house this time of the day. The sheriff's department was miles away. Town was miles away. Did we have a phone book for the area?

"Stupid. *Stupid.*" This was my fault. I hadn't even bothered to gather up emergency numbers and keep them by the phone.

I ran to the bedroom and dumped my purse out onto the bed, dug through the mess for the sticky note with Chrissy's work number on the back. By the time she picked up the phone at the pharmacy, I was in tears on the other end. I blurted out the story between sobs and moans of regret. A voice in the back of my head admonished, *See? See? What made you think you could be someone's mother?* Meanwhile,

Chrissy repeated details to the pharmacist, her voice taking on a breathless sense of drama that heightened my fear and reinforced the idea that I wasn't panicking over nothing.

Before Chrissy and the pharmacist could decide whether it would be better to relay information to the county sheriff's department or round up some volunteers to search for Nick, a silver BMW convertible melted out of the heat waves on the driveway. The low undercarriage scraped the grassy hump in the center of the road, sending up a silty cloud of caliche dust that overtook the car. Wandering peafowl scattered in all directions as the incongruous vehicle whipped into a parking spot beside Jack's ranch truck. Jack was in the passenger seat, the driver a distinguished-looking man in a suit. The two of them were engaged in what looked like a business conversation.

I dropped the phone and ran outside, throwing open the gate before they were out of the car. If I'd previously been intimidated by Jack West, in that moment I wouldn't have cared if he were Attila the Hun. I wanted someone to help me find Nick. Alive and well and unharmed.

"Nick's gone!" I blurted. "I can't find him anywhere. I've checked the house and the yard, and . . . and I was in the kitchen . . . and then I realized I hadn't heard him . . . and I don't know how long . . ." The story tumbled out, almost unintelligible. I felt time ticking away, the possibility of this turning out to be an innocent, harmless incident growing thinner and thinner as the minutes passed.

Jack patted the air, his expression hard to read in the shadows of his cowboy hat, his voice matter-of-fact. "Kids wander off. Where's the last place you saw the boy?"

I repeated the details again.

He turned to the man in the business suit, who was standing with his hands clasped, his face impassive, as if he were waiting for Jack to tell him what his reaction should be. "Jankowski, grab the radio in my truck, there, and see if any of the hands are around. Track down Daniel, too. Could be he came by and picked up the boy and didn't check in."

"Daniel would never do that," I insisted. "He always lets me know if he's taking Nick. We always tell each other. He wouldn't . . ." I stopped mid-sentence. Jack was already walking away. I followed along as the man in the suit, Jankowski, crossed to Jack's truck.

"Yard gates weren't open?" Jack seemed strangely detached from the situation—as if the outcome didn't worry him in the least.

"No, they were all *closed*. Nick can't open the latches, and there's no way he could climb over the fence. But he's not in the yard. I just don't . . ."

Jack held up a hand, silencing me. He scanned the area, seeming to listen for something. A peacock strolled by, dragging a folded fan of tail feathers, and he watched it pass. "You seen the dog lately?" In the past month, Pecos had gone from *my* dog to *the* dog, in Jack's vernacular. "Dog wouldn't just leave the yard without the boy."

Inside, I was screaming, *Stop standing here talking! We have to do something!* Jack started toward the yard, toward the one place I was certain Nick *wasn't*. "They're not there. I looked. I searched everywhere." My mind flashed a picture of Nick wandering into the surf. We didn't have time to waste looking where I'd already searched.

"You check in the garage buildin'?"

"I *said* I've been *everywhere*. They're not in the yard."

Right now, Jack looked as though he didn't care whether Nick lived or died. What kind of man was he?

"I can't raise anyone on this thing," Jankowski yelled, and even he seemed more concerned than Jack.

181

My stomach fell. The world spun. I felt like I was going to be sick. We needed help, and we needed it now. "We have to call the sheriff, or somebody, before any more time goes by."

Jack held up a hand to silence me again. I wasn't inclined to obey this time. I whirled toward him, intent on taking control of the situation.

"You check in the little house?" he asked.

"What . . . no, it's . . . the doors are locked." If Nick had somehow managed to let himself into Jack's house, surely he would have heard me when I was running around the yard calling his name.

A slow heel turn swiveled Jack toward the gate, and he strode through, dismissing me in midsentence. Left with little other choice, I followed to the little house, again protesting the waste of time. His glance was dismissive as he took a skeleton key from the porch light and turned the old-fashioned lock. The door creaked open, and he paused to replace the key, his countenance still annoyingly calm.

A soft sound jingled in the silent air, barely audible. I listened again and heard nothing except the fall of Jack's boots against the hollow floors, his passage quieted by seventies-vintage linoleum in an avocado-green print. The kitchen décor seemed to be of the same era, the wallpaper covered in sprays of tiny sunflowers. The L-shaped row of cabinets looked to be a deep shade of olive green, now gray with dust. A saucepan sat on the stove next to a china canister that read *Oatmeal*, and a dust-covered metal spoon struggled to reflect the weak afternoon light filtered through partially disintegrated lace curtains.

A child's cereal bowl and mug waited on a cream-colored breakfast table by the window. The chair was pulled out slightly, as if someone had left to grab the milk from the refrigerator and forgotten to come back. Without wanting to, I slid my gaze over the breakfast set. *Fruity Pebbles* ran in multicolored letters along the rim. Nick's favorite cereal.

Where was the boy who'd owned that bowl? Why would it have been left on the table if he'd gone to Mexico with his mother for a long-term trip? Why did it look more like someone had been here making his breakfast, and then suddenly disappeared?

What if Jack's wife and her little boy had never gone to Mexico at all? What if they'd never left the ranch?

I turned and watched Jack moving through the room, emotionless, not looking left or right. Had something unthinkable happened here? Had he done something unthinkable . . . and then left this place as . . . as what? A shrine? A trophy? A strange act of denial?

Behind me, the other man, Jankowski, stopped in the doorway. I didn't blame him. This tiny house was filled with the presence of the woman and child who had been here—Jack's wife and her young son.

I wanted to turn and run out the door, but I couldn't. If Nick was in here, I had to find him, but how could he possibly be? The back door was locked. The other doors were, too.

Jack stepped through a darkened passageway into another room. Taking a breath of mildew and stillness, I followed him into the shadows, then emerged in a tiny living room with two sofas, a console television, and various antique end tables. The shades were pulled over bay windows at the opposite end, casting pallor over everything.

A beautiful painting hung over the sofa—a little blond-haired boy squatting in the grass, picking flowers. Rain lilies, like the ones that had bloomed in our yard. A lump rose in my throat as I followed Jack through another doorway into a hall that was narrow by modern standards, the striped wallpaper making the walls seem to close in. Jack traversed the distance in three long strides and crossed through another doorway into a sunlit bedroom. He stopped just inside the door, and I stopped just outside it.

Moving a few inches closer, I studied the interior with both foreboding and fascination. It was a child's room, a boy's, the bed constructed of miniature wagon wheels, the dresser fronts decorated with wood-burned cattle brands, the toy box and the shelves beside the closet door stocked with tiny trucks and tractors from a mixture of eras—some even old enough that they might have belonged to Jack.

Clothes hung in the closet. T-shirts, jeans, a suede jacket with fringe. A boy's clothes. There was a photo beside the closet door. A woman with long blond hair, kneeling by the lakeshore with a little boy, both of them smiling at the camera. Firefly Island lay behind them, across the water. I knew exactly where the picture had been taken. I'd been there not long ago with Chrissy and Tag.

My head swam. I reached for the doorframe, steadied myself, felt a wave of grief mixed with the rush of desperation and adrenaline inside me.

Jack motioned toward the floor. I pulled my gaze downward, unwillingly grazing over another picture frame on the corner of the desk. A smiling little face underneath a cowboy hat. He couldn't have been much older than Nick then . . .

I glanced downward still, past the legs of the desk, across the round rag rug that covered the wooden floor, and then, near the footboard of the bed, I saw them—Nick and Pecos, sound asleep on the floor, surrounded by an assortment of toys.

They'd been in here . . . playing?

"Looks like that answers your question," Jack said, and Pecos opened his eyes. He rolled upright and surveyed the room, seeming surprised and slightly embarrassed to find himself here. Noticing Jack, he ducked his head and tucked his ears.

"Must've climbed in through the doggy door on the side of the house." Jack turned to leave the room, and for an instant, there was emotion on his face. Grief? Pain? Regret? I couldn't tell. As quickly as it came, it was gone, but suddenly I understood that there was a reason he'd known to look inside the little house even though the doors were locked. Nick wasn't the first child to come in that way.

"I'll get him." I moved past Jack, stubbed my toe against a little red tractor, and watched it skitter across the room. Nick had trespassed where he shouldn't have, touched things that had been closeted away for years. "I'm sorry." My voice choked with a mixture of feelings I couldn't even begin to sort out. "I . . . I had no idea he could . . . get in here." Threading through the toys, I tried to decide whether to pick them up or leave them. The photo of the little boy and his mother pulled at me again. I didn't want to look. I didn't want to touch anything. I just wanted to grab Nick, get him out of this place, explain to him why he should never come here again.

Jack didn't answer, but walked back through the house without a word. I picked up Nick and followed, passing down the hall and across the living room, not looking at the painting above the sofa. The dog followed quietly behind me, as if even he knew we were treading on memorial ground.

Outside on the back steps, I finally caught a breath as Nick yawned, stretched, and blinked, slowly coming to life. Smacking his lips, he took in the yard, his face a mask of confusion as Jack locked the little house again and put the key away.

The sounds of a car door closing and another vehicle rumbling up the driveway echoed against the buildings as we walked back around the corner. When I stepped onto the path, Chrissy was hurrying toward the yard, her eyes wide, her red curls flying in the wind. "Oh my gosh, you found him!" Leaving the gate hanging, she ran to meet us. "Thank God! I've been callin' everyone I could think of to come help you search."

From the looks of things, she had. Two vehicles were racing up our driveway already, and a third had just turned in the gate. The posse had arrived.

Never go to bed mad. Stay up and fight.

—Phyllis Diller
(Left by Mama B, for the couple not talking in Cabin 3)

Chapter 13

The evening after Nick's disappearance wasn't a pretty one in our house. Daniel and I fought because while Nick was missing, Daniel had been AWOL—so consumed with trying to recalibrate a fixed-speed centrifuge that he'd turned off the phones in the lab.

My Firefly Island epiphany evaporated like smoke, and I heard myself hissing, "There's something wrong here, Daniel, and you're so caught up in your fascination with Jack West's scientific genius that you're blind to it. You didn't see what I saw in that little house. It's like a shrine, and then out in the garage, I found a cookbook. I think it was *her* cookbook. There was a letter in it she was writing. She talked about needing to get away from here, about being afraid. You have a family to think about, Daniel. Nick and I need you to put us first. It's like Jack West is pulling you further and further away from us. I feel more like your hired *nanny* than your wife!" They were horrible words—the worst I could think of. In that moment, I meant them to be. I was going for shock value, hoping Daniel would wake up if I hit him hard enough.

For the first time we ended up not speaking, and we slept in separate places.

In the morning, Daniel was gone before daylight. I woke exhausted, aware that I'd been tossing all night, dreaming that Nick was wandering along the lakeshore alone, unaware that just across the cove, hidden in the dark undergrowth of Firefly Island, someone was stalking him. Someone dangerous.

A moment later, I was in a grocery store, but there were no customers. I was running from aisle to aisle, screaming for Nick. Then I saw him walking out the door hand-in-hand with the little boy from the photos in Jack's cottage. I screamed, tried to run, but my legs wouldn't work.

Frightening, vivid dreams came one after another, a relentless assault.

In the morning I went straight to Nick's room to check on him. He was sleeping in after his big day afield, his fist curled close to his face, his blond curls spread out on the pillow, soft, angelic. His face was so peaceful, his lips playing with the smile from some dream that must have been very different from mine. He deserved so much more than two people who couldn't seem to pull it all together.

In the kitchen, the pages had been turned in the red-and-white-checked cookbook, the letter tucked haphazardly in a different place than before. Daniel must have looked at it, then gone to work, not the least bit concerned.

I pulled it out, read those few sentences, realized again that they could have meant almost anything, could have been written by anyone. . . .

The phone rang, and Trudy was on the other end.

"Hey, everything okay?" She sounded at once both concerned and cheerful. "I woke up thinking about you this morning." Trudy and I always had that sixth sense that connects sisters like an invisible thread. "I checked the blog, and The

Frontier Woman didn't report yesterday. Thought I'd make sure you hadn't been carried off by coyotes."

"Last night's report wouldn't have been pretty." I passed through the kitchen, saw the peach pies, baked but untouched. "We had a major blow-up." I spilled the story. "I woke this morning feeling awful—and not just about the fight. Just when I think I'm finally settled in . . . then, I'm not. Trudy, there's either something wrong with this place or there's something wrong with me."

"Okay, let's just back up a little." Trudy was the voice of reason, as usual. "Not that the letter thing doesn't give me the creeps a little. I can see how you could read almost anything into it, but it's not like you to be so . . . reactionary."

I sighed, wanting to pick up the pie-making utensils and smack myself repeatedly on the forehead. "I'm sure I'm being mental. Maybe I'm just tired. I'm having all these wild dreams—not just the bad ones I told you about. One night, I was helping with the cattle roundup, only I was riding a spotted cow. Anyway, every day seems like a roller-coaster ride. One minute I'm psyched about the blog or about working on the house with Al, and then the next minute, I have this out-of-nowhere urge to crawl in a hole and cry my eyes out. It's just weird." I reached into the cabinet for a mug, thinking that some coffee would smooth away the rough edges. I didn't want to greet Nick first thing in the morning in this kind of mood.

"Mal, are you two using birth control?"

I almost dropped the phone. "What?"

"You heard me."

Outside, a peacock strutted by, its fan of tail feathers as otherworldly as Trudy's question. I stared at the bird for a minute, grasping for an answer. "Where is *that* coming from? Of course we're using birth control. The last thing we need right now is a *pregnancy* to worry about." As soon as the words were out, I realized how wrong they were. On the other end of the line, my sister would have given anything for a pregnancy, for a baby. "I'm sorry, Trude. That sounded really bad. I should go before I say anything else stupid. Any news on the in vitro, by the way?"

"No bad news, which is good so far, but let's not get off track. We're talking about you. When Carol was pregnant, she was exactly like that. So were Meryl and Missy. The dreams, the wild emotions, the . . ."

"I'm on the pill, Trudy. Believe me, I take it regularly. Daniel and I haven't even talked about whether we want more kids, and now definitely isn't the time." Our lives were so tenuous already; I couldn't even imagine what a pregnancy might do.

Trudy was like a dog on a choice fillet. "What was that thing the week before the wedding . . . that day I called you, and you'd been to the doctor?"

"That was the dentist, and it was a root canal. What does that have to do with anything?"

"Oh, *man* . . ." Trudy's response was laden with gravity, her hesitation weighty. "Did they prescribe antibiotics for that?"

"Yes, they did, and the first one gave me hives. I thought I was going to have to go to my wedding looking like Shrek, by the way." It seemed funny now, but at the time, it felt more or less like a tragedy. Waking up with hives during your wedding countdown is tantamount to a bride's worst nightmare. "Anyway, they called in a replacement, and it was fine. I finished them up on the honeymoon. No more problems with the tooth. Thank goodness, because I don't know where the nearest dentist is around here. I'm going to have to look into that."

"Oh-h-ho-oh, man," Trudy was half groaning and half

laughing now. "That's how my friend Melinda got pregnant the fourth time. Antibiotics and birth control pills don't go together. Didn't anybody ever tell you that?"

Somewhere deep in my brain, a tiny little alarm bell sounded. I thought back to that day at the dentist. "No, Trudy, I remember the nurse asking me if I was on birth control pills. I'm sure they gave me something that wouldn't be a problem."

"But you just said you switched—after the hives."

"Well, I'm sure they gave me something *else* that wouldn't be a problem. The dentist isn't an idiot, you know." The answer sounded more combative than I meant it to. I wanted Trudy to stop the inquisition, already. Unwillingly, I began counting up weeks, trying to remember if, in all the chaos since the wedding . . .

"Listen, just pick up a home pregnancy test and make sure, all right? And don't do any painting or bug spraying or crawling around in closets until you know."

"Trudy, everything's fine. I *know* it's fine." My stomach clenched around the words, forcing a nervous little laugh.

"No, you don't. I can tell by the way you're saying it. Don't take any more birth control pills, either."

"Trudy, enough already! I'd better sign off. Nick's waking up."

"I mean it. Either you take care of this, or I'll tell Mom." She hung up the phone before I could argue, leaving me with that frightening ultimatum. In our family, *I'll tell Mom* was the death knell of every argument. Nothing, but nothing, was worse than that.

Trudy's threat hovered as Nick wandered in for breakfast. The more I tried to put it out of my mind, the more it nagged, like a fly that lingers because you keep swishing blindly at it rather than going after a fly swatter.

"We gonna go pick beans today!" Nick chirped, after scarfing his cereal. "We gonna go pick gween beans wif the lady."

I groaned. Of all the things he could have remembered about yesterday, he had to remember the thing about bean picking with the summer enrichment kids. Keren had mentioned it again when she'd shown up with Chrissy's posse of neighbors.

"Mrs. Zimmer," I corrected, trying to decide how to let Nick down easily.

"Wif Mrs. Zimmer!" he cheered, sliding from his booster chair and very carefully carrying his empty cereal bowl to the kitchen. Pulling his stool over to the counter, he climbed up to reach the sink, turned on the water, and informed me, "I washin' my bowl. You gotta go get dwessed." His eyes twinkled as he glanced back at me. "You can't go in yous jammies!"

How could I possibly tell him I'd changed my mind about visiting the summer enrichment kids?

I couldn't, of course. I wanted to be a promise keeper in his life, not a welcher.

"You're right." I gave him a big hug, and his little arms squeezed hard, warming me to the very depths of my soul. But even that joy came wrapped in a tissue paper layer of uncertainty. *Why isn't this enough?* I didn't even know who the question was for—my soul, my heart, God? Why, every time I thought I'd settled into this new life, did a whisper in the back of my mind tell me not to let my guard down? Was it this place, or was it just me? Was I afraid for our safety, or was I afraid of becoming *just* a wife and a mom? Was I worried that I would lose everything, or worried about losing my image of myself?

I pondered it as I dressed and then drove to town with Nick playing happily on my iPod in the backseat. What I wanted, I supposed, were concrete answers. I wanted someone to open a window into the future and say, *Look, there you are a year from now. And see, you're just fine.*

When we reached town, I parked my car in the shade of an alley behind Main Street. Nick jitterbugged with excitement as we walked around the building to where the kids were sitting in a circle on the sidewalk. The shade of an awning fell over them, shielding them from a summer sun that was intense, even at nine o'clock in the morning.

Keren smiled at us as we strolled up the sidewalk to the group. "Everyone, we have a guest with us today. This is Mrs. Everson and Nick. Can y'all say hi?"

The kids swiveled, and Nick hung back a little, clinging to my hand, momentarily overwhelmed. Tucking his chin and letting his blond curls fall over his eyes, he stopped walking. A bullet train of thoughts raced through my mind. *Maybe we shouldn't have come. Why is he being so shy? This isn't like him.* Nick was used to going to day care. What if his social skills were flagging already? What if playing by himself all the time, with only a dog to talk to, was ruining him . . .

I waved and smiled at the kids on Nick's behalf. "Hi, everybody!"

The sea of faces checked us out, wheels turning behind pairs of sparkly little eyes. Without even realizing it, I'd started cataloging the group, taking note of clothing that was dirty or tattered, hair that looked like it hadn't been combed or fixed or washed in a while, smiles with teeth that were decayed or covered with hideous silver crowns, skin mottled with bug bites, a child in what looked like pajama pants and a T-shirt that was dirty and didn't match. Her dark hair hung in a lopsided ponytail. She was scratching her head. I thought of lice. I looked at Nick's beautiful blond hair.

The little girl smiled a silver-crowned smile.

I thought of Nick's beautiful baby teeth. His perfect smile.

On the other side of the group, three little boys were sitting together, wearing name-brand clothes. Hair trimmed and combed. Faces washed. Legs not covered with scratched-and-healed bug bites.

I found myself steering Nick that way, stepping off the curb to circumvent the group as Keren tried to refocus their attention.

A little dark-haired girl in a wrinkled, washed-to-death sundress smiled at Nick and patted the sidewalk, her blue eyes curving upward in recognition. Her sandals were too small and her hair hung in uneven pigtails that looked like they'd been in for a couple days. I tried to decide whether I'd seen her before. She seemed to know Nick.

"Birdie, look up here at me, please," Keren admonished, and the little girl turned around again.

Birdie, the granddaughter of Len, the mentally slow man we'd seen in the convenience store our first morning in Moses Lake. I only remembered the name because it was so unusual, and because I wondered what sort of child would belong to such an unkempt man. I felt sorry for her without even knowing her.

Nick pulled away from me, his fingers slipping through mine, sweaty and sticky, so small. I wanted to hold on, to keep him close, to keep him away. He was gone in an instant, tucking himself into the space beside the little girl. She patted him gently on the back, smiling. If he noticed the bedraggled ponytails or ragged sundress, it didn't show. He smiled back. To him, every person he crossed paths with was a potential friend. I wished I could be as open as he was.

He didn't even look back when the kids hopped to their feet and lined up to follow Keren through the iron gates into a wide courtyard between the antique mall and the little bookstore. I walked through the gate behind the kids, already forgotten. Where a few minutes ago I'd been worrying about Nick's social skills, now his fluid friend-making hurt my feelings. He'd already left me for another girl. One closer to his own size.

Tears prickled, and I blinked hard. On some level, I knew I was having more of a reaction than made sense. Of course little kids liked other little kids. Getting all weepy about it was completely irrational. This morning's conversation with Trudy came to mind, though I'd been trying to block it out. Could all of this be some sort of hormonal insanity?

It was way too much to think about, and anyway, I was sure everything was okay . . . I was . . . pretty sure . . . wasn't I? Of course. Of course I was. My stomach had been solid as a rock—no sign of anything like morning sickness. In my family, morning sickness was legendary, so common that anytime one of my sisters mentioned stomach upset, my mother practically started knitting booties.

Once inside the garden, the kids took their plastic baskets and began carefully measuring and picking green beans, just as Keren had shown them. A bean-based disagreement erupted not far from me, and since Keren and her teenage helpers were otherwise occupied, I felt compelled to referee. Before I knew it, I'd been drawn completely into the wonder of watching kids harvest something they'd grown from seed. Keren's gardening program wasn't just a teaching tool, it was a tiny miracle.

In the sunlight and shadows of what could have just as easily been a forgotten space, I discovered something about those kids I'd earlier been judging based on their clothes, their hair, their grooming. They were beautiful—as beautiful as Nick, as much fun to spend time with, as filled with curiosity and a desire to see the wonder in everything around them.

Unlike Nick, so many of them were desperate for attention, hungry for hugs, anxious to hold hands, thrilled to have an adult to spend time with. It was, I realized, impossible not to feel good in the presence of these kids, not to feel good *about* them, not to want good for them.

A little boy named Sergio and I were soon fast friends. Sergio wasn't one of the kids in the name-brand clothes and expensive shoes. He wore jeans that were an inch too short, suede cowboy boots scuffed clean through on the toes, and a Vacation Bible School T-shirt he must have inherited from someone else, because according to the date, it was three years older than he was. He wanted me to come to his house and meet his grandma, who I gathered was raising him.

"Her's comin' pretty soon sometime," he said, after he'd asked whose mom I was, and I'd pointed out Nick. "My mama. The police gotted her. Sissy goed to her daddy house. She comin' for my birt-day, maybe tomorrow."

A lump rose in my throat. I pretended to be busy looking for beans on the climbers up high. I could feel the questions in those brown eyes as they watched me. I didn't have any answers. I didn't know what to say. "When is your birthday, Sergio?" I asked to shift the subject a bit. I picked a bean up high and dropped it into Sergio's little red basket. He smiled at it, and then at me.

"I dunno."

"Are you five?" I was guessing. Sergio seemed a bit older than Nick.

Sergio set down the basket and held up six fingers.

"Oh . . ." All I could think was that someone who's still counting on stubby little fingers shouldn't know about jail, sisters who have to go live with their fathers, and birthdays that come and go with promises unfulfilled. "That's really big." But in reality, he was so small. So very, very small.

"You come to my house!" he offered again, his sweet little mouth lifting into a smile. "You come . . . and you boy." He pointed at Nick, who was busy washing beans with Birdie, the two of them squatted down by the water pail, carefully scrubbing off the dirt. Birdie showed Nick how to open the pod. Clearly Nick had never seen the inside of a bean before.

Keren passed by and leaned over to explain the contents to them, then took Nick to a table by the wall, where bean plants were growing in Dixie cups all lined up in a row, names written on in magic marker.

"Sergio, did you grow a bean plant in one of those cups over there?" I asked, and Sergio couldn't wait to show me what he'd created all by himself.

With a little help from God.

Chapter 14

Throughout the morning in the garden, Sergio held fast to my hand, looking expectantly up at me. After a while, I had inherited another little fan. Sierra, a sandy-haired fourth-grader who was one of the older kids in the group. She let me know that she was writing a book, and I would now be in it. I told her I'd just discovered the joy of keeping a blog, so the two of us had something in common.

Somewhere in the conversation, I also concluded that, like Sergio, Sierra came from a family with issues. She had always lived in the country, but right now she was staying in town with someone she called "the foster lady." I gathered that this was not the first time Sierra had experienced a foster stay. She wanted to make sure I knew that none of that was her mother's fault. "Them stupid deputies come and got us," she informed me flatly. "My mama tried to get us away. We got in the car and drove off down to the river bottom, but they found us anyhow. Jerks." But she didn't say *jerks*. She used an off-color anatomy term that shouldn't be in any kid's vocabulary.

"I really don't like that word," I choked out, mimicking my sister Carol, who could discipline her brood without ever raising her voice. "It's not a good word, especially for a *smart* girl to use. Smart girls don't need to say things like that."

"'Kay." Sierra shrugged as if she'd heard it all before. "You gonna go to the church with us after this and have green beans? The lady gives us sheets to color, and we see how to cook the food." She stood on her toes, motioning for me to lean over so she could whisper in my ear. "They tell the little kids it's all stuff from the garden, but it ain't. There's too many of us for it all to come outta here." Sierra rolled a surreptitious glance at Sergio, then smiled a private smile, as in, *These kids are so dumb, but I've got it all figured out.*

I pretended to be surprised. "You're a smart cookie."

Sierra quirked a brow at me. "You talk funny. Where you from?"

"Washington, DC. We moved here a little over a month and a half ago."

Sergio grabbed my hand and tugged me sideways, trying to search under yet another bean plant that had already been plucked clean. "That your boy?" Sierra asked, giving Sergio a doubtful look. Sergio was dark eyed and dark skinned, probably Native American or Hispanic.

"No, that one over there." I pointed to Nick, who was on the other side of the courtyard, happily planting his very own seeds in a cup with the Binding Through Books sisters, who'd apparently shown up to volunteer for the day. Nick had been carefully avoiding me all morning, afraid that I might say something objectionable, like, *It's time to go home.*

Sierra smacked her lips apart, then motioned to Sergio again. "Oh . . . I thought maybe you took in kids, or somethin'. But that one over there looks like you."

"Nick is my stepson." I wasn't sure when I'd stop feeling

the need to explain that to people I'd just met. Mentions of family resemblance between Nick and me always brought an unwanted awkward feeling.

"Huh." Sierra shrugged. "I had a stepdad one time, but he was a jerk. My mama had to get her a restrainin' order to keep him off us, but then we moved in with Lenny. Lenny keeps lotsa guns and stuff. But Lenny got us in trouble with the CPS, so there you go." Flipping a hand in the air, she laughed a little.

I felt sick. I looked at Sierra, with her bright hazel eyes and long spindly legs that seemed to be already pressing into adulthood, and my throat burned. I thought about the things I knew at nine years old, about the world I lived in, about the words I understood. *What good are plants in a Dixie cup to her?* I thought. *What good is anything going to do?*

Keren called for the kids to line up, and I was glad.

"Come up to the church with us." Keren tapped my arm as she passed by. Watching her lead the crew through the gate and up the sidewalk, her voice a happy sing-song as she called out gardening vocabulary words, I couldn't help wondering how she could do this every day. Didn't these kids' stories, their words, their faces, their needs overwhelm her?

We arrived at Lakeshore Community Church sweaty, sticky, and tired. The cool air inside the meeting hall beside the old chapel felt like heaven. I held my hair off my neck and stood under a vent as the kids jostled for seats at folding tables. My Binding Through Books friends, Alice, Paula, and Cindy, and several grandmotherly-looking church volunteers helped the kids settle in. Then an elderly woman everyone called *Mama B* stood in the church kitchen behind the pass-through counter and began introducing the art of snapping beans.

Keren wandered back and forth behind the children, keeping them quiet and directing them as they began snapping their little bean piles. I wondered again at her thoughts. One thing I had learned in DC was that passions—good and bad—came from somewhere. Where did the passions of this enigmatic young woman come from? What brought her here every day to work with kids who had such an uphill battle ahead of them? She couldn't have been more than a year or two out of college. The slight uptilt in her voice when she finished sentences made her seem more like one of the teenage helpers than a teacher in charge of a class.

She stopped beside me after lunch was finished and the kids were busy coloring the recipe sheet. A wink and a smile made me feel like we were old friends. "Well, I think the day was a success for Nick," she observed.

"He had such a good time. Thanks for letting him come. We both enjoyed it, actually. Now I'll know what to do with the beans I bought at Walmart yesterday. I've never actually seen a green bean in the wild before."

Keren chuckled. "Well, one thing girls do learn in my family is how to cook. I can't remember one single day growing up that wasn't full of pots, pans, and dirty plates." Bracing her hands on her back, she stretched, for the first time seeming fatigued by all the morning's activities. "I used to dream about things like corn dogs and frozen pizza."

"Now, that I can do. You need to know how to cook frozen pizza or whip up a box of macaroni and cheese, I'm your girl. I did do all right on the peach pies, though, thanks to you. They're a little lopsided, but they look pretty good. There are more peaches on the tree, if you can use some."

She nodded, pausing as one of the kids brought a coloring project for her to see. After admiring the work and making a few suggestions, she grabbed chairs for the two of us, and we sat down by the wall. "I might have to take you up on that. James gets pretty burned out on eating the leftovers his mama sends home from lunch. He works for his folks in the dairy barns, so his mama takes care of the midday meal. There's usually something in the fridge when I get home at night. James has lost ten pounds in the two years since we got married, though." She paused again to admire student artwork. "I think my mother-in-law is afraid I'm trying to starve her boy to death, but really, James wants to drop some weight. It'll all be easier once we've got our own place." With a self-conscious glance at me, she added, "Not that James's parents aren't great and everything. They've been so good to us."

"That's all right, I get it." I nudged her with my elbow, which wasn't the sort of thing I normally would do. It was easy to be comfortable with Keren. "When things were looking a little iffy with the job here, my mother said we could move into her rumpus room. But as you can see, we're still in Texas."

Keren's wide smile dotted her cheeks with dimples. We chatted until it was time to take the kids outside to play in the park behind the church. After that, they would be loaded onto the bus, which would take them back to the school. From there, some would go home with parents, some would walk to a couple of foster homes nearby, and some would be ferried home on a summer school bus route.

Keren and I sat on a picnic table in the shade while the kids enjoyed the last few minutes of their day. Al pulled into the parking lot and honked, then came down the hill wagging a small paper bag in my direction. "There you are. Feedstore got your fox urine in."

"Well, there's a sentence you don't hear every day." I laughed. I'd been blogging about the squirrels in the attic for a while now. Al had suggested the fox-based brew as a guaranteed deterrent. Despite the inherent gross-out factor,

I was willing to try almost anything. The happy sound of squirrels partying in the attic at all hours gets old eventually.

Keren cast a quizzical look as Al took the bottle from the sack and tried to hand it to me. "Here's your Foxy Moxy."

I pulled my hands away. "I'm not touching that stuff. Seriously. Yuck. I'll make Daniel do it."

"Don't be such a *girl*." Al set the sack by my feet.

"I have my limits. They go right up to fox urine, and then stop."

Al scoffed, and the fox urine languished in the shade while the three of us watched the kids play. I couldn't wait to blog about Foxy Moxy and see what Josh, Kaylyn, and my sisters had to say about it. None of them would believe this one. Just a few months ago, I was working on The Hill, contributing in my small way to legislation that would affect millions of people, and now . . . fox urine. I'd have to take a photo of the bottle before Daniel opened it. I'd be happy to go my whole life and not know what the contents actually smelled like.

For the first time that day, Nick sought me out. His face gleamed with anticipation as he ran across the playground. He arrived at the picnic table out of breath, and presented me with a dandelion.

"It's a wing!" Nick pointed to the stem, which had been woven into a circle to form a ring. "Miss Alice and me maked it." He pointed to Alice Steele, who'd been stationed by the lakeshore along with Paula and Cindy to keep kids away from the water. "It's for my mommy!"

An unexpected burst of emotions pushed tears into my eyes. "It's beautiful. Thanks, Nick." Holding the tiny, fragile token in the palm of my hand, I touched the flower petals and felt everything else fall away. It didn't matter that there were squirrels in the attic, or that I'd lost Nick for almost three hours the day before, or that Daniel and I were still in a fight. For an instant, there was only Nick and me and that ring—a wild, growing thing that had sprouted in glorious color all on its own, developing unseen and almost unnoticed as the world passed by. Like the love I felt for Nick. For this boy. This son of mine.

"Put it on you finger. It's for my *mommy*," Nick said again, as if he wanted to make sure I knew.

Slipping the ring into place, I leaned over and kissed the top of his head. "I love it. I love it so much, Nick. More than anything," I whispered the words into the sweaty scents of dirt and green things, leftover shampoo and childhood. *I love you more than anything* was on the tip of my tongue, but before I could get it out, Nick was already gone, off to join the other kids again. Watching him skitter away, I felt the process of loving and parting and holding on and letting go that would be our future together, his and mine. In that moment, I understood so much about my mother that I never had before. I knew why she'd had such a hard time releasing me into the world. Allowing the last little bird to fly the nest. No wonder I had to travel to the other side of the globe to finally break free.

I felt the hot-cold moisture of a tear on my cheek, saw it fall past the dandelion ring and land on my knee.

"Geez, if it's that big a deal to you, I'll climb up in your attic and put the Foxy Moxy out myself. Don't cry about it," Al joked. Both she and Keren laughed, and I sniffle-laughed along.

"Wow, I wasn't ready for that," I admitted, swallowing hard and wiping my eyes. "That's the first time he's called me *mommy*, just on his own like that."

"Smart kid," Al assessed flatly.

Keren laid a hand on my back and rubbed gently, and

suddenly I felt as if there were no better place in the world to be than here. The conversation between us stilled, but the silence felt comfortable, relaxed. We sat side by side on the picnic table, enjoying the view and the kids' antics. My little friend, Sierra, had elected herself director of a freeze tag game. Confidently standing on one of the cement picnic benches, she barked out instructions, while Cindy, Alice, and Paula lined up the kids.

"She'll be president of the United States one of these days," Keren commented, then drew in a long breath and let it out slowly, her shoulders rising and then falling. "If she can just get past where she comes from."

"Well, this summer program is a start." Al's gaze scanned the group. "The more you can get these kids out of Chinquapin Peaks and show them a bigger world, the better. If they don't ever see a normal life, they'll never know how to make one. But it's got to be long-term and consistent— that's what the school board needs to understand. Spending a bunch of money to bring in some pro athlete to speak or some actor in to talk to them is great, but there has to be regular follow-up. The research conclusively proves that fact every time. It might look to the school board like we're just growing beans here, but the truth is that we're growing kids."

I glanced sideways at Al. *The research conclusively proves . . .* Those words didn't sound like Al at all. And was it my imagination, or had the Texas twang vanished for a few sentences? I had the impression, as had happened a few times before, that Al was not at all what she seemed to be, that something lay hidden beneath the façade of rusty pickup trucks and well-worn cowgirl clothes.

Her gaze cast my way, and I pretended to be watching the kids.

"We need to get this program funded for the full school year and into next year." Al's words came with a long, slow Texas drawl this time. "If you had a greenhouse, you could grow all through the winter."

Keren's shoulders sagged a little more. "There's no money for a greenhouse. The school just can't afford anything more, especially with all the state budget cuts. They're talking about not having the horticulture class in middle school at all next year, which would pretty much mean the supper garden program is finished. I'll either be teaching an elementary homeroom all day, or they'll just combine classes and I won't have a job at all."

"Well, we'll see about that." Al removed her cowboy hat, then dropped it on the table before using the crook of her elbow to swipe sweaty strands of intermingled brown and gray. "I'll have a few things to say to that school board before they start laying off good young teachers."

"James wants me to quit, anyway." Keren's expression was unusually glum, a wrinkle worrying her brow. "Really, everybody does—his family, my family. Everyone wants to know when we're going to start having babies. As soon as we got to our second anniversary, it's like we crossed some invisible line." She looked down at her hands, locking them together. "If the horticulture program gets cut, maybe it's God's way of saying it's time."

Self-consciously, I rubbed my stomach, thought of my conversation with Trudy, felt myself tumble into Keren's push-pull of career and family. For just an instant, I wanted to tell the two of them what Trudy had said, admit to the dilemma that had been cycling in the corner of my mind all day—similar to Keren's, but opposite. If, *heaven forbid*, I had to announce an accidental pregnancy so soon after an impromptu marriage and a cross-country move, my family would be calling the men in white coats. I had no idea what Daniel would say or how his parents would feel about it. And, on top of that, there was the mystery of Jack West and the question of whether we were really safe on the ranch at all.

It might just be God's way of saying it's time. . . . An accidental pregnancy for Daniel and me at this point couldn't be anyone's idea of a good plan.

"Or else your family needs to mind their own business," Al said to Keren, and I took that as confirmation. Trudy just needed to mind her own business. There wasn't any way I was pregnant.

"Maybe," Keren admitted. "I mean, I get where they're coming from. It's not like our family is old order conservative or anything. They were fine with me going to college when I got the scholarship, but I guess they just thought that after college I'd settle down and do the normal thing."

"You're young, Keren," I pointed out. "You've got years to think about having kids."

Keren nodded, squinting contemplatively at Chinquapin Peaks, far in the distance across the lake. "Do you ever just . . . have the feeling that God's using you right where you are?"

Al answered with a shrug that had a sense of *harrumph* to it.

I felt compelled to come up with an answer, but contemplating the mind of God was hardly my specialty. I looked down at my finger, thought about the dandelion ring. That first day in the rotunda, had God envisioned the dandelion ring . . . started a seed growing, far away on a lakeshore in Texas, so that the flower would be there when Nick was ready for it? Had He made sure that Alice would be here to aid Nick's tiny fingers in weaving the ring? Had He envisioned everything about this moment?

Did He plan things so intricately? Adjust the timing of seeds, and summer enrichment classes, and sisters visiting over books?

A school bus rumbled into the parking lot, and Keren jerked upright. "Oh my word! Line up, kids, the bus is here!" Cupping her hands around her mouth, she called the kids a second time.

"I'm Birdie's ride home today," Al said, as we stood up. "Sheila was going to keep her over at the Waterbird until Len could come get her, but Sheila's got a cold today, and she thought it'd be better if Birdie just went on home. No sense in her getting sick."

Al moved to the loosely forming kid line and extricated Birdie, who came out towing Nick by one hand. Before the rest of them could leave, I got a hug from Sergio and a high-five from Sierra. On her way up the hill, Sierra walked backward and pointed at me. "I'm gonna put you in my story!"

"I can't wait to read it," I called back.

The kids boarded the bus. Mama B, the Binding Through Books sisters, and the church ladies waved good-bye from the back steps, and the park grew strangely quiet as the helpers dispersed to their cars. Birdie and Nick crouched down together, watching an inchworm move across the cement footing of a picnic table.

"You ever been up in Chinquapin Peaks?" Al leaned over to pick up a candy wrapper that had dropped from one of the kids' backpacks.

"I really haven't been anywhere but the hardware store, the house, the Waterbird, and the Walmart in Gnadenfeld," I admitted.

Al nodded toward the parking lot. "Come ride along with us. You'll see some things." It was more of a command than a request. Al wheeled an arm as she walked up the hill. "C'mon,

Birdie, let's load up." She didn't check to see if I was following; she just assumed I was.

Grabbing Nick's backpack and my bag of Foxy Moxy, I started after her. I knew enough about Al to know that if she wanted me to go to Chinquapin Peaks with her, there was a reason.

*You can't cross the sea merely by standing
and staring at the water.*

—Rabindranath Tagore
(Left by Danny and Elaine, racing sailboats in the rain)

Chapter 15

I had a feeling that Nick would be asleep before we made it out of town, and he was. Birdie soon joined him, and Al and I drove along in silence awhile. We traveled several miles along the road that paralleled the river, then we turned off, then turned again and again, weaving our way past hills, trees, and small ranches.

As we drove, the pavement dissolved into gravel and the homes became few. Gravel melted into narrower gravel, smooth surfaces becoming pockmarked trails that wound lazily up steep slopes and into rocky valleys where clearwater creeks cascaded over beds of loose limestone. In the backseat, the sleeping kids bobbed back and forth as the truck bounced over chuckholes and rattled across miniature canyons left behind by rushing water.

"Is this the *normal* way of getting up here?" I asked after we'd driven thirty minutes or so. I knew it must be. People did live up here. While the foothills had been dotted with ranches where cattle and goats dozed in the shade, up here the signs of human habitation were more hardscrabble—aging trailer homes with old tires holding tarps over the roofs, rusting school buses converted into dwellings, ancient camp trailers that were obviously being used as permanent residences, tiny homes with peeling paint, leaning front porches, and the carcasses of old cars half buried in the weeds. In small lots scratched from cedar and scrub brush, skinny horses, goats, and cows searched in vain for edibles. Dangerous-looking dogs chased the truck or barked from behind ragtag yard fences made from shipping pallets and road signs.

"This is the way." Al's answer was flat, matter of fact. "The meth boilers and the pot farmers don't live up here for nothing. It's remote. They like it that way." We topped a hill, and she pointed out the window, where the view stretched for miles. In the distance, Moses Lake shimmered cool and peaceful, like a spill of glitter at the edge of fabric tumbling forth in shades of green and gray.

"There's some beautiful country up here, too." Al's voice seemed far away for a moment. "And plenty of good people, just doing the best they can with what they've got. Like Birdie's grandpa. He's a veteran, a good guy, suffered head trauma in Vietnam, so he's limited somewhat, but he's working hard to raise that little girl. Birdie's mother dropped her on Len's doorstep about a year ago, and now the mom is in prison on a meth conviction, among other things. She won't be coming back anytime soon. If it weren't for Len, Birdie would be in foster care. There are a lot of kids up here with stories like that."

"Wow," I sighed, still taking in the view. It seemed so serene, yet the kids I'd met today and the things I'd learned made it clear that for all the beauty here, an ugly reality hid also.

"One of the worst things is the access in this area, really. Like with Len's place—it's so far back in the hills, the school bus can't even get there when the roads are bad and the low-water crossings flood. On top of the other strikes against them, kids in Chinquapin Peaks miss a lot of school, partly because they can't get there. The school has been begging the county commission to spend money on the roads up here for years. The people in charge always make excuses to commit funds on the other side of the lake where there's already money, if you know what I mean. Blaine Underhill from the Ranch House Bank just got elected to the county commission, though, and he's making some headway against the old guard." Pausing, she pointed a finger at me. "I should introduce you to his wife, Heather, come to think of it. She's a city girl, like you. You two would enjoy each other. You know that big white house on the edge of town, the one with the Harmony Shores sign at the gate?"

I nodded. I had noticed the place. It was beautiful, a stately icon of the bygone era of southern belles and two-story porches with tall white pillars.

"They've refitted that into a bed-and-breakfast. Good people. Heather commutes to Dallas some for her architecture business. I'll find out her work schedule and get you two together."

"Thanks." Sometimes I wondered if I would have survived this long here, had Al not taken me under her wing. Other times, I couldn't imagine why she wanted to bother. I had to seem like such a nuisance, always needing something, and with no skills to contribute to the relationship, unless Al ever happened to need someone who had experience writing congressional legislation. Not very likely. Still, I had the underlying feeling that Al was interested in me for a reason, but I couldn't imagine what it might be.

"Not a problem." Al turned off the road into what looked like a wagon track winding off into a field. Tall grass scraped the undercarriage of the truck as we passed, and branches squealed across the windows like fingernails on a blackboard. "Anybody who has to put up with that sorry so-and-so you work for deserves a little extra help."

As usual, I didn't answer. The animosity between Al and Jack West was legendary around town. They were not good neighbors. Al only came to my house when I knew Daniel and Jack would be gone for the day, which was just about every day, so Al and I had plenty of time to work.

Birdie's house, when it came into view, seemed pretty typical of what I'd seen so far in Chinquapin Peaks, although it was in better shape. The small, square home listed slightly to one side, but the roof was new, the porch posts were parallel, and the place had a fresh coat of paint. Ruffled curtains hung inside the paint-spattered windows, giving the place a homey touch.

A mule brayed from a corral as we rolled to a stop, and Birdie's grandpa appeared in the barn doorway. I remembered him from my first day in Moses Lake, when Pop Dorsey in the Waterbird store had suggested that I hire Len to help with construction projects in our house. I'd been mortified at the time. Now, here I was, rolling up to his farm in a pickup truck. Who would have thought?

Today he was wearing overalls with what looked like blood smeared on the front. My skin crawled, and I gaped in complete revulsion. That really was blood, and it was wet . . .

Al opened her door and stepped out. Didn't she see the blood? I stayed where I was. The man was carrying . . . a knife. The knife had blood on it, too. I smiled and tried to look friendly, but I was inclined to do my visiting from inside the truck.

In the backseat, Birdie and Nick woke up. She was already wiggling out of her seat belt when Al opened the door beside her.

"I ubb-been ubb-butcherin' up hogs," I heard Len say. "I udd-don't s-s-smell too ugg-good. S-sorry."

Shuddering, I pressed back against the seat, staring at the knife. *Butchering hogs?* My stomach lurched and I was uncharacteristically lightheaded. Behind me, Birdie wrestled with Nick's seat belt, trying to help him out of his booster. She was telling Nick he could have a ride on the mule.

"No. No-no." I swiveled around to lay the Mommy-panic-hand over Nick's buckle. "We're not staying, sweetie. We have to go home now."

Nick's bottom lip jutted out. "I wanna go see Birdie's haw-see!"

"I can ugg-get 'im real f-f-fast." Len's bushy eyebrows lifted over his gray eyes, and he motioned amiably toward the corral, the knife flashing in the sunlight. "He's a ugg-good m-mule." The words came with a reassuring smile, flecks of tobacco dotting his teeth.

My head swirled like a car on the Tilt-A-Whirl, the sights and smells of the place overtaking me in a sudden assault. I saw stars. "I'm . . . I'm sure he is. Thank you, that's really kind of you, but . . ."

"Oh, for heaven's sake, it'll only take a minute." Al flicked a look of appraisal my way, and beyond the swirl of panic, I realized this was a test, and if I didn't step up, I would be lumped into a certain category. *Who are you, really?* Al's look asked.

Who are you, really? The question penetrated, echoed, demanded an answer. It nipped at me in ways I wasn't prepared for, pinched in places I didn't like. Was I really so entrenched in the world I'd been raised in, so set in my ways that I couldn't look beyond the surface of another person and see a human being? Was I that shallow? Was I The Frontier Woman, or wasn't I?

I had worked in downtown DC and shopped in fish markets in Asia. Was I really afraid of a little hog butcherin'?

Yes, actually.

And there was Nick to consider. This place looked so . . . *unsanitary.*

The word made me think of my mother. My mom who, as much as I loved her, wanted me to live and die within the confines of an upscale burb, preferably no farther than sixty miles from where I'd been raised. Hadn't I spent my entire life trying to break free of that mold? Maybe I wasn't as far from it as I thought. Everything in me wanted to stuff Nick back into the seat belt and speed away from this place, tell him he couldn't be friends with Birdie because she wasn't our sort.

Something strange happened to me as I sat there in Al's truck with Birdie, Nick, Len, and Al watching me. A barricade fell. A hard place cracked open. These were only people. People living in a different way than I did, but trying to be kind, to offer hospitality. "Sure. Sure, okay. I guess we have a minute."

In the backseat Birdie and Nick squealed gleefully, and outside, Len nodded at me, seeming pleased. "We'll be uff-fast," he said, then was off to get the mule. On the way, he stopped at a water pump near the barn, washed the blood from his hands, and deposited the knife.

For some reason, I thought of a tapestry in the little white church where Daniel and I had married. Jesus, gathered with a crowd of listeners, some wealthy, some in rags. All sizes, all ages, all colors, all worthy of His presence, of His attention and efforts. Why should I be any different? Why were some people worthy of my attention and not others? Why was I so afraid?

Could I change? Could today be the start of a kinder, gentler me, with my eyes and hands open to new people and new adventures?

This was what The Frontier Woman would do. She would experience the whole thing and take pictures.

So, I did.

We ended up staying for more than a quick mule ride. I even climbed onto the mule and clung to the saddle, laughing while Len led me around the barnyard. Al took photos with her phone. Meanwhile, Nick also experienced the tractor, held a fluffy yellow chick in his hands, played in Birdie's tree fort, and helped pick tomatoes in the garden where Len grew produce to sell. He ended his tour in Birdie's bedroom, where her toys were stored in a little bookshelf next to an antique iron bed that took up most of the room. Inside, the house was small but freshly painted. The furniture was old but clean, and the tiny kitchen was stocked with home-canned goods. A game of Candy Land, in progress, had been left open on the coffee table, and Birdie's drawings of herself were pinned to the refrigerator, as well as several of the walls—stick figures fishing, walking in the woods, picking flowers, flying a kite. The evidence of a happy home, a child who was loved.

I left with all the reference points in my mind slowly shifting. In DC, where upscale families had everything money could buy, I'd known plenty of privileged kids who needed that kind of undivided attention but didn't get it because their parents were busy with other things. Growing up, I'd been surrounded by families who had everything . . . but time for one another. Even though my mother's level of borderline-obsessive involvement in our lives had practically driven me crazy, I'd always known that we were the lucky ones. I'd probably never told her that. Sometimes you don't appreciate the things your parents have done for you until you're a parent yourself. I wanted Nick to have what we'd had—what Birdie had.

Nick . . . and a new baby? I laid a hand over my stomach as the truck bounced along on the road home. I pondered the possibility, then pushed it to the back of my mind. Now just wasn't the time for a baby. Daniel and I were in such a mess here. We still had so much to learn about each other, so much to work out. I did want a baby someday, but later. Much later. We weren't ready yet. Just yesterday, I'd lost track of the one child we already had, and at present, Daniel and I weren't even speaking. So far, we had no resolution on the issue of work hours.

Not exactly ideal conditions for, *Guess what, honey?*

But what if . . .

"You're quiet all of a sudden." Al's comment broke into my thoughts.

"Just enjoying the view, really," I answered as we topped a small peak. Below, the river wound through hills like a thin blue thread, spilling into the lake downstream.

"Something to see," Al agreed, and we drove on without talking. For once, I appreciated Al's penchant for silence. When we neared the edge of Moses Lake, she slowed before we really needed to, as if she were trying to prolong the ride. "I've got some time tomorrow, if you want to tackle that last closet."

I thought of dust, paint fumes, germs, mouse droppings . . . babies. "Oh, I . . . I can't tomorrow. I . . ." I tried to come up with something other than, *My sister made me promise not to, because she thinks I'm pregnant. Isn't that ridiculous?* "I want to write something up for the blog about Keren's supper garden program. Some of my friends in DC have deep pockets, or they know people who do. I thought if I went back to the summer enrichment class tomorrow and took some pictures . . . I don't know, I thought I might be able to help find some funding. If I do a good write-up on the blog, I can send out emails and point some of my parents' friends to it, too. Quite a few of them could pop for a whole greenhouse and not even think twice about it. I know Nick's going to wake up and want to go to the class tomorrow, too. He really liked it."

Al looked away, and I sensed something. Disappointment, maybe. I wondered sometimes how Al felt about her life, if she was happy being by herself with all those animals. The few times I'd tried to ferret out details about her past, about whether she'd ever been married or had a family, I hadn't learned much. Once, she'd mentioned that a French guy she dated in college had introduced her to polo, and for a while she'd been pretty serious about the sport. Polo didn't seem like Al at all, but I suspected there had been a different Al at some time. I wondered how she'd ended up here, alone, living on this land that had been passed down through her family.

"Daniel working tonight?" she asked.

"I'm sure he is. He's never home for dinner, unless Jack's out of town." Given the way Daniel and I had left things, he probably wouldn't go out of his way to hurry back tonight, either.

Al nodded, and surprisingly, she refrained from kibitzing about Jack. Complaints about Jack had bonded Al and me like glue. Jack was as lousy a neighbor as he was a boss. He'd actually taken legal action against Al over a fence that had been in place for forty years. Al had won the dispute. Now they liked each other even less.

"Might as well stop off for a burger at the Waterbird, then," she suggested.

Nick, who'd been busy in the backseat playing with turkey feathers and fossils Len had given him, tuned in and repeated, "The Water-burb? I wanna some fwies and a candy!" Nick never missed a chance to visit the Waterbird and collect a free sucker from Pop Dorsey. He'd also become attached to the collection of old men who hung around playing dominos, drinking coffee, and talking about fishing.

"Sure, that sounds good." The thought of going home to another long, quiet evening on rat patrol wasn't all that tempting, really. The vermin problem in the house was better than it used to be, but we hadn't obliterated it yet and wouldn't until we'd finished the last closet. We couldn't finish the closets until I made good on the promise I'd given Trudy.

The ancient, flickering sign on the front of Hall's Pharmacy caught my eye. "You know what, drop me at my car, and I'll meet you over there. I need to grab something in the pharmacy. Nick can just ride to the Waterbird with you, if that's okay." I held my breath, hoping Al wouldn't suddenly remember that she needed something in the pharmacy, too. I didn't even want Nick with me for this little purchase. He watched too many TV commercials. I could picture the two of us in the female aisle, Nick calling out, *Two lines pwegnant, one lines not!*

"Sure, no problem." Al steered toward the curb and let me out at Hall's. Like a spy on a clandestine mission, I waited for her to round the corner, pretending to have been drawn in by a rack of tourist magazines out front. Inside the pharmacy, I did my business as quickly as I could, thankful that Chrissy worked at the pharmacy in Gnadenfeld, not this one.

The elderly woman behind the counter smiled at me as she picked up the test and turned it slowly over and over and over in her hands, looking for the price tag. She leaned toward the microphone for the store PA.

"It's thirteen ninety-five," I blurted, then pulled out a twenty and shoved it at her. *Keep the change. Really. Just put that thing in a sack. Now.*

She opened a sack, then paused and looked up as the Binding Through Books sisters came in the front door. I shifted impatiently, glancing at the box, watching it disappear slowly into the bag. The minute she slid it my way, I grabbed the sack and shoved it under my arm like a man forced to buy feminine products for a wife who's home sick.

"Well, hey!" Paula greeted me. I thought she gave the bag a curious look, but maybe I was just paranoid. "How about that little blurb about *The Frontier Woman* on the *Woman's Day* Web site? That was pretty neat."

"Now I feel like I've had somebody famous in my lake house," Alice added. "We might have to bronze your lawn chair." She nudged Cindy, and the two of them giggled, the way sisters do when they get each other's jokes.

"We'll add a little plaque." Cindy drew an imaginary frame with her fingers. "*The Frontier Woman sat here.* We can sell tickets to see it—help pay for renovations on the lake house."

They giggled again, and I laughed with them. "I don't think we're quite to that point yet, but the magazine coverage did bring in a bunch of new followers on the blog. It was pretty exciting. I thought my techie friends were going to pop a cork. I'm hoping I can parlay that into some support for the supper garden program."

"That's a great idea. Just remember us one of these days when you're on *Good Morning America* talking about your adventures." Alice winked. "Tell them you need three extra tickets to New York. We'll stand out front and hold a *We Love the Frontier Woman* sign. We can tell everyone we knew you before you were The Frontier Woman. We loved the story about the cattle roundup, by the way. And the one about making goat's milk soap. I never knew how the pioneers did it, or that they put yucca in the soap. That was interesting."

Paula nodded, jumping into the conversation. "We look forward to seeing what The Frontier Woman's doing every morning. Now, instead of just talking about books, we talk about what you're doing. We're your groupies."

"Keep it up," Cindy added, and for a moment their enthusiasm was a little overwhelming. I'd never imagined, the night I wrote that first story about this wild, off-the-map life of mine, that anything like this would happen. I had actual groupies. How cool.

"I will, thanks."

The sisters and I parted ways, and I hurried to my vehicle in the alley. Safely inside, I tucked my package beneath the seat where Nick wouldn't ask what it was. Throughout dinner at the Waterbird, a little visit on the dock with Nick's favorite crew of fishermen, and then the drive home, I felt the presence of the pregnancy test. Contraband, right behind my feet. The Waterbird burger I'd nibbled on during dinner began churning in my stomach as we turned into the driveway.

Ten minutes. In ten minutes, I could know for sure, put this fear to rest. As soon as we were in the house, I'd give Nick a quick bath, settle him in bed with his night-night book, grab my secret package from the pharmacy, and slip off by myself . . .

But Daniel's ranch vehicle was waiting by the yard fence when we drove up. The lights were on in the house. I had the momentary thought that Trudy had called him about her suspicions—that she'd ratted me out. It was silly, of course. Trudy wouldn't do that.

Tucking the package and my phone into my purse, I zipped it shut, my mind hurrying ahead as I wrestled with the sticky buckle over Nick's lap. What was Daniel doing home? Was something wrong?

Scenarios spun to life. I imagined walking in, hearing Daniel say, *He fired me today,* or *I've had enough, I quit. I'm not doing this anymore.*

I imagined, *This thing, us, it isn't working out, Mal. We jumped into it too fast. . . .*

Stop, I told myself. *Stop already. You're being ridiculous.*

But when I opened the door, Daniel was striding across the kitchen toward it. He looked strangely wide-eyed and wild-haired, edgy and frazzled.

"Daddy!" Nick cheered. Daniel collapsed to his knees and scooped Nick up, his arms wrapping around so that Nick's tiny body disappeared into Daniel's.

"Hey, buddy." Daniel's voice was thin and choked. His lips pressed together, holding back some emotion. His lashes brushed his cheeks momentarily.

"What's wrong?" My mind conjured up more scenarios— death in the family, sudden world crisis, a call from back home. Cancer, heart attack, tragedy. Something must have happened for Daniel to be waiting for us in such a wild state, and for him to grab Nick and hang on as if the world were coming to an end. "Daniel, what's wrong?"

"Where have you guys *been*?"

"What?" I deposited my keys into my purse, heard them land against the pharmacy bag before I closed the zipper again. Most of the time lately, Daniel didn't have a clue where Nick and I were, nor did it seem to bother him. If Nick and I had plans of our own—house projects with Al, shopping in Gnadenfeld, or spending time down at the lakeshore with Chrissy and McKenna, it took the pressure off Daniel. He was free to be wrapped up with Jack and his work.

Rubbing my hands up and down my arms, I tried to smooth away the uneasiness. "I took Nick to the summer enrichment class in town today, then we rode with Al way up into Chinquapin Peaks to drive one of the kids home—you wouldn't believe that place, by the way—and after that, we had supper with Al at the Waterbird and did a little fishing with the Docksiders. Why? Is everything okay? You look like . . . well, I don't know . . . like someone just held you up at gunpoint or something."

Nick started to wiggle, and Daniel squeezed him into another hug before letting him shimmy down and trot away. Daniel faced me with his hands on his hips. "For heaven's sake, Mal, I've been trying to call you for hours. I thought something had happened to you . . . or Nick." He motioned to a phone book open on the counter. "When it got later and later in the evening, I started calling hospitals. I called Al's house and Keren's. She said you and Nick should have been headed home hours ago. I drove back and forth to town, looking for your car. I went down to the shore to make sure you weren't there. I've been going out of my mind." He flipped a hand toward the counter, in a motion that somehow reminded me of my mother.

My instant reaction was to get indignant, to say something like, *Well, welcome to my world. We sit here and wait for you every single day. We never know where you are. Half the time I call you, and you don't pick up the phone. . . .*

His frenzied gaze met mine, and I looked into his eyes, those soft, beautiful eyes, and the fire in my belly went to mush and spawned little butterflies. "You were looking for us?" The words came in a soft coo, tremulous and tender. I set my purse on the counter, thinking that I wanted to slip into the strong, warm spot that Nick had just vacated. The oven was hot when my hand brushed it. "Why is the oven on?"

Daniel's shoulders stiffened again, and he threaded his arms. "I made supper for you. I've been trying to keep it warm all this time, but you never came."

The butterflies inside me lined up and did a Disney-movie dance. I was twitterpated. "That's so sweet." Taking a step toward him, I added a little *I'm sorry* pout lip.

"Oh *no. No, no, no* . . ." He kept his arms crossed, barricaded. "You are not forgiven. You took at least two years off my life tonight."

"I love you." I added the goo-goo eyes. "My car was there in town, but it was parked around back in the alley all day. I had my phone plugged into my car charger and I forgot about it. I'm sorry we scared you." The man of steel was about to crumble, I could tell. "We were at the Waterbird later, but you must have come back home by then."

"You make me crazy, woman." But he was unlocking those big, strong arms, reaching for me.

"You make me crazy, too." Slipping into that space that I craved, I stood on my toes for a kiss, whispered against his lips the words that my mother had advised me should always come shortly after an argument, "I'm really sorry. Forgive me?"

"You're still in trouble," he whispered back, then kissed me fiercely.

We made out in the kitchen like a couple of teenagers until we heard Nick pushing one of his toy cars across the icky yellow carpet in the dining room. When Daniel released me, I was on fire from head to toe. I fanned my face as Nick crawled through the kitchen, making motor sounds and pretending he was Al, driving to Chinquapin Peaks to pick up a mule.

Turning off the oven, Daniel poured coffee for us, and we sat on the porch swing, enjoying the night breeze and gazing at the stars while Nick and I told the story of the day. By the time we were finished, Nick was more than ready for a bath and bedtime. Daniel did the honors while I cleaned up what was left of dinner—chicken, rice, baked potatoes, and the green beans I'd bought the day before. It hadn't even occurred to me that Daniel might know how to cook them.

After Nick was in bed, we took a blanket outside and lay under the stars, just talking. Nick and I had been so busy telling the story of our day, I hadn't asked Daniel about his. "So, how in the world did you manage to get away from Jack early enough to actually cook dinner?"

"Jack went to Houston. He got a phone call and took off in a hurry this afternoon. Something about his son."

"His son?" I repeated incredulously. According to Chrissy, Jack and his son didn't speak, and if Chrissy said it, it must be true.

Daniel's shoulder shifted under my head. "I didn't ask him too much about it. He wasn't in the mood."

"So I guess you didn't talk to him about coming up with some reasonable parameters for work hours." As soon as the words were out, I wished I'd left them for later. This night, this moment, was so perfect, so peaceful. We needed peace more than anything. We needed each other. Like this.

"No, not yet." His weariness was unmistakable. He was tired of being the pulling rope in a tug-of-war between work and home. "Jack's just finally starting to turn me loose with his research in the lab. Now isn't the time to rock the boat. Just let me do this my way, okay?"

"Okay." The word faded off into the night as our fingers intertwined on the blanket. Overhead, the bling had been rolled out, the stars glittering against a carpet of black. "It's just that you're brilliant, talented, and valuable, and he should acknowledge that."

Daniel turned over and propped himself on an elbow. "You forgot *handsome.*"

"And handsome," I giggled, even though I knew he was only trying to distract me from complaining about the tyrannical work hours. "Really handsome." He was. Really.

He kissed me as the moon waxed overhead and the crickets chirred. A whippoorwill lent its voice to the night music, and horses milled in the pasture down the hill, making soft sounds of satisfaction. In that moment, everything seemed perfect, as if the world were no bigger than the two of us. In one of Kaylyn's romance novels, it would have been the scene in which the heroine knew she could never belong to anyone but him.

By the time we went inside, I was logy and sated, filled with a contentment that was beyond understanding.

We slipped into bed and into the magic of a dance that was both passionate and sweet. I fell asleep in my husband's arms for once without a worry in my mind, my heart running over with a rightness so complete that I could only understand it as a moment of grace. Where could such love have come from, if not from God? Who else could have concocted this crazy plan for me, this unlikely life? If God did have a place for me in the world, this was it. With Daniel.

Thank you, the prayer whispered in my mind as Daniel's breaths lengthened. *Thank you for all of this. For everything about this day. For kids in the garden. For Sergio and Sierra. For the view from Chinquapin Peaks, for Birdie, Len, and the mule. For Nick's smile. For the dinner I missed. For my gypsy king . . .*

I fell asleep with the list still scrolling by.

In the early morning hours, I dreamed that the kids from the supper garden were here on the ranch, helping to pick vegetables in one of Jack's test plots. It seemed so real that, as I was drifting to consciousness, my mind clung to the idea, turned it over and looked at it from a few angles. Sitting on the porch last night, Daniel and I had talked about whether some of the families in Chinquapin Peaks could be hired to farm test plots with West Research seed. The land up there was certainly rugged enough.

The scent of fresh coffee tickled my senses, and I felt Daniel's weight atop the quilt. When I opened my eyes, he was resting against the headboard with a cup of coffee in his hand, watching me. Outside, the first rays of morning blushed the sky, outlining long, wispy clouds in bands of gold.

I had the strangest feeling that he had been there awhile, watching me sleep. "You're awake early." He took a sip of coffee and smiled again, his lips moist.

"You're here," I whispered through the grogginess. One thing I really loved about life in Moses Lake—I didn't have to get up at five a.m. to shower and rush off to catch mass transit.

"Going in a little late this morning." He winked at me, and the rush of misty-morning love was overwhelming. Setting his cup on the nightstand, he leaned over to kiss the top of my rumpled head, then swung his legs off the edge of the bed and stood up. I noted with disappointment that he was already dressed in jeans and a polo shirt, ready for work. He'd be heading out soon.

"Don't get up. I'll grab a cup of coffee for you." On his way around the bed, he leaned over and kissed me again, whispering against my lips, "I like you there, looking all . . . snuggly."

Sighing, I watched him go, then braced the pillows and pulled the quilt up high. I felt all snuggly. I did.

What a perfectly wonderful morning.

Closing my eyes, I listened to the sounds of him in the

kitchen—the soft clatter of cups, the tap of the coffeepot against the base, the ring of the stirring spoon.

An electronic beep disturbed my reverie. My cell phone was dying again. Apparently the battery was going bad. I'd have to remember to order a new one. Even though reception was sometimes spotty, there was no way I wanted to be on these rural roads without a phone.

Daniel dropped something on the floor, grumbled about it. I wondered if he'd spilled the coffee. I considered getting up and going to the kitchen, but decided against it. If I got out of bed, the magic would be gone, the morning underway. If I waited here, hopefully he would come back once he'd cleaned up the mess, whatever it was.

When he crossed the yellow carpet, his steps sounded hurried. Disappointment plucked a note inside me. His mind was already rushing off to work; I could feel it without even seeing him. He stopped in the doorway, leaned against it. I prepared for him to say something like, *Jack just texted. I'd better get going, Mal.*

But when I turned to look at him, his face was strangely ashen. I wondered if some heretofore unknown horror in the kitchen—like a rattlesnake, or something—had caused the commotion in there.

"Daniel? What's the ma . . ." And then I saw what he was holding. The sack from the pharmacy, the words *Pregnancy Test* clearly visible through the filmy plastic.

The series of events clicked together in my mind—the phone, my purse, something toppling on the floor. In all the excitement last night, I'd left my purse sitting on the counter.

"What's . . . what's this?" His gaze didn't meet mine. Instead, he stared into the room, unfocused, shellshocked.

I swallowed hard. *Be calm. Be calm. Let him know it's no big deal.* "Nothing. Trudy's just worried—something about antibiotics and birth control pills, and she threatened to sic Mom on me if I didn't make *sure* I wasn't pregnant. She's all uptight about it because I'm doing so much painting and spraying and stuff."

"But you don't think you are . . ."

"No, of course not. Really. It's fine."

"It's just that . . . the timing, you know?"

"I know." I couldn't disagree at all, but I wished he would stop looking at me like that—like a Mack truck was headed his way at a high rate of speed and his feet were stuck in heavy tar. "Don't worry about it, okay?"

"Well . . . well, maybe you should . . ." He held up the sack, rolled his eyes toward it, but didn't quite look.

"I'll do it later today." I wasn't ready to face the idea quite yet. I needed a little time to work up to it.

He set the test on the nightstand like a hot potato. "You're supposed to . . . do it . . . first thing in the morning." He actually blushed along with the words, but the color quickly drained away.

In a crush of thoughts, it occurred to me that he had been through this before—a wife, a pregnancy test, an unwanted result. A marriage toppled and left in pieces.

I couldn't let him know how nervous, how uncertain I was. I couldn't let him think that, if the test came up positive, we would fall apart. "Oh, sure. Of course. No big deal." I took the bag and headed to the bathroom, shut the door and leaned against it as I opened the package with trembling hands.

The instructions quivered so much I could barely read them. Sweat broke over my skin and dripped down my back. Outside the door, Daniel was pacing the room, his footfalls going back and forth, back and forth.

I wanted to scream at him to stop it. To just leave me alone a minute. But there was no point. There was no point in doing anything but finding out for sure. Waiting wouldn't change the truth.

And in ninety seconds, I knew the truth.

We.

Were.

Pregnant.

A person often meets his destiny on the
road he took to avoid it.

—Jean de La Fontaine
(Left by Reverend Hay, whose mother thought he'd be a doctor one day)

Chapter 16

Two weeks of carefully stepping around the elephant in the room and several home pregnancy tests later, we'd finally accepted the fact that we were on our way to being a family of four, planned or not. Perhaps *accepted* was a fairly strong word. I had ceased all painting and handling of bug sprays. Daniel had taken over the catch-and-release mouse eradication program, and after going to the summer enrichment program and meeting Len a few more times, I had made arrangements to hire him to finish lining the closets and to caulk around any other pipes or wiring where vermin might be getting in. Daniel had promised to talk to Jack about the issue of paying for the labor and outfitting the house with new carpet. Daniel and I didn't need to be spending the money, especially with a new baby on the way, and I couldn't imagine laying a helpless, vulnerable new baby on the icky yellow carpet.

In truth, I couldn't imagine a new baby at all. Over and over, I stood in front of the mirror alone, ran a hand over my stomach, tried to grasp the concept of cells dividing and multiplying, each uniquely designed, pre-ordained to create a brand-new human being, a tiny person. A combination of Daniel and me. How could that possibly be happening without my knowing it, without my feeling something? Other than strange dreams and wild emotional swings, wilder now that I knew what was happening, I had absolutely no symptoms of pregnancy.

I wondered if it was some sort of indicator—proof that I lacked the essential maternal instinct required to forge the bond between mother and child.

I couldn't share those feelings with Daniel. I was afraid of what he would think of me. While he seemed to be slowly settling into the idea—slipping his arms around me from time to time, cupping his hands over my midsection and saying, "It'll be all right, you know. Babies don't have to be planned to be wonderful."

"I know," I told him each time, leaning into him, trying to picture the future.

But all I felt was fear. I'd been barely holding it together when there was no second child to contemplate. The worst thing was, I couldn't talk to anyone about it, not even Trudy.

Especially not Trudy. I hadn't even figured out how I was going to tell her. How would she feel—after everything she'd been though trying to have a baby, with all her hopes tied up in the most recent in vitro—when I suddenly turned up pregnant and wasn't happy about it?

What would my mother say? What would everyone say—Kaylyn, Josh, all the former coworkers who followed the blog and still thought I was a little nuts for coming here? My sisters . . . Daniel's family . . .

How in the world would we tell everyone?

I practiced writing blog posts and emails about our unexpected, expected arrival. I deleted every one, caused them to disappear into the ether, like vapor.

Daniel harassed me about scheduling a prenatal doctor's appointment. I made excuses not to do it—too busy helping Keren with the supper garden program, it was goat-shearing season at Al's place and I wanted to take plenty of photos for *The Frontier Woman*, Jack's ranch hands were sorting cattle again at the headquarters, Keren's summer kids were inviting their families to a garden tour on Saturday. If I could do a good enough job on the photography, maybe I would try my hand at writing a magazine article about the supper gardens. So far, I'd had good response on the blog. Some donations had come in, and my emails to family friends with deep pockets had produced interest. My dad had even offered to talk to a few people.

Now just wasn't the time to break the baby news. Telling everyone seemed like such a huge step, such a game changer. I'd just started finding ways to get myself out of the house, to build new friendships, new interests. I was looking forward to letting Nick start preschool in the fall, to having more time for *The Frontier Woman* and for helping Keren write grant proposals. Plus, there was still the whole question of Daniel's job here and Jack West's sordid history.

It was all so much to assimilate. I felt as if we'd failed to clear one hurdle before jumping another. And then I felt guilty for even thinking that way. A baby was a gift, not a hurdle.

Why was I still so conflicted about this?

On Sunday we went to services at the little church in Moses Lake. The volunteer ladies at the supper garden program had been inviting us for a while, and Nick had been pestering to go. He liked the cookies the ladies made. He liked the crafts and the friendly people there. Now I felt the need in a way I never had before—not for cookies and crafts, but for guidance. I wanted God to take away the muck of unwanted feelings inside me and make me feel the way I should feel.

I needed to confess to someone the things I couldn't tell anyone.

"Up and dressed on Sunday and headed into the chapel," Daniel joked as we walked through the door of Lakeshore Community Church. "My mother will be proud." Among other things, with Jack gone these past two weeks and Daniel having free time, he'd been talking to his parents more. I felt bad that we hadn't told them about the pregnancy, but the fact that we hadn't officially been to the doctor seemed like a good enough excuse. At least we could say, *Well, we just wanted to be sure before we told everyone . . .*

"It's not Easter or Christmas. *My* mother would probably be shocked," I quipped, and then winced at how irreverent the comment sounded. Bad, bad, bad. Who was I to be raising children?

Daniel squeezed my hand as we settled into a pew and the organist started playing.

The service started, and I followed along in the program, so as not to look like someone who only showed up in church on special occasions. The pastor was warm and well-spoken, the atmosphere inside the little chapel peaceful and reverent, and the music inspiring. Nick marched right up front with Birdie and the other kids for the children's sermon, then happily trotted off to a preschool room with the under-five set before the pastor, a friendly-faced, thirty-something scarecrow of a man I'd met during the summer enrichment visits, took the pulpit. I was so distracted by my own issues, I really couldn't focus on Reverend Hay's sermon at first. I just kept waiting for . . . something . . . for a sign, a confirmation, for holy lightning to strike and fix me. I wanted God to whisper in my ear, to say, *Don't worry, Mallory. When this baby comes, you'll know just what to do. It's all part of the plan. . . .*

But it didn't happen, even though the sermon finally did compel me to focus. Reverend Hay was a skillful orator and a passionate leader. Still, when the service concluded, I felt as lost as I had earlier.

There was a potluck meal afterward—something that happened monthly, apparently. As we made our way out the door, Reverend Hay invited us to stay for lunch, and before I knew what was happening, we were headed next door with the rest of the congregation.

In the potluck line, I ended up next to the reverend, of all people. He crossed the room and wiggled his way into line right behind me. Mama B, who regularly helped feed the supper garden kids, patted tall, skinny Reverend Hay and remarked, "We need to fatten him up a bit, don't we, hon?"

"Oh, well, you know these men can never get enough food," I said innocuously.

"You must be a cook." Mama B smiled at me, then pointed a finger, her brows drawing together. "Everson . . . Everson. I'm trying to place that name. Now, who are your people?"

"My peop . . . my what?" I honestly wasn't sure what she was asking.

"You have family around, or you just in for the summer?" she translated, a relaxed cadence stretching *you* into two syllables, *ye-ew*.

"Mallory and her husband moved here recently," Reverend Hay explained, motioning to Daniel and Nick, who were talking with Nester, one of the fishermen from the Waterbird. "Daniel's working out at the West Ranch, and Mallory writes that blog that . . ." Birdie trotted up and spirited Reverend Hay away before he could finish the sentence.

Mama B studied me with concern that even Coke-bottle glasses couldn't hide.

The middle-aged woman behind her, whom I now recognized

from some of my visits to the hardware store, leaned over Mama B's shoulder to get in on the conversation. From beneath a helmet-head of blond hair, she flicked an appraising look back and forth between Daniel and me. "Ohhhh . . . *you're* the ones at the old ranch headquarters. Well, I thought I recognized ye-ew. You've been in the store quite a bit, haven't ye-ew? I'm usually back in the office, but I do try to poke my head out once in a while. Sorry I've missed ye-ew."

"That's all right." Was it my imagination, or had Daniel and I suddenly become a whole lot more interesting?

The woman reached around Mama B to shake my hand. "I'm Claire Anne Underhill, by the way." Her fingers were loose and limp against my palm, barely going halfway in.

Claire Anne Underhill glanced Daniel's way again, her eyes traveling up and down, and I felt oddly defensive. What was behind that look? "Well, I'd heard that Jack West had hired himself somebody who looked a *whole lot* like his son, and I'll be a June bug if that's not the truth." She stepped out of line to get an even better look at Daniel. "He *is* a dead ringer for Jack West's son. Pitiful to have all that money and be at odds with your family, don't you think?"

Claire Anne's hand traveled back to her own body, her perfectly manicured nails toying with the diamond pendant on her necklace. "I don't know if anyone's filled you in on the history there, but word is that Jack West financed Mason's campaign for state senate years ago, and then Jack expected favors. When Mason wouldn't compromise himself, Jack disowned him, and they stopped speaking. Can you imagine that? Putting your only son in such a position? It's no wonder that wicked old man is alone." The snarky little giggle that followed actually made me feel a little sorry for Jack. Considering that he spent a lot of money in town, and quite a bit of it went to the hardware store, she had some nerve. I drew back when she leaned toward me and added, "Of course, I guess Mason is just lucky he got away before he ended up six feet under, like the wife and the stepson."

A shiver ran over me, and my brain tripped and staggered, searching for a reply. How did one respond to something like that? Really, in view of my present condition, I'd been trying not to think about Jack West's sordid past, or what might be buried somewhere on the ranch.

"My word, Claire Anne. That ain't appropriate." Mama B had an air of command that didn't invite argument. "It's Sun-day and we're standin' in a church and yer mouth is floppin' like the tail on a flea-bitten mule."

Claire Anne's eyes flared, and she threaded her arms, still studying Daniel. "Well, he *does* look like Mason West, Mama B. I mean, not that he's identical or any-thang, but they do favor . . ." The sentence drifted off, as if she were tasting the possibilities, savoring them, thinking about what she might say around town. "I hadn't had a close look until now, but it is peculiar."

"Claire Anne . . ." Mama B's frown was a silent warning, but it seemed to be lost on Claire Anne.

"It's just really so sad to have so much and be so . . . unhappy, that's all." She splayed a hand against her chest, one pink fingernail tapping the diamond lightly.

I focused on the necklace and the matching tennis bracelet, and an idea struck me suddenly. Keren had complained a time or two that she'd tried to get the hardware store to help her with supplies for the gardening program, but she'd had no luck. "You know, you're so right. What good is money if you can't do some good with it? My grandmother used to say that."

"Truly," Claire Anne agreed, tossing her hair, but it was glued in place.

"Grandma Louisa never missed a chance to support the community, after she moved back home to Charleston."

Claire Anne's eyes brightened, and she regarded me with a new level of interest, her thickly coated lashes fanning against pale peach eye shadow. "Oh, I do love Charleston. So beautiful. So historic. So . . . cultured. And the churches . . ." Giving the aging fellowship hall of Lakeshore Community a down-the-nose look, she cupped a hand aside her mouth. "Nothing like that here." Her pursed lips added, *Well, you understand, of course.*

"Grandma Louisa loved her old home, just off Broad," I commented. "She loved everything about it. It always bothered her, the dichotomy between wealth and poverty in the city, though."

"Well, of course, it would." I could feel Claire Anne stepping blindly into my trap. The reverend was headed our way again, which would make it that much more effective. One thing I'd learned from my father—there's no better donor than one who's trying to impress someone else. Occasionally, being a lobbyist's daughter did pay off. I'd watched my dad work his deal-making noose countless times.

"Of course, that's true in so many places."

"Yes, yes, it is. People must do what they can, mustn't they? Wouldn't it be wonderful if someone with Jack West's means would contribute to solving the social problems around here? We have such an issue with the riffraff up in Chinquapin Peaks." Her lips snapped closed as Reverend Hay slipped into line with us again.

I pictured the faces of the kids in the gardening program. The riffraff. "I've heard." Claire Anne gave me a *hush up* look, her gaze darting toward the pastor. I pretended not to catch her drift. "And I was so glad to know that the hardware store planned to play a big part in the supper garden program, donating supplies and what-not. That's just awesome. There's something so empowering about equipping people with the tools to meet their own needs."

Claire Anne's face blanched, and her mouth dropped open, then snapped shut, then opened again. Her blue eyes swam in a sea of white. I'd rendered her temporarily speechless. The victory was . . . rather sweet.

"I'm sorry . . . did I get that wrong? Maybe Keren said it was Walmart that was donating the supplies. We've had so much going on since we got here, it's all sort of a blur." While I had her on the mat, I figured I might as well go in for the full nelson. "I've been raising donations for the program through my blog, *The Frontier Woman*, and through some other contacts in DC. I was just thinking that, as money comes in, maybe the hardware store could let Keren buy supplies at cost. That would make the money go so much further."

Reverend Hay glanced down at me, the hint of a smile tugging his thin cheeks, an eyebrow curving upward as in, *The new girl knows a few things*. "What a fine idea," he interjected. "The better the families in Chinquapin Peaks do, the better the community does as a whole. Kids can't learn when they come to school hungry."

Claire Anne strafed me with an ocular machine gun, tipping her chin up. "Well, of course they can't. I think the gardening program is a *lovely* idea. Truly. But I do hope that, while you're bringing it to the *world's* attention online, you'll give equal time to the many fine amenities of Moses Lake. We wouldn't want the masses to see this as . . . well . . . a disadvantaged area, for instance." Another glance flicked toward Reverend Hay. "Not that I'm against helping the disadvantaged, of course. I just question whether those families can be counted on to follow through. Honestly, when you can't even wash your child's hair or make certain they aren't bringing *lice* to school . . . I don't mean to sound cynical, of course."

"If we never take a chance on people, we'll never know." Reverend Hay smiled pleasantly at Claire Anne. "Of course, you understand that, or the hardware store wouldn't be helping the program. Widows and orphans. There are plenty of those in Chinquapin Peaks, just like in the Bible."

"Of course." Claire Anne had the look of a woman biting her tongue and tasting blood. Clearly, I'd just been crossed off her friend list, Charleston connection or not.

"I'll be sure to mention it on *The Frontier Woman*, too— the sponsorships from Underhill Hardware, Walmart, and other places," I finished, doing the thing my father always did just after snapping the trapdoor shut—drop a little treat into the cage, so your prisoner doesn't turn violent.

"How lovely." An eyetooth flashed, and Claire Anne's nose crinkled as she looked around the room. "Oh, there are those sweet sisters from the Binding Through Books club. I hear they're going to be in the pages of *Woman's Day* magazine. Excuse me a little moment. I must find out what month, so I can order copies. It's not every day that Moses Lake makes the national news." Ducking out of line, she threaded her way through the tables and chairs, exiting the playing field, thoroughly beaten.

Mama B turned her attention to me and smiled. "You got a little cowgirl in you." She shook a finger. "Not too many people can rope Claire Anne in. You go by the bank and talk to my grandson, Blaine, about a donation. You tell him Mama B said so. He just got elected to the county commission. He's been workin' to get some attention for the roads up in Chinquapin Peaks, so bad weather don't keep the kids out of school. You can put that on your *Frontier Woman*—I been readin' that, by the way. I think folks'd be interested in what a hard time Blaine's havin' getting any money spent up in Chink."

"Welcome to Moses Lake," Reverend Hay added, and nudged me. "And you thought politics was just a big-city thing, I bet."

We moved along in the potluck line before I could answer.

Daniel and I ended up at a table with Stan, my favorite feed-store guy. He introduced us to the local game warden, Mart McClendon, and his wife, Andrea, who it turned out were the parents of Dustin, my teenage friend from the hardware store. Andrea was a social services counselor and spent a lot of time working with families up in Chinquapin Peaks. We talked about the lives of the kids and how remote the place was.

"It's worse with the bridge out of commission on County Road 47," Andrea pointed out. "Access is so much more restricted. Some of my clients are on school buses for almost two hours in the mornings and two hours in the afternoons. Little kids. Kindergarteners." She tapped the tabletop with a fingertip. "Fifty thousand dollars—that's what the county commission won't come up with. The federal government already committed the rest, because it was flood damage. That bridge directly affects several hundred families. I wonder if those stuffed shirts on the county commission even think about how difficult an extra thirty minutes or hour commute is for workers who make ten dollars an hour processing chickens at the Proxica plant in Gnadenfeld, or how an extra hour a day on the bus limits a kid who's already academically—"

"Did I hear someone taking my name in vain?" cut in a voice, and a young couple joined us at our table.

"Not you, Blaine," Andrea clarified. "The rest of those idiots on county commission. We *like* you."

The man—dark-haired, nice looking, thirty-something—laughed. "You must be talking about your pet project again."

"Yes. My bridge."

"You just need to tell them that my wife is going to haunt them until they rebuild that bridge," the game warden, Andrea's husband, joked. He laid a hand over hers, like he was trying to keep her from winding up. Daniel gave me a *what-in-the-world-have-we-walked-into* look.

"I got a bridge!" Nick piped up. "In my sandbox!"

All of us looked at him and laughed, and the tension broke. We talked about the food and about the expansion to the church fellowship hall, which Blaine's wife, Heather, was designing. She was also doing the architectural renderings of an addition to the Moses Lake School, which brought up the subject of education again, which led to another discussion of the bridge. By the time Nick started getting restless in his booster chair, Daniel was ready to escape the onslaught of small-town issues, of which he'd been blissfully unaware while spending his time closeted with Jack.

"Guess there is no utopia, no matter how far off the beaten path you go," he remarked as we drove home, Nick drifting to sleep in the backseat.

"Just kind of a microcosm of the usual issues," I agreed. "But you know, what's different here is how cheap some of the solutions are. Ten thousand dollars for a greenhouse for Keren's gardening program. Less than a hundred dollars to help a family get a few backyard chickens and a coop so they can raise their own eggs year-round. Fifty dollars for gardening equipment and seeds. It's just not that much money."

"No, it's really not." Daniel glanced over at me, his lips curving into a wry twist. "I heard you rope in the hardware store lady, by the way. Nicely done. But are you sure you want to get wrapped up in all this?"

Gazing out the window, I took in Chinquapin Peaks, so beautiful at a distance, such a puzzle of stark contrasts up close. "I don't see how I can ignore it. These are the kids Nick will go to school with. It's going to affect him, whether we want it to or not. He'll be sitting in class with the kids who didn't get enough to eat that morning, or the ones who are growing up with parents who don't care, or the ones who have been yanked back and forth between foster care programs. We're involved, whether we want to be or not."

Daniel nodded. "I just meant that you're getting a lot of irons in the fire, with the house problems, Nick, and *The Frontier Woman*. And now gardens, bridges, kids in Chinquapin Peaks, and . . . the baby news."

The last words, *the baby news*, pressed me back against the seat. Somewhere along the way today, that had slipped from my mind in favor of everyone else's issues. I'd given up hoping for holy lightning to strike, and instead distracted myself with other things. "Irons in the fire," I deflected. "You're starting to sound like Jack."

"Well, you don't have to insult me . . ." He smirked, those beautiful eyes catching the light, glowing bright, like emeralds.

If there was such a thing as holy lightning, it struck me then, but not in the way I'd expected. I thought of the question Keren had asked as we sat watching the children play during my first visit to the summer class. *Do you ever just have the feeling that God's using you right where you are?*

Looking at my hands in my lap, contemplating the idea, I considered the possible uses for those hands. "Sometimes I feel like I'm here for a reason—here in Moses Lake, I mean." A blush stole into my cheeks, and I glanced at Daniel, gauging his reaction. "I mean, I don't mean to sound like I've gone all prophetic and profound or anything, but sometimes, I think I'm here because of those kids. With the contacts I have—with the contacts *we* have—maybe we can make a difference."

Daniel's hand slid over mine. "You're the most amazing

person I know, Mal. If you've got a feeling about it, then you need to go for it."

"What if I said I feel like . . . kind of like . . . it's something I'm meant to do?" It seemed weird to say it out loud, sort of presumptuous even, but I *was* feeling something, and it was something bigger than me, larger than my own concerns.

Daniel didn't answer at first.

He probably thought I'd gone round the bend. I probably had. I could always claim hormones . . .

"Then that's probably what it is."

A lump of emotion rose in my throat. No one had ever believed in me like Daniel did. All my life, people had been babying me, protecting me, cautioning me to keep my plans small, to stay on the safe side, to work within the box, to stay in my own neighborhood. "Will you be okay with it if I talk to Jack about the supper garden program . . . whenever there's a good opportunity, I mean? And maybe about the bridge in Chinquapin Peaks? Jack must be the biggest landowner in the area. He could put pressure on the county commission. For heaven's sake, he could pay for that bridge without even batting an eye." My heart sped up just at the thought of talking to Jack. He had at least four different personalities, ranging from vaguely aloof to paranoid and hostile. Even so, I felt strangely empowered, unexplainably larger than myself.

Daniel's fingers toyed with mine. "Can I *stop* you from talking to Jack?" He followed the question with a wry look.

"Probably not."

"Then I guess it's okay."

When we got back to the house, we took Nick to the lakeshore for the afternoon. We built a small fire, cooked hot dogs, chased lightning bugs, and created a lantern jar. I thought again of how perfect things would be if every day could be like this one. If there were no Jack West to worry about.

After Nick and Daniel were asleep, I awoke consumed with the need to put the day into words—to write and write and write. I wrote about the potluck at church, the strange collection of townsfolk we'd met, and the kids in Chinquapin Peaks. I wrote about the people who wanted solutions for them and those who saw them only as a problem, an inconvenience. I wrote about Reverend Hay's observation that if we never give people a chance, we never know what they're capable of. I wrote about the seeds we plant, and how we can never be sure which will grow and which will lie fallow, but seeds in the hand have no chance to grow at all. The only way to guarantee a harvest is to take a risk.

Long after the moon rose and drifted out of sight above the window, I was writing and scheduling pieces for *The Frontier Woman*. In the dark of midnight, by the light of a single lamp, I wrote about the baby, about the fact that what I really wanted, what every mother wants, was a better world for my child, for this son or this daughter—this little piece of my heart who would grow within my body and tear from my body and travel into the world, with all its hills and valleys, with all its blind corners and unexpected precipices.

When I finished writing, I pulled my legs into the chair and sat reading what I'd created. I deemed it ridiculously emotional and sentimental, but I saved it anyway, tucked it in a small corner of my hard drive, where I might pull it up one day and show it to my son or daughter, and say, *See, I had hopes for you before you were ever born.*

The most difficult mountain to cross is the threshold.

—Danish proverb
(Left by Donna Sue, on a lakeside getaway with Mary Kay)

Chapter 17

In the cyber world, the difference between keeping a secret and revealing it is the touch of a button—a few lines of code, an accidental click, a careless email forward, a glitch in programming logic that causes something unexpected to happen for reasons no one can explain. If there was one lesson I should have learned after starting *The Frontier Woman*, it was that one.

When the phone rang early Monday morning, my head was pounding as I reached toward the nightstand. Daniel's side of the bed was empty, the house quiet, Nick apparently sleeping in after our big day at the church and the lake. Outside, the morning was cloudy and the light muted, so that it seemed earlier than seven o'clock.

Grabbing the receiver, I fell back against the pillow, rubbed my eyes, and muttered, " . . . Ellll-oh?"

"What. Is going. On?" Trudy was on the other end, and she did not sound happy.

"Trude? Huhhh? Wha . . ." I blinked, tried to clear the

sleep clouds from my eyes, but they were red and sore from my late-night blog-o-rama. There was a note from Daniel on the nightstand. *Jack called, coming back today.* My head pounded harder. No wonder Daniel was up and gone so early this morning.

The nirvana I'd felt last night while writing articles about the supper gardens and the kids in Chinquapin Peaks flipped over in my stomach and became a sense of dread. "Oh, man, I think I stayed up too late. I have a blog hangover."

"Yeah, really?" Trudy was not amused. "Well, if you don't already, you will when I get through with you. And when Mom gets to you, you're going to be dead meat, little sister."

Adrenaline pushed through my body, thick and slow like syrup, waking me up piece by piece. Trudy was really in a mood this morning, and it was somehow aimed at me. I hoped this over-the-top emotion didn't have anything to do with another failed in vitro. She wouldn't talk yet about the fact that this one had made it farther than any of the others, and as day after day passed with no bad news, I was hopeful. "What's Mom upset about? What did I do?" It takes a special kind of skill to get in trouble with your family from hundreds of miles away. "Listen, Trudy, I'm not feeling so great this morning. Can you just tell me what's wrong?" *Please, please don't let her foul mood have anything to do with bad news about the in vitro.* How could I sit here and console Trudy about the loss of another chance at a baby, when I was hiding my own pregnancy?

"Well, maybe it's *morning* sickness."

I rolled onto my knees, suddenly ready to bound off the mattress and dance around the room. "Trudy, you're pregnant? Really? How long have you known for sure? Can we tell people now?"

"We're not talking about me, but apparently *you're* in the

family way. And that's a good question: How long have *you* known?"

I hovered in an awkward squat on the bed, a dozen questions and a plethora of emotions washing over me at once. Daniel had told people? Without talking to me? Without asking when and how I wanted to share the news? Trudy knew already? And my mother. Ohhh . . . my mother! "Trudy, what are you talking about?"

Her response was a disgusted snort. I knew exactly what expression would accompany that look—her short, pert nose crinkling, her lip jerking upward to reveal that orthodontically perfect smile. "And you go putting it on your *stupid blog* and *announce* it to the world without even *telling us* first? Really? *This* is how I find out. If you've got half a brain in your head, you'll get on there and take that post off before Mom sits down with her morning coffee and checks in with *The Frontier Woman*. And then you'd better call and give Mom the news, because there's no telling who else has already read it."

A bass drum reverberated through my body. *Boom, boom, boom, boom*, beating the seconds away. "I didn't put that on the blog . . . I mean, that was just . . . I was just . . ." I was out of the bed and running for my laptop before I could finish the sentence.

"Mallory, there was so much stuff on there this morning, it took me forty-five minutes to catch up. Imagine my surprise when I got all the way to the end and found this . . . well, diary entry basically . . . with you pondering parenthood. At first, I thought you were just talking about Nick, and then I realized, *You're pregnant.* You're pregnant, and you're telling the world, and you haven't even told *me*. I was right, by the way. It was the antibiotics."

"Trudy . . . hang on a minute . . . I'm trying to . . ." Tucking the phone on my shoulder, I flipped open the laptop, waited impatiently. "To get to the blog." Surely she was just calling my bluff, trying to get me to admit to a positive pregnancy test. Every time she'd asked me the past two weeks, I'd hedged and told her there was nothing to report.

"What, you're not going to just take my word for it?" she taunted. "It's not like I could make this kind of stuff up. You . . ."

"Trudy, just a *minute*!" My hands were shaking, and I couldn't even think of my own password.

"I wetted my bed," Nick's squeaky whine echoed through the house, and then there he was in the doorway, drowsily rubbing his eyes, his Spiderman pajamas dripping a little round stain on the icky yellow carpet.

"You wet your bed?" I repeated, trying to think of the blog password. CongressAvenue1. That was it.

"Not *me*," Trudy quipped, "but apparently, there's been something going on in *your* bed."

"Trudy, just . . . let me . . ."

I set down the phone. Nick was coming across the room, dripping all the way, his eyes two big, soulful saucers, brimming with tears. "I dweamed I was swimmin'," he sniffed.

"Nick, it's okay." I turned back to the computer, waiting, waiting, waiting for the blog dashboard to load. "Just go take everything off and put it in the bathtub."

His lip trembled, and a tear spilled over, drawing a glistening line down the smooth skin of his cheek. "I messed-ed up my Spidey-mans. My new ones from Nanbee and Gwampa. My big boy wa-a-ones." The sentence crumbled into a sob. The pajamas had come in the mail from Daniel's parents two days before. Nick would have worn them morning, noon, and night if he could.

The dashboard inched onto the screen, I looked at Nick. The dashboard inched, I looked at Nick.

"I'm not a big boy-e-e-e."

"Nick, honey." I abandoned the computer and crossed the room, then pulled him close, cradling his head against my ribs. "It's okay. That just means it's time for the Spidermans to go in the washer and have a bath, and you know what? They get even more comfy after they're washed."

"I'm not a big boy-e-e-e," he whimpered again. Before the wedding and the move, Daniel had determined that Nick needed to move out of Pull-Ups pants at night and into regular undies. Daniel had reinforced the switch with copious amounts of *big boy* talk.

"Honey, even big boys have accidents sometimes." I turned him around and steered him toward the bathroom. "But guess what? We can just run a little bath, and get out some clean clothes, and the washing machine will be so happy, because it gets to have the Thomas the Tank Engine sheets *and* the Spidermans all at once. I mean, if you were a washing machine, you'd think that was awesome, right?"

Nick looked at me like I was nuts, but in short order I'd removed the stinky Spidermans, turned on the bathwater, and cheered Nick up with soap crayons. By the time I got back to the computer, it was more than clear that I'd published a blog-a-palooza of information last night. Before I'd even finished cleaning up the dashboard, the phone started ringing—Trudy again. Following that, I heard from my mother, Kaylyn and Josh calling on speakerphone with friends from their office, three former coworkers, my two middle sisters, and finally Corbin, phoning in because Carol was tied up in a Junior League meeting and couldn't call. She'd texted him and told him to find out what was going on. By then, hours had passed, and Nick was happily playing in the backyard.

"You live an interesting life," Corbin commented. "First,

you move into an alleged murderer's backyard, and now there's a baby on the way. Kind of sudden, isn't it?"

Leave it to Corbin to state the brutally obvious. "It wasn't planned, Corbin, okay? You can tell Carol that. I'm sure she thinks we're completely nuts, but we're not." I instantly felt bad for being short with Corbin. Of my brothers-in-law, he was the one I was the closest to. He'd covered the political beat for years, so we had something in common. "It was an accident—antibiotics and birth control pills don't mix, it turns out. Remember, I had that root canal right before the wedding?" Carol would never understand, no matter what I said. Carol's children were perfectly spaced, three years apart. Undoubtedly, no bed in her house had ever sat for hours with befouled sheets, while tinkle-soaked pajamas waited in a wad on the bathroom floor.

"Good to hear," Corbin replied pleasantly. "I'll relay that to your sister. Find any dead bodies around there yet?"

"Ohhh, Corbin," I groaned, letting my head fall into my palm. "Not today, all right? Listen, call waiting is beeping. Tell Carol I love her and not to worry about us, okay?" Right now I just wanted to get off the phone. I hadn't had so much as a cup of coffee. My head felt swirly and my stomach was about as happy as a bear coming out of hibernation. Nick's bed had probably dried into a crusty, smelly mess by now.

I ended the call with Corbin and pushed the flash button. Al was on the other line. We went through the baby conversation again. I had the distinct impression that the baby news was less than pleasing to Al. "All I can say is, if you're gonna have one, make sure you take the time for it after it gets here." Al's words were strangely hard-edged, almost bitter.

"Well, it wasn't planned," I explained for what seemed like the hundredth time. Whenever this poor child did come, everyone in the world would know it was an accident.

Al muttered something, and a sliver of discomfort needled under my skin. Who was she to question my ability to take care of a baby, anyway? She didn't have any children. And besides, weren't babies born every day to mothers who had to figure it out as they went along?

"Keren says to tell you they missed you and Nick today at the summer class." Al's tone was flat, as if I'd offended her in some way. "She says thanks for what you wrote on your blog about the supper garden program, the kids, and the bridge up in Chinquapin Peaks."

"Tell her I'm really hoping it'll bring some action, but I'm sorry the blog was such a mess today. I didn't mean to publish it with all that . . . personal stuff and . . ."

Outside the window, Daniel's truck came racing up the driveway, and I cut the conversation short just as he walked through the back door. He closed it behind himself and stood with his hand clutching the knob, his eyes blinking wide. "I just had a phone call from my mother."

"Ohhh, shoot," I groaned. I'd been so busy dealing with the shockwave on my side of the family that I hadn't even thought about Daniel's parents. "I'm an idiot. Your mother probably thinks she has the worst daughter-in-law ever." Not only had Daniel's mother been forced to relinquish Nick to a woman she barely knew, now I was proving to be a monumental doofus, as well.

"Are you kidding? She's thrilled." Daniel paused to scratch his head, dark curls falling through his fingers. "She thought it was a little strange to find out about it on your blog, and she wasn't exactly happy I hadn't called her first thing." He pulled his lips on one side, frowning. "I thought we weren't going to tell anyone for a while, though."

"I didn't mean to," I moaned. "I was up last night writing stuff . . . just . . . just kind of for me, really . . . thinking about the day, the baby, and Chinquapin Peaks . . . and, well, everything. I was just rambling, trying to work it all out in my head. I meant to publish a piece about the supper garden program and maybe a little bit about the bridge and the long school bus rides, but somehow, I stuck it all on there. Trudy called first thing and informed me of my blunder. I've been dealing with my family all morning."

Laughter pressed past Daniel's lips. Considering Jack was back, he was in a remarkably good mood. Maybe Jack hadn't returned after all. Maybe God had realized that a baby news bomb, numerous family confrontations, and a wet bed were enough for one day.

Daniel released the door handle and came across the room, his chin tilted sympathetically. "Bet that was interesting. What did your mother say?"

"That any woman with a modicum of sense would've known about the antibiotics thing. She's sure that, between the dentist and the pharmacist, someone must have warned me, and I just blew it off. She's convinced that I thought I knew better than everybody else, just like always, which proves her point that I do need to keep my mother in the loop, now, always, and for the rest of my born days, amen. She also made the point that, if I would have told her about the root canal instead of hiding it from her, she'd have warned me to take precautions." Daniel's cheeks twitched, and I rolled a look at him, warning him not to say anything cute. "I didn't tell her about the root canal when it happened because she was already in such a twist about the wedding. I figured one more thing would push her over the edge. Anyway, now she's back to wanting us to move home and set up housekeeping in the rumpus room."

Daniel chuckled.

"Don't laugh." I sighted the gun finger at him. "She's

planning to have my dad use his connections to find the perfect job for you."

"Eewwww, I wonder what I'll be doing." His wry grin attempted to lighten the moment.

Folding my arms on the table, I hid my face in them like a grade-school kid. "I'm sure my mother will let you know."

The icky yellow carpet crinkled, stiff and sticky under Daniel's shoes as he came closer. His touch was featherlight, sweeping my hair aside before he kissed the back of my neck. "I love you," he whispered. "We'll be okay. We're not the only people to ever have a baby before we meant to. Nick wasn't planned, and look at him. I wouldn't trade him for anything."

I knew he was right. I was overthinking all of this. It wasn't like we'd be having the baby tomorrow. We had months to prepare. But, somehow, knowing that a baby was coming made everything else seem more critical, more pressing. We were on a timeline now. Within just a matter of months, everything had to be perfect.

"You're right. I know you're right." I was embarrassed, as much as anything. When you grow up being teased by four older siblings, you don't handle public screw-ups well. "So, what else did your mom say?"

"They want to come for Thanksgiving. Dad's excited about seeing the ranch. They're hoping Chad might think about bringing his bunch, so we can all be together."

"Wow." Amid the warm, sweet anticipation of a family Thanksgiving, there was panic over the house, the fact that there was no place to sleep that many people, and unless they wanted macaroni and cheese and peach pie, I wasn't sure what we'd eat. "You guys must have talked quite a while. Where in the world was Jack all this time?"

"Otherwise occupied." Daniel moved to the chair beside me, leaning over it rather than sitting.

"Okay, what's going on? Spill. This is not the usual mood for a day with Jack. How in the world did you have time for a phone call? And how did you get away to come home for lunch?" Usually after a return from Houston, Jack was wound like an eight-day clock, irritable, driven, and suspicious of everyone. He decompressed by patrolling the ranch and berating the ranch hands, complaining about the lab and the test fields, and changing the parameters for Daniel's job.

"Jack's not alone this time." Tapping his thumbs to his lips, Daniel gave me a look that was somewhere between hopeful and perplexed. "His son is with him."

"The one he doesn't speak to? That son?"

"They're speaking now, apparently." Daniel stood and stretched the knots from his back. He looked so good when he did that. "They seemed pretty chummy, in fact. Jack spent the whole morning giving a tour of the laboratory and showing him the growth environments and the test plots. The great thing was, I got to follow along and finally see everything. Jack didn't even seem to care. When he and Mason left the lab, he hung the keys right there on the pegboard by the door, with all the other ranch keys. I helped myself to a full lab tour while they were out driving around the pastures."

"Okay, you're talking about the son who's the state senator or something, right? Or does he have another son?" Maybe I'd misunderstood something along the way.

Outside, Nick was sitting on the porch of the little house having an intense conversation with Pecos. Daniel smiled at him. "Far as I can tell, this is the son everyone keeps mentioning. Mason West. I didn't ask too many questions. If it keeps Jack off my tail, I'm not gonna breathe too hard on it." He pointed at Nick. "What do you think they talk about?"

"Nick and the dog? Or Jack and the mystery son?" I wasn't really ready to change subjects. Maybe it was the strange karma of the day so far, but this new development made me uneasy in some way I couldn't quite define, as if some sixth sense were warning me that disaster was on the way.

"Either one."

Outside, Nick stood with his hand on one hip, pointing and delivering orders to Pecos.

"Well, right now I'm afraid he might be pretending to be Jack. Scary thought." As soon as I said it, I knew I shouldn't have. There was no sense in raining on Daniel's parade. It was nice to see him feeling good about things for a change. "Sorry. If Jack's happy, I'm glad. Really."

"I'm just hoping this reconciliation with his son is a long-term thing." A wrinkle of concern straightened Daniel's smile, then disappeared. "It'll make my job a whole lot easier. Sounds like the son is planning to be here awhile. Apparently he's staying in the cabin on Firefly Island—working on a book or something. I heard him tell Jack he didn't want to bunk at the big headquarters because he needed a quiet place to write."

"Huh . . ." So someone *was* allowed access to the mysterious cabin on Firefly Island. The place looked pretty primitive, at least from a distance. It didn't seem like the sort of accommodations a man accustomed to hobnobbing in political circles would choose. "Well, considering the plethora of No Trespassing signs and the fact that there's an elephant-proof gate on the causeway, I guess he's not in much danger of being surprised by company."

Daniel shrugged. "Guess not. Jack knows about the baby, by the way. He heard me talking with my mom."

My cheeks prickled again, even though it really wasn't anything to be embarrassed about. Women got pregnant every day. I'd just never pictured myself this way—jobless, stay-at-home mom, pregnant. "He didn't get upset, or anything?"

Jack hardly seemed like the type to approve of niceties like paternity leave.

Daniel leaned across the space between us, cupped my chin. "Stop worrying. Jack said congratulations." Tweaking the end of my nose, he kissed me quickly, then turned and headed for the kitchen.

I sat staring out the window, watching the golden light of midday drench the grass, and thinking that maybe my barrage of awkward prayers yesterday had been answered. Maybe holy lightning had struck after all.

Whatever our souls are made of, his and mine are the same.

—Emily Brontë
(Left by Marvin and Gracie, fifty-fourth anniversary in Cabin 3)

Chapter 18

Bliss. I don't know what else you'd call it. Life in Moses Lake was suddenly bliss. Jack and his son spent time riding, fishing, tooling around the lake in one of Jack's boats. Daniel worked regular hours . . . well, farmer's hours, anyway. He was up early in the mornings and left at dawn to make his rounds in the test plots and beat the heat. Sometimes he met us at the Waterbird for lunch, and we wiled away the high-noon hour listening to Burt, Nester, and the other fishermen telling stories.

Once, Jack and his son even came to lunch with Daniel. Mason West was a nice-looking man in his mid-forties. He did resemble Daniel in many ways—same build, similar facial structure—although Mason was about ten years older, with forehead lines and a dusting of gray at the temples. Like most politicians, Mason was well-groomed and well-spoken, confident and charismatic. He had just enough of his father's larger-than-life cowboy persona to present the ideal picture of a Texas politician: part charm, part bluster, and a dash of good-ol'-boy thrown in for added measure.

Two weeks passed, and even Chrissy couldn't find a reason to complain, which was saying something. "I woulda got his son down here long ago, if I knew it would, like, turn Jack West into Mr. Happy Pants," she told me as I stood at the pharmacy counter in Gnadenfeld, picking up prenatal vitamins after my first doctor's appointment. I was bummed that Daniel had stayed home to watch Nick. I didn't know I'd be hearing the baby's heartbeat and seeing a new little life, no larger than my thumb on the ultrasound screen. The doctor had recorded it all on a DVD for me. I couldn't wait to get home and show Daniel and Nick.

"Kind of amazing about Jack, isn't it?" I agreed. Even Chrissy's penchant for finding the worm in every apple couldn't dampen my mood today. I was overflowing with the glory of the moment. "I always wondered if Jack was just really . . . chronically lonely and depressed. It would be hard, losing part of your family in such a violent way, and then never being able to really clear your name, and then being estranged from what family you have left. All the money in the world can't fix something like that."

I should have known better than to share my new rose-colored view with Chrissy. Glancing left and right, as if the walls might have ears, she leaned across the counter. "Yeah, don't let them fool you. You gotta wonder why a guy who's been trying to stick it to his dad for years is suddenly all buddy-buddy. I mean, really? I've been mad at my daddy since he left my mama and married that witch of a woman, and even when we do talk a little, there's no *way* we'd all of a sudden be hangin' out at the ranch, going fishin'. Pah-lease. Give me a break. If Jack West had half a brain, he'd see through that stuff and wonder why Mason's really here. The only time I call my daddy is when I want somethin'."

A sting of apprehension pricked my fluffy, floaty cloud of

maternal bliss. A nagging unease had been skulking around for two weeks now, flat, silent, and stealthy, like a scorpion trying to find a way in through the newly sealed closets that Len had just finished for me. Even as day after day passed pleasantly by, worry was looking for an entrance point—just a little crack, a tiny gap.

I wouldn't let it happen. Things were finally good. I wouldn't let Chrissy dim my merry sunshine. "Well, I doubt there's anything Mason needs. He's been pretty successful on his own, from what I can tell." I'd talked to a couple of former DC coworkers, done a little asking around about Mason West. He was an up-and-comer. After a dozen successful years in state politics, he was in a perfect position to make a U.S. senate bid and, considering his clout on the state level, he'd have a good shot at it. My guess was that, before putting himself on the national stage, Mason had made the wise choice to clean up his family baggage. Solidarity with his father would be politically beneficial. A happy family goes a long way in an election, and deep pockets like Jack West's couldn't hurt, either. I wasn't going to say that to Chrissy, of course. Anything you said to Chrissy was liable to end up on a billboard somewhere.

"Well, hey, at least you're getting new carpet out of it." A snarky little smile wrinkled Chrissy's pert nose, compressing a fan of girlish freckles. "Smart move, hitting Jack West up when he's in such a good mood. I should try that."

"Well, the carpet in the house was really bad," I defended, but in truth, I did feel like I was the lucky beneficiary of Jack's current state of near euphoria. He actually seemed strangely interested in the fact that Daniel and I were expecting a baby. When Daniel had asked him about having the carpet replaced and paying Len for further remodeling work, Jack had given him carte blanche for repairs and for ordering a houseful of new carpet from the sample books at the hardware store. Claire Anne Underhill was so thrilled that she'd pretty much forgiven me for trapping her into donating to the supper garden program. "I'm not sure Jack had even looked at the house to know what kind of shape it was in, to be honest," I told Chrissy. I couldn't help it—my opinion of Jack was softening, even as I tried to keep my defenses up.

Chrissy shook her head, her lips puckering. "Just get it while you can, girlfriend. I'll admit he's never acted this nice before, but Jack West always goes back to being Jack West. How'd the doctor visit go, by the way?"

Her smile was genuine then, and we talked for a while about the due date and the ultrasound. Leaving the pharmacy, I couldn't wait to get home and share the DVD with Daniel and Nick. As I drove home along the rural highway, the fields seemed greener, the sunlight brighter, the river more serene, the sky a deeper blue. The world around Moses Lake was suddenly altogether different, more beautiful, more . . . glorious. That's how I felt. Glorious. Nothing could spoil it.

Pulling into the ranch and finding Daniel gone and Mason West sitting on my back porch watching Nick play in the sandpile did put a damper on my happy little world, though. A strange, uneasy feeling passed over me.

Daniel had left Nick here with this man we barely knew? What could possibly cause him to do that?

If I hadn't been in a state of cottony bliss, panic would probably have quickly followed the question. As it was, I pushed the car door open quickly, shifted around to get out, and whacked my head when the door blew shut on me. I had to stand there for a minute catching my breath, and by that time, Mason was making his way through the gate, asking if I was all right.

"Yes, I'm fine. Really. That was dumb." I blushed and

smiled, and Mason smiled back, lifting his sunglasses and setting them atop his head so that I could see his eyes, hazel like Jack's. I wasn't sure I'd ever seen him take his sunglasses off, even indoors.

"The wind out here will drive you crazy." Holding the gate open, he swished a hand, ushering me into the yard. "Could've happened to anyone." He held up a finger with a Band-Aid around it and said, "Evidence."

"Car door?"

"Gate. Yesterday, looking at the cattle with my father. Now I remember how cumbersome those latches are." He smiled again as he followed me into the yard, and I caught myself looking over my shoulder, flashing a grin. Maybe it was the fact that Mason looked a fair amount like Daniel, or maybe it was that he was clearly good with women, but I needed to watch myself with Mason. I was never sure if he was just being friendly, or if he was looking to flirt.

I wasn't a good one to judge. I wasn't the kind of girl guys usually flirted with—too serious and into the business end of things. Working around politicians, I'd learned to be. I'd also, for years, watched my mother navigate the slippery slope of interest from my father's associates. She was a master at being friendly, but letting them know where the boundaries were.

The first rule in that game—mention your significant other early and often. "Where's Daniel?" I looked around, as if I'd just noticed that his vehicle was gone.

"They're at the lab. My father had some idea, and you know, Jack West's ideas wait for no man." I caught a hint of something underlying that comment. There was no time to decipher it before it vanished behind the mask of casual amiability. "Your little boy was taking a nap when we came by. I volunteered to wait here until you got in."

"I'm sorry you had to do that." Discomfort crept in on

quick, nimble spider legs. I didn't want to go back to the days of Daniel being at Jack's beck and call. He was supposed to be off work this morning, watching Nick. *Jack West's ideas wait for no man* . . . I had a feeling Mason knew exactly what I was thinking.

He inclined his head sympathetically, shrugging off my apology. "They haven't been gone long. No worries. The little guy woke and he seemed to want to come out here, so we did. I think he was a shade worried when he found his dad gone, but we took care of it." A wink and a shrug directed my attention to the sandpile, where Nick was playing with some antique-looking Tonka tractors, a tiny pickup truck, and a horse trailer. I took a couple steps closer and realized where those things had come from. Jack's little house out back. Those were the toys Nick and Pecos had spirited onto the bedroom floor during their episode of doggie-door breaking and entering.

An alarm jangled in my head like a three-cornered dinner bell. I remembered the expression on Jack's face when we'd found Nick asleep on the floor in the undisturbed little-boy bedroom of Jack's dead stepson.

"Oh, I don't think Nick should have those." I set my purse on a plastic chair and started in Nick's direction. No doubt, an epic meltdown was on the way, but I had to get the toys cleaned up and put back in their places before Jack returned.

Mason reached out and caught my arm, stopping me as I passed him. The distance between us was suddenly intimate. "It's fine." He looked down at me, his eyes intense. "The little house needs to be cleaned out. It's unhealthy, don't you think? All those things still in their places, like someone's coming back for them?"

I glanced down at his hand on my skin, feeling cold, then hot, the sensation traveling over me in waves. "I think that's

Jack's decision." Backing away, I broke the contact between us and crossed my arms over my chest, using body language to signal that I was in no way open to anything Mason might have in mind . . . if he did have something in mind.

"Relax," Mason assured. "I've already talked to my father about emptying out that house. He knows." Again there was a flash of something I couldn't read. It came with those two words, *He knows.* Then it was gone.

"Well . . . then I guess . . . it's okay."

"Look what I got!" Nick came out of his imaginary world long enough to hold up the Tonka truck and livestock trailer. "It gots cows in it!" Opening the doors, he dumped out a load of plastic cows.

For some reason, all I could think about was Jack's stepson playing with those things. The dead boy. He became real to me in an instant. A child young enough to live in a pretend world. Like Nick.

Gone without a trace.

My head pounded and swirled. Sweat dripped beneath my T-shirt.

Mason's hand slid under my arm. I tried to shrug it off, but he wouldn't let go. "I think you'd better sit down." His voice was smooth and calm, not ruffled in the least by my reaction.

"I'm fine." But I followed him to the porch and took a seat in the shade. No matter what, I didn't want to end up in the house with Mason. Even more now my nerves were on edge. I couldn't pin it to any one thing—nothing Mason had said or done was in any way a threat.

"Better?" he asked, sitting in a chair beside me, leaning over and bracing his elbows on his knees, as if he were trying to get a good look at my face. His expression was a model of friendly concern. Compassionate, even.

"Yes, thank you." Pressing a hand to my forehead, I tried to smooth the tangle of thoughts. "It's just a whole lot hotter here in Texas than I'm used to."

"Not quite DC, is it?" He sat back in his chair, increasing the distance between us.

"Yeah, not quite." I decided I was probably being ridiculous. What in the world would someone like Mason West want with someone like me?

"Sorry you left the staffer's job behind?" His question took me aback. I hadn't realized that he knew so much about me. The surprise must have registered on my face, because he explained, "Your husband mentioned that he was afraid you really missed it."

"Oh . . ." It was a little strange to think I'd been the topic of conversation between Daniel and Mason at some point— that Daniel had been telling them I was having a hard time adjusting. It felt like a tiny betrayal. "Daniel worries too much. Actually, the longer I'm in Moses Lake, the more I discover that it isn't all that different. There's plenty of political controversy here, too. It's just on a different scale." A connection formed in my mind. Mason was a state representative with strong party contacts and higher aspirations. If he threw a little weight behind the bridge issue in Chinquapin Peaks, local politicos would be likely to fall in line, trying to gain favor. One thing any politician covets is a connection with a politician at a higher level. It's all a game of favors. My father had taught me that.

The press loved politicians who weren't above getting their hands dirty—taking on real-world issues that affected families. Chinquapin Peaks was full of families. . . .

"Really? How so?" He cocked his head away, squinted at me, his look both cautious and acutely interested. "I wouldn't think there'd be anything in Moses Lake you would find interesting, after having been involved on the national level."

I had the little tingle that comes with knowing the fish is nibbling at the bait. There was more of my father in me than I'd ever realized. "You'd be surprised. Actually, I meant to say something about this to Jack, but we've been so busy recently." In truth, I'd seen very little of Jack since he returned with his son, other than their comings and goings and that one lunch at the Waterbird. "I sent some information to the *Dallas Morning News*. I haven't had a reply yet, but I think they'll be interested. It's an issue that affects quite a number of people."

Mason scratched near his ear, then braced a finger there. "Sounds intriguing." He didn't seem intrigued, really. More like worried. Maybe I was playing dirty pool, trying to drag him into local issues while he was on vacation, reconnecting with his father after so many years. "So tell me what passes for political underground in Moses Lake."

Well, he did ask . . .

I took a moment to put the information into logical order in my mind, maximizing the lure of possible photo ops that could be beneficial to a state representative with an electorate to cultivate. *Supper garden program, cute kids, Chinquapin Peaks, social issues, access problems, horrendously long bus rides, high failure rates in school, a bridge that could make so much difference . . .*

A kindly state representative with ties to the area . . .

A Bridge to Success—that would be a perfect tag line for an article . . .

All-in-all this had the makings of a great human-interest story.

I was just winding up to spill the details, when Nick squealed, "Daddy's heeeeere!"

Daniel's truck rattled up the driveway, bearing only Jack. I shifted to the front of my seat, wondering what he had done with my husband.

Mason didn't move. "Go ahead and finish what you were saying. He'll wait." It was more of a command than a request. It came with eerie intensity.

Mason glanced toward the sandpile, and for a horrifying moment, I wondered if he was hoping that Jack would see Nick with the toys. I'd forgotten about the toys.

My throat clenched.

Mason hooked one leg over the other, brushed dust off his jeans, and rested an arm across his lap, waiting for me to continue. I wondered what kind of game he was playing. "No, really, it's not urgent." I stood up just to make the point. "But there are some issues locally that would be worthy of attention. A little outside interest might help to move the logjam. My father always says that nothing gets a little wheel moving like a big wheel."

The quote brought a smile and a nod. Standing up, Mason slipped two fingers underneath the pearl snap on his shirt pocket, then handed me a business card. "I like the way you think. Give me a call in the morning. We'll talk. My father and your husband have some business to do first thing to-morrow—something about harvesting a plot, then running growth comparisons. But I'll be at the big house taking care of some business. Better yet, why don't you come by? I'll have the housekeeper fix some breakfast for us." His fingers brushed mine as I took the card, but I barely noticed. Jack had exited his truck and was proceeding toward the gate. Nick was just a few feet away, playing beneath the pome-granate bushes.

"Thanks, but I'll have to just call," I said. "Nick has a sum-mer class in the morning. I usually stay and help." I wasn't sure if Mason had heard me or not. His focus shifted, homed in as Jack walked through the gate, stopped, and looked at Nick and Pecos in the sandpile.

"I wonder what Dad did with your husband?" Mason remarked. "Some of those fields they planted are in the strangest locations. Hope everything's all right." Not only was the comment odd, but it was also flinty-cool. I looked up just in time to catch a countenance that matched the words. Just as quickly, it was gone, replaced by a pleasant look that was aimed at Jack.

"You get your business done?" Mason strode ahead to the gate, and I followed in his wake, acutely aware of the sweltering afternoon sun bearing down.

"What's this?" Jack motioned to the sandpile, his face hidden in the shadow of his hat.

"I got a tw-uck and tw-ailer!" Nick held up his treasures. I felt like I might pass out.

Mason's lips curved upward into a smile, his head inclining solicitously. "I took a few things out of the little house. Nick, here, was a bit lost when he woke up, and you'd taken off with his dad." The sentence ended in a chuckle that didn't seem to have much humor in it. "I figured you wouldn't mind if I got a start on cleaning the place out a bit."

Jack stood motionless, his shoulders stiffening, the muscles in his neck and jaw taut as if he were trying to restrain some emotion.

"We can put them back, if that's better," I offered hurriedly, stumbling over the words, moving toward Nick and the toys. "I'm sure Nick enjoyed playing with them, but they're not his."

Big blue eyes widening and mouth dropping, Nick clutched the truck and trailer to his chest, then reached back and hid the bulldozer behind his body.

"Nick . . ." I admonished, but I could feel a meltdown coming on. This was going to get ugly. In front of everyone.

Mason gave me a private look with a quick headshake that could have had a myriad of meanings. "Of course not. They're a gift. It's better that they're used rather than going to waste, right, Dad? Just like the cabin on Firefly Island. No sense having things sit idle. Locking them up and letting dust gather doesn't change the past."

I glanced back and forth between Mason and Jack, trying to read the invisible power play between father and son. In those few sentences, Mason had not only confirmed the reason that toys and belongings from twenty-five years ago rested enshrined in the little house, he'd also answered some of my lingering questions about Firefly Island. That place was a shrine, as well, a time capsule shrouded in meanings only Jack understood. What made him preserve the belongings of his wife and stepson, exactly as they had been?

Guilt? Grief?

Jack's shoulders lowered slowly, the line of his jaw softening. Pulling off his cowboy hat, he swiped an arm across his forehead. "No . . . no, 'course not. Place needs to be cleaned out. Might as well use what can be used. There might be some clothes and things in there about his size . . ." He nodded at Nick, but the sentence drifted off. I was glad. I didn't want to think about Nick wearing the dead boy's clothes.

"Thank you." I swallowed a weird soup of reactions. "I know Nick will take good care of the toys, won't you, Nick?"

Nick's face was open and honest, a little shock of blond hair falling over his lashes as he hugged both arms around the truck and trailer. "I wuv these." He rested his cheek against the truck's miniature headlights, and if his gratitude could have been sweeter or more genuine, I couldn't imagine how. He was absolutely, heart-meltingly earnest.

Bracing a hand on the fence, Jack slowly squatted down, his hulking form seeming to fold into place piece by piece as it cast a shadow over Nick. I stood transfixed, watching Jack reach out a big, brawny hand and lay it on Nick's head, the two of them connecting gaze to gaze. The moment seemed to slow, the day quieting around us. I wondered at Mason's reaction. I wanted to check, but I couldn't tear my focus away from Jack and Nick, from the war of emotions evident on Jack's face—tenderness, grief, and monumental sadness.

"You take care of those," Jack said softly. "A boy loved those very much. A very good boy."

Nick nodded solemnly, seeming to understand the seriousness of the moment. "Ho-kay," he whispered.

I thought about reminding Nick to say thank you, but no words seemed to fit. My vision of Jack shifted and changed, melting and taking on a new form. The suspicions I'd harbored, the rumors I'd heard . . . all of it seeped away, disappearing like vapor in the heat of the day. There was no way this man, this broken mountain who could kneel down and look at Nick that way, could have had anything to do with the murder of the little boy who once owned those toys. It simply wasn't possible.

"All right, then, that's that." Mason interrupted the moment, swinging his arms impatiently, letting his hands clap together. "What say we move on with our agenda for the day?" He stepped back as Jack slowly worked his way to his feet, groaning with the effort.

"Thank you for the toys," I told Jack as we walked toward the driveway. I'd just remembered that there was a gallon of milk in the car, along with my vitamins and a few other things I'd picked in Gnadenfeld.

Jack nodded. "Someone oughta use them." Clearing his throat, he affected the usual stoic frown. "Your husband drove the tractor to the lab with some samples in the front end loader. He'll call you for a ride, after a while."

"Oh, okay, thanks." We parted ways at my vehicle, and I grabbed the gallon of milk, along with my sacks from town. From the periphery of my vision, I was aware of Mason getting into the ranch truck, and Jack hovering by the driver's side door, watching me. Closing the back of the Jeep, I stopped and looked his way.

"Too many hormones." Jack pointed to the milk, as if he were voicing the observation and thinking it through at the same time. "Not healthy for babies and kids. Big dairy wants you to believe it's harmless, but it's not."

"Oh, well, okay." I wasn't sure if he was waiting for me to dump the milk out in the driveway, or what. The comment was so out of character for Jack, I didn't know how to respond to it. "I'll be sure to . . . buy . . . organic next time."

"Still pasteurized," he grunted, and then he was gone.

I stood there with my hormone-laced milk, thinking, *I need a drink.*

A really, really big glass of milk. With chocolate.

Lots of chocolate.

Greatness is not in where we stand,
but in what direction we are moving.

—Oliver Wendell Holmes
(Left by Jay, who drove a truck to earn his pay,
and learned some things along the way)

Chapter 19

The world's most unusual gift arrived three days later. I was out in the yard with Nick, enjoying another sudden bloom of rain lilies. Overnight, they had popped up and carpeted the grass, and the first thing Nick wanted to do after we came home from summer enrichment was pick bouquets and put them all around the house again.

On the back porch, the intercom buzzed, indicating that the front gate was closed and someone was out there. I answered, thinking it might be Keren, who'd been working with me on some article ideas about the gardening program. I was hoping that a few human-interest pieces about specific families involved in growing supper gardens might help to generate media interest. So far, I hadn't had any luck getting major media coverage for the program, although readers of *The Frontier Woman* were clamoring for updates on the kids in Chinquapin Peaks and their plans for family gardens.

The voice on the intercom definitely wasn't Keren's. The words came in the thickly accented pidgin of Spanish and English that was typical of many of the guys who came up from Mexico to work on ranches around the area. "I gottee dees mee-lk cow for jou, *pero este* gate es close."

"You've got my what?"

"Mee-lk ca-owww." He slowed the words down. "From de cow sale dis morn-een. Jou buy her. I gottee the b-eel of sale. It saying, de-liber her here."

It occurred to me that maybe Al was at the gate, and she'd solicited someone's help to play a joke on me. I'd shared Jack's comment about the hormones in milk last week, and for once, Al was actually in agreement with Jack. She'd been threatening to bring me my very own milk goat, and I'd been telling her that if she did, I was going to sneak over to her house with the goat and put it in her living room. My one attempt at goat milking was a funny blog and a bad memory. "I think you're at the wrong place. I didn't order a milk cow."

"I gottee de-liber her here. She for Mal-lo-reee E-ber-soon. Mee-ilk cow. Cow is *para ti. Hace mucho calor* out here. Bery *hot*, okay?"

"I *didn't* buy a *cow*," I said sweetly, smirking to myself. I was not going to be sucked into this. Al was probably watching through those ever-present binoculars of hers, just waiting for me to open the gate.

"I gotte de-liber her. I gonna tie her to dees fence, okay?" The man actually sounded perturbed. "She kick-een my trailer."

"Okay, okay, wait." Even if I didn't open the gate, I'd have to go down there, on the off chance that some poor cow might be tied to the gate in the afternoon sun. Maybe the deliveryman didn't know this was all just a gag. "Hang on. I'll buzz you in."

I pushed the button and moved to the yard fence, shading my eyes and looking down the driveway. Nick, his fingers clutching a batch of rain lilies, followed me. He had learned some time ago that a cute ranch kid standing at the fence was a magnet for delivery men with packs of gum, bags of suckers, or rolls of stickers to give away. Pecos, who knew that the UPS man carried Beggin' Strips and Milk-Bones, waited with us, his nub tail wagging hopefully.

The usual swirl of white caliche dust followed a truck and livestock trailer up the driveway. Apparently, Al had gone all the way this time. There was actually a cow in the trailer. I could see it moving around as the vehicle stopped and the delivery man exited with a clipboard in hand.

"You gotte *escribé*." The deliveryman made a motion for me to sign the delivery ticket.

A plaintive *moo-ooo-ooo* traveled through the air.

I held my hands palm-out, giving the international sign for, *No way, dude. That's not my cow.* "I . . . didn't order . . . a cow. I promise. No . . . uhhh . . ." I searched my limited Rolodex of college Spanish. I was much better with French and Italian. What was the word? "No . . . uhhh . . . *comparlo.* No." I thought that should translate to, *I didn't buy it*, but the poor man only thrust the sheet at me again.

"I gotte leeb here." He made the motion of unloading the cow. "Muy caliente." Pointing to the trailer, he pantomimed the last words, even though I understood them well enough. *It's hot.* No telling what the temperature was inside that trailer. The cow looked miserable.

Balancing the clipboard atop the gatepost, he hurried toward the trailer. I caught the clipboard as it slid off.

"No, but . . . wait . . ." There was no point in arguing, though. The man was determined. In fact, he couldn't seem to move fast enough as he secured my new cow in the barn.

I called Al as soon as the truck and trailer rolled away. "Very funny, sending the cow. You can come get it now, though. The man said it needs to be milked, and not that I know anything about cows, but she looks uncomfortable—like she might explode or something."

Al didn't answer at first. I was waiting for laughter, but instead she said, "Hang on a minute, Mallory," and brusquely left me dangling on the line while she ordered food at a drive-through.

Apparently, she wasn't staked out somewhere on a hilltop, enjoying the drama of the cow delivery. She actually seemed confused. "So, what's up? What'd the old so-and-so have a cow about now?" She was referring to Jack, of course.

Nick tugged at the hem of my shirt. He wanted to go back out and see the cow. She was charming, as cows went, I supposed. She had big brown eyes and long eyelashes, and she seemed to like children. "The *cow*, Al. Really. That was funny and all, but if someone doesn't do something . . . well, *can* cows actually explode? The guy didn't speak much English, but he used the sign language for *She needs to be milked*. I know what *gorda* and *mucha leche* means. I did take a little Spanish in college. Come pick her up, okay?"

Nick tugged harder on my shirt. "I wanna see the cow-w-w-w," he whined. In all the excitement over rain lilies and then the cow, we'd neglected naptime.

"Nick, shhh," I snapped. "It's not our cow, it's Al's. It's going to Al's house to live."

A huge pout lip formed, and Nick's forehead lowered over his eyes. Releasing my T-shirt, he crossed his arms and staged a sit-in on the kitchen floor.

"Nick, cut it out. We can't keep the cow."

"It's not mine," Al insisted. "I'm a strictly a sheep and goat girl, remember? Shoot, I hardly even know what to do with a cow."

Nick uncrossed his legs and pummeled the kitchen floor with his heels, sending a dirty look my way.

"All right, you know that's not okay." I pointed the mommy finger at Nick. I was learning not to cave in to the threat of snotty hum zingers at inopportune times and in public places. "If you're going to throw a fit, go do it in your room."

"Well, I would, but I'm over in Gnadenfeld, getting a sandwich." Al was laughing on the phone now.

Nick flopped over on his stomach and started wailing.

"I told you what to do about that kind of thing," Al offered. Somehow, she was an expert on parenting techniques, too. "Just tell him to throw the biggest fit he can come up with, and cheer him on while he does it. The minute he thinks you want him to throw the fit, he won't want to anymore. Reverse psychology. It works. Learned that from Foster Cline and Jim Fay, *Parenting With Love and Logic*." One incongruous thing I'd discovered about Al was that she'd read more books than anyone I'd ever met. She had a penchant for self-help and psychology. "I'll come by and take a look on my way home, but it's not my cow."

"Well . . . but wait . . . who . . ." Then I landed on a completely new thought. "You don't think that Jack . . ."

"Can't hear ya. Give me an hour or so. I'll call Keren and see if I can bring her, too. This oughta be fun." Al hung up, and I was left with the phone and the fit. Nick wore himself out and quieted to a whimper, and I put him down for a nap. Then I called Daniel at the lab.

"Do you think Jack would have sent us a cow?" I blurted.

"A what?"

"A cow, Daniel. A man showed up with a cow, and it had my name on the delivery notice. Please tell me this cow isn't supposed to be here . . ."

"Jack did go to an auction this morning. But I can't ask him about the cow because he just left with Mason. Something about looking at a site to build a lake house. I guess

Mason's thinking he might spend more time here." Daniel sounded happy and hopeful, but the more often I rubbed elbows with Mason, the more vaguely uncomfortable I was around him. The day after he'd given Nick the toys, I'd had a phone conversation with him and tried to bring up the bridge in Chinquapin Peaks. The only thing Mason seemed interested in was luring me over to the big house for breakfast. I'd politely declined again.

I hadn't said anything to Daniel, but Mason was definitely angling toward something. I just couldn't figure out what it was.

"So, do you think that Jack sent me a *cow*?" I asked.

I heard metal clinking, and what sounded like one of the centrifuges in the lab whirring. "Anything's possible. He's on a buying spree. I just got two four-foot crates of used lab equipment he found on eBay. Looks like it came from some university. I'm trying to figure out if there's much I can actually use, and the thing is, Jack doesn't seem to care. When he came by here and saw it this morning, it was like he'd almost forgotten that he'd bought it. He said, whatever I don't want, just donate it to the school. So I'd say a milk cow is a definite possibility. Jack's happy, and when Jack's happy, I guess money flows. Nobody knows for sure, because nobody's ever seen Jack like this. Do you need me to come help you with your new cow?" He was laughing when he said, it.

"No, Al's coming."

"Well, fine, I've been usurped by Al again." He sighed, trying to give the impression that he was greatly wounded by the fact that I'd called Al first.

"Do you know *anything* about milking cows?"

"Only what I learned off *Gunsmoke*." He chuckled, then added, "You're probably better off with Al, and I should try to get some things done here before the parade of roses ends.

I'm going to drive out to the test plot in the Cedar Break pasture and gather some samples. Jack said he and Mason would grab some for me, but there's no telling where they're at right now. They might have forgotten all about it. I should be back in the lab in an hour or so, if you need me. I want to run tests while I can."

We said good-bye, and I hung up the phone, leaving the undercurrents of Daniel's last comment unexplored. We both knew that Jack's recent phase of nirvana, or joy over his family reconciliation, or whatever was happening couldn't go on forever. Sooner or later, we would all have to find out what the landscape of Jack West was going to look like after Mason's return.

The days of new wall-to-wall carpet and free cows were undoubtedly numbered.

I tried not to ponder that too much as I did some things around the house and waited for Al and Keren to show up. An hour and a half later, when we walked into the barn together, the subject of Jack's recent outlandish behavior came up. It was bound to, considering that the gift cow was standing right there.

"The old fart has gone round the bend this time," Al observed while Keren checked the cow over, then found a crate to sit on and washed out a bucket to use for milking. The cow looked greatly relieved that someone qualified had arrived.

Nick leaned in to watch, bracing his hands on his knees, fascinated as Keren settled in and began the milking.

"My sister's doctor told her not to drink raw milk when she was pregnant," Keren pointed out. "Of course, they tell all the farm girls that, and a lot of them do it anyway, but you should be careful."

Crossing my arms over my stomach, I leaned in and watched the milk scooshing into the bucket. I'd never really thought about where milk came from. In the store, it looked so . . . pristine and white and . . . sanitary. "I think I'll just buy organic." In general, I preferred to believe that food just appeared in the world, neatly packaged in hermetically sealed containers. "I'm hoping it's a misunderstanding about the cow. Maybe Jack wanted it or something. Surely, he wouldn't buy me a *cow*."

Both Keren and Al turned incredulous looks my way, as in, *This is Jack West we're talking about, remember?*

Al scoffed, then sifted a horseshoe from the dust on the barn floor and handed it to Nick. "The way that old coot's been acting lately, I wouldn't be too sure. He passed by me when I was coming out my gate the other day, and he waved. Actually *waved*. I heard he went into the Waterbird last Friday and asked a couple of the Docksiders how the fishing was."

Keren nodded. "Our bull ran through the perimeter fence last week, and instead of calling and threatening to sic his lawyer on us, Mr. West sent a couple of the ranch hands to help us pen up the bull and fix the fence. He didn't even ask us to pay for the repairs." Her eyes were wide with disbelief.

Leaning against the side of the stall, Al hooked her thumbs in her pockets. "This keeps up, the old man's not going to be any fun at all to have as a neighbor." She pulled a face and I chuckled, but I felt guilty for laughing at Jack. In spite of all that we'd been through here, there was something incredibly sad about Jack's life.

"I feel sorry for him." Keren offered a mirror of my thoughts. "He must have been so lonely all these years. I can't imagine what it would be like, not having your family. I mean, we might have our little differences in our clan—there are so many of us, for one thing—but family means everything. I don't know how we'd survive without each other."

Al turned toward the corner, hiding something. If she had

any remaining family, she had never mentioned them. Her life, in some ways, seemed a lot like Jack's, though I would never have said that to her.

She cleared her throat before she spoke. "Well, I hate to say it, but he's putting his eggs in the wrong basket with that son of his. That man is trouble."

"Oh, I hope not." Keren cast an anxious frown at Al.

Al's expression was flat, her lips a thin, confident line. "If Mason West is spending this much time away from the wine, women, and song down in the state capitol, he's here for a reason. And it's not to reconnect with his daddy."

A chill ran over me. Chrissy had said the same thing, and with the same sense of certainty. "Then why? Why do you think he's here?"

The milk bucket went silent, and Keren looked up, waiting.

Al shrugged. "I'm not a mind reader or a fortune-teller. I'm just saying, look at the man's record. He's a slash-and-burn politician—more coal plants, more strip mining, more access to public lands so his cronies can make money off resources that should belong to the public. Less money to teachers and schools, and more money to testing companies to produce state tests. Over a hundred million, last year alone. Who do you think the investors in those testing companies are? His contributors. His cronies. Mason West has made himself a multi-multimillionaire by serving up favors for the right people. He's living the high life down there in Austin, and now he's looking at a national bid. You tell me if you think he's got any real interest in this ranch, his daddy, or in the development of grain that'll make some farmer in Africa able to grow corn on the savannah. Mason is here for a reason. If I knew what it was, I'd . . ."

My cell phone rang, the sound echoing through the barn, high-pitched and out of place, stirring the guinea hens from the rafters. Both Keren and I jumped, and then I slid the phone out to look at it. Daniel. Probably calling to check on the cow milking. I popped it onto speakerphone.

The minute he said my name, I knew something was wrong.

"Daniel, what's the matter?" There was noise in the background, either voices or the radio. He wasn't in the lab. "Where are you?" I was aware of Al, Keren, and Nick watching me.

"Jack's had an accident," Daniel's reply was rushed and breathless. "We're on our way to the hospital in Gnadenfeld. I'm following the ambulance." Al pushed off the wall, and Keren steadied the milk bucket.

"An accident? What happened?" The day suddenly felt surreal, as if everything around us had stopped moving.

"I don't know all the details. Something happened on the cliffs above the Cedar Break plot. His truck slipped out of gear and rolled over the edge. I've gotta go, Mal. I'll talk to you at the hospital." He hung up, and I stood there staring at the phone, trying to process. A sense of dread and disbelief filled the sunny day with sudden shadows.

Al's gaze met mine again, and she pulled her bottom lip between her teeth, slowly shaking her head. "Wonder where Mason West was when that happened."

The words were an unnerving echo of my thoughts. I was wondering, too.

Men and fish are alike.
They both get into trouble when they open their mouths.

—Jimmy D. Moore
(Left by Roger the dog, often the smartest one in the room)

Chapter 20

When I arrived at the hospital, Daniel was in a waiting area with several ranch hands and various people who appeared to have been part of the emergency response team that had rescued Jack. The air in the room was stretched gauzy thin, the discussion taking place in careful whispers intended not to ripple the fragile fabric. Conversations stopped and glances turned my way as I entered. Daniel stood up and met me near the door.

"Where's Nick?" he asked, anxiety sketching lines over his forehead.

"Al stayed with him at the house. The Jeep wouldn't start, so I drove Al's truck over here. How's Jack?"

Daniel moved to the wall near the door, and I followed. "We're waiting for the doctors to tell us. It was bad, Mal. His heart stopped on the way to the hospital, and they had to resuscitate him. They're doing CT scans now, checking for internal bleeding."

I glanced around the room, trying to process everything, struggling to put together the pieces. All I could think of were Al's final words before she tossed me her keys and told me to take the truck.

Find out where Mason was when it happened.

I scanned the anxious faces in the room, looked at Chrissy in the corner, sitting on the arm of a chair, her body curled protectively over Tag's. Was she thinking the same thing I was thinking—that her husband could have been in that truck with Jack?

"Where's Mason?" Ears seemed to shift my way when I mentioned the name.

"Talking to the sheriff's deputy about the accident." Daniel shrugged vaguely toward the hall. "I'm not sure where they went."

"What happened, exactly?" I searched Daniel's face for the things he wasn't saying. He was worried, and not just about Jack's prognosis. There was something deeper that he was afraid to give voice to.

Stroking his bottom lip with his thumb and forefinger, he blinked slowly and turned his attention from me to the window, as if he were trying to look across the miles and see the Cedar Break cliffs for himself. "Apparently they were parked at that test plot above the lake. Mason got out to take some pictures and step off some square footage for the lake house he wants to build. Jack stayed in the truck and slid over to the passenger side to stretch out and take a catnap. According to Mason, Jack had been up with the stomach flu last night and hadn't slept much. Anyway, when Mason turned around, the truck was rolling toward the cliff. He tried to get to it, but he couldn't make it there in time. Jack attempted to bail as it was going over the edge. He hit a patch of cedars about twenty feet down. That's the only reason he survived the accident. That's Mason's version of what happened, anyway."

I watched Daniel's teeth worry his bottom lip, saw the

tension in his fingers as he combed them through the dark curls of his hair.

"But you don't believe him. . . ."

Pulling in a quick breath, he shrugged and shook his head. "I don't know what I believe. Why did the truck just slip out of gear like that? Jack's ranch truck was pretty new. It's not like the gears are worn out. And why didn't Mason hear it when it started rolling? It's pretty quiet out there, normally, and it's rocky. The tires would've been moving over gravel."

"What are you saying? You think Mason might have . . . left the truck out of gear on purpose?" The words were hard to even say. The idea seemed so melodramatic and farfetched. Why, after all these years, would Mason come here to reunite with his father and then attempt something so sinister?

Our strange conversation the day Mason had given Nick the toys from the little house slid through my mind. I crossed my arms over my stomach, squeezed my elbows hard against my ribs. Maybe Daniel thought I was out of my mind, bringing up a suspicion like that, but that nagging feeling I'd had about Mason was now exploding like fireworks in my head. There was a history of people meeting strange fates in the West family. As frustrating as life under Jack's thumb had been, I couldn't help but remember the tender look on his face as he knelt over Nick's sandpile.

Daniel tasted his lower lip again. "Jack was *driving*, though, or Mason says Jack was. And typically if Jack's in the truck, he does insist on being at the wheel. If the truck was left out of gear, that would mean he was the one who did it. Apparently he got his foot hung up in the seat belt, trying to jump out the door, and that's what actually dragged him over the edge. One thing different, and Jack wouldn't have survived at all."

In the hallway, an orderly rattled by with a supply cart.

I watched it pass, thought of Jack broken and battered. I imagined the net of thick cedars catching him, saving him from the rocks below. "But something is still bothering you." I touched Daniel's chin, turned his face toward mine, and stretched closer to him. "What are you not saying, Daniel? If you know something more, tell me. We have to figure this out before anything else happens. *You* could've been in that truck. You could've been in that truck with Jack. What are you hiding from me?" In that moment, I felt the depth of my love for my husband, the fierce devotion to our life together, to our life here. Somehow, in the past weeks, this place, this man, had become home for me. I wouldn't let anyone threaten that.

He closed his eyes, took a moment to think, then looked at me again. "It's just that Jack never parks the truck pointed toward the lake like that. My first day here, he specifically told me not to. He related some story about his wife and his stepson going out Christmas tree hunting in one of the pastures years ago. They left the truck out of gear, and it rolled over a cliff into the lake. No one was in it, but it almost ran them over. Supposedly it's still down there under the water somewhere."

"Did you tell the sheriff's deputy that?" I thought of the letter in the cookbook. *Her* letter. If the letter was hers, could that accident be the reason she was afraid, the reason she was planning to flee the ranch with her young son?

"I haven't talked to the deputy, and they haven't asked me any questions. I don't know if they're looking at it as anything more than an accident. Jack has mentioned a few times that the sheriff's department in this county isn't very proactive. Mart McClendon, the game warden, was there and helped with the rescue. He asked me a few questions about how I thought it happened, but that was about it."

"You should have told him what you just told me." Overhead, the air-conditioner clicked on, and cold, antiseptic-scented air slid over my bare shoulders, raising gooseflesh.

Daniel slid a hand over my skin, a placating gesture. "Let's just take things a step at a time. In the weeks Mason has been here, he hasn't done anything to make me think he would try to . . . stage a murder. Because that's what it would be. No way you would expect anyone to survive going over that cliff in a vehicle. I was at the Cedar Break right after the accident—remember, this afternoon, I told you I was going out there to gather some samples? When I drove up, Mason had already called 9-1-1. He had help on the way. Why would he do that, if he wanted Jack dead?"

I slid into Daniel's arms and pressed hard against his chest. "I just keep thinking that you could have been in the truck. What if you'd been out with them today?" For an instant, I saw a future without Daniel—Nick growing up with no father, this new baby never knowing Daniel at all. No more mornings of drowsily rolling over in tangled sheets and reaching for Daniel, curling my body against his, feeling warm, protected, complete.

I realized how lucky I was, how much I loved him. It didn't matter where we lived—ranch house in Texas, hut in Borneo, tent in Timbuktu—as long as we were together.

"I'm okay. I'm fine." His kiss fell soft on my hair, and I took in the scent and the feel of him—the laundry soap from our washing machine, the shaving cream from our bathroom, the musky cowboy-hat-shaped soap that Daniel's brother had given him at his bachelor party, the faint smell of new paint from our freshly repaired closets. Ordinary scents. Beautiful scents.

"You have to be safe, that's all," I whispered. "I think you should tell someone what you told me."

"Let's see what they find out about Jack, first." Daniel's

answer ruffled the hair near my ear. "If he comes to and is able to talk, he might shed some light on what happened. I don't want to stir up trouble where there may be none. It's possible that Jack just wasn't paying attention to what he was doing, and he parked in the wrong place. He's been pretty manic since Mason came. Maybe he just had his mind on other things."

"Maybe." But every cell in my body was screaming that this wasn't accidental.

"And to tell you the truth, Mason was beside himself after the accident. I know what I'd do if that were my dad, and that's pretty much the state Mason was in. If he was faking it, he's one heck of an actor."

But maybe he is, I thought, and then the idea seemed off-base and unkind. Perhaps I was creating ridiculous drama where there was only an unfortunate accident. "Okay." I leaned into my husband and hung on, waiting, trying not to overthink things too much, but I couldn't stop.

Twenty minutes ticked by, then thirty, then an hour, as the people in the room moved from place to place, from hushed conversation to hushed conversation. My mind returned over and over to that day on the porch with Mason, to words that seemed to have double entendre, to gut feelings and subliminal impressions. To the letter from the cookbook, the obvious fear. I'd assumed that, if the letter was hers, she was afraid of Jack. What if that wasn't it at all? What if she was afraid of Mason? He would have been a young adult then. What if he saw the new wife and the cute stepson as competition? What if he didn't want them around?

My father always said that a gut feeling will tell you more about a man than what he says. *If you're ever in doubt, go with your gut, Mallory.*

My gut was still saying terrible things that I didn't want

to believe, whispering warnings as the number of people in the room increased. Reverend Hay showed up, along with Mama B.

Claire Anne Underhill from the hardware store arrived a few minutes later, obviously trolling for information. "Lucy Rivers told me it's all over the police scanners, and a Dallas news station even sent a *helicopter* to film the story. They're bringing a crane in to get the truck back out of the lake." Her eyes widened, sparkling like small blue gems beneath her neatly hairsprayed bangs. "It's just so fortunate that Jack was able to get out when he did. Has there been any report on his condition? I've been so worried. If we hadn't been in the middle of a delivery at the store, I would have closed up and driven here right away. Mason must be beside himself. Just beside himself." She scanned the room like a beauty pageant contestant making sure to work all sections of the audience. "Where *is* Mason? Is he all ri-ight? Does he need anything?"

"He's with the sheriff's deputies. But if he does need anything, all of us from the ranch are here," Chrissy said, strangely territorial considering her usual sentiments about Jack.

Claire Anne helped herself to a seat by the window, not about to be squeezed out. "It's just like those know-nothings from the sheriff's department to trouble the poor man at a time like this. Really, I have half a mind to contact my stepson and tell him to give the sheriff a call. Maybe they'll listen to someone from the county commission. Mason West is a state representative, for heaven's sake. If they're not careful, they'll give Moses Lake a bad name. What with the drug arrests up in Chinquapin Peaks last year and the Proxica Foods scandal, this county doesn't need any more bad publicity." She checked the door again. "Is there no news about Jack's condition?"

"We're still waiting for the doctors to tell us something,"

Reverend Hay answered, because no one else did. He had the patient look of a man accustomed to not letting his parishioners rattle him.

"It's just so tragic," Claire Anne lamented. "Such a terrible accident. I hope Mason is bearing up all ri-ight." She peered through the doorway again, checking the hall. When Mason West didn't magically appear, she settled back in her seat, her long, coral-colored fingernails toying with a loose thread on the arm of the chair. Silence descended over the group. Another twenty minutes ticked by. Al texted my cell to see if I knew anything. I told her we hadn't heard.

"This is ridiculous. I'm going to figure out what's happening," Daniel finally whispered in my ear. "They must know something by now." He pushed off the wall and left the room. Chrissy watched him go, then rose from her chair and came to stand by me.

"Where's he goin'?" She kept her voice low, glancing over her shoulder at Claire Anne. "Was that something about Mr. West on your phone just now?" She motioned to the cell. I hadn't even realized I was still holding it. My thoughts were spinning down the corridor with Daniel, wondering what he would find.

"He just went to see if there's any news. The text was only Al Beckenbauer, asking if we'd heard anything."

Chrissy blinked. "Why would *she* care? She and Jack West can't stand each other."

"The man fell over a cliff, Chrissy," I said sharply. Chrissy would grow up to be like Claire Anne Underhill one day, if she wasn't careful.

Tucking a shock of red curls behind her ear, Chrissy ducked her head. "Sorry. I'm just worried, you know? Tag and I need this job. If anything happens to Jack, Mason will get rid of the ranch in a heartbeat. The day Daniel went with Jack to pick up that new seeder in Fort Worth, Tag was counting cows on horseback up by the Twin Mountains, and he saw Mason driving around the pastures with some guy in a suit. They were pointing and talking and shaking hands, and stuff. Tag watched them for a long time. He said it looked like a business deal." She cut a look my way, lashes narrowing. "And now, Jack has an accident, like *two weeks* later?"

"Let's just wait and ask questions when Jack wakes up, all right?" After seeing Jack so euphoric about his reunion with Mason these past few weeks, I couldn't imagine what would happen if he heard the ranch hands making accusations like this.

Chrissy looked down at her feet and scuffed a pink flip-flop along the ugly linoleum tile. "I just hope Jack gets back up out of that bed. I mean, I complain about the man, but I didn't want something terrible to happen to him." Moisture rimmed her eyes, and she swallowed hard. "It makes me think that you never can tell what's gonna happen—when everything might change in a heartbeat, you know? I mean, Tag and me had a fight last night, and this morning when he left, we weren't even talkin'. When I heard about Jack's accident, I thought, What if that were Tag, and I never had the chance to take it all back?"

I touched her arm, and suddenly she seemed like the bratty little sister I never had. "Something like this makes everyone take stock. So much of what seems to matter on a regular day wouldn't even make a ripple the day after a car accident or a cancer diagnosis. The trick is to remember that on all the regular days, I guess. My grandmother gave me that advice years ago when she was diagnosed with cancer. I don't always remember it as well as I should."

Chrissy sniffled, her chest shuddering. A tear traced the outline of her cheek when she looked up again. "I wish Tag and I were more like you and Daniel. You guys are so . . . nice to each other."

I wish Tag and I were more like you. . . . It had never occurred to me that anyone might be watching us, that we might be teaching lessons as we were learning lessons, and when we learned well, we might teach well. When we didn't, we weren't just hurting ourselves; we were polluting the world with bad examples. "It's a process. My parents had their issues, and they drove us kids crazy with their expectations sometimes, but they were always kind to each other. I think that's the best thing they did for us."

Chrissy batted away a tear, her lips twisting ruefully. "My parents fought like two cats in a tow sack. I never wanted McKenna to see stuff like that. I never thought about it too much until y'all came here. The other day when I put McKenna to bed, she said she wished Tag and I were nice like you."

Emotion squeezed my chest. All this time, I'd thought that Daniel and I were groping our way too clumsily through marriage. Maybe we weren't doing so badly. "Oh, hey, we're still in the design phase. Everyone's family looks better from the outside."

A text buzzed on my cell phone, and I paused to look at the message from Daniel. *Jack stable now. Back there in a minute.*

"It sounds like good news," I breathed, showing Chrissy the text. She promptly shared the information with the rest of the room. Reverend Hay lifted his hands, and Mama B cried out, "Praise God!"

"Mason must be so relieved," Claire Anne observed, anxiously checking the hall again. "I wonder if there's anything we can do for him. Maybe I could organize food to go to the ranch house. Family members shouldn't be worrying about cooking at a time like this."

"They have a *cook*," Chrissy pointed out blandly. "Besides, there is no family except Mason, and he's staying out on Firefly Island. Good luck taking food out there."

Claire Anne gave Chrissy a sour look. "Well, it's only proper to ask. What sort of a town would we be if we didn't rally around a neighbor in a time of need? I'm sure there are some ways we can help. I wonder where Mason is now. . . ."

"He's probably got bigger things on his mind than casseroles, Claire Anne," Mama B interjected. "Just leave him be. Don't sound like there's a lot we can do right now."

Claire Anne's thin, perfect fingers kneaded her pink leather clutch bag. "Well, we could at least . . ." She paused hopefully as Daniel entered the room, then registered disappointment when she realized he wasn't Mason.

Daniel shared the report on Jack's condition: broken ribs, cuts, bruises, no internal bleeding. "The thing they're most concerned about is swelling in the brain from the head injury. They're keeping him in an induced coma and giving him meds to try to relieve the pressure on the brain. If they can't control the swelling with meds, they'll have to relieve it with surgery. They're optimistic going forward, but they won't know the extent of the brain injury until he regains consciousness, and they're not sure when that will be."

Claire Anne stood up. "Well, where is Mason? Is he all ri-ight? I should tell him we're prayin' for his daddy. It wouldn't do for him to think that no one even came by. I mean, especially considerin' the amount of business that West Ranch does in this county."

"Mason is with Jack in ICU. They're not letting anyone else in." There was something Daniel wasn't telling the group. I could see it in his face. "It's just as well for everyone to go home. They don't expect anything more to happen tonight. Best-case scenario is that they're able to relieve the swelling on the brain with meds, and they won't have to do surgery."

The room cleared slowly as people retrieved their belongings and left. I sent Al a text with the news about Jack, then stood with Daniel until everyone was gone.

"You should go on home to Nick," he said as I slid the phone into my purse. "There's nothing more to do tonight." Outside the windows, the day was dimming, golden sunlight slanting through the glass in angular streams.

"But you're staying . . ." I looked at Daniel, his shirt still spattered with dirt and Jack's blood, and I knew he wasn't planning on going anywhere.

"I feel like I should."

"Because . . ." What wasn't he saying?

"I'm not sure." He rubbed the back of his neck, stretched it side to side. "I just feel like I should. I can't really explain it. This whole thing still bothers me, and I guess it will until Jack wakes up and can tell me what happened. I'm going to hang out by the ICU. There's a table and a couple chairs in the hall there. Someone needs to be here . . . besides Mason."

Trepidation walked up my spine again, looping and tightening the muscles like my mother's quick crochet stitches. "Did the sheriff's deputies leave?"

Daniel's cheek twitched the way it always did when he was irritated. "Apparently. When I went up there to see about Jack, Mason was sitting outside the ICU by himself."

"How did he seem?"

"Upset. Nervous. Kind of like a cat on hot tar, to borrow a phrase from the Docksiders at the Waterbird. When I asked him what the sheriff wanted, he said it was just routine—they needed the details to fill out the accident report." Daniel caught my hand in his, lifted it, and kissed my fingers. "I'm just going to spend the night in the chair up there. Don't worry about it, okay? You shouldn't be worrying right now."

I pointed a finger at him. "Daniel Everson, don't you go

babying me because I'm—" It still felt so strange to say the words. "In a family way."

"I wouldn't think of it." He caught my other hand, kissed those fingers, too. "Have Tag or one of the guys bring some clean clothes up here for me, okay? In fact, could you send a couple sets? I asked Mason if he wanted me to have one of the ranch hands go pick something up from Firefly, but he didn't take me up on it. He said he'd go himself when he could."

Daniel kissed me tenderly, and I left the hospital feeling off-center. The remains of the day were strangely beautiful as I crossed the parking lot to Al's truck. Opening the door, I turned to look over my shoulder one more time. Something fluttered in the corner of my vision—a piece of paper trapped partially under the truck tire, the wind teasing it, threatening to carry it away. I retrieved it, looked up and down the parking lot, then turned the paper over in my hand. It was a check stub from a literary and entertainment agency in LA. It had Al's address on it, but the name was different. Alex Beck.

Alex . . . Beck . . .

The name stirred the dusty corners of my mind and left behind a vague agitation, as if those words should mean something to me, but I couldn't quite put a finger on it.

Why did Al have another name, and why did that name seem so familiar . . . ?

The question shadowed me as I drove the rural highway home from Gnadenfeld, the river basin and cream-colored limestone cliffs peeking through yawning trees, playing a magician's trick. There one minute, gone the next. Hiding secrets.

Here, everyone seemed to have secrets.

When I reached the ranch, Al was gone. She'd left to take care of the evening feeding at her place, and Keren had taken over watching Nick. They were at the table, coloring in one of

Nick's coloring books. Nick was freshly bathed and already in his pajamas.

Keren offered to take Al's truck back to her, and I agreed. My body was weary, and my emotions were tangled like a kite string after a crash. I just wanted to eat something, then melt into bed—to sleep and not think about the day.

"Have you ever heard of Alex Beck?" I asked as I walked Keren to the door.

She paused before stepping out, pale brows gathered over blue eyes. "I don't think so. Why?"

"No reason. I was just trying to figure out why it seemed familiar."

She shrugged, then gave me a hug. "Well, it's kind of similar to Al's name—maybe that's why it's ringing a bell."

"Maybe," I said, the name scratching back and forth across my mind, sanding off a layer of old lacquer as I watched Keren walk away.

No harm befalls the righteous,
but the wicked have their fill of trouble.

—Proverbs 12:21
(Left by Rotten and Emma Lou, rescue dogs who've learned a thing or two)

Chapter 21

That night I dreamed of secrets—deep, terrible secrets. In my dream, I saw a man in a hooded trench coat. He was digging in the thick, loamy soil along the water's edge. Slowly, I moved closer, trying to discern his identity. Lightning flashed overhead, and the air crackled against my skin. I slid a hand across my stomach, swollen, late in pregnancy, heavy. I felt the baby's heartbeat beneath my fingers, a fragile flutter like the doppler stethoscope at the doctor's office.

Thunder eclipsed the sound.

The man by the shore stretched upright, then looked over his shoulder. Breath caught in my throat, and I hid behind the cedars, the branches catching my hair. I couldn't see the face inside the hood, but I could feel him searching for me, scanning the brush cover before returning to his task. My arms rounded my stomach protectively, and I crept closer after the man's back was turned, my bare feet falling silently in the moss.

The hole was large, rectangular . . . a grave, but shallow. Lightning crackled horizontally across the sky, illuminated the ground. I froze, stared into the hole, saw something white. A shroud, the outline of a body.

Who? Who was buried there, in this shallow grave so near the water?

The man continued his work, not burying the body, but digging the dirt away, finally bending and lifting the shrouded form as if it were weightless, then carrying it to the shore and setting it on the water. A gust of wind blew over the lake, stirred the surface, moaned through the oaks and cedars. Rain fell, soaking the shroud over the body, revealing the outline of a face.

Who? Whose face lay under the cloth?

I took a step closer, then another and another, and watched the body float farther and farther away.

Then I was on a cliff, looking down.

The body neared a small brown boat that was bobbing wildly in the storm. In the boat, children were playing, unaware of the danger—Chrissy and Tag's daughter, little Sergio from the summer class, Sierra, Birdie, and Nick. They were planting a garden in the bottom of the boat, laughing with each other, oblivious to the body floating near them, unaware of the hooded man on the shore.

"Watch out!" The wind whipped my voice into the air, sending it over the cliffs and away. "Watch out! Get off the water!"

The children couldn't hear me, and even if they had, there were no oars in the boat, no way to bring it to shore.

The man turned, his head swiveling. I drew back, wrapped my arms protectively over my stomach again, and then I was falling, the ground crumbling beneath me, sending me sliding toward the water. I was falling, and falling, and falling, the roundness in me gone. The baby, gone . . .

I woke with an outcry, gasping for breath, and slipped a hand under my T-shirt and felt the skin, searching for the thickening still so faint that I could hide it beneath my clothes. My own heart thrummed within my chest. I tried to sense the baby's heartbeat, as well.

It was only a dream. Just a dream.

Everything's okay.

I wanted to call the doctor, rush to the hospital, have a test, hear the baby's heartbeat just to be sure.

It's okay. We're all right. It was only a dream.

Or a message. Did God still speak to people in dreams? Terrible, unthinkable dreams?

Something threaded through my mind, something Keren had told me when I'd interviewed her about the supper gardens. She'd dreamed of the gardens first. *God talks to people in dreams in the Bible,* she'd said. *Daniel, Ezekiel, Paul, Solomon . . . Why couldn't He talk to me, tell me something I'm supposed to do, something that's meant to happen? Job 33:15 says it right out—He speaks in dreams . . .*

But this dream, my dream, wasn't a pleasant vision of kids and gardens. It was terrible, ominous. Like a warning, a threat.

The kids in the boat, the storm, the baby . . . our baby. Gone.

The body floating on the water. It was a warning. A death warning.

Drawing my legs to my chest, I squeezed the covers hard around me like a barrier, tried to push the visions away, but I couldn't.

Finally I threw the covers aside, crossed the room in the moonlight, my footsteps silent on the cool wood floor, like the footsteps in my dream. The closet door creaked loudly as I opened it. Down the hall, Nick stirred in his bed, and I paused, listening as he settled in again, then I turned on the closet light and sifted through a container of wedding gifts that had yet to be sorted and used.

My fingers circled a shoebox with scraps of lacy wedding wrap still clinging to the corners. A sense of calmness fell over me, quieting my heart as I opened the box. Inside lay Grandma Louisa's bridal Bible with the pearlescent Lucite cover. The scent of my grandmother's Charleston house wafted up, teased my senses with salt air, Spanish moss, dust, must, and the long history of Ellery brides. *This Bible always goes to the last bride in the family,* Mother's voice was in my ear now. *Each bride carries it, and the last one keeps it for the next generation. It's from Grandma Louisa to you. I have to say, you made it wait a while. . . .*

The light cascaded over my skin, the Bible reflecting the moonlight through the window and seeming to glow with life as I slid my fingers across the cover. I parted the pages, searched the table of contents, and found the book of Job, the chapter and verse Keren had quoted when I interviewed her about the supper gardens.

> *For God speaketh once, yea twice, yet man perceiveth it not. In a dream, in a vision of the night, when deep sleep falleth upon men, in slumberings upon the bed; Then he openeth the ears of men, and sealeth their instruction, that he may withdraw man from his purpose, and hide pride from man. He keepeth back his soul from the pit, and his life from perishing by the sword.*

A warning . . . was this nightmare a warning?

And of what?

Somehow, I had to find the truth, to sort through the secrets hidden beneath the surface of Moses Lake. I knew it in a way I'd never known anything in my life. This was the reason I was here.

Something terrible waited if I failed.

The sensation lingered as the night passed, sleep whisking over my mind, a ragged and featherlight veil. When I woke in the morning, I was tired and sore. Nick was standing beside the bed, cuddling his favorite stuffed Dalmatian under his chin, the plastic eyes watching me along with Nick's.

"Where's Daddy?" His voice was barely a whisper, as if he were afraid to disturb the stillness in the house.

"Daddy stayed at the hospital last night. Remember I told you that Mr. West had an accident and the doctors have to take care of him for a while? Tag came last night and got clothes to take to Daddy at the hospital, and he fixed the battery cable on our Jeep while he was here. Remember that?"

Nick blinked at me with huge eyes, a little pout lip jutting out. "I wanna my daddy," he whimpered, as if he sensed my uneasiness, as if he felt the undercurrent of fear that had floated with me through sleep.

Pushing against the bed, I sat up, my back in a twisted coil and my shoulders aching. I felt like I'd been run over by a bus. "Oh, honey, Daddy's okay. He'll probably come home in a little while. We could call him on his phone and see how Mr. West is doing, how about that?" The previous day swirled through my mind, the details growing crisp as the haze of sleep faded.

"Do you and puppy want to find my purse and get my phone for me?" I needed a moment to myself, just to think.

Nick wandered off with the puppy's rear end tucked under his arm. When he came back, he wasn't alone. He had my phone, the stuffed puppy, and a real one. Pecos was trailing behind. "Nick, Pecos is an outside dog," I said.

Nick looked at me with those big, sweet eyes, and I knew it was hopeless. I let the dog stay. He sat politely beside the bed, gracing the room with the scent of creek water and cattle pens, while I called Daniel and got the report on Jack's condition.

No change, basically. Mason had been in with Jack during the night as much as the nurses would allow. He thanked us for bringing him clean clothes.

I didn't ask Daniel any more questions. It didn't seem like a good idea to talk about it with Nick listening, and I wondered if Mason might be somewhere nearby Daniel. If any of my suspicions were valid, the last thing I wanted was for Mason to know that we had doubts about him.

"Are you coming home this morning?" I wanted Daniel to say yes. Outside, the early sun was dimming, clouds sliding over Chinquapin Peaks. A storm was on the way. I didn't want to spend the day alone. I needed to talk things through with Daniel, to see if, between the two of us, we could make some sense of this. I wanted to tell him about the dream and have him chuckle and say it didn't mean anything.

"Until Jack wakes up, I plan to stay here." There was a change in his voice. I sensed that Mason was there with him.

"Nick wants to talk to you," I said and handed the phone over.

Slipping from the bed, I stood looking at Grandma Louisa's Bible on the night table. The dream, the Scripture, the warning repeated in my mind, a strange contrast to Nick's innocent questions about Jack's accident. Nick thought he could rescue Jack's truck and put it back together like one of his Hot Wheels cars.

He wandered into the dining room, and I went to the kitchen and poured the cereal, absently listening to snatches of conversation. Daniel and Nick were discussing the fact that, with Jack in the hospital and Daniel gone, Nick was head-man-in-charge at home. Nick, standing by the window in his T-shirt and Toy Story undies, gazed at the lawn and scratched his rear end as he discussed whether he might need to take care of the mowing. "I gotted my mow-air." Holding his hands in front of himself, he pantomimed pushing his little plastic mower, as if Daniel could see. "I gotta milk my cow, too, Daddy . . ."

Ohhh, the cow . . . The poor thing was probably out there suffering right now. Keren would already be on her way to school to prepare for her summer enrichment kids. I'd have to call Al. How much different could milking a cow and milking a goat be, really?

I'd just started to smile, felt a little, private laugh, when the questions about Jack's accident rushed in like a cloud shadow, covering everything with a watercolor wash of gray. The laughter fell away, out of place now.

What in the world were Daniel and I going to do about all this? Should I share our suspicions with anyone? Normally, I might have told Al, gotten her advice, but even Al was perhaps not who she seemed to be. What was she hiding, and why did I feel like that name, Alex Beck, should mean something to me?

What was I missing here? What was just beyond my fingertips?

I knew that name. I did . . .

I moved Nick's cereal and the milk to the dining room, set everything on the table, then flipped open my laptop and entered a name into the browser window. *Alex Beck*. Over six million entries came back—everything from genealogy and family tree makers, to stories about a new teen singing sensation and unfortunate web ads for a porn star by the same name. None of it seemed to have anything to do with Al Beckenbauer. After five pages of entries, I gave up and closed the computer. Whatever was going on with Al really wasn't the most pressing issue right now. The real issue was Jack, and the accident, and whether Mason had anything to do with it.

When Nick finished chatting, I picked up the phone and paged through the contacts, then dialed Corbin while pouring milk on Nick's cereal. How much did Corbin know about the case against Jack West, twenty-five years ago?

My brother-in-law's voice registered surprise when he answered the phone. "Hey, Mallory, what's going on?" The question came with an underlying note of concern. It wasn't normal for me to call Corbin—especially not first thing in the morning on a work day.

"Nothing . . . well, there is something, but . . . Okay, let me stop and start over. I'm not calling because there's a family emergency or anything. Don't queue up any panic-mail to Carol, okay?" If Carol or Mom heard that a ranch truck had just gone off a cliff with a passenger in it, they'd be ordering up a moving van and cleaning out the rumpus room by noon today.

"Oh . . . kayyy . . ." The line crackled with Corbin's expectation as I moved to the bedroom and closed the door.

I took a breath, then spilled the whole, strange story of the last few weeks—Mason's arrival, the change in Jack's demeanor, his state of near euphoria, all the money spending and gift-giving, and then the accident, the sheriff's deputy talking with Mason, Daniel's suspicions, the fact that he'd chosen to stay nearby Jack at the hospital, and the old letter I'd found in the cookbook.

"It's just . . . like, a gut feeling. We don't have any proof, except that early on, Jack told Daniel not to ever park the truck so that it was pointed toward the cliffs. Apparently, Jack's second wife and his stepson made that mistake when they were out Christmas tree hunting on the ranch decades ago. The truck started rolling and careened into the lake. They weren't in it, but it almost ran them over. It seems like a lesson you wouldn't forget, doesn't it? Now I wonder if that's what the letter in the cookbook was about. Maybe she was running from Mason, not Jack."

"That's certainly a valid question," Corbin agreed. "So, how can I help?"

Outside, a peacock called, and I jumped, then checked the room around me, looked out the window, had the strange feeling that someone might be watching from the shadows. "Hang on a minute, Corbin." I peered into the yard, moved to the kitchen and leaned close to the window, scanned the driveway for any signs of human activity. I walked through the house and located Nick. He'd finished his cereal and settled himself in the front room, watching PBS and playing with the toys that had come from Jack's house. Pecos lay beside him, his ears perked with interest as Nick carried on imaginary conversations between the characters in his pretend ranch drama. He'd included everyone—his dad, Jack, Tag and Chrissy, all the ranch hands. Even the loyal pickup-riding cowboy dogs were part of the story.

For an instant, I forgot about the phone call, the hospital, the questions. I slipped into Nick's imaginary world, took in the squeak-squeak of tiny axles as his hands propelled the toy trucks, the purr of his lips making motor sounds, the thinner look of his fingers, changing daily it seemed as the last baby dimples faded from his knuckles . . .

The child who'd once owned those toys became real in my mind again. The little boy, who for reasons we could only guess at, never had the chance to grow up. Could Mason possibly be involved in something so heinous? Could he have been there the day their truck rolled over the cliffs? Could he have made another attempt as they vacationed in Mexico, and been successful that time?

The question haunted me as I retreated to the bedroom and shut the door again. "Corbin, how much do you know about Mason West? I mean, what's the scuttlebutt on The Hill? I know he's connected on the federal level, that he has aspirations in national politics. Have you heard anything?"

"Well, the name's not unfamiliar to me. . . . Let me think a minute." Corbin paused contemplatively. "You're asking in relation to the accident? As in, you really do think he had something to do with it?" Corbin's interest level was perking up, his reporter-nose sniffing out a story.

"Corbin, this has to stay between us."

"Of course, of course. You know I'm stuck spending ninety percent of my time on local stuff in this rathole, anyway."

I was reminded again of Corbin's burning desire for that one big story that would get the *New York Times*, *USA Today*, or the *Washington Post* to look his way. "I mean it, Corbin."

"I know. I know. I've heard the name, but that's about all I can tell you off the top of my head. I'm not sure if I remember any mention of him in the double murder case against Jack West all those years ago, but I do feel like there's something more recent. Can't quite bring it to mind, but some kind of coverage with his name attached. Let me do a little poking around, see if I can find anything on the research service and whatnot. I'll call you back in a few."

"Thanks, Corbin."

"What's a brother-in-law for?"

Nick rattled the bedroom doorknob, and I jumped like a spy caught in the throes of a secret mission. "Corbin, I'd better go. Nick needs me."

"All right, Mallory. Listen, keep these questions to yourself until I have a chance to do some digging. You're dealing with powerful people here, you know? And when little people dig around in the hidden business of big people . . . well, accidents seem to run rampant around there, don't they? Players like the Wests like to keep their secrets buried."

Nick pounded on the door because he couldn't turn the handle far enough to open it. "I'll be careful, I promise." If there was one thing I'd learned in DC, it was that when you're dealing with powerful men, you need to be careful whose territory you tread on.

I opened the door, and Nick was on the other side, dressed in an odd combination of shorts, a T-shirt, his Junior Adventurer vest, and cowboy boots. He gave me an expectant look. "Misser Al's here!" he said and led me to the back room, then pointed at Al, who was sitting on the back porch, patiently scratching Pecos's head.

"We gonna go milk my cow, 'kay?" Nick jittered in place, excited.

Al waved from the porch as I opened the door and Nick bolted through. "Thought you might need some help with the cow this mornin'. Figured I'd better drop by." She looked me up and down, taking in my sweats and slippers. "Looks like you're not ready to go to the barn yet. Nick and I'll get started on our own." She held a hand out to Nick, and he pulled her out of her chair.

I thanked her, then stood in the doorway watching them walk toward the gate, and thinking, *Alex Beck . . . Alex . . . Beck . . .*

By the time I'd dressed and made it to the back door, Corbin was calling my cell again. I juggled the phone while pulling on the rubber boots I'd bought for barn use. "Hey, Corb, did you find anything?"

"Yeah, just a little. Mason West does have some hefty national connections. There's a long-term relationship with the Reirdon family, as in *Senator* Reirdon, as in committee-chair-of-anything-that-matters Reirdon. Mason West and Reirdon's eldest son were college roommates and fraternity brothers, so the connection goes deep. Reirdon helped Mason get his start in politics. There's a tight relationship there, and these are not people you want to mess with, by the way—I'm assuming you're aware of that already, having worked in DC. You know that Reirdon had an intern disappear back in the late nineties, and she was found in an alley, murdered after an Internet date? Rumor was that she was meeting a reporter, not a date that night. Her family said she would *never* go on an Internet date, and that she had a boyfriend back home. You really need to be careful about sniffing around these people, okay?"

"All right. Thanks, Corbin." This mess was getting more complicated, more ominous by the minute. Powerful connections, murdered interns . . . Everywhere I turned, there was a new secret. Was any of this related to Jack's accident? To Mason's reason for being here?

I stood staring out the window, my fingers drumming on the glass. "By the way, Corbin . . . does the name Alex Beck ring any bells?"

Corbin chuckled into the phone. "Whoa, now that's a blast from the past. I'm surprised you don't remember that one."

I hesitated, unsure I could handle one more surprise. Maybe I was better off not knowing. "I feel like I should know it. . . ."

"Your dad couldn't stand that woman." Corbin's tone was lighter now. "Reporter. Bleached blond. Did the DC beat for that *Nightcap* news show? Eighties, I guess, maybe early nineties. Remember? *Hard questions, hard-hitting news.*" His tone deepened and took on reverb. I recognized the slogan. It wafted from my memory banks like the scent of high-school cafeteria food, bringing with it snippets of memory.

Corbin was being gentle. My father not only couldn't stand that show, the blond-haired woman reporter was practically the bane of his existence. She had a penchant for exposing lobbyists and legislators cuddled up together on expensive dinners, trips, golf games, flights on private planes, and other bonding activities. She outed lobbyists guilty of failing to file the proper reports, exposed them to civil penalties, and occasionally uncovered criminal violations of lobbying law. She wrote books exposing Washington's dirty laundry, past and present. She delighted in such things, and as a result, my father's blood pressure notched up several points every time her face appeared on his TV screen.

"*That's* Alex Beck?" I stammered, still trying to paint the woman's face in my mind, to reconcile it in any way with the Al I knew. She was roughly the right age, but other than that . . .

"Mmm-hmm," Corbin murmured contemplatively. "Can't remember what ever happened to her. She dropped out of sight for some reason a long time ago. There was something . . . but I can't quite tell you what."

I wasn't sure I wanted to know. "Thanks, Corbin. Listen, I've got to go." I hung up without even waiting for an answer, put a hand on the doorknob, then just stood there, thinking. Could Al possibly be Alex Beck? *The* Alex Beck? Was that why her past before coming to Moses Lake was such a mystery? Why she never wanted to talk about any of her history?

Was that why she was always so interested in Jack, and now Mason?

Inside the cowgirl rancher, was the rabid reporter still lurking, just looking for the right story to make a comeback?

Most of us, I suppose, are a little nervous of the sea.
No matter what its smiles may be, we doubt its friendship.

—H. M. Tomlinson
(Left by Captain Jake, guiding tours on the lake)

Chapter 22

I watched Nick struggling to carry his bucket, balancing his weight against it as he walked, staggering in the little cowboy boots I'd bought him on one of our trips to the Walmart in Gnadenfeld. He was gazing up at Al with a look of unfettered adoration, chatting away, his forehead lifting in a question.

Al laughed and shifted her bucket from one hand to the other, then roughly tousled his blond curls, causing him to stumble sideways and pop a splash of milk from the bucket.

"Hey!" he protested.

"Little milk's good for you. It'll make your skin pretty." Al shrugged the braid over her shoulder and batted her eyes at him in a maneuver that seemed completely unlike her.

At least, unlike the Al I knew.

Alex Beck must have known how to put on makeup, how to assume a persona. I tried to remember, tried to visualize the face on TV—the one that usually elicited a scathing comment and a disgusted snort from my father. I remembered fluffy blond hair, and that she was pretty, but I couldn't recall the details of her face. It didn't matter, really. I couldn't equate that face with Al's. How could they be one and the same? How could this sun-browned, no-nonsense, earthy woman have ever been Alex Beck?

"I'm not pwitty!" Nick protested, shaking his head earnestly. "I'm a boy-eee!"

"You are?" Al teased. "All this time, and nobody told me that."

Nick peered up at her, his face narrowing, lips pursing into a tiny bow of consternation. "I always been-did a boy!" he shrieked, and then laughed, staggered, and sloshed more milk.

"Well, I guess you don't want to come help me boil up some goat soap this morning, then, do ya? You might get some on you and wind up with pretty skin." Al rolled out the invitation before I could step into the conversation and stop her. "Guess I'll just have to see if Birdie can help me today."

"Birdie's comin' to you house?" Nick gyrated, milk splashing onto the gravel as he and Al stopped near me.

"I'm going to give this cow's milk to Birdie's granddaddy . . . if it's okay with your mama." Al directed the question my way. "I caught up with Len in town this morning, early, and I told him about the cow. He said he'd take the milk and distribute it around in Chinquapin Peaks, if you want. He's got some families he supplies with fish, deer meat, garden produce, cow's milk, and that kind of thing. I thought Nick could help me get the milk separated and bottled at my place, and then we'll work on some soap until Len shows up for the milk. I figured you'd be going up to the hospital again today, and Nick would need someplace to hang out. I stopped by there this morning and saw your husband, by the way. No change, sounds like. Your husband said Mason was right there all night, hovering over the ICU like a good son." One eye ticked shut, and there was the usual hint of animosity.

"I gotta get my hat!" Nick answered Al's invitation and promptly set his bucket down in the driveway.

I caught Nick before he could skitter away. "You know what, sweetheart? Why don't you go in and watch your show for a few minutes? *Thomas the Tank Engine* just came on. Al and I need to talk."

I felt Al's gaze on me as Nick jogged to the house and disappeared inside.

"You want to tell me what that was all about?"

I fought the urge to leave all my questions unspoken. Al's past really wasn't any of my business . . . unless her interest, her willingness to take me under her wing since our arrival in Moses Lake was really a way of getting to Jack, of looking for the kind of story that could break big, bring back a career.

I let out a long breath, then spilled the question, "Who is Alex Beck?"

Al's chin snapped up, and she eyed me mutely for a moment before setting down her milk bucket. "I'm not sure I understand what you're asking." Color burned up her neck and into the shadow of her sweat-stained cowboy hat, underlying the sheen of moisture on her skin.

I knew I'd stepped into something large and earthshattering, but there was no going back now. "Are you Alex Beck?"

Exhaling, she crossed her arms over her loose-fitting work shirt. "Why do you want to know? What business is it of yours? Did someone say something about it? Someone around here?" A quick glance toward her truck made me wonder if she was thinking of walking out on the conversation. Unlocking her arms, she rammed her hands onto her thin hips and muttered something under her breath.

"No one said anything to me." What was going through her mind right now? What was she feeling? "I saw a piece of mail yesterday when I drove your truck. It was . . ."

She stiffened immediately, whirled toward me, her eyes flaring. "So, I loan you my vehicle, and you snoop through my private papers, stick your nose into things that have nothing to do with you? Search my mail?" Her accusation echoed across the barnyard, shredding the morning quiet. In the tree overhead, a peacock cried out and flew across to the orchard.

"Hang on a minute. First of all, I wasn't snooping through your mail. It fell out of the truck, and I picked it up."

"I'll bet."

I clenched my fingers, determined not to tumble over the precipice of emotion that had been looming ever since Jack's accident. "Whether you want to believe it or not, that's the truth. I saw the name. It rang a bell. I asked my brother-in-law about it when I called him about Mason West. He refreshed my memory a little. That's it."

"And now you're talking about me to other people. Nice." Al's lips thinned, the creases alongside her mouth deepening. "Real nice. That's what I get for helping you. I should've left you on your own to get by here in Moses Lake."

My stomach sank. Something between Al and me had just been broken beyond repair. "Listen, it's not that I'm not grateful. I just need to know that . . ."

"Some things aren't your business." She stabbed a finger in my direction, and I stumbled back a step. By the yard gate, Pecos stood up, growled low. Al ignored the warning. "That name doesn't have anything to do with you."

"Doesn't it?" I pressed, anxious to finish the conversation, to be done with it, whatever the result. "That's what I need to know. *Does* it have something to do with us? Are you here because . . . ? You've mentioned Jack and the murder case to me before. Is that more than just idle curiosity?"

"Oh, so now you're *accusing* me?" Al threw her hands up, then let them slap to her sides. "Of *what*?"

"I don't know, Al." The anxiety that had been caged for almost a day now burst forth, wild, uncontained. "All I know is that there's one man in a hospital bed, and you don't think it's an accident, but you won't say why. My brother-in-law is telling me I'd better watch my step, and my husband is camped outside the ICU, trying to protect Jack, and everywhere I turn there's a new secret. Yes, I'm worried. There's *something* going on here, and I don't know what it is. I just want the truth. About something. The questions you're always asking me about Jack and about Mason since he got here . . . Are you working on some kind of story? I'm not accusing you of anything. I'm just asking for the truth."

Spitting air, she turned and started toward the truck, then stopped and spun around, her chin jutting out. "You want the *truth*? The truth is, you don't belong here, Mallory. You never did. Go home to DC, where all that matters is face value, and you never know who your friends are. You must fit right in there." Her voice echoed through the empty farmyard, bouncing off the trees and the barn, slowly slipping into silence as she slammed the door of her truck, started the engine, and peeled out, sending a shower of gravel bouncing against the milk buckets and my legs.

My heart rapped in my throat as I watched the dust settle on the milk, the pale caliche drawing tan swirls on the surface. Somewhere in the distance, a peacock let out a long, lonely call as Al's truck disappeared down the driveway.

You never know who your friends are . . . you must fit right in there . . . The words stung. I didn't want that to be true of me. I didn't want to be someone who didn't trust, who nursed suspicions, who dug into backgrounds while greeting people with a smile.

But I couldn't afford to be naïve, either. I had a family to think about—Nick, Daniel, and the baby coming.

Last night's dream haunted me.

Maybe Al was exactly right. Maybe we should leave. Even if Jack did recover and come home, who was to say that there wouldn't be another accident, and that the next one wouldn't involve Daniel? If Mason had something to do with this, if he was willing to attempt the murder of his father, why would he even think twice about Daniel's life?

The laboratory was literally full of dangerous chemicals— ammonium nitrate, chlorine compounds, diesel, and other fuels—everything needed for an explosion. Daniel had joked a time or two that, if Homeland Security found out about the place, he and Jack would end up in jail. Someone with Mason West's connections and his access to the ranch could arrange an accident in a heartbeat. . . .

Before I'd even considered what I was doing, I was on the way to the hospital with Nick strapped unhappily in the backseat. We met Daniel in the downstairs lobby, where Nick settled in at the Lego table while Daniel and I talked nearby. The news on Jack's condition was as good as could be hoped for. The doctors had been able to control the swelling in his brain without surgery. He was still unconscious. When his medications were reduced, perhaps later today, we'd know more about what condition Jack would wake up in, or whether he would wake up at all.

"Mason is in there every chance he gets, but the nurses are keeping it pretty limited. They have Jack under close supervision, thank God." Daniel glanced toward the elevator, as if he was planning to storm the ICU. "Mason isn't letting anyone else in. I think he wants to make sure he's right there, if and when Jack wakes up. He's worried about whether Jack will remember anything about the accident, I can tell. One of the first responders stopped by late last night to see how Jack was doing. I heard Mason talking to him, trying to find out whether Jack was conscious during the rescue or in the ambulance, and what he might have said. Mason was working really hard to play the good ol' boy card, but the volunteer fireman was really cagey. He's suspicious, and Mason didn't miss that, either. He was sweating bullets after they talked. He really wants me to stop dogging him, too. That's clear enough."

Daniel walked away a few paces, then came back, checking the lobby and leaning close to me. "After the fireman left, Mason kept trying to persuade me to go home. He actually patted me on the shoulder and said it was above and beyond the call of duty for me to stay here. When I wouldn't leave, he lost it for a minute, said he was in charge now. He all but fired me. I told him that when Jack wakes up and fires me, then I'll go. I thought he was about to wind up and slug me right there in the hall. I wish he had." His shoulders squared, the muscles in his forearms tightening visibly. I imagined the confrontation, imagined Daniel's lightning-quick anger making him brash and careless with his words. If Mason had any doubt about Daniel's reasons for hanging around the hospital before, he probably knew for certain now.

Daniel ran his tongue along the edge of his teeth, as if he were relishing the fight, tasting it. "I'm going to keep pushing him until he cracks. He's close."

I reached out and caught my husband's arm, thought of everything that was at risk. I thought of Corbin's warnings. "Daniel, listen. You have to go to the sheriff's department and turn this thing over . . . or . . . or tell Mart McClendon and let him relay the information the way he thinks is best, but get out of it. Please. I have a terrible feeling about where this might end. Corbin told me that Mason has powerful connections to people you don't want to mess with. We need to leave. Go back to DC. The job isn't worth this. There are other jobs."

He drew back indignantly, his eyes a metallic gray in this light. "I can't just walk out. The guy who gave me this job is flat on his back in a hospital bed, for heaven's sake. What kind of a man would I be if I left now?"

"The kind who puts his family before his job." My voice rose enough that Nick looked up from the Lego table. Clenching my teeth, I took a breath. Everything was running through my head—Corbin's warnings, the fight with Al, the dream, the passage from Grandma Louisa's Bible.

He keepeth back his soul from the pit, and his life from perishing by the sword . . .

If I told Daniel about the dream, he would only mollify me. He'd say I was being pregnant and emotional.

He craned away, his shoulder brushing the rough plaster of the hospital wall. "Where's all this coming from?"

"I hate this place, Daniel. I'm sorry. I know that's not what you want to hear. I hate all the drama, the unpredictability. All these people and their secrets." Al's words repeated in my head, the volume ramping up. She was right, I didn't belong in Moses Lake. "We'll never have a normal life here. It will always be like this. I want a normal life—regular work hours, weekends off, a house that's ours, and friends down the street for Nick."

"Nick loves it here." His brows pinched together, his expression conveying that he thought I was being silly. "And the last time I checked, you were starting to like it, too. What happened to working on funding for the gardening program and taking on the hunger problem in Chinquapin Peaks? What about helping kids like the ones you've been writing about on the blog? What about showing the rest of the world how the odds are stacked against kids growing up rural and poor?" His gaze drilled into me, pierced me, called up memories that made me ache inside—the garden, the kids, Sergio, Sierra,

Birdie, and Len. My husband, this man who understood me like no one else, knew those things were inside me, even as I tried to deny them. "All that fire just . . . went away?"

My throat stung and tears gathered in my eyes. "I'm scared, Daniel. I'm afraid for us. We don't know what we might be dealing with here. If Mason did do this to Jack—to his own father—what would stop him from coming after you? Us? We have Nick to think about, and the baby. What if Mason really was involved in the disappearance of his stepmother and that little boy . . ."

"Shhh." Daniel took me in his arms, pulled my body close to his. "I'm going to take care of us. I promise, Mal. I will."

I clung to him, gulping back tears, trying to gain control as he tucked me under his chin, his arms holding me tight, his heartbeat pulsing against my ear. The depth of my love for him, of my need for him poured over me, both painful and sweet, both comforting and frightening. If anything happened to him, I didn't know how I would keep going. Couldn't he see that? Couldn't he see that *we* were what mattered most?

Finally, I straightened and wiped my eyes. I didn't want Nick to look over and see me this way.

Daniel smiled down at me, stroking a tear from my cheek with the pad of his thumb. Something was on his mind. The downward squeeze of one eyebrow betrayed it. "You know what? Maybe you and Nick should go—just grab a few suitcases and take a little vacation back to Maryland. There's plenty of room at your mom's, and you've been missing your sisters. By now Trudy must be about ready to tell everyone that the in vitro was a success this time. You could be there for that. You can compare pregnancy notes together."

I pulled back, my mouth dropping open. "You're . . . trying to send us away . . ." In that instant, I understood everything. Daniel knew how risky this game of cat and mouse with

Mason was, but he wasn't willing to give it up. "*You* won't go, but you're sending us away. You know how dangerous it is here."

He lifted his palms, held them out to fend off my accusations. "I didn't say that."

"You didn't have to. I can see it all over your face."

"Mal, don't read more into it than there is. I thought you'd enjoy a vacation, that's all." His gaze darted away, then back.

I stood there staring at him, a cold tide of disbelief and resentment filling all the warm places where love and trust had been a moment before. "Yeah, thanks a lot." Taking a step away, I turned from him, strode across the lobby, and gathered Nick.

"Mal, hang on . . ." Daniel stopped in the entryway.

"You know what, never mind," I shot back, and behind the reception desk, the greeter paused in her work, sending a look of concern our way. I was beyond caring who heard. "If you decide *we* matter more than whatever it is you *think* you need to do, we'll be at home. Packing." I didn't wait for an answer but just turned away and left.

Mercifully, Nick was easy to distract with a hot dog and a movie when we reached home. By the time it was over, he was dozing on the sofa. I tucked him into his bed for a nap, then went after the suitcases we'd stored in the old garage. I'd dusted them off, done a batch of laundry, and packed the suitcases half full of clothes before Nick woke up. The sound of his bare feet coming down the hall brought the feel of precious, quiet mornings when Daniel and I lingered in bed, listening to the doves in the cedars, the loons on the water, the cows lowing to their calves in the fields, the roosters in the barn singing up the sun, and then finally the soft stirrings of Nick in his bed before he came padding into the room, dragging his favorite blanket behind him.

I realized that I'd been imagining the new baby's life this way—filled with slow, sunny mornings, the music of the loons, the scents of damp, hidden canyons and flowers sprouting in the leaf litter. I'd been imagining our life here, in this wild, strange place that was like nothing I'd ever planned.

I stood with a shirt half-folded in my hands, watched Nick come into the room and climb onto the bed. Cuddling his stuffed Dalmatian under his chin, he regarded me with big, drowsy eyes, his static-filled curls hovering around his head like a sunny halo.

I finished folding the shirt and set it in the suitcase.

"What you doin'?" The last word came out in a long, slow drawl that reminded me of Birdie and McKenna. *Do-een.*

"Packing some clothes so we can go on a trip." I walked to the closet to look through the shoes, because I couldn't face Nick anymore. Why was I so conflicted about this? Why was I torturing myself with doubts? Daniel was the one who was wrong. I was right, wasn't I? Shouldn't our family come first? We weren't some kind of vigilante squad. We were just regular people, and we were out of our league here. "You remember the rumpus room at Grandma Hale's—with all the toys? Where you slept on the little sofa? We're going there. And maybe we'll drive on out to see your Nanbee and Grandpa Everson, too. That'll be fun, won't it?"

The bedsprings squeaked as Nick bounced closer. "We can't go dere, silly!" Grinning, he straddled the stuffed puppy and lifted his hands. "I gotta go to school tomorrow in two week." Two fingers demonstrated his understanding of the number. Nick was beyond excited that we'd signed him up for the preschool program at Moses Lake school. He was literally counting down the days.

Guilt nipped at my heels as I moved to the closet to sort

through shoes. "Well, we don't have to worry about that right now. We'll get on a plane, and we can be there in no time."

Get on a plane . . .

If I was really serious about this, I'd have to do something about plane tickets and a ride to the airport. Maybe Chrissy or Tag could drive us. I didn't even know where the closest airport was. . . .

I *was* serious about this, wasn't I?

I had to be. Someone had to think about Nick and the new baby. Someone had to be rational.

"I'm hungry," Nick complained, and I was glad he'd gone off the topic.

"Let's take a break and go get something to eat." I'd been in such a spin since Al's visit that morning, I hadn't even thought about the fact that I hadn't eaten since breakfast, and other than the hot dog with his movie, neither had Nick. He was probably starving.

"I want onion wings!" He squiggled happily off the bed. "And a fwies and a lollypop!"

I realized that Nick thought I'd meant *go*, as in to the Waterbird. The idea didn't sound too bad all of a sudden. In reality, it was too late in the day to wrap my mind around booking a flight and figuring out how to travel to the airport. I needed to get out of the house, to really think. Maybe the drive would clear my head, and when we came back, I'd be ready to look for airport information and tomorrow's flight schedules.

But I knew why I was delaying—why I was putting off the inevitable. The fact was that no matter how upset I was with Daniel at the moment, I couldn't leave him behind. Somehow, I had to persuade him to come with us. "Let's go to the Waterbird." I held a hand out to Nick, and he slipped his fingers into mine, small, fragile, and filled with trust. Daniel and I needed to be worthy of that trust.

On the way to the Waterbird, I tried to sort out the muddle in my thoughts—to untangle facts from feelings. But they all were so twisted together, so inseparably interwoven. Daniel was putting his job ahead of Nick and me again, even to the point that he was willing to separate from us, to put himself in danger. To put us in danger of losing him. The truth of that dredged up a sludge of resentments that made it difficult to see anything else.

I wanted him to consider us first. Was I so wrong to expect that? Was it selfish? Was I asking for too much, demanding too big a sacrifice? Was I reacting like the spoiled, catered-to caboose baby who'd had everything her way, who'd been on her own all her adult life and never had to compromise with anyone?

But hadn't I compromised these last months—compromised almost to the death of everything that made me who I was? I'd left a job I enjoyed, my life, my family, my comfortable apartment, my dreams for myself. I'd become a mother, a laundry washer, a house fixer, a peach-pie baker, a support system, a cow caretaker. The suits and shoes and purses I loved were still in a box in the corner of a closet, because I had no place to wear them. I had no identity outside the house, the ranch life, the everyday activities that comprised the mythically idyllic life of The Frontier Woman.

Would it always be this way? Would I always be trying to force myself into a mold that didn't quite fit, because it was the only space available in Daniel's life? How long could that go on before you resented the very person you loved?

The questions, the future, haunted me as we pulled into the Waterbird and I helped Nick out of the car. The hillside view of the lake in the afternoon sunshine failed to soothe my rough edges, to quiet the nerves vibrating under my skin. I couldn't shake the feeling that something terrible was lurking just out of sight, and our only chance was to destroy it before it destroyed us.

Inside the store, the Docksiders were gathered in their favorite booth, with Birdie camped out in a chair at the end of the table, sharing their fries.

Nick did a back-and-forth on the doormat, trying to decide whether to go to the counter to see Pop Dorsey or hurry to the back booth to catch up with Birdie and the Docksiders. The men were busy talking, cracking fresh-roasted peanuts, and drinking coffee. Nester Grimland was doing something with feathers, string, and a strange-looking metal apparatus. Birdie, on her knees in her chair, was both watching and helping. She sorted a red feather from a Ziploc baggie and handed it to Nester, and he pinched it, twisting it in the long stream of afternoon sunlight from the windows on the Wall of Wisdom.

"Yep, I sure think that one'll do just fine." Nester gave approval to Birdie's choice. "If I was an ol' fat bass, I'd jump right at a hand-tied fishin' fly with a red feather on it, for sure."

The lure was more than Nick could resist. He was off like a shot, and a moment later, he'd squirmed onto the chair next to Birdie. She slipped her arm around him, her little hand patting him on the back as they smiled at each other.

I went to the counter and ordered two small-fry cheeseburgers with onion rings—ketchup and tomato only on the burgers. No mustard, no pickles, no onions. Two small vanilla Dr. Peppers. Two scoops of Bluebell Homemade Vanilla ice cream. Our usual.

Something about the normalcy of the routine made me feel better, and the lull of the Waterbird slipped slowly over me. I stood gazing out the back windows, watching boats race across the water's glistening surface as vacationers on water skis drew cascading swirls in the water.

Daniel and I had talked about getting some kind of boat, once the bio patents started coming in. If everything worked out with the patents, we'd be able to afford things we could only dream about now. . . .

Pop Dorsey slid our drinks across the counter. "Here ya go, darlin'. Sheila will bring the rest out to ya in a bit. Everythin' all right today?"

"Sure," I said, and Pop registered doubt. I wondered what I looked like. I hadn't even glanced in the mirror before leaving the house. "Busy day," I added as an excuse.

"No more news about Mr. West, I s'pose?" Pop slid a stack of napkins and two straws my way.

"Nothing since this morning. Daniel hasn't called to report any change." Daniel hadn't called at all, and the silence stung.

"Well, we're all prayin'. That's the best thing." Pop met my gaze for a moment, his eyes cloudy with age, yet acute. "Jack West may be an ornery old cuss, but he's lucky to have you young kids lookin' after him. Even an ol' growlin' dog needs love and care. Sometimes an ol' growlin' dog needs it most of all."

Guilt rushed over me as Pop wheeled away in his chair. I carried the drinks to the corner and sat staring at the quotes on the Wall of Wisdom as I waited for our food. Meanwhile, Nick entertained himself at the Docksiders' table, helping Nester and Birdie tie fishing flies. When our hamburgers came, Nick didn't want to leave his perch, so I handed over his burger basket.

The Waterbird conversation ebbed and flowed with the usual rhythms—weather, fat bass, fishing holes, badly behaved tourists who threw trash in the lake, giant catfish large enough to swallow a human. I relaxed into the hum of it and the serenity of the lake, trying to imagine the fact that the same God who guided the rhythms of wind and water might be trying to guide me.

What was He saying?

I closed my eyes and tried to hear.

But there were so many voices. How could anyone ever know which one was God's and which ones you were creating yourself?

Stay. Go. Worry about your own problems. Take on everyone else's. Love. Resent. Forgive. Withdraw. Be suspicious. Be trusting. Uncover lies. Leave them be. Be nice. Be forceful. Don't offend anyone. Be honest.

Where are You? Where are You, really? What do You want from me?

What if what You want isn't what I want?

Am I always supposed to give in, let other people walk all over me . . .

"Mommy?" I felt Nick's hand tapping my shoulder. When I turned to look, all eyes at the Docksiders' table were turned my way. I realized that someone must have just asked a question.

"What?" I blinked, brought my mind back. "I'm sorry. I was out of it for a minute there."

Nester lifted a fishing fly. "Okay if we take the little guy down to the water with us to try out these new flies? We'll keep a good eye on him, I promise."

"Pleeee-ase?" Birdie added, and pressed her hands together, begging.

"Sure." Down the hill, the dock was drenched in late-day sun, the weathered picnic tables waiting for fishermen to happen by. Maybe a little time by the water would clear my head, since I couldn't seem to do it for myself. "Sure. I'll be down there in a minute, as soon as I finish my hamburger. Nick, don't you want to eat your ice cream first?" Few things could separate Nick from his Bluebell Homemade Vanilla.

Pushing his food away, Nick shook his head. "I gotta fish!"

"He's a boy after my own heart," Burt Lacey cheered, then stood up and leaned over my table to retrieve Nick's ice cream. "Here, I'll tuck this in the bait cooler." He winked at Nick. "When you grab it back out, young fella, just make sure you grab the one with ice cream in it, not worms."

"Eeewww!" Birdie squealed, and Nick clapped his hands, delighted by the idea.

A moment later, the group was proceeding toward the door, fishing supplies in hand, their booth still littered with newspapers, feathers, and assorted bait-making tools.

Len hesitated by my table. "W-what's all them ubb-boats out at F-firefly Island fer? They ubb-been f-fishin' out there in the li'l ubb-bay?"

Nester paused in the back doorway, holding up the rest of the party. "I been wonderin' that myself. What's all the hullabaloo out there? Everything on that island's been locked up for years—well, except for a few old fellas who *might* sneak on the place at night with their lantern lights to hunt coons once in a while—and now all of a sudden these last couple weeks, there's boats in and outta there like Grand Central Station."

"Really?" The swallow of soda in my mouth suddenly tasted strange.

Nester nodded, heading off Birdie as she and Nick tried to sneak by. "Been a houseboat anchord up for over a week now, right in the bay there by Firefly. Real nice rig. Saw a couple guys goin' back and forth to the island on a little skiff. I've got a pretty good view of the other side of Firefly from my back porch. Those fellas don't look like they're here to fish, but that's what they *say* they're here for. Burt and I motored out there one day, just to snoop around, and it looked like there was several fellas havin' a business meetin' and sharin' cocktails up there on deck. We hailed the boat and asked 'em how was the fishin', and they said it was real good. Everybody knows there's no fish in that cove off Firefly Island this time a' year."

"And you've been seeing boats come and go from the island for a couple *weeks*?" The wheels in my head were turning—peeling out and laying down skid marks, actually.

"A couple. Maybe three."

Ever since Mason arrived. Yet, as far as any of us knew, Mason's visit here was simply a reunion, a time to reconnect with his father. So, who was the man Chrissy's husband had seen with Mason, driving through the ranch? Why were boats coming and going from Firefly Island?

I raked my food trash into a pile and pulled my phone out of my purse. "Nick, you hold somebody's hand. You be good down there and do what Nester, Burt, and Len tell you. I'll be watching from here, and I don't want to see you near the water by yourself, okay?"

Nick nodded solemnly, then clicked his heels together and saluted me. I couldn't imagine where he'd learned that. "Ho-kay!"

"We'll watch him, Mama," Burt promised.

As they disappeared out the door, I brought up the browser on my phone. Time to do some pawing around on the Internet and see if I could find any clues as to what Mason was really up to out there on Firefly Island.

You don't create your mission in life—you detect it.

—Viktor Frankl
(Left by Jenny Guilliam, retired from lifelong English teaching)

Chapter 23

I needed to get myself onto that island. Tonight, while Mason was still occupied at the hospital. Something was about to happen. Something big. But so far I hadn't been able to put all the pieces together. Maybe some clue in the cabin on Firefly would tell me why Mason was really here and what he was up to.

Exhaling a breath through my fingers, I studied the sticky notes I'd written and pressed hastily to the dining room wall after returning home from the Waterbird. The bits of information from my Internet research were seemingly disconnected, but they had to add up to something.

Business meetings on Firefly Island.

Mason's return to the ranch.

Jack's accident.

Ties between Mason and Senator Reirdon. Reirdon's son and Mason had been more than just fraternity brothers in college. They'd quietly supported various business ventures and political action committee agendas in order to please wealthy constituents and to benefit one another's interests.

They'd acted and interacted and done business together to the ragged edge of what was legal. There had been ethics complaints in the past, but nothing stuck.

Mason had made himself a very rich man in the last several years. In interviews and on campaign materials, he'd even boasted of the fact that he was a self-made man—that he hadn't gotten the money from his father. He'd gone so far as to say that he didn't want his father's money.

But now here he was, schmoozing Jack West and taking time to play the devoted son. Why?

The soft strains of *The Lion King* wafted in from the living room, echoing the theme of family betrayal. I tapped a fingernail to the tabletop, absently keeping time with the "I Just Can't Wait to Be King" song. Nick wasn't even in there watching it. He'd gone home to play with McKenna after Tag and Chrissy had stopped by to tend to the milk cow.

There was something skimming the surface of my thoughts like one of Nester's fishing flies—something I couldn't quite pull in. What was it?

My cell phone rang, and I jumped, then pressed the button and left it on speaker, since no one else was home.

Corbin was on the line. He'd called to relay some additional information about Mason West's history—mostly things I'd already figured out. Ethics complaints, accusations of influence pedaling. Suspicions about some of the money he'd made in big real estate deals. Mason was a shrewd businessman who knew how to dance along the line between morally questionable and outright illegal.

"He likes big utilities," Corbin pointed out. "Their PACs are some of his major supporters. The last ethics complaint came from an environmental group accusing Mason of paving the way for ten new coal-burning power plants whose PACs had been generous with the political contributions. The legislation was pork-barreled into some bill about economic stimulus money and funding for low-performing schools. Pretty dirty trick."

"I just can't figure out what he's up to here in Moses Lake," I confessed. "I know so little about this area—what the issues are, or what he might have to gain. I've been taking shots in the dark all afternoon, just pawing around on the Internet to see what I can learn. I did hear in town that he's been having some kind of business meetings in the cabin out on Firefly Island. I'm going out there tonight to see what I can find."

"Hold on. You're doing what?"

"I'm going to the cabin on Firefly Island—tonight, while Mason is still at the hospital with Jack." At least as far as I knew, he was. I'd have to call Daniel and check before I went to the island. What would Daniel say if I told him what I was planning? "There may not be another chance."

The line crackled with hesitation. I could almost see Corbin rocking back in his chair, holding the smartphone away from his face, making bug-eyes at it. "Okay, now just wait a minute. Don't you think that's a bit too Magnum, P.I.? As in, a little risky? What if he finds out you were there?"

"He won't. I'll tell Daniel to call me if anything changes at the hospital, and it's no problem getting onto Firefly. There's a pegboard in the lab with keys to everything on the ranch. I can just grab the key to the causeway gate. If I go across in the dark, and come back in the dark, nobody will even see me." Unless the men from the houseboat happened to be there. Who *were* they? Was the boat still anchored in the bay? Were they coming and going from Firefly when Mason was gone, or only when he was at the cabin? "Anyway, I'll be careful." I wasn't sure whether I was trying to convince myself or Corbin.

There was rustling and shuffling on Corbin's end of the

phone. "You know what, just let me see if I can get a flight. I'll come out there, and . . ."

"No, Corbin. I need to do it now. The sheriff's deputies questioned Mason at the hospital, and so did one of the first responders. He knows that Daniel is suspicious. If there *is* anything at the cabin, he'll clean it up the first chance he gets. I'm going tonight."

"At least get Daniel to go with you. You shouldn't be out there alone, Mallory. You're not super-sleuth Scarpetta, you know. You're pregnant, for heaven's sake. Do you have any idea what Carol would say if she heard about this? Or your mother?" His voice wavered, implying a shudder on the other end of the phone.

"Don't you dare tell Carol. Or Mom. And for heaven's sake, don't say anything to Trudy. She's practically put herself on bed rest, she's so worried about not jeopardizing this in vitro, and she's halfway convinced that I should do the same. I'll be fine, Corbin. If anyone sees me and asks what I'm doing, I'll just say I thought I should bring some clean clothes to the hospital for Mason." What if Mason decided to return home for clean clothes . . . tonight?

He wouldn't. Of course he wouldn't. He was more concerned about what Jack would say when he woke up. "I'm just driving across the causeway and driving back. It's not like I'm going to swim over to the island, Corbin. I'll be fine."

"You need to promise me you're not going out there alone."

"Okay. Okay. I won't go by myself. I'll get someone to come with me." Who? Who in the world could I get? I couldn't imagine involving Keren in something like this. If any of the ranch hands got caught helping me trespass on forbidden territory, they'd be out of a job. The rest of our friends in town were more like casual acquaintances we'd met at the church or various stores. I couldn't just call one up and say,

Hey, want to help me do a little breaking and entering? What if Mason did find out . . . or even Jack at some point, and they decided to press charges?

"I mean it, Mallory." Corbin was clearly on the verge of calling my mother. On the other end of the phone, *protective brother-in-law* was struggling to trump *curious reporter.*

"Yes, really. I hear you." Al. Al was the person I needed. Al would go along on this little mission in a heartbeat. She would relish it, even. The risk of future prosecution wouldn't mean a thing to her, and if there was one person she seemed to dislike even more than Jack West, it was Mason.

"I don't know about this. . . ." Corbin's inner angel and devil continued their wrestling match.

"Just think if there really *is* a story, though." I baited the hook, tossed it my brother-in-law's way, pictured one of the Docksider's brightly colored fishing flies trolling slowly over the water . . . so tempting. . . . "What if there really *is* something juicy going on?"

"That's what I'm worried about."

Outside, the dog barked at a peacock flying over. The birds were moving into the trees, selecting their roosts for the night as the sun sank toward Chinquapin Peaks. By now, all the ranch hands would have finished feeding cattle in the pastures and gone home. I needed to start moving. "I'll be *okay*."

"Call me as soon as you're back, and remember, you promised. You're not going out there to some island in the dark by yourself."

"Aye, aye, cap'n." I copied Nick's salute, though Corbin couldn't see it.

"Very funny. Keep me informed tonight, all right? Now I'll be on pins and needles."

"I'll stay in touch." My mind spun ahead, making plans. Al. I wanted to call her—not the angry, stone-faced Al from this morning, but my friend, Al. I wanted to tell her everything that was going on, and have her say something like, *Well, c'mon, cowgirl, let's go. I've been dying to get on that island for years now, anyway.*

But it was entirely possible that I'd severed that relationship forever, and even if I hadn't, how could I be sure that, by inviting Al into Mason's secrets, I wouldn't be bringing more trouble on Jack than he already had? What if Al really was after a story? What if Jack woke up and the headlines were splashed with smarmy details about Mason? I couldn't imagine the depths of Jack's heartbreak if he were to learn that Mason was responsible for the accident—that Mason had come here to take advantage of Jack, rather than to reconcile with him. The last thing he needed was a reporter offering up his family drama on the front page. Corbin, I could control, but I had no idea what Al, with her intense dislike for Jack, might be capable of.

How could I be sure?

"Hey, Corb?" I caught him just as he was starting to sign off. "Did you remember anything else about Alex Beck? I mean, I know my dad used to practically spit at the TV when she was on, but did you remember anything about the reason she quit?"

"Why do you want to know?" With Corbin, there was no such thing as an idle question.

"I just need to, okay? I think she's my neighbor, but she doesn't go by Alex Beck anymore. I'm trying to figure out why."

"Your neighbor . . . Al? The cowboy-woman?" Corbin choked. "The one with the goats? Trudy sent Carol your blog about milking goats with her. Did you, really . . ."

I'd forgotten how well the family telegraph worked in the Hale clan. "Hey, Corb, I'm kind of in a hurry, you know?"

"Okay, hang on. I can probably find out some information for you." I heard his computer keyboard clicking. "This have anything to do with the whole Firefly Island thing?"

"I'm not sure," I admitted. "I just want to know why she'd be here in Moses Lake, going by another name, living such a . . . different kind of life. And why she's been so interested in spending time with me here on the ranch. I mean, I kind of remember Alex Beck on TV. She was this rabid reporter, chewing up whoever she had on her show to interview. That doesn't seem anything like the Al I know, but when I mentioned the name to her, she didn't deny it."

"Whoa," Corbin breathed, and the note of gravity in his voice concerned me.

"But don't say anything to anyone, okay? Don't go making your next big story out of it, or anything."

"No, I mean, *whoa*." Corbin's voice lowered ominously on the last word, the sound almost grief-stricken. "I'd forgotten all about this. No wonder she dropped out of sight and doesn't want to be recognized. I'm sending the article to your phone."

"Corb, just tell me. I don't have time for all the cloak-and-dagger stuff, all right?"

"Man, yeah," he breathed. "I was back in school getting my master's then. It was during the House impeachment proceedings against that district judge from Colorado. Don't know if you remember that. You were probably still pretty young. A federal judge had been handing out some pretty favorable rulings benefitting oil and gas companies that were big contributors to members of the House Energy Committee. There was a lot of supposition that some powerful names might come out if the indictment was handed down and the thing went to trial in the senate. Alex Beck was on that case like a dog on a bone. I mean, she was all over it. My journalism professor loved her. Your dad absolutely hated that she was getting so much coverage, digging into the background on the judge and his friends. Anyway, she was covering the proceedings that summer, just back from maternity leave, and—I don't know, I think the nanny quit or something—but Alex Beck forgot to stop off at day care, and it was ninety degrees the last morning of the thing. Her baby was found dead in her car four hours later by a city policeman. It was all over the news, and of course she had plenty of enemies, so the DA came after her full force."

An icy, horrible chill walked up my arms, a recollection. "Ohhh . . . I remember that now—not the name, but I remember them finding the baby and all the footage on the news. My mom was so sick about the whole thing, she wouldn't even let us talk about it. Maddie was just tiny then, and after that story, Mom was scared to death that you or Carol would forget her in the car when you went somewhere, remember?"

"Yes, I remember," Corbin admitted. "When I saw that story on TV, I just sat there thinking that could've been Maddie. I had my mind on a million other things every day—work, school, my next story. I never put Maddie in the car again without looping a little hair ribbon right there on the door handle so I'd be reminded. Anyway, if your neighbor is Alex Beck, I don't blame her for wanting to leave all that behind. Her trial was a media circus that eclipsed anything happening in Congress—I'm sure that was their hope when they pushed the DA to bring it to trial. She was a pariah. People were standing outside every day, carrying signs, yelling at her, calling her a baby killer and that kind of thing. It was eventually ruled accidental, but what does it matter when your baby's dead, you know?"

A length of chain twisted tight in my belly, cold and unyielding. "Yeah." I felt sick. I wanted to throw up.

I wanted to call Al and take everything back. I shouldn't have opened my mouth until I knew what I might be cracking into.

"It makes sense that she decided to drop out of sight and become someone else. Really." Corbin's voice was a faint hum on the edge of my thoughts.

"I'd better go." I breathed in, breathed out. I wouldn't blame Al if she never spoke to me again. No wonder her reaction was so swift and cutting when I brought up her past. She didn't want any reminders, and now I was one.

"I mean it about calling me," Corbin reminded. "And about being careful. You don't know what you might be dealing with. I could fly down there tonight, Mal. . . ."

"I'll be okay." The last thing I wanted was to involve the family in this strange mess. I'd never forgive myself if I put Corbin in any danger. Aside from that, if Carol found out that Corbin knew something was amiss here and he hadn't alerted her, she'd have a hissy that would only be surpassed by the one my mom would throw when she discovered it. I had to sort this out myself.

I hung up the phone, considered dialing Al's number, then lost my courage. Instead, I took Daniel's key ring from the desk drawer and went to the lab to get the keys for the cabin and the causeway gate. The security system was easy enough to manage—I'd learned the pass code during my visits there with Daniel—and the rack inside the lab door was right where I remembered it, dozens of keys to padlocks and farm equipment all hanging on a meticulously labeled pegboard.

I ran my finger along the rows, scanning the labels.

Firefly Cabin. Check.

Causeway Gate . . .

Missing.

Who had taken it, and when? Jack's strict rule was that

master keys were to be kept in the lab. According to Chrissy, he'd almost fired Tag for keeping a master key in his truck overnight.

Was Mason hiding the key so that no one could surprise him on the island, or was someone else on the ranch planning to see what was happening on Firefly?

My cell phone rang, and I jerked as the sound echoed through the office, rebounding off the locked metal door that led to the lab. Somewhere beyond the door, a piece of machinery clicked on and hummed.

Chrissy was on the phone, asking if Nick could spend the night. "My little nephew's here, and Nick and him are havin' such a blast together. McKenna's playing little mommy. Now they all want to build a tent in the living room and then later they want to watch a movie. Tag can bring him back to you on his way out to feed the cows in the mornin'."

Normally I would have been hesitant to let Nick spend the night away, but this time I quickly agreed. Nick was better off somewhere else this evening, and Chrissy might be annoying, but she kept an eagle eye on McKenna.

I considered asking her if she knew who might have the causeway key, but then I decided against it. Nothing Chrissy heard remained secret for long.

We said good-bye, and I thought again about Al. With no causeway key, a boat was the only way to get to the island. Al would know how to make that happen. I needed her now more than ever.

My courage swelled and flagged as I left the ranch and drove the road to Al's place. Dust billowed in my wake and swirled on the winds of a storm worsening over Chinquapin Peaks, propelling me down Al's driveway in the deepening twilight. Within a few hours, it would be raining. Moses Lake was predictable, in its own way. I'd learned to understand it. The worst weather always came over Chinquapin Peaks, the storms dropping torrents of water as they traversed the hills, then settling into gentle rain on the lake, and finally whipping over the ranch, blowing through the flatlands and pastures in wild gusts.

If I didn't get to Firefly Island in the next couple hours, it wouldn't happen tonight, and maybe not for a day or two. When a storm stretched over the whole of Chinquapin Peaks, it usually stayed awhile.

My heart was in my throat as I slipped through the yard gate to Al's house. A baby goat hobbling on a splinted leg trotted from behind a bush and bleated at me. It nibbled on my pants as I made my way to the front door, knocked, then stood there with a lump in my chest and heat burning over my skin. Inside the house, the television was playing loud, but no one came to the door. I knocked again. The goat butted my knee insistently. I scratched its head, waited. Nothing.

Was she ignoring me or was the house empty? All the lights were on. Al wasn't the type to leave things running when she wasn't home. She was always lecturing me about the environmental load of every kilowatt of electricity, the number of years it would take to biodegrade a Styrofoam take-out container, the potentially harmful chemicals in shampoo. She'd already pointed out that I needed to buy BPA-free baby bottles when the baby came along.

If I'd even taken a minute to think about those conversations and everything else Al had done for me, I would have realized that she had offered me something precious. She'd extended friendship in every possible way, but when I'd had the chance to do the one thing a friend should do, I'd failed miserably. Instead of thinking the best of Al, I'd cast a net of suspicion. I'd thought the absolute worst.

I'd made everything about *me*, about defending myself,

about making sure that, if Al had befriended me as a way of getting to Jack's secrets, I came out on top. Success and protecting my own interests were all I could see.

It hadn't even occurred to me to believe that Al might have reasons for keeping her secret. That even Al might have fears and wounds beneath the hardened, weathered exterior.

"What the devil are *you* doing on my porch?"

Her question spun me around. My feet tangled with the goat's, and it stumbled off the porch, bleating in protest and hobbling on its splinted leg.

I came down the steps with my hands held out, whether to help the goat or plead with Al, I wasn't sure. "Al, listen. I'm really sorry. I'm so sorry. I didn't know that . . . I didn't realize why . . ." There were no right words to say. The lines I'd practiced on the way over seemed insufficient now. "I was wrong. I was so incredibly wrong. I shouldn't have said what I did. I shouldn't have even thought it. Working in politics, you get so used to being suspicious, to looking at everyone's motives. I don't want to be like that. I don't. You've been a good friend to me, and I needed a friend. You've kept me alive out here." I swept a hand to the wild, empty, beautiful expanse of land around us. *Home*, now. "I don't know what I would have done without you, and I shouldn't have assumed . . ."

"Assumed *what*?" Her cheeks hollowed inward, her jaw jutting toward me. "That you knew what my motives were? Well, maybe you were right. You ever think of that? Maybe you were dead on. Maybe, when I moved here all those years ago and realized I had an accused murderer living next to my grandparents' old place, I wasn't one bit happy about it. Maybe if I could get rid of Jack West on my fence line, I'd use you or anyone else to do it." Loose whips of salt-and-pepper hair slashed across her face, and she brushed them away impatiently, her jaw taut. "You hit it right on the head,

Mallory. Congratulations. Now get off my porch and get off my place."

Despite the words, I knew the truth. Beyond the hard look, there was pain. Incredible, searing torment, brokenness I would never truly be able to understand. I couldn't imagine what it would be like to lose Nick, to have to go through the rest of my life without him, knowing I'd caused it, knowing I would continue to live in this world while he wouldn't. To be prosecuted, tried in the court of public opinion. To lose everything, everyone. To end up hiding away for years, trying to escape the past.

"Al, I'm sorry," I tried again. "I shouldn't have said those things. I understand if you don't want to talk about it. We don't have to. Ever. I mean, I'm here as a friend if you ever want to talk, but I understand if . . ."

"No, you don't, Mallory. You don't understand a thing." Her laugh snaked into the wind, sharp-edged and icy, out of place with the summer heat still radiating off the ground as the day dimmed. Lightning flashed so far away that the thunder was inaudible. "I took a chance on you." The truth was coming now, closer to the surface.

"I know that. I didn't handle it well. That's my fault. It's one of those things I need to work on. I see my own point of view, and most of the time I don't look for anyone else's. What I said to you—I was way out of line. I was wrong."

Al angled her face away, regarded me from the corner of her eye. "I just agreed with you. You had it all *right*, Mallory. Congratulations. You're smarter than you think you are. I'm after your boss. Why don't you run along now and tell him that?" She fanned me away as if I were the goat, nibbling on her bootlaces.

One thing was obvious. The rift between us wouldn't be mended today, and maybe never. Overhead, the security light clicked on. While we were standing here arguing, time was slipping away. "All right, well, if that's true, then there's something you'll want to know." If I couldn't get Al to go to Firefly Island with me one way, I'd try another.

"If it comes from you, I don't want anything to do with it." She opened the yard gate to let me out, then she caught the goat, sweeping it under one arm as it tried to make a quick exit. "In fact, if you're involved in any way, I'm not."

I steeled myself and plunged in. The question now was, did Al's dislike for Mason West outweigh her anger toward me? "You'll want to be involved in *this*. Mason West is up to something big. He's been holding secret meetings the whole time he's been in Moses Lake. I'm going to figure out why he's really here, before he can get away with it. I'm going to Firefly Island. Tonight."

There is, one knows not what sweet mystery about this sea,
whose gently awful stirrings seem to speak
of some hidden soul beneath.

—Herman Melville
(Left by R. L. Jakes, writing a screenplay about the lake.)

Chapter 24

The storms were moving closer. Thunderheads boiled over Chinquapin Peaks, rising and churning, blotting out a heavy half moon that seemed to belong to a quieter, gentler night. Beneath the dock, Moses Lake frothed and churned, clawing at the wooden pillars and the rocky shore. The summer night had turned unusually cool, the air smelling of the coming storm, windy one moment, then silent the next, seeming to pause and wait, breathless.

"Is it them?" I whispered, pulling the dark sweat shirt closer around my middle, feeling vulnerable and conspicuous as Al and I slipped from the cedars and moved along the swaying dock. Aged and abandoned, it listed in the water, the plastic barrels sinking lower beneath our weight.

"Not likely anybody else would be out tonight." Al's answer was flat and short, letting me know that, even if we were partners in this strange mission, we were no longer friends. She pulled out a light and flashed it on the water twice, and the boat flashed twice in reply. The whole thing would've seemed comically cloak-and-dagger if I weren't so nervous.

With the causeway locked, I didn't know how I'd explain our presence on Firefly Island if we got caught.

We'd just have to make sure that we didn't.

The boat drifted to the dock, the motor idling softly. A sound, something like an owl hooting, skimmed over the water.

"Nester, cut that out," a gravelly voice replied.

Laughter stole into my throat, and I snort-chuckled nervously against my hand. Of all the people Al might have arranged to get us to the island, Burt Lacey and Nester Grimland seemed like an unlikely choice, but Al had pointed out that, due to the low water levels this summer, there were obstacles close to the surface, especially on the side of Firefly Island opposite the bay where the houseboat had been anchored. The Docksiders knew this lake, every inch of it. They could get us there and back safely, even with the weather turning ominous.

I was learning, once again, the most important lesson that my time in Moses Lake had taught me: You can't always handle everything by yourself. Sometimes . . . oftentimes . . . you have to rely on other people. To survive, really survive well, you have to be willing to accept help and to give it. It was a hard lesson to internalize. I'd been fighting all my life to prove I could do it—whatever *it* was—all by myself. Without my parents holding my hand or my big sisters telling me how.

But pride doesn't go very far when you need to get across the water in the dark, and you don't have a boat.

Nester and Burt's rig, a small aluminum fishing craft just large enough for four people, pulled up to the dock. Nester shifted fishing equipment and life preservers aside to make room, and Al and I climbed onboard.

"Y'all just settle in there on the bench by the live well," Nester instructed, his hat brim hiding all but his gray handlebar mustache and chin. "Put them life jackets on. The storm's comin' in quicker than we thought. We coulda brought Burt's big boat, but it's loud. With this little thing, we can troll in and outta there, and them fellas holed up on that houseboat won't hear a thing."

"They're still anchored there?" I was hoping the storm might have sent Mason's associates elsewhere to anchor their houseboat.

"Looked like it. We went by the other side of the island on our way here—made like we were night fishin'. Houseboat was there, and the lights were burnin' below deck. Little skiff was tied up behind the boat, so they aren't on the island tonight."

"Good." I buckled my vest and pulled it tight. If Daniel could see me right now, he'd kill me. When I'd called the hospital to tell him I planned to go to Firefly tonight, I hadn't exactly mentioned that the causeway key was missing. If Daniel knew, he'd be back at the ranch inside a half hour, trying to stop me from going. I needed for him to stay at the hospital, and to make sure that Mason stayed there, too.

I could still hear Daniel protesting my plan. "This is crazy, Mal. It sounds like something out of *Nancy Drew*. And you're pregnant, remember?" I knew he would say that—as if being pregnant rendered me incapable and incompetent. He sighed into the phone then. "Listen, Mal, I'm sorry for the fight earlier. When I told you to go home to DC for a little while, I was just . . . thinking of you and the baby and Nick. It's not that I want you all leaving without me, but if I keep up the pressure on Mason, I can get him to crack. He's worried about me, and the closer Jack comes to regaining consciousness, the jumpier Mason gets. Give me some more time."

We'd gone back and forth until Daniel had finally agreed to call my cell if there was any sign of Mason leaving the hospital. In the meantime, Al had arranged the boat and gathered flashlights, a pocket camera, and dark clothes.

Now, here we were, the boat thrashing side to side, cutting through the waves, water splashing against the bow as it rose over a swell, then crashed down again, then rose, and fell, and rose.

"Hang on, girls," Burt advised, and I squeezed the side rail even tighter, the cool metal bending my fingernails backward. "It's gonna get rough once we clear the point."

Going to get rough? My stomach turned over. I felt like I was ready to lose my supper already. That kind of thing didn't happen to Nancy Drew. It would have been funny, if it hadn't been so serious.

As we cleared the little cedar-clad point that hid the abandoned dock, the swells kicked up and the boat's engine revved, rivets and joints crackling in the full-on wind and waves. Spray splashed over me, and the back of the boat dipped so low that the water was just below my fingertips, glistening dark and full of churned-up debris. I watched something float by beneath the surface—a piece of cloth. A scarf, or part of a swimsuit, maybe. It slid through the glow of the lights, slipping by like a shadow, seeming to stretch and contract in the water, taking on life.

I thought of my dream and the Scripture in Grandma Louisa's Bible. The warning.

I held on. Closed my eyes. Tried to stay calm.

The boat's lurching ebbed as we moved closer to the island, the craggy cliffs and thick cedars of Firefly slowly blocking the wind until there was none. The waters nearer the shore were eerily still when Nester cut the engine. Burt moved to the front of the boat, silently piloting us in with an electric motor so that our entrance was almost soundless, even the gravel only scratching dully on the hull as we beached.

Al took off her life vest and made her way toward the bow as Nester caught an overhanging cedar and pulled us in alongside a tangle of logs and debris.

"All right, nobody had oughta see us here," he whispered, leaning close. "Burt and me'll hole up here by the cedars. Lake patrol comes by, we'll just pretend like we was out night fishin' and had to pull up outta the weather a minute. Better step out on the right and climb across them downed logs, see? Don't wanna leave footprints to tip em' off."

Burt grunted as he maneuvered over the boat railing and stepped into the mud. "Heaven's sake, Nester, you ought to get a job in Hollywood. Not likely to be a lake patrol tonight, and the footprints will be gone by morning. Those clouds are fixin' to cut loose a toad strangler. It's that storm we oughta be worried about. You girls hurry on and do what you've gotta do. We'd better be heading back across that point in thirty minutes, not much more. The weather's coming faster than you think, and from what Al said, I'm guessing we don't want them to find us sitting here on the shores of Firefly Island in the mornin'."

"We'd go with ya, but we'd probably just be in yer way," Nester added. "Besides, last time we sneaked out here coon huntin', some woman saw our lights and thought it was a ghost or a UFO. She called the sheriff, and Burt and I about ended up in jail. We get caught trespassin' again, we're dead meat. Don't even know what yer lookin' for, anyway."

"Neither do we," Al grumbled, and she started for the woods, clicking her flashlight on as she reached the blackness under the canopy of oaks and elms.

"We'll hurry," I promised, then tossed off my life vest and trotted after her. Nester was more dead-on than he realized.

None of us had any idea what we were looking for. I only
knew that there was something. Something I was supposed
to find on Firefly Island.

Wind rustled in the live oaks overhead, bending the branches
as we made our way through the woods. Al walked uphill
ahead of me, moving with an uncanny confidence. There was
no path to follow, yet she seemed to know exactly where to
go, deftly weaving her way around tangles of briars and nests
of roots hidden in the darkness of the forest floor.

Ahead, the undergrowth of brambles and seedlings fluttered and swayed, parting in a gust of wind, then closing like
a curtain. The glimmer of a security light shone through the
leaves in the distance, then vanished. I stopped a moment,
trying to get my bearings, waiting for the light to come into
view once more. The cabin was farther from the edge of the
island than I'd thought. . . .

When I looked down again, Al's flashlight was gone. A
fist of apprehension caught my throat. The woods closed in
around me, the rustling becoming more than just the breeze
passing by. Was someone . . . or something there? Behind
me? Beside me?

Beyond my flashlight beam, it was interminably dark, the
moon blotted out by the building storm. Something skit-
tered across the forest carpet. I swiveled without moving my
feet. A shiver raised gooseflesh on my skin. I thought of all
the things that could happen in the woods on an inky-black
night like this.

The wind quieted, and I strained into the darkness. Ahead,
a boot skidded on wet rock, sending a pebble bouncing downward. I hurried toward the sound, keeping my flashlight low.
Within a few dozen steps, I'd crested a hill. Al was traveling
down the other side into a canyon, her light held close to her
body so that the beam illuminated only the ground beneath

her feet. At the bottom of the hill, she stopped, circled her light to hurry me along, then continued on.

I didn't catch up until Al stopped at the edge of the clearing, where a single security light illuminated the cabin. It was nothing fancy—just a small cedar-shingled shack with old plate-glass windows and a tin roof. All one room, from the look of it. The lights were on inside, but threadbare white curtains hung over the windows, blocking the view. The porch, other than the portion near the door, was littered with debris. Amid a clutter of fallen leaves, a rocking chair with a broken arm moved gently in the wind, swaying back and forth as if someone were sitting in it. I imagined that I could see *her* there—the woman from the photos in Jack's little house. The wind caught her hair, lifted it, and swirled it away from her face as she gazed off into the trees.

I blinked, and she was gone.

On the porch, the remains of an easel leaned haphazardly against the wall, the wood gray from the weather, one of the legs broken. That was hers. It had to be. Just as in the house behind ours, this place had been left unchanged since she died. It remained frozen in time, waiting.

Why would someone like Mason want to stay here? He must have been desperate for privacy so that he could conduct his business, whatever it was, right under his father's nose. The fact that Jack had allowed him to use this cabin, a place shared with no one else for so many years, only proved how deep, genuine, and desperate Jack's love for Mason really was—how much he wanted this reconciliation with his son. Why else would he offer up a home he'd protected for so long?

"Looks pretty quiet," Al whispered. "Let's go see what we can figure out from the windows. You check the one on that side. Be careful. Keep quiet." She motioned to the far end of the cabin, and we pressed through the brush, the tentacles of wild grapevine tugging at our clothes.

On the far side of the cabin, a single window radiated dim light, drawing a faint circle in the murky air. I crept toward it, then leaned over slowly and peered through the gap in the curtains. The interior of the cabin was small—bed on one side along the wall, tiny kitchen on the other, a wicker sofa with faded cushions and a rocker in between, white wicker end tables and a little dining set that matched. The chairs were covered with lacy floral seat cushions in shades of yellow and green, the colors faded now. At one time, the house had been decorated to a woman's taste—rustic and earthy. Cute. A studio where an artist might work in quiet and natural light. During the day with the curtains open, the room would have been bright and beautiful. There were canvases everywhere, in all stages of completion. Studies of flowers, deer, bald eagles on the wing, a little boy with his knobby legs curled under him, playing with a tiny toy pickup truck. I recognized it. It was parked beside Nick's bed now.

This was *her* place. Her haven. Her private island. Peaceful, like the paintings.

I turned away before I could delve more deeply. If Mason really was using Firefly Island in some sort of plot against Jack, she would hate it. She would hate every bit of it.

A steely determination filled me, carried me around the cabin, onto the porch, to the door.

"Hold on a minute." Al circled the opposite corner and jumped agilely onto the porch, not bothering with the steps. "Let's be careful, here."

"I don't want to be careful. I want to know what's going on." Anger and righteous indignation made me bold where I had been fearful, confident where I had been unsure. I'd seen something under the table, just before turning away from the window. A file box. It looked new.

I was about to find out what was in it.

The old floorboards creaked and complained as Al and I entered the cabin, my tennis shoes moving quietly, Al's boot soles landing with dull thuds.

"Over there," I whispered, pointing to the dining table. Paper—some sort of map?—had been spread out across the wicker tabletop. It dangled over the edges, fluttering in the breeze of a clattering window air-conditioner with a missing plastic grill.

Al and I crossed the room and stood over the table, studying the contents together.

"What is it?" Mason apparently hadn't been very careful about hiding it. Of course, he had no way of knowing anyone would come to the island.

"I don't know, but it's not for around here. This property is up in far Northeast Texas, near the state line." Al pointed to the blue ink words at the edge of the map, then traced a long, straight set of lines, obviously a road. "Look at the county names. This is for some kind of development. A plot map. What's this area marked off in the center, do you think? No plots are mapped off there."

I studied it a moment. "Water, I'll bet. It looks like they're going to build a lake." One thing about my dad—he believed in taking free business-related vacations whenever they were offered, and he dragged the entire family along. Countless times I'd sat trying to wait politely while developers seeking advice, political favors, or investors attempted to work their sales magic on my father, wooing him with mock-ups of lakes, green spaces, and golf courses surrounded by high-end lots and mini ranches. Dad had done pretty well by joining some of those investment groups. Others, he had shunned. Some of those eventually became the stuff of legendary lawsuits involving politicians in office and all manner of shady deals.

Al traced a finger along the jagged shore of the paper lake. "All right, so he's meeting here with someone, and they're working out a property development with a lake involved, up in the northeastern corner of the state. Why all the cloak-and-dagger treatment?"

"That's the real question, isn't it? My dad's had some pretty wild stuff pitched at him in relation to property deals, though. You'd be surprised what goes on." I reached under the table for the file box. "Let's see if there's anything in here." The plot map crinkled as I set the box on the table and worked the lid free. The container was filled with mock-ups of advertisements and brochures for an upscale development offering lakefront lots and other posh amenities—equestrian trails, club houses, a floating restaurant, parks, and community centers.

"Kingdom Ridge." Al unfolded one of the brochures, squinting at the text. "'You really *can* have it all.'" Rolling her eyes at the cheesy slogan, she tossed the brochure back in the box. "Just what we need. More perfectly good land chopped up and filled with cookie-cutter houses." She tapped a finger to the price point listed on the ad mock-up I was holding. "Starting in the half mil range. Not the stuff of the common man."

"Yeah, no kidding. But the question is, why would this bring Mason here? Look at the dates on these ad dummies. Some of these are slated to run later this year. With all this on his plate, and his political career and a potential senate run, why does Mason come to the ranch and decide to reunite with his dad after fifteen years? There has to be a connection."

Something tapped on the window, and I jerked upright, dropping the brochure in the box. Beside me, Al was cucumber calm, seeming not the least bit worried about being caught here.

"Storm's kicking up in the trees." She nodded toward the window. "We need to finish and get back to the boat."

"All right, you look through that side of the cabin, and I'll look through this side. See if there's anything else." I wasn't sure what I was hoping for . . . but something. Anything to explain what Mason was up to and in what way it involved his father. Maybe Mason had some sort of similar plans for the ranch? Maybe he wanted Jack out of the way so that he and his partners could make West Ranch their next big project—divide it up for vacation homes and ranchettes?

But if he already had a big project going, why start eyeing the ranch now? Mason seemed like an intelligent man. He was calculated and smooth. Not the type to spin more plates than he could deal with at any one time.

Maybe he needed money for his project? Maybe he was hoping to get Jack out of the way and inherit? Maybe he'd been trying to convince Jack to invest, and when Jack wouldn't, he thought he'd go for the inheritance, instead?

An estate like Jack's could take time to settle, though.

What was Mason looking for here? What?

If the cabin had any more clues to offer, they were well hidden. While we searched, branches slapped the windows and scratched along the tin roof, the high, whining sound mixing with the wail of the wind. On the porch, the rocking chair swayed wildly, the motion erratic and angry.

My phone rang, and even Al jumped. "Turn that thing off," she snapped.

"Daniel's watching at the hospital." I slid the phone from my pocket, looked at the screen, and answered the call. Daniel.

"You need to get out of there, if you're still on Firefly." His voice was breathless and frantic. "Mason left the hospital.

He was down the hall, talking to someone on his cell phone, and then the next thing I knew, his car was pulling out of the parking lot, and he was in a hurry. Maybe he knows someone's in the cabin. If that's where he's headed, you don't have much time to get back across the causeway."

"He couldn't possibly know we're here." Could he? Unlike Jack's other properties, Firefly Island had no alarm, no surveillance system. Did it? What if the men in the houseboat were watching the cabin? What if they could see movement in here? What if they were on their way to the cabin right now?

Potentially, Mason had already attempted murder more than once, and perhaps been successful. The fact that no one could prove it didn't mean it wasn't true—or that he'd hesitate to make Al and me disappear.

"Don't go back to the ranch house tonight." Daniel's ominous undercurrent circled me like a cold draft. "Go to Al's place, instead. Better yet, go to Keren's or a hotel. I just want you somewhere safe. I'm going to get in to see Jack while Mason's gone. If I keep my head down, I don't think they'll even notice it's me and not Mason. Jack's been awake for a while, it turns out. Mason has been lying to me. He doesn't want me in there."

"Be careful, Daniel." My heart lurched, the fist of fear squeezing tight. What in the world had we involved ourselves in?

"It's you I'm worried about," he said softly. "Just get somewhere safe, okay? I never should have let you go to that island."

My heartstrings pulled and tugged. When all of this was over, and Daniel and I were together again, I would never, ever complain about the petty little challenges of an ordinary day. Dirty closets and roach powder in kitchen cabinets hardly seemed an issue anymore.

"I love you, Mal. Get out of there now."

"We're already gone." A quick once-over to make certain everything was back in place, and Al and I hurried out the door. Outside, the mist drove sideways now, wet leaves and twigs falling and sticking in my hair as we hurried into the brush cover. At every turn, I thought I heard people following us—behind each tree, around each bend. Each flash of lightning illuminated strange shapes among the trees.

A crack overhead sounded like a gunshot as we scrambled up the side of the canyon. I dropped my flashlight, and it clattered down the trail behind me, lay there shining a half circle over the damp leaves.

Al switched off her lamp, squatted, and pulled me down beside her as the sound reverberated through the trees and a flash of lightning crossed the sky. "Let's go!" she yelled, and we groped blindly in the darkness until we'd topped the hill and started down the other side. Branches tugged at my clothes and whipped my skin, but I didn't care. Below on the shore, a light shone through the trees.

Please, please, I prayed. *Let that be the Docksiders, not someone else.* What if the men from the houseboat had found them already? Who were those men, and what might they be willing to do to keep things quiet?

A loon's call trilled through the night as we came closer, and I caught a breath. Burt and Nester were waiting. We were almost there.

My sweat shirt was plastered wet and cold against my skin, and the rain had started in earnest by the time we climbed into the boat. A shiver rattled through my bones, and I tried not to think about the crossing. The storm had come in harder and faster than expected. We were far from home free, but we had to get off Firefly Island.

Burt tossed a tarp our way as he started the engine. "Hang

on, girls. Get your life vests on, and you might want to cover up with that. This is gonna get a bit dicey." He pulled his slicker tighter around his face.

"Don't y'all worry, though. We're professionals." Nester compacted his cowboy hat lower on his head before he untied the boat and pushed off.

My teeth chattered and my heart pounded as Al and I pulled the tarp over our heads and huddled in the back of the boat. When we left the shelter of the island, spray bounced wildly against the canvas, rain pelting in drops so large they struck the fabric like marbles. The boat roared over swells, lifting and splashing downward. Thunder rumbled and lightning split the sky over Chinquapin Peaks, fanning out in all directions.

"Hang on!" Burt yelled, revving the engine higher. "She'll make it through. Come on, Bertha! Come on, you scurvy girl. Don't fail me now, darlin'!" The motor roared and coughed, struggling to propel the boat against wind and tide.

Something bumped the sidewall, and I squealed, clinging to the railing, the tarp, and the seat all at once. If I ever, ever got out of this, I would never do something so stupid again. Ever, ever, ever. Amen.

Light shone against the canvas. Were we near shore already? I peeked through an eyelet ring. There was nothing but water. Churning water, everywhere. Beside me, Al stretched upward. Raindrops shot in as she pulled the tarp away slightly.

"Stay down, back there!" Nester called. "Somebody's spotlightin' us from the causeway. He'll lose us once we go around the point."

Al and I huddled low again. The boat pitched and danced. My heart pounded, and the chill needled my skin. My mind filled with unwanted images of what it would be like to be tossed into the cold, dark water, with waves closing in over-head.

The rocking eased as we rounded the point, but by the time we reached the dock, the lightning show was like nothing I'd ever seen, jagged spears splitting sideways and fanning out across the sky. Burt and Nester tied the boat securely to the old dock and left it, rather than crossing the water to go home.

Inside Al's truck, we huddled wet and bedraggled, catching a breath as Al turned the key and the engine roared to life. The tires slid in the greasy caliche, the truck grinding wet gravel and threatening to bog down as we drove away from the lakeshore.

"W-w-we n-need somep-p-place with Internet s-service . . . and a c-c-computer," I stuttered out, my teeth chattering wildly. My fingers trembled on the phone as I texted Corbin and Daniel to let them know I was safely back in Al's truck. "D-D-Daniel says n-not to go back t-t-to the house ton-n-night."

"Waterbird's got Internet." Nester leaned in from the backseat as we turned onto the gravel logging road that had led us most of the way to the old dock. "Pop Dorsey and Sheila's got a couple of them carry-along computers. Pop likes to play bingo online, and Sheila teaches some college classes that way. They'd be closed by this time a' night, but if we rap on the door, they'll let us in."

"Let's go," I said, and Al wheeled the truck sideways at a dirt-road intersection. The rear tires slid, sputtered, and drifted, and I was momentarily compressed against the door. Then the tires caught, and we were rocketing forward, machine-gunning mud and rocks, and heading for the Water-bird. Burt called ahead, and when we arrived, Pop Dorsey and his daughter, Sheila, were waiting with two laptop computers open at the Docksiders' favorite booth.

Only after Nester began sharing the story of our night did I realize that, by coming here, we'd let more people in on our secret. It didn't seem to matter anymore. I had a feeling that this thing was about to grow bigger than any of us could hope to contain. My only worry now was whether we could unearth the details before Mason figured out who had invaded his den on Firefly Island, if he didn't know already. We had to find something incriminating. Soon. So far, Daniel hadn't been able to get any details out of Jack at the hospital. Jack was weak, groggy, and still confused about how he'd ended up in ICU. Mason had already been filling in the details for him. The details according to Mason.

Al and I sat before the computers as Nester recounted the drama of our crossing in the storm. Pop Dorsey and Sheila were wide-eyed with interest.

Al quickly shoved her computer away. "Don't have a clue what to do with this thing. I don't even keep one in my house anymore."

Sheila squeezed into the booth beside Al. "Here, I can help. What are we looking for?"

"See if there's anything about a planned recreational development called Kingdom Ridge, northeast of Dallas, near the Oklahoma border." I fished my cell phone from my pocket again. "I need to call my dad and get some ideas. I'm not sure what we're looking for." There had to be some reason Mason was conducting meetings in secret. If we dug in the right places, sooner or later we'd hit pay dirt. Hopefully, Dad could tell me what the right places were.

I dialed my parents' number, hoping I'd get my father and not Mom. Usually by now she was in bed asleep with a book on her chest while Dad alternately dozed and watched the late-night news recap in the great room. Hopefully she wouldn't hear the phone ringing in Dad's office. She had never allowed a business phone upstairs, because Dad's clients and contacts tended to call at all hours of the day and night.

Dad answered on the fourth ring, his voice drowsy and thick. He was surprised, of course, when I was the one calling. "Everything all right? Hang on, let me go find your mom." Generally, crises were Mom's domain. Dad's job was to listen, nod, act curmudgeonly, and offer to pay for things.

"No, no, Dad, I called to talk to you. Don't wake Mom, okay? I have a . . . technical question."

"Technical question . . ." Dad was doubtful, but there was a hint of intrigue in his tone. He missed the old wheeling and dealing days.

I realized that everyone in the room was looking at me, trying to follow the conversation. I switched to speakerphone. "Dad, what kinds of things might cause a problem with a property development? I'm talking about a large recreational plan—ten thousand acres, crossing state lines, manmade lake, golf course, that kind of thing. Very upscale. What kind of holdup might come along?"

"You and Daniel thinking of investing in something, because in this economy . . ." The sentence ended with the cautionary clearing of the throat that conveyed Dad's disapproval without his saying it. "Never make investments after ten o'clock at night. That's always been my rule. Sleep on it and let it ruminate a few days, Mudbug."

Al lifted a brow at the nickname I'd inherited when I ran away and hid during a crawfish boil in Charleston. The whole concept of cracking the head off something and slurping out the brains was a little much for a city girl.

Right now, though, I wanted to get at Mason's brain, to figure out what he had brewing there. "We're not investing, Dad. I just need to know. What might get in the way of a development like that? What might bring on some . . . sneaking around. Some under-the-table deals?"

Dad considered the question for a moment. "Well . . . any number of things. Water-rights issues, with the building of a lake involved, access issues, of course—roads, right-of-way disputes, and that sort of thing—possibly zoning, fire control, environmental issues like natural watersheds, financing and debt capacity of the developer. Any of those can hamstring a big project like that. Eminent domain issues, habitat for any kind of endangered species—doesn't matter if it's tree moss or little green beetle bugs, that can be one whopper of a snag. Issues with mineral rights, easements for things like pipelines and power transmission . . ." Dad hesitated, waiting for me to speak. I was busy making notes on the back of a take-out menu. "That enough, or you need more? Could you narrow it down for me a little?"

I pushed strands of wet hair off my face, looking at the list, trying to imagine which might apply to Kingdom Ridge. "I'm looking for something big. Something that might have implications on a federal level. Something that might involve calling in favors—where connections in the House or the Senate could make a critical difference." Both Dad and I knew what I was talking about.

"Well, now you've got my interest. What's this place called, and how does it involve my baby girl?" Dad was suddenly wide-awake, ready to swoop in and take control and handle everything for me. My independent streak flared. Once Dad started asking questions around DC, word would circulate.

"I'll tell you all the rest later, Dad. I'm just working on a story." My attempt at sounding casual was pathetic, but it seemed to convince Dad. "For right now, could you just give me some ideas? The most likely things?"

He answered with a disappointed grunt. Dad still hated it when I wouldn't just be his little Mudbug. "Federal . . . federal . . . Well, if I were looking at why someone might be calling in favors on that level, I'd look specifically at endangered species, anything of historical or archaeological significance on the property, anything that might stoke up the Environmental Protection Agency, any abutments to federal properties like park land, military facilities, preserves, or federal research facilities." He paused again. I could almost hear him scratching the five o'clock shadow on his saggy chin. For a minute, I wasn't wet and cold in a booth at the Waterbird, I was curled up on the arm of my dad's big chair, laying my head on his strong shoulder.

"Thanks, Dad."

"You know, anytime you need me you can call." The wistfulness in those words was unmistakable. My mind stumbled ahead to some day far in the future, my children grown, my house empty.

"I know, Dad. I love you." I blushed a little, the moment feeling gushy with everyone staring at me.

"Power corridors." It wasn't exactly the *I love you* that I'd been expecting in return. "There've been some interesting issues with a couple large-scale development plans out west over the years, where Congress had previously established a massive power corridor right-of-way through the property. No power lines in place at that point, but a pre-established corridor location like that one is the kind of obstacle only congressional action can help you deal with. You want to move something like that, you need friends in high places . . . and some luck."

Power line corridors . . . *Holy mackerel!* I'd heard something about that, not that long ago. What was it? Why was that ringing a bell? "Tell me more about that, Dad. How would you get rid of an obstacle like that? What would a developer do?"

Dad chuckled in his *well-you-know-that-as-well-as-I-do* way. "Pony up the campaign contributions, host a few fund-raising events for committee members with power, give generously to their PACs, and then mention—and when I say *mention*, you know and I know there are a lot of people in this town who'd go far beyond what's legal here—that you've got a problem with the power corridor plans. Typically, relocating something like that is the type of issue that'll be tucked quietly in the non-germane amendments to a bill where nobody's going to bother to read the fine print. You understand how that works, daughter."

Did I ever. My mind was ringing like a firehouse bell. The back of the Clean Energy Bill—all the pork attached by Congressman Faber's office. Faber was from Arkansas. He and Senator Reirdon had served on at least one joint committee together, and probably more. The Reirdon family were long-time friends of Mason West. If we checked Reirdon's contributors and Faber's contributors, no doubt Mason West, or interests connected to Kingdom Ridge, would be there. That didn't explain why Mason was here now, hovering around Jack, but it might get us started. "Okay, thanks, Dad. I think you just helped me out in a big way."

"It's what I live for," Dad answered ruefully, and then we said good-bye.

I turned to Sheila and Al. "Look up the contributions to Congressman Faber and Senator Reirdon. Look for anything connected to Mason West, interests he owns, or Kingdom Ridge Trust." While they were busy searching and making notes, I pawed around for information on a planned power corridor through Texas, Oklahoma, or Arkansas, possibly involving the border area where Kingdom Ridge was located.

It wasn't hard to find. The Gateway To the Coast corridor was massive, a mile-wide right-of-way for high voltage transmission lines traveling from Texas, all the way to the big cities in the northeast. Communities and property owners everywhere were raising petitions, claiming that the planned route for the corridor had been changed without reason. The proposed new route was not only more costly, but it traveled through a federal preserve. It also grabbed thousands upon thousands of acres of private land, rather than making use of existing power rights-of-way . . . including the one that ran through the property that would become Kingdom Ridge.

Who wants to spend a half million on a vacation home that will someday have massive high-voltage transmission lines dangling over it? According to the map, the power corridor was supposed to run right over the lake at Kingdom Ridge. Of course Mason West and his partners, whoever they were, couldn't let that happen. They needed to find a means of moving the corridor right-of-way before they could begin selling lots.

Faber's pork in the back of the Clean Energy Bill would be a perfect way to do it. Tuck the relocation of a portion of the power corridor into a nice little bill about wind farms and renewable energy—the sort of bill no one would ever look that closely at.

I needed to get another look at the bill. But all my files were back in DC, in my old office, under new management. I couldn't just call up and say, *Listen, I know it's the middle of the night, and I don't work there anymore, but can you let me snoop around in my files for a bit?*

I drummed on the keyboard, trying to think of another approach. Somehow, I had to get to my old files . . . and who knew more about computers than anyone else I'd ever met? Who loved them, lived for them, and talked about them endlessly while sharing round-robin desserts at a corner booth? If there was anyone who could help me, it was Josh, the Wizard of Computer-Oz.

I texted him instead of calling, realizing that it'd be just as well if everyone wasn't in on the conversation.

Hey, you there?

His answer was almost instant. *Yeah, we're all at the pub. What kind of pie do you want us to order you?*

I pictured the old crew, cooped up at a corner table at the pub. The setting felt foreign now. The lopsided booths at the Waterbird seemed like home.

;o) No pie, but do you remember that time you hacked my email and grabbed a bunch of my stuff to prove to me why I shouldn't email my work stuff to myself as a way of backing it up? Any chance you still have those files? The email hacking lesson had taken place after I met Daniel—when I was working on yet more amendments to the Clean Energy Bill. It was probably a long shot that Josh still had the files around, but with Josh, anything was possible. Truth be told, he could probably hack the new assistant's email at my old office, but there was no way I would ask. I didn't want the two of us to end up occupying side-by-side jail cells in federal prison.

The phone rang a moment later. Josh was on the other end. "I deleted those files. Remember? You threatened to send the FBI after me."

I stood up from the table, pretended to be going to the cafe counter, where Pop Dorsey had prepared a fresh, hot pot of coffee. "So, did you *delete* them, delete them . . . or did you delete them in the way of deleting them where people like you can still actually find them on some hard drive somewhere?" Another lesson I'd learned from Josh. Even after standard deletion, ghosts remain unless the hard drive is sanitized by some special means only gurus understand.

"Uhhh . . . who wants to know?" Josh's answer was sheep-ish at best, but more like culpable.

"Just me."

" . . . because there's been a hot girl watching me in the gym three days in a row, and I thought it was just because I've lost thirty pounds. Do I need to worry about Homeland Security throwing me in the back of a black sedan and taking me to an unmarked basement somewhere?"

Any other time, I would have laughed at Josh's joke, but right now I was focused on other things. "Come on, Josh. Do you have the files or not? I need my copy of the amendments to the Clean Energy Bill."

"Oh, those are a sure cure for insomnia . . . oops, I mean not that I looked at any of your private files or anything."

"Josh . . ."

"Yeah, I can probably get it. For one thing, my system runs incremental backup every night. Everything that's on my hard drive goes there. I'll check for you when I get to work tomorrow."

"No, I need it now." I poured a cup of coffee, the damp clothes still making me shiver. The warmth from the coffee pot felt good.

"I'm not at my computer right now."

Wrapping my hand around the steaming liquid, I lifted it to my lips. On the other side of the room, Al, Sheila, and the Docksiders were pointing at Sheila's laptop screen and furiously making notes, whispering among themselves with looks of *Eureka!*

"Come on, Josh, I know you've got your iPad with you." Josh never went anywhere without his little man-purse full of gadgets.

"So, you want me to hack into my own data drive and get a file for you with a Bluetooth keyboard and an iPad?" Josh protested. "Now *that's* a challenge." I pictured him rubbing his hands together and cracking his knuckles with relish. "Text the filenames to me, or at least some combination of letters you're sure were in the filenames, and I'll let you know when I have something."

I did as Josh asked, then crossed the room with my coffee, looking over Al's shoulder as she made notes. "Well, he's definitely funneling money to these guys. Nothing that's obvious beyond the legal limits, but I'll bet if we dig here, here, and here—" the tip of her pen tapped the screen, indicating several PACs and named corporate donors—"we're going to find Mason West connected in more ways than one." Al's inner reporter was showing.

"I think I'm onto something, too." I rested my cup on the back of the seat and stretched my neck. Now that there was a pause in the wild rush, the night was catching up with me. Outside, the storm had quieted to a gentle rain, as if Moses Lake were waiting for something to happen. A yawn pulled at me, and I felt my eyes tugging. I wanted some dry clothes and a hot bath . . . and my own bed. But I couldn't go home.

"If we find anything, we need to make it as public as we can, as soon as possible," Al pointed out. "The minute it's all out there, the motivation to come after us is gone. In fact, they'll stay as far away from us as possible, to avoid looking guilty."

I moved to the other computer, logged into my email, thought, *Come on, Josh.* Minutes ticked away. Ten, fifteen. I imagined Josh at the Gymies' favorite pub booth, bent over his iPad and little keyboard, surrounded by nine kinds of pie, his fingers flying.

"Y-y-y-yes!" I cheered when Josh's email came through, and then a text. Attached to the email were two documents, comprising several hundred pages of the amendments to the Clean Energy Bill. I held my breath as it downloaded, and I opened it, my mind slipping back into another life. The day I'd met Daniel in the rotunda seemed so long ago.

How could that girl have ever guessed that she would end up here in Moses Lake, holed up in a combination bait shop, convenience store, and café, married, pregnant, hopelessly in love, and wondering if somewhere, someone in some other office deep within the bowels of the Capitol building had slipped the words *Gateway To the Coast* neatly in with the amendments, never to be seen again.

I plugged the words into the search window, and then . . . "There it is." The quiet relocation of the Gateway To the Coast power corridor, snuggled in with all the other pork, where you'd have to be combing the fine print in order to discover it. "I think I found exactly what we're looking for."

We're here to make a dent in the universe.
Otherwise why else even be here?

—Steve Jobs
(Left by Josh and Kaylyn, finally in Moses Lake for that ranch vacation)

Chapter 25

It sounds so strange when you say it all out loud—speak it into the air and let it hover there, the entire journey from the white space at one end of the map, where a girl rushed through the Capitol building, not even noticing the sights and sounds of spring, to here. Such an unlikely journey, a life-changing road trip of epic proportion.

The lights glare, mesmerize me, and for a moment as the cameraman at CNN's Washington Bureau counts down, my mind slips away and glides over the waters of Moses Lake with the red-tailed hawks and the bald eagles. Who could have imagined such a journey? Who but God could have laced together the twists and turns, the blind curves, the valleys and peaks? Who could have ever looked at that blond-haired girl in her favorite suit and designer knock-off shoes, and seen a mother, a wife, an advocate, a blogger, a woman-of-the-moment . . . The Frontier Woman?

No one. No one but the God who knit us together, who knows the very fiber of who we are and who we can be.

Beside me, Keren glances my way, widens her eyes, and

takes a breath. Her hand touches mine. Her fingers are shaking, but she looks determined, nervous but poised in her soft blue suit, her hair pulled neatly into a bun.

She tucks her hand into her lap as the cameraman finishes the count and points the gun finger at the host. The host recaps the story for all those who haven't been following the press coverage of the congressional investigation. When a scandal involves a congressman, a senator, a state politician, several well-known wealthy investors, and potentially even a state governor's office, there's no end to the media frenzy.

"Take us back to that night before the story broke." The host turns from the camera to me, his lips quirking slightly to one side. I know where he's going with this. "So you're sitting in the local bait shop with two laptop computers, the bait shop owners, a neighbor who raises goats, and two retired fishermen, and you uncover an alleged influence-pedaling scandal of massive proportion. Set the scene for us. What happens next?"

I sit up a bit straighter, shake off the lingering weariness of testifying before Congress, flashbulbs popping like Christmas lights. I remind myself that I am an Ellery woman, descended from the line of Grandma Louisa. Ellery women are always confident and poised in public. Aside from that, an Easter gathering with the family looms just ahead. They'll all be critiquing my performance here today, as will Al, who traveled along on this trip—though she stopped short of attending the congressional proceedings or accompanying us to the TV studio. *Too many memories*, she says, and I don't blame her. It's enough that she has come along for moral support. There's a sweet irony in the fact that she and my father will sit down together at the dinner table tonight. My mother has insisted that my *new friends* must join us for a gathering before returning to Texas. I imagine that, as this interview takes place, my mother is tormenting the catering staff and buzzing around the house like a honeybee on steroids.

The breath I take in smells faintly of baby powder, Dreft, and Johnson's shampoo. No More Tears. Emmie's sweet scents. In the hotel room, she's curled up in front of the TV with Al. Al is pointing and saying, "Look, look, Emmie, there's your mom!" Emmie looks at the TV through her sweet, dreamy baby eyes. Her daddy's gypsy green eyes. She jabbers and coos and blows little bubbles with her lips. She smiles, because somehow Al can always make her smile. There's a bond between them that began when Al drove me to the hospital, in labor three weeks earlier than expected. Considering that she'd stood in through the worst of it before Daniel could get there, an official position as godmother seemed a fair reward. It's a distinction that Al and I share. I am a godmother to Trudy's first child, Aaron. There's finally another boy in the family. Nick is thrilled.

Standing just off-camera, Daniel smiles at me, as in, *Come on, tell the story. They're gonna love this one.* Beside him, my father gives me a thumbs-up. He smiles and picks Nick up so that Nick can get a better look at one of the cameras. He puts a finger to his lips to remind Nick to be very quiet as I answer the question. "Well, of course, when we started putting together all the details, we knew we had to make it public as soon as possible—certainly before the Clean Energy Bill could be released from committee and brought to the floor for a vote. We all knew we couldn't let that happen."

"You, the bait shop owner, and the fishermen," the host dabbles in a joke. I can't blame him. Beside me, Keren laughs politely.

"And the woman who raises goats," I add. A little levity makes for a good interview. "But in all seriousness, when we learned that the alternate route took in a far greater number of privately owned acres, traveled through a federal preserve, vastly increased the corridor's cost to taxpayers, and followed almost no existing power line rights-of-way, we realized that the public had a right to be made aware of the facts. Aside from that, for us personally, there was the issue that the new corridor plan routed a mile-wide swath of high-voltage power lines through the state park and across several family ranches. Because most of those ranches are small, the landowners don't have the means to legally fight the plan, but many of those ranches are of historic significance. The rerouting plan was being kept as hush-hush as possible to avoid any action from larger landowners in the area who might have the connections and the funds to stall the corridor plan legally." I stop without mentioning West Ranch and Jack West by name. I imagine Jack back at the ranch, still recovering from the knowledge that his son's only purpose in their reunion was to distract Jack, to be sure he didn't find out about the power corridor and use his money and influence to protest it.

Even with that knowledge, Jack has so far refused to accept the idea that Mason might have caused the pickup to roll over the cliff on purpose, or that he could have had anything to do with the disappearance of Jack's second wife and her young son. Jack insists that Mason was not responsible for either incident. If the truth is otherwise, he is not willing to disclose it yet, but if Al has anything to say about it, that day will come.

There's more of the old Alex Beck inside Cowgirl Al than I would have guessed, and she's on Mason West's history like a catfish on stink bait, as the Docksiders would say. She's certain that she's on the trail of evidence that will finally solve the disappearance of Jack's wife and stepson. She's convinced that Mason is guilty, and I believe she'll prove it sooner or later. Now that she's oddly on the side of looking out for Jack's best interest, a strange tango has developed across fences back at the ranch—a dance of aggression and resolution, hate and . . . maybe love? Every once in a while, I wonder if almost anything could be possible in Moses Lake. Even two lonely hearts finding each other across enemy lines.

At least Mason is long gone from the ranch. He has plenty of other things to worry about now. Like the end of his political career and a potential stint in prison for the Kingdom Ridge scheme.

"Aside from that . . ." I continue on, leading to another point I want to make. There's a reason why Keren is here beside me today. " . . . there was the fact that the new corridor would route power lines through the economically sensitive area of Chinquapin Peaks. Hundreds of families already struggling to survive would be displaced with nowhere to go. I've been covering Keren's work with the kids of Chinquapin Peaks for a while now on *The Frontier Woman*, and when people who'd been donating to her supper garden program found out about the power corridor, they were outraged."

I nod toward Keren, addressing the next question to her as much as to the host. "Why should the taxpayers tolerate far greater expense—and sacrifice both federal land and state park land—to reroute a power corridor through virgin territory that is topographically less suited to the building of power lines? When something like this happens on the backs of poor families and ranching families who have worked their land for generations . . . when plans are made in secret and kept secret, so that a handful of multimillionaires can rake in billions selling luxury vacation home lots, the public should be outraged. Elected officials should be in the business of protecting our citizens, not selling their influence to the highest bidder. When something's wrong, ordinary people have to speak up."

The host nods, sharing a fierce look with me. He likes the idea of seeing government graft exposed. It's what he lives for.

His smile says as much as he formulates the next comment: "And as a former insider, you were in a perfect position to understand what was going on and to bring it to light."

I think about that for a moment, imagining Josh sweating off twenty more pounds, wondering if the email hacking thing will somehow come up on national television. "I was in the right place at the right time, but it was a team that brought down the rerouting of the power corridor. A team of neighbors."

I picture them now. There's a watch party going on at the Waterbird. When it's over, Nester and Burt will head out to troll the waters near Firefly Island in search of the perfect fish. Pop Dorsey and Sheila will serve up coffee and lollypops, handing out Sharpie pens to visitors so that they can leave a signature or a favorite quote on the Wall of Wisdom. The ranch hands will go about their day, Tag making sure to stop by and milk that silly cow. It's Wednesday, so he'll share the milk with the church ladies, who are gathering in the fellowship hall to have a Bible study and talk about their latest charitable project. In my mind, even Claire Anne Underhill is there with them, smiling. She's pleased that Moses Lake has finally made national headlines. Maybe now she'll forgive me for all the discounted supplies she's had to provide for the gardening program.

The announcer uses the word *neighbors* as a segue into a discussion of Keren's supper garden program—a little personal interest to bring this big, big story down to a human level. Down to the fate of one small town, and faces like Sierra's and Sergio's, and even down to the tiniest of things. Seeds, and the hope that lies inside them.

Dozens of gardens will rise from the soil of Chinquapin Peaks this spring, if the rains come.

Beyond the glow of the spotlights, Daniel smiles at me in a way that whispers, *Let's go home.* That errant curl falls over his forehead, and I am filled with love, with wonder. I am in awe of this journey, this trip across the map from one life to another.

I smile back at this man, my husband, and I wonder where the roads will lead as the years pass, the miles drifting by beneath our feet. Will we live all our lives along the quiet, glistening shores of Moses Lake, or are there other things in store? Other journeys? Other discoveries?

For the first time I can remember, I'm satisfied not to know. To wait, and to watch. To see, as Keren says beside me now, what God can do with a single, ordinary life.

When it's given over to love.

Acknowledgments

It's a funny thing about books. You start out with a blank page, and yourself, and an imaginary person or two. The story world is small at first.

Over time, the world inside the story grows to include more people and places that don't exist. But it also grows to include wonderful people who enter from the real world in all sorts of different ways. There are those who lend advice on research issues, those who help to proof and edit, those who design the covers and sell the books, and of course those who eventually read the book. If you're here, you've just become a citizen of Moses Lake. Welcome! We're so glad you've come. The journey would not be complete without you . . . and without a few other people whom I would like to acknowledge here.

First of all, thank you to my beta-reading crew, Teresa Loman, Ed Stevens, Sandy Strong, and Sharon Manion. Nobody could have a better group of first readers or encouragers. Each one of you is a treasured presence in my life, and also in Moses Lake. Thank you for sharing these story worlds with me.

To my boys, who lived some of the real-life adventures in this story with me when their daddy walked out of the bedroom years ago and said, "I think I've just been offered a job in Texas." Thank you for teaching me not only about motherhood, but about really important things, like how to make clay pots out of the goo at the side of the driveway, how to catch grasshoppers for fish bait, and how to properly enjoy a new bloom of rain lilies on the lawn. I'm so grateful for the little boys you were, the wonderful young men you have become, and the lessons in life and love that you have taught me.

In terms of print and paper, my thanks and admiration goes out to the group at Bethany House publishers. To Dave Long and Sarah Long, thank you for being talented editors and just great people to work with. To the group in marketing, publicity, and art, thank you for using your talent in support of this and so many other books. Without your skill and dedication, books would never reach readers. To my agent, Claudia Cross, at Folio literary management, thank you for taking these literary journeys with me over the years.

To Alice Steele, and her sweet sisters Paula and Cindy, who won the chance to join the cast of Moses Lake in this book, thank you for sharing your Binding Through Books club with Mallory and the residents of Moses Lake. I know they're glad to have you here, reading books together in Alice's new little cabin on Moses Lake. I hope you enjoy your time alongside these wonderful waters. May they take you on an adventure!

Last of all, but never least of all, I am grateful to so many reader friends far and near, who have helped populate Moses Lake. Without you, the lake would be a lonely place. The Docksiders and I love it when you stop by. Thank you for all the sweet notes about the books, for all the wonderful book club nights, and for recommending my stories to your friends.

You can't imagine how much it means, when the story goes out into the world, and people give it a wonderful home in their reading lives and their imaginations. I hope you enjoy this latest adventure in Moses Lake. May your time there be a blessing, just as you have been to me.

God's way of connecting people is, indeed, the most magnificent part of any story.

Discussion Questions

1. In the beginning of the story, Mallory thinks she has life all figured out . . . until life turns a blind corner. Has your life ever taken a sudden turn you weren't anticipating? How did you react to the change?

2. When Daniel gets the job offer in Texas, Mallory finds herself forced to choose between her career and her love for Daniel. Do you think she made the right choice? How much should we sacrifice to make someone else's dreams come true?

3. Mallory has struggled all her life to step out from the shadows of her older sisters and to escape her parents' control. How much of her decision-making do you think is based on her position as the caboose baby in the family? Do you think birth order determines personality? Have you seen this in your own family?

4. Mallory's mother advises her to "get over herself" and apologize when she and Daniel have their first big fight.

Mallory feels that her mother is asking her to stuff down her feelings and be a doormat. Do you agree? What was your mother's best advice for resolving marital disagreements?

5. Mallory struggles with the feeling that she is "losing herself" to the demands of marriage and motherhood. Do you think too much is asked of women, in terms of sacrificing themselves for family? Is it possible to have it all? Where do you think the balance should be between the traditional 1950s housewife and the modern mom?

6. When Mallory meets Cowgirl Al, Al takes her under wing even though Al lives a fairly reclusive life. Why do you think she decides to befriend Mallory? What bonds them together?

7. Mallory's first struggle in Moses Lake is making the ranch house habitable for the family. She likens it to coming to Texas as a pioneer. How well do you think she does in adopting the pioneer spirit? Have you ever felt like a pioneer trying something new? Do you have a funny "critter" story to share?

8. Both Mallory and Al are struggling to leave the past behind. Do you think it's ever possible to fully move beyond the past? How can we accomplish that? Should we?

9. When Mallory begins to document her adventures in *The Frontier Woman* blog, she finds that she begins to look for adventure in her life. How can journaling, blogging, or documenting our experiences change the way we look at life? How has blogging changed our culture? Is it a change for the better or for the worse?

10. Keren struggles with the pressure from her family, but in a different way than Mallory. She feels that God is using her right where she is, even though her family doesn't fully support her decision to put so much of herself into her career. Mallory also wonders how we can know which voice inside us is God's voice and which voice we may be creating on our own. When we feel a calling that other people do not support or understand, how can we know if it's God's voice we're hearing?

11. When Mallory finds out who Al really is, she jumps to conclusions. Do you think she is justified in this? Have you ever jumped to conclusions about someone based on evidence, and then been sorry later?

12. In the end, Mallory uncovers a political scandal that she is in the unique position to combat. She feels that she finally understands some of God's reasons for sending her to Moses Lake. Have you ever been surprised by God's plans in your life?

Lisa Wingate is a popular inspirational speaker, magazine columnist, and national bestselling author of several books, including *Tending Roses, Talk of the Town, Good Hope Road, Dandelion Summer,* and *Never Say Never*. She is a Christy Award finalist, a seven-time Carol Award nominee, and the winner of the 2011 and 2012 Carol Awards. Her work was recently honored by the Americans for More Civility for promoting greater kindness and civility in American life. Lisa and her family live in Central Texas.

Visit *www.lisawingate.com* to sign up for Lisa's latest contest, read her blog and excerpts from her novels, get writing tips, contact her, and more.

More From Bestselling Author Lisa Wingate!

To learn more about Lisa and her books, visit lisawingate.com.

Moses Lake, Texas, is the last place Heather Hampton ever wanted to go again. But when her career hinges on an unexpected trip back to her tiny hometown, she discovers a family steeped in secrets—and a startling connection to the handsome local banker.

Blue Moon Bay

When a mysterious little girl is suddenly seen with the town recluse, two unlikely people see a chance at redemption and hope. Harboring deep wounds, yet drawn together in their quest, Andrea and Mart's search for the girl's identity has consequences neither of them expected.

Larkspur Cove